P9-CQA-676

THE LION SEEKER

The LION SEEKER

A NOVEL

KENNETH BONERT

HOUGHTON MIFFLIN HARCOURT

BOSTON   NEW YORK

2013

First U.S. Edition
Copyright © 2013 by Kenneth Bonert

For information about permission to reproduce selections from this book,
write to Permissions, Houghton Mifflin Harcourt Publishing Company,
215 Park Avenue South, New York, New York 10003.

www.hmhbooks.com

First published in Canada by Alfred A. Knopf Canada,
a division of Random House of Canada, in 2013.

Library of Congress Cataloging-in-Publication Data
Bonert, Kenneth.
The Lion Seeker : a novel / Kenneth Bonert. — First U.S. edition.
pages cm
ISBN 978-0-547-89804-9
1. Jews — South Africa — Fiction. 2. Johannesburg (South Africa) — Fiction.
3. South Africa — History — 1909–1961 — Fiction. 4. Historical fiction. I. Title.
PR9199.4.B6743L56 2013
823'.92 — DC23
2013019330

Printed in the United States of America
DOC 10 9 8 7 6 5 4 3 2 1

For my parents

The traveller who goes there from our land, tired and weary of the oppressor and of the vicissitudes of life that dog his every step, can forget his poverty, his squalor, his degradation and his humiliation. In Africa he breathes a new life, a life of freedom and liberty, a life of wealth and honour, because there is no discrimination between a Hebrew and a Christian there. Every man can attend to his labours diligently and find a just reward for his toil.

— 1884 report from Lithuania in the Hebrew journal
HaMelitz, by N.D. Hoffman

Gitelle: *A Prologue*

WHATEVER CROUCHED BEYOND THE LAKES and forests of her green life was unseeable as night. She had never studied a map till it came time to leave forever and then her fingertips traced ceaselessly over what her mind could not picture. The mysteries beat in her like a second heart. The pinprick of her village lay closer to the borders with Poland and Latvia than she'd ever known; the whole country was but a slither in a howling world. There were salt oceans, desert kingdoms. She had the words and the colours on the map but nothing more.

When they stopped at the cemetery on the way out, the carriage driver Nachman said, —A tayter nemt mir nit tsoorik foon besaylem. Dead ones never come back from the grave. The old saying meant what's done is done but was turned upside down in his wry mouth: here it was the living who would never come back to these graves at the far end of Milner Gass, near the spring and Yoffe's mill, flashes of the lake silver through the dark trees.

A closed sky kept spitting and everyone wore galoshes against the mud. The peeling birches creaked and dripped; candle flames twitched and fluttered. Her daughter, good girl, stood nicely beside her but Isaac on the other side kept squirming against her right hand bunched in his little jacket. This was a boy who hadn't stopped jerking and kicking from the second he came out of her with thick hair gleaming like fresh-skinned carrots and his biting mouth screaming enough for twins. Almost five now, about to travel across the earth to meet the father he'd never seen.

Gitelle made them look at and put pebbles on the gravestones of their grandmother and then all their great-grandparents. That was enough: another five centuries or more of buried Jewish bones spread away from them beneath the hissing branches. She adjusted her veil and turned back to face the living – her tutte Zalman Moskevitch, her sisters, the nieces and the husbands. Isaac wriggled free like a cat and ran off. She didn't bother shouting: the boy needed a leash not more words, hoarse or otherwise. Some of his aunties caught him. Another two of them came up to her. Trudel-Sora hoisted Rively onto her hip and went away while Orli held out her arms. Youngest of the sisters, Orli was plump in the lips and hips and smoothly olive skinned; her black eyes, now liquidly gleaming, matched her thick long hair. She hugged Gitelle close, groaning, and said, I think you're the first one ever who didn't need a hanky on her leaving day.

Are you surprised?

Of course not.

Gitelle nodded. How strange tears would be today, after everything. All the years spent gagging on the taste of her breath against the shame of the veil, her words dribbling from her like spatter from an overbubbling pot – such sorrows, encompassed by this place, should not include her leaving too. Never that.

What are you thinking of?

The future, said Gitelle. The living. My husband. What else is there to think of?

Orli smiled: her teeth unpeeled were white as river stones and brilliant in her olive face. Sister, not everyone's as strong as a tree stump.

Is that what I'm supposed to be now?

It's what you always have.

She had threaded her warm soft arm through Gitelle's and pulled it close as they walked back though the gravestones.

A sodden squirrel stood up to stare at them, quivering. Gitelle said: Listen. If I can do this so can you. Don't waste time. Be brave. Don't ever stop trying. I was twenty-seven before I met my Abel. They said with the way I am such a thing could never happen. And after we had Rively, you think he wanted to go? Men are lazy as stones. I had to nag so much I nearly twisted my own head into craziness – borrow the money, get moving, wake *up*. And how many years now it's taken him, drip drip drip, to send back just enough for our tickets . . . But see, here I am, I don't complain. Today it's my turn, my leaving day. You understand what I'm telling you, Orli? Remember this day. Don't ever give in. Don't ever go slack. Your leaving day will come sooner than you think. All of yours will. It's the only way we'll ever see each other again, and we will. We have to.

Orli was drying her cheeks with her free hand. But it was always fated, she said. You and Abel. Like everything.

Gitelle snorted, rippling the line of the veil.

What? There *is* fate. You two prove it.

Prove what exactly?

How The Name makes His perfect matches for us, in every generation of souls. A heart for a heart, even a wound for a wound. Every shoe must have its foot.

Gitelle was silent, felt her sister's eyes on her face.

Forgive me, said Orli. Foot and shoe. I didn't mean—

Ah Orli, said Gitelle, lisping into the cloth. You think *that's* what bothers me? My dear sister, you need to forget all that romantic trash if you're ever going to grow up. Now's the time to start.

Outside the cemetery the horse cropped at wet weeds with a stretched neck; Nachman had his collar up and his chin on his chest. There was a wait to find Isaac who'd gotten loose again and was giggling somewhere off in the lindens on the opposite side. First would come the station at Obeliai, then a train to Libau on

the coast. She had packed goose feather pillows for the freighter's
hard benches and plenty of lemons because lemons are the cure for
seasickness: advice from the ones who'd gone before. Africa. She
wondered what an ocean will be.

In Southampton on England's coast they boarded a Union Castle
liner with a lavender hull and two fat smokestacks. It took twenty
days to reach the bottom tip of the pistol-shaped African conti-
nent and on every one of them Isaac found ways to raid the upper
decks of first class, returning to steerage with pockets stuffed
with glazed tarts and fresh cheeses and Swiss chocolate, with
strange and impossibly sweet fruits Gitelle had never seen before.
When he wasn't raiding he fought other boys or kicked the shins
of the duty officers. His masterpiece was starting a fire in a life
raft with a flare gun. The crew called him Devil Boy and the captain almost had him confined. They didn't understand it was only
that he was born with a little more kaych in him than others, a
little extra life energy bubbling and frothing inside like hot milk
to get out. When she wiped his face in bed every night with a
damp cloth she got him to keep still by promising him the freckles were coming off, and every morning he'd run excited to the
mirror to verify her claims.

Cape Town was on a bay raked by salt winds, its streets laced
over the roots of a flathead mountain. Colours burned the air:
blood flowers, thorny eruptions of vermilion, limeyellow smears
on the rocks like veins of fresh paint. The red sun had sandpaper
beams. She saw human beings burned the colour of coal or dark-
brewed tea or cured leather; she smelled their alien sweat and their
tangy cooking, heard the mad bibbering of their manifold tongues.
A strange music that made her heart sag in the fear of this shattering
place. But later she saw pretty whitewashed houses in a row near
the waterfront, with palm trees in tranquil garden squares, and she
dared hope that Abel had secured them similar lodgings.

Johannesburg was two hot dry days to the north by train, through country that stunned her like a blow: the cactus hills, the khaki desolation of the plains, the distant hazy sky pierced by that red sun, a madman's glowering eyeball.

Her husband was the same but he was swaddled by grime, like a gem wrapped in dirty rags. He lived in a squalid cottage in the self-made Jewish ghetto along Beit Street in the inner-city neighbourhood of Doornfontein. Here it was as if a poor Lithuanian village had torn itself up from the cool forestlands of the north to root again in the baking dust of the deepest south. There were three small rooms behind his workshop, with a surly Black woman living in a tin hut out back. Gitelle gave herself over to tenderness with her beloved for only a day, no more. His long fingers and his gentle eyes. Then:

What do you need *her* for?

Everybody has one, a shiksa girl. It's the way here. People even poorer than us have them.

What does she do?

Do? She cleans, she cooks.

Is that what she calls it.

She fired her that afternoon and set to work cleaning out the pigsty of what Abel Helger's life had become without her, the poor beautiful man overwhelmed by the accretion of filth that is always the creeping growth of negligence. The children helped her boil water and scrub the floors and walls, even the cracked concrete of the tiny backyard. They emptied the useless Bantu woman's room (she had taken only what she could carry for her long journey home) and made a kerosene bonfire out of the reeking blanket and stained overalls, tossing onto it strange bottles and totems, things that looked like shrivelled insects which Gitelle warned the children away from and handled with just the extended fingertips of one gloved hand, her nose crimped above her dark veil.

Wherever they scrubbed, thick soot came off; when they beat a rug with an old tennis racquet there was a dense cloud of the albino dust that settled on everything from the mines close by. Gitelle opened windows to let in light and air. She shopped well and cooked good kosher food, hearty soups with marrow bones and barley, gefilte fish and cholent, beef with prunes, greasy potato latkes with sour cream and cinnamon and sugar. She baked sitnise bread, razeve bread – black and rye loaves – and fragrant braided challahs on a Shabbos eve with an egg wash to make them golden. She swept constantly, swiped the dust off the windowsills constantly, made sure the children went to bed with their bodies bathed and their hair washed, the teeth clean in their bright grins.

But there was one area that she could not reach and that was the workshop. Here was an unsanitary jumble of Abel's things and here he drew his masculine line. She did wrest control of the very front, where customers came in for her to greet, but the shop itself remained an unhealthy chaos, and worse – far worse – it was also where Abel's so-called friends congregated each day (except for Shabbos, when he was at shul). These were a group of men who'd settled onto him like parasite birds on the back of a rhino, fellow Litvaks all, most from the same Zarasai region, who didn't seem to work at all – how could they, sitting around on their tochuses in the workshop and eating and drinking, making useless chatter all day long. They seemed to have only one subject: their minds always mired in der haym, in backhome, that other country, that fallen time. It scared her more than any freeloading, this dank unhealthiness of living in the past. Life is the here and the future. These men were like a kind of death. Abel's past loneliness excused their initial presence; now she waited for their dismissal. But months passed and even her deliberate rudeness had no effect, the way she grunted back at their greetings, how she banged their plates down, their glasses.

She had to remind herself they had wives she saw in the streets, wives with cutting tongues. This was a neighbourhood full of watching eyes. Always she must take care to be seen as a good wife to her husband – for the sake of the business if nothing else, though truly the last thing she wanted was to disgrace him, demean him. She loved Abel. So she ground her teeth behind her veil and did her duty, left the workshop alone save to serve the men in it the way she was expected to serve. She was the new one to this place, after all, a greener off the boat, and an object of maddening pity in the streets where people still stared at the veil, still made sad faces and shook their heads at the sound of her sloshy words. She knew how their rumours said she suffered from some hideously deforming disease. Let them talk.

Meanwhile her energies transformed the front of the shop. Her husband's dealings, bless him, were a mess: debts forgiven or unknown, charity jobs for sob stories. She gave the business discipline, started writing everything down, and money began to drip steadily in. Like a bull terrier she guarded this accumulating cash, keeping it from her husband's hands and especially the hands of the parasites. She bought a new strongbox with a good lock and a slit in the top so money could be deposited but not withdrawn. The box was always locked if she was away from it and the only key was always in her purse tucked into the groove of her deep bosom. Soon there was enough saved to purchase a used black-and-gold Singer machine like the one she'd worked with in Dusat. She set up a sewing room in the maid's hut in the back, stocked it with fabrics she bought from the Indians on Fourteenth Street in Vrededorp, and began to make and sell dresses and fill alteration orders for a few tailors she went to see. The money from this piecework she spent on used goods at the market on Diagonal Street or at jumble sales. She stored them behind the piles of fabric: cracked vases, wonky coffee tables, broken picture frames – whatever nobody wanted. When she had time she fixed them up and sold them for a profit, quickly reinvested in more goods.

As soon as enough of her money was saved, she went to see a doctor for a consultation, a big surgeon named Graumann. This Dr. Graumann examined her and promised he could remove the need for the veil. His fee was too high; but he said he would take on her case for what she could afford. The news made her weep aloud for the first time in too many years to count. For so long she had worn the gloomy veil that cupped the lower part of her face like a hospital bandage – with its laces passing behind the ears to tie off at the nape, the bottom of it left loose for reaching under to eat or drink – that it had become a part of her being. It marked her out as a patient, a kind of leper. She had gotten free of Lithuania, yes, but she had not yet gotten free of the veil which ever in her mind chained her to that miserable place, that gloomy choking hopeless past.

She had the surgery against the advice of Abel who said he worried it might go wrong; but it went as she hoped it would, as Dr. Graumann had promised. No, she would never be normal, but after the surgery her words sounded as they should and she was prepared to let all of her face be seen by anyone who wanted to look at it.

Once healed, she burned the veil in the yard, as she had burned the shiksa's trash. She felt the clean-burning sun and the dry hot air on her chin, her lips. She went for long walks in the streets, walking around like everyone else. If someone looked at her, she looked them back in the eyes till they looked away. Slowly came the feeling that she had become another person, as if she had been born a second time in this country. Her feet were under her: she stood on her rights. She began to speak up more loudly more often.

But all the while the situation with the men in the workshop had not changed except to worsen. They were always in her way, cluttering the house, chattering uselessly about the old days, the old stories, the old country, a useless deadly nostalgia, circling.

The workshop was a kind of escapist bubble for them, like an opium den, a place to inhale each other's memories and exhale their own as they swallowed Abel's brandy and ate his food. Still, she must go on serving them for the sake of her husband and the appearance of being a good wife, but all the time now she was screaming inside her skull. She had changed; she had no more tolerance left for them at all. Her rage, pressed down, seared at her nerves and gave her bellyaches and heartburn, left her thrashing in her sleep like a victim of nightmares to wake with a stiff jaw and a headache from grinding her teeth all night.

Came a day when enough was enough. The inevitable day. One of *them* called her back when she was at the kitchen door. She had forgotten to take his ashtray, he said. His filthy stinking ashes. Out of habit she turned halfway back, she almost went to him. And then, no, she hit the door with her shoulder and passed right through the kitchen and out the other side into the backyard (hardly saw little Isaac spying from the doorway, hardly felt herself brush him aside on her way out). There was a thing in amongst the second-hand goods that she had bought that weekend at a clearance sale on Commissioner Street, and it called to her now beneath the level of words. Funny, she had hesitated buying it, it wasn't the kind of item she'd be able to sell easily, and yet. And still. The weight of it in her square hands. Now again she hefted it and felt resolve pour into her strong squat body. She turned, started back to the house. Nothing could have stopped her then, not even herself.

PART ONE

Doornfontein

I.

SKOTS SAYS IT'S FUNNY how soft the bottoms of Isaac's feet are – man he's always getting thorns or glass stuck in them that everyone else just runs right over. He says it goes with Isaac's funny hair like grated carrots and all the freckles on his face that make it look like them white cheeks was sprayed with motor oil or something; goes with those funny shorts about twenty sizes too big that he can only wear cos his da has made all those extra baby holes in the belt for him. Skots laughs and says also maybe the soft feet have to do with Isaac's skin that turns red as anything from one little tiny poke of the sun, and also look how skinny your legs are man, like two spaghettis.

They are all sitting in the burnt-out piece of veld behind Nussbaum's kosher butchery, eating a pigeon that Isaac shot off the phone wire with his catty when everyone else missed, and suddenly everyone goes all quiet, Isaac feeling them watching him. All he can hear is the noise from Beit Street, a tram clanging and rumbling, Yiddish shouts from the men selling fruit or bread or coal or ice.

Isaac looks slowly at Skots. —You calling me something hey Skots?

Skots seems to ponder the question, bunching and opening his toes in the dust at the edge of the firepit they'd scratched and packed with tomato-box wood since turned to greyblack ashes. Pigeon bones and pigeon grease lie on top; singed feathers still smoking.

Isaac says, —If you not bladey calling me something you better shut your bladey trap, know that Skots.

The others wait. Isaac watching Skots, thinking maybe he'd be a Stupid and try jump at him like last time, Skots a taller older boy with muscles in his arms like hard little apples. But that other time he'd gotten the thumb in his teeth and bitten so hard, to the bone, making Skots cry like a girl, saying I give, I give. Isaac gets his heels under him and leans forward.

Charlie, looking from one to the other, quick and nervous, says, —Hey hey you all know what? And starts telling them about a man was so crazy, so moochoo in his head, that he was doing these *very bad things* that he, Charlie, has seen with his own two eyes.

—What bad things? says Isaac, staring at Skots.

Charlie doesn't want to tell, but after they press him and he tells them everything, Isaac starts to feel hot and sick. His eyes and his throat grow full. He doesn't care about Skots no more, or about anything else. He stands up. —Lez go get him! Lez get that bladey bastid.

When Isaac runs, the others follow. No hesitation. They pass through the alley next to Nussbaum's and into the noise and motion of Beit Street, the Yiddisher jabber of the sellers and the horses pulling carts and the bicycles ching-chinging and the Packards hooting and the doubledecker tram with its twirly stairs rumbling off down the middle of the street, scratching loose blue sparks from the wires above. On the corner, cages of gabbling chickens are stacked high and farther down the iceman with heavy gloves is unloading blocks wrapped in straw from his horse cart. There are tables of vegetables and the noises of sawing and banging from Dovedovitz and tinking noises from Katz the tinsmith while down the next alley the blacksmith's forge glows orange hot, and all along in front of the long covered stoep there are Xhosa women on the side of the street sitting with their legs sideways on their bright blankets with their trinkets of ivory and stinkwood. Behind the glass of the butcher shops there hang black logs of salt-cured biltong and fat bottleblue flies mass on the blooded gobs of sawdust swept into the gutter with the smelly chunks of horse kuk.

On the far side of Beit Street, beyond the shops, they run between row houses with roofs of corrugated iron. It gets quiet here: just their breathing, their patting feet. Lizards on whitewash in the bright sun. They run till the asphalt ends and the dirt is hard as steel, pocked with holes or the glitter of quartz. Here at the end of the road is an open-sided square of tin houses with a single water tap in the middle on the open dirt, where women line up with squalling babies lashed to their backs and clinking buckets in their hands. Men sit on newspapers in the afternoon glow, children wrestle and shout. Someone is playing a guitar made of rubber bands and pieces of a detergent box.

They slow. Isaac touches the catty in his back pocket, a nice one he made from some inner tube stretched on a Y of strong wood; shoots stones beautifully hard and straight. He turns on Charlie. —Where is he, wherezit?

—Hang on, says Charlie. They watch him run to the far corner of the square where there's a gap in the tin and he looks around, then comes jogging back shaking his head. —He not there yet.

—Lez go back and play by the chains park there.

—Lez go to the churu man and tell him kuk banana.

—We staying here, says Isaac. We staying here till he comes. Charlie, you keep an eye.

They wander down to a door where Isaac lets Skots go first. Dark coming in from the bright and sudden close smells of mielie pap and sour piss. Now he sees the table made of cardboard boxes with a bedsheet on it with pictures of strawberries and cigarette holes. Auntie Peaches is there: she passes them sweet real coffee in an old Horlicks jar – coffee he's not allowed at home but Mame will never find out. Coffee to wash down the taste of the charred pigeon. He takes his sip and passes on. Bad coughing rips through the tin wall. Auntie Peaches pokes his tummy. —How's the little devil hey, hey? Little devilhead, little troublemaker.

He rolls on his back with his knees up, giggling. This is happiness in the close feel of this homely space. But Charlie comes shouting: —Ouens, ouens, hy's hier die bliksem!

Guys, guys, the bastard's here.

Outside the sun burns a white disc through a passing cloud as they run to the corner and turn into the alley there, sausages of kuk underfoot to dodge. At the end is the rubbish place that used to be a hole but is now a little rubbish mountain and in front of it is the madman.

—Is the puppy man, says Davey. Thaz the puppy man.

—I know him, says Nixie. He try sell them every day all around.

Puppyman is tall and wears only armless dungaree overalls with holes in them, too big for his lean frame, his cap is stuffed in a back pocket and his head is bald in spots and he is missing one sock and the heel flaps on one shoe. He sways on his feet with a small bottle in one hand. On the ground in front of him is a tall cardboard apple box. Things are moving in that box. He bends down and takes out a little dog that's white with black spots, puts it carefully on top of two stacked bricks and stands looking down at it.

—Come on, says Isaac. But his heart is hammering very big in him and he goes slowly and can feel no one wants to come with as they follow behind. Puppyman looks bigger and bigger the closer he gets. Puppyman has deep wrinkles everywhere in his face like they cut in with a knife. Isaac says to him, —Scuse hey, what you doing with that liddel dog?

Takes a while for Puppyman to find his focus, squinting down at Isaac. —Why you care? You wanna buy?

—How much? says Isaac.

—Ach you got no monies, lightie. Piss off now. *Voetsak!*

The pup is standing up on the bricks, the whole of its fat-bellied body trembling; then it squats at the back and some pee runs off the bricks. It's true that Puppyman doesn't look right in the head. His eyes are yellowish and full of red veins and it's like they are covered over with glassy webs. He takes a drink from that bottle and talks some kind of nonsense to himself. His breath smells like petrol. There's dirt crusted in some of the blobs of his hair, and bits of maybe paint or something also. He has red blistery sores on one side of his mouth and not many teeth.

—You the puppy man, says Isaac. You musn't hurt that dog.

—I'm the puppy man, says Puppyman. Is what I am. Is true. He turns and takes a long step, swings his leg like a soccer player: a grunt with the meatbone thud, the puppy only huffs one tiny squeak. It arcs high, drops onto the rubbish and rolls, flops, lies still and strewn as a rag. Puppyman lifts the bottle, wipes his mouth and talks low to himself.

Isaac feels sick right through.

—All you little buggers go piss off, says Puppyman. Is my stock, I does what I want with my own stock. Isaac stares at the box behind Puppyman. Another one moving in there, a bigger one. Puppyman mutters and turns to it. He is so tall and the muscles in his shoulders stand out like they carved in wood and the elbows look pointy as spears, the forearms wrapped in veins like snakes.

Isaac lifts his arms. Behind him Nixie says, —We better go hey. He drinking meths, that.

Skots: —He big and mad.

Charlie: —He's cooked in the head. He gone moochoo.

Nixie: —Lez go tell someone.

—Izey? Hey Izey, no man. *Izey!*

But Isaac is already moving.

2.

BUXTON STREET, NUMBER FIFTY-TWO, a corner house. Isaac stops at the front door and the dog on the leash of onionsack string sits at his ankle. Through the window next to the door Isaac sees the business desk with the adding machine, the big black order book and the cashbox. The wall calendar says 1927 in red letters and also *JHB* which are some of the letters he knows how to read even though he hasn't started school yet. Means Johannesburg which is Joburg, where they live. He puts up a hand to cover the glare and looks past the front into the workshop where he also sleeps at night on a foldaway cot. Tutte is there at his bench, bent over; his left foot flat and his bad foot resting up on the low stool. All around him the boxes heap up, holding the gutted clock and watch parts, the springs, cogs, clock faces, clock hands. There's tiny brass tubes in there that give a nice chime if you tap them with tiny hammers, so tiny you can put them on the fingernail of your pinky. On the bench he sees the long half-circle of the lathe attached by a spring cord in a figure eight to the electric motor that powers it. There's mineral oil in long-nosed bottles, piled rags overspilling a shoebox. Tutte uses some screws that are thin as hairs, as eyelashes. Tutte with the magnifying loupe sticking from his right eye like a permanent growth. Tutte – he fixes time.

But when Isaac looks down at the white dog he knows it's not ganna do any good to even ask him.

———

There's a long laneway behind all the houses. Number fifty-two is on the corner where the alley makes a turn and opens onto Buxton Street, Beit Street just a little way up. Isaac turns into the alley and starts down. His back hurts when he walks, right in the middle where the bottle got him, and he's sure there'll be a lekker fat bruise there tomorrow if there isn't one already. Yas, but he was lucky that the big man tripped and fell over. He can't hardly believe he did what he did – all happened so quick. He pushed him and got the dog and ran and when he looked back Puppyman was getting up and chucking the bottle. He'd ducked his head down and that's when he got whacked hard, didn't feel it then only later once he'd climbed up over the rubbish and behind him the others gave it to Puppyman with their catties so that he chased them instead.

He had climbed down the far side of the rubbish and gone over the railway tracks and made a big circle coming home. Stopping a few times to give the little dog water and rinse him off in a horse trough. So little and shivery it is. He ties the leash to a nail in the brick wall, feels its hot little chest and the heart inside going pumpapumpa. You alive still. I got you.

He goes on by himself and the alley turns and he comes around the side of his house to the gateway at the back without a gate, just a gap in the low wall of cracked purple bricks. He stands there watching her in the backyard, a solid wide woman with thick arms in the short sleeves of her handmade dress, one sleeve stuffed with her handkerchief, the muscles in her forearms crinkling as she works, hanging up the wash. Her mouth has that familiar bunched expression, one side smeared pink with scar tissue that runs over the cheek to the jawbone like melted candle wax. The forehead is wide and freckled like his, and the gingerish hair, darker progenitor of his own, is worn back and clipped flat. Without looking at him she says: —Nu, voo iz der chulleriuh?

Where is what? he says, the same language automatic.

You heard. Don't pretend. That piggish cholera, an animal to kill us all in our home.

It's not true.

There's a snigger: Rively at the kitchen door. He punches at her, the bladey tattletale. She musta seen him outside with it.

Now Mame's looking at him, her wide warm face shaking slowly at his rage. My little Isaac, she says, and she smiles her halfsmile, one side clawed down by the scar. He runs to her, folds against her, feels her square hands on his back and her kiss on his crown. You're the beautiful little one, she says, only you. You're my boy, my rainbow, aren't you?

Mame, Mame. I got him for you.

Are you my clever one?

He's wrapped his little arms around her hips and her hands are at the back of his head, the heat of her soft belly eases through the apron into his pressed cheek.

It's all right, love. You take me and show me what you have brought for your mame. Because you are my Clever.

Yes Mame, I'm your Clever.

Tell me the two kinds in this world.

The Clevers and the Stupids.

That's right. And what are you?

I'm a Clever, Mame, I'm your Clever.

Come, Clever. Show me.

They go hand in hand to the puppy dog, sitting flat on its back legs, loose tongue unscrolled.

It looks a thirsty one, she says. How did you get it?

I asked for him. For free I got him.

Someone gave for free in the street?

Yes, free. A present.

Who was it?

He doesn't answer. She's looking down, scrapes loose a sound like someone readying to spit. He sinks and reaches for the dog but she yanks him back. —Sish! she says. Disgust! Don't touch your eyes. Can go blind. Now we'll have to boil up water to wash you good.

Wash?

Filthy animal from you don't even know where it's been. Gives you warts. A fever.

He shakes his head. The dog is watching him, his face. It tries Mame and its tail quivers then droops.

Backhome I remember how the poyers used to put such a dog with a stone in the lake and finished.

No!

She turns his chin, looks down at him. What you so upset? If I told you to go and do *that*, your mame, would you?

No.

—Neyn?

—Neyn!

You see, so you don't listen to Mame. If you had said yes to me, because you're a good boy, so then you could keep him.

He thinks on this, gnaws his bottom lip. Feels his eyes start to glisten. No, I would have, Mame. I would listen and say yes.

Don't make up grannystories now. It's written a thousand truths can't clean one lie. Come inside.

He pulls against her, stretching down. The dog whines, licks at his fingertips.

See how you don't listen, not even what I am telling to you this second. Leave it.

Pleading, he reaches for another language: —Oh Ma. Oh Ma *please*. He's not dirty. Auntie Peaches gave him to me and I washed him also, look how clean.

She stiffens as if slapped. Turns very slowly. What did you just say?

———

Now they are moving across the crowded jumble of Beit Street traffic then down the long stoep under the tin roof. Ma pulling him by the hand and the little dog on its string behind. At the end of the block: Is this the place? Is this it? But he can't speak. People are looking. Mr. Epstein the tailor next door comes out with a tape measure looping his skinny neck, his sharp nose twitching, pretending not to listen. A tram rumbles past while a truckload of dirty workers sitting on burlap sacks of coal passes on the other side, the men singing Zulu together, a mingled wave of sound deep and sweet and sad through the traffic. Outside Siderman's dry goods they're brooming shmootz off the edge of the stoep.

Mame shakes his arm. This the place or not?

It's the churu grocery on the corner and he peers in. Where they come to steal naartjies and Cadbury's chocs. Round rock candy gobstoppers that everyone calls niggerballs. They come in here, the five of them, and one will sing a mocking song to make the churu get cross and chase him while the other ones lift the things. Singing,

> *Hurry churu*
> *Hurry curry*
> *Kuk banana*
> *Two for tickey*
> *No bonsela*

Churu, dirt word for Indian, never fails to get the man shouting and lunging. Mame is starting to get cross herself. Why did he have to tell her this place? It just jumped into his mind.

Now he looks inside and the proprietor behind the desk, with thick eyelids half down against the evening light, lifts up his fly swatter as a warning. Isaac's face he knows. Calls him the little redhair rubbish.

—She's not here, Isaac says.

Where is she then? says Mame. You know where she lives?

—No Ma.

How can you not?

—Ma, she was here, here's where she give him to me, I–

He stops because he's seeing someone behind her. She is coming to the churu shop like they sometimes do. He had been counting on no one being here, but here she is crossing the street and Mame turns to watch where he's watching. Not Auntie Peaches or Marie. Auntie Sooki.

What are you looking?

Nothing.

Who you looking? What?

That's when he steps out and waves – can't help it. Auntie Sooki slants her head, lifts a hand to her brow to see him in the cutting light. He shouts, the right tongue automatic: —Allo daar Auntie!

She sees him then. Lifts her other arm. She's stopped in the middle of the road to let the bikes and the Studebakers and the Chevs go by. When they're passed he sees her big loose grin, her hoarse voice carries: —Allo Izey. Howzit my boy! Howzee my boy!

Isaac is running off the stoep to her when his teeth clack, his head jerks. Mame's grip digs into his arm and then they're moving so fast away that his feet skip and the strung dog yelps to keep up. He thinks don't cry, mustn't cry. Sees the face of Mr. Epstein flash past, the eyes huge in their staring.

Farther down they veer through traffic unstopping like he's not supposed to, and she doesn't slow, not once, all the way home.

Supper will be late tonight. Isaac is sitting with Mame in her room and the door is shut and she's speaking very softly but very firmly, gripping his chin to make him look in her brown eyes. Say it again, she tells him.

—Auntie Peaches gave me the dog.

She is the mother of your friend.

—She's Skots's ma. That was Auntie Sooki by the churu. I think she's the sister of Auntie Maggie, who's Charlie's ma.

A deep breath, her chest lifting. I want you to listen. Those women are not your aunties. You have aunties. That woman, she is a *Coloured*.

—I know Ma, you said it.

Listen. A Coloured is half of a Black. It's coffee in your blood. We are Whites. We are Jews but we are Whites here. If People see you with Coloureds and hear you talk like that about *aunties* who are Coloureds, then they will think maybe we have coffee in our blood also. You understand?

—Ja Ma.

Don't *ja Ma*. Listen. We are Whites, like anyone. No one can think we have coffee in the blood. That's dangerous. Do you understand me?

—Yes Ma.

She stares at him, into him, for so long he starts to shiver. Who is this *Skots*?

—I go by his house sometimes. To play, like. My friends.

Where's this house?

—In the Yards, he says.

Ma is silent for a long span; her breathing whistles a little in her nostrils. You go in the Yards. Do you go into their houses?

He trembles and won't look. Her fingers pinching his chin. Look at me, Isaac. You don't mix in with dirt people in the Yards. Ever. You could be killed or anything. The filthy Yards. Bring the diseases home and make your family sick.

He can't hold it in anymore, the tears come. They tumble through his snivelling. Mame pulls him close then and kisses his head, his brow. Her lips are so rough on one side. Oh my good boy, she says in his ear, my good fine boy. I only wish you knew your real aunties, it rips my heart you don't know your own. Auntie Trudel-Sora, Auntie Orli, Auntie Friedke, your uncle

Pinchus and uncle Shlayma, Auntie Dvora and Rochel-Dor. Your
cousins. The most important thing.

I'm sorry Mame, he says in Jewish in his weeping. I'm so sorry.

I know, my boy, my beautiful.

She makes him look at black-and-white pictures in the albums,
images of women he can only just touch at the far edge of his
memories. These are your only aunties. Your father, bless him, has
no one. Don't ever talk about any other aunties.

Sitting next to him on the bed and turning the stiff pages.
This is Rochel-Dor. This is her husband Benzil. This is your
grandfather Zalman of peaceful memory, he was the butcher and
a clever scholar, you remember? This is by the bridge . . .

She makes him put his fingertip under each black-and-white
face and say the name that belongs to it. Uncles, cousins,
especially aunties.

Orli. Friedke. Trudel-Sora.

Say the name. Say it aloud.

Rochel-Dor. Dvora.

One day they will be here with us. We will have a house for
them and they can stay as long as they want or need to. In our
own house we'll decide who stays, not miserable creeping little
Greenburg, sniffing for his rent every month, the moping cholera.

—Yes Mame.

Outside, Tutte is knocking again. Gitelle, the girl is hungry.
I'm hungry.

I'm coming, she says. Another minute. This is more important.

From the kitchen table Isaac can see the dog tied in the backyard
next to the water bowl he set for it. Mame sees him looking as she
dishes up thin slices of brisket with pumpkin latkes and mashed
potatoes. Rively is asking Tutte a question about God, if God ever
talks to people at shul. Tutte nodding very slowly. Yes but you

have to know how to listen because God whispers. *Have you heard him Tutte?* Of course, all the time. *When Tutte?* Like when I was working just today. *What did He say, Tutte, what did He say to you?* He says what He always says, that He is looking after us. *Why doesn't He talk to me, Tutte?* He does, but you have to be quiet to hear Him, my mind is only quiet when I pray or I work. He turns up his long fingers and wiggles all of them like an insect on its back and Rively giggles. When my fingers are talking for me in my work then my heart is quiet, and my head, and that's when I sometimes can hear Him whispering. It's written that it's this whisper of God that sustains the world. Whispering underneath everything, always the whispering, because if it ever stopped the world would go out like a light. *Tutte, I want to hear Him whisper.* You will, my beautiful girl. You only have to have a good heart and to do what you love to do with a good heart, that's all you need in this world.

Mame clicks her tongue, almost angry, to get Isaac to look away from the window. She settles down behind her plate and they all start eating; only Tutte murmurs the blessings first, only Rively hesitates, watching him. —Geshmuck number vun, Tutte says, after swallowing. Delicious number one: a line from an old joke about a fat woman on Muizenberg beach that Isaac's never understood. Mame seems not to have heard and keeps on looking at Isaac. She starts to talk about the Clevers and the Stupids. The Stupids who live like pack mules, poor and hopeless, the Clevers who rise in the world like Mr. Jackman who started with one cart here on Beit Street and now owns the biggest department shop in all Africa, a whole block there in town, anyone can walk and see it. The Clevers like the men who own the gold mines. Mr. Barney Barnato was a poor Jew who came to Africa with nothing but dust in his pockets, and then there was Sammy Marks and the Joels and the Beits, Mr. Hersov and the giant Mr. Oppenheimer. Now they are the richest men in the world. Every diamond on earth is under their thumbs, and most of the gold.

Yes, says Tutte, smiling, but tell me, do they eat as well as we do? Not like this. And how many pairs of shoes can they wear at once? How many beds do they sleep in? How happy are their children?

Mame clicks her tongue, irritated. For a Clever, she says, anything is possible but for a Stupid life is misery.

When she talks this way Isaac knows she'll start to talk about a house again soon, that they need a house, up in the northern suburbs, a private house of their own, of the family's; but she surprises him. She is smiling her clawed-down halfsmile and tapping the serving spoon on the dish of mashed potatoes. Now Isaac, she says in that warm deep loving voice, you tell us, if one person gets rid of a dirty animal that makes diseases and costs to feed, that makes a stinking mess that must be cleaned all day, that can *bite children* God forbid, then is that person not a Clever? And if someone else must take in the animal and get sick from the diseases and have to clean up the messes and pay for the food for the animal, then is that person not a Stupid?

—Nu, zog mir, she says. Zog mir der richtike emes.

So tell me. Tell me the real truth.

—Ja hey Isaac, says Rively. You tell us.

Isaac twists a face at his sister but after a while he knows that Mame is right. He stops looking to the window. He wants to be like Mr. Jackman who is a Clever and if Mr. Jackman wouldn't keep a dog, as his Mame keeps saying, then he won't want one either. Her logic, too, is as watertight as the lavender hull of a Union Castle liner: the dog brings expenses and trouble and you can't do anything with it, like get milk from a cow (like the beautiful cow called Baideluh that Tutte always talks about that they had backhome). You have to be a Clever. Today he's done like a Stupid.

The dog starts crying outside, a rising woowoo that breaks at its peak then settles back to mounting whimpers.

Do you see? says Mame. Do you see what problems he is making already?

When supper is over he and his mother go out to the dog. It is clear she has a plan for it, her movements brisk. Isaac watches her untie the leash from the wall but when she pulls it the dog and its tail droop and it looks at him and yaps and Isaac runs across and falls over it, squeezes its huddled warmth tight against him. I didn't even give a name yet.

Listen Isaac, don't stir me now. Don't make me boil. Be good.

I'm not, Mame, I'm not.

He looks up and she's moving to the sewing room. She's moving fast and all of a sudden it hits him that it's just like it was with the couchers: it's going to be the couchers all over again! He starts to shout as loud as he can, he leaves the dog and he chases after her with his arms spread. No Mame, no! Don't do it, no, Mame!

Mame puts on the light in the cramped hut, turns to face him with a screwed-up face. What are you hammering in my head for? Calm down.

You mustn't, Mame!

Mustn't what? What are you crying about?

As she talks she reaches into a hiding place behind a half-splintery folded table and brings out a bottle of brandy, then another. Isaac stops shouting, leans against the wall.

What is it? says Mame. What's the matter?

He doesn't answer but watches her wrapping the bottles briskly in newspaper so they won't clink inside her handbag. She puts the handbag strap in the crook of her plump arm, her chin points. Your friend, she says.

He turns and the little dog is standing there watching his face. Mame comes out and picks up the dog's string, hands it to him. She walks off and he doesn't move. She stops and looks back. Isaac.

He follows her and the dog follows him. Drooping both.

Okay, oright, ja: the dog will not stay. He's resigned. Seeing her go for the sewing room like that – it lit up the fearful memory of that other day, harsh and real enough to burn away all the protest in him. More than.

Old carpets draped on a sagging frame that reeked of smoke and sweat, that's all it was, pressed against one wall of the workshop opposite Tutte's bench. And the warm feeling from the slumped men there on it, their grizzled faces and hairy hands. He loved to watch them, how they tipped bottles of Chateau brandy and used their penknives on plates of pickled fish or to cut up fatty chunks of Goldenberg's kosher polony or salty crackling logs of biltong. The way they argued over the scattered news pages. How they taught him to play klaberjass with a dog-eared pack showing ladies in bathing costumes (slapping the cards down hard, shouting *Shtoch! Yus! Menel!*), and how they smoked their oval Turkish Blend cigarettes pinched in a circlet of thumb and forefinger. His father would look up and sometimes add a murmur to their lurching debates from the workbench where he was bent over the watches; never more.

Simple Fivel had the gap in his teeth and the tongue curling through to the tip of his nose. Kaplan used to bend over the side hacking up black jelly into a saucer always positioned by his left foot. Mandelbaum had no teeth at all, his gums alone crunching peanuts and even Mame's taygluch – syruped doughnuts baked candy hard – while he winked at Isaac, making him giggle. They were the men of old and their hoarse voices breathed to him the wisdom of narrow streets and distant times and fading places, they wore their hats on the backs of their heads and went at life with a sideways elbow, a knowing whistle from the corner of the mouth. Scrapers, survivors. Full of jolly battering. They told no stories that were not jokes. There is a way to laugh at anything and they had it, a glaze of double meaning he could never quite penetrate but always sense. And when they laughed, their heads rocked back and the couch squeaked and shifted. Farting Ellenbogen the crook. Yishi Strudz doing tricks with hanky and spoon. Swarthy Leitener the strongman buckling horseshoes, a drop of shvitz quivering on the tip of his arced nose.

While they laughed he saw that their sad drooping eyes did not change, their faces grizzled and pouchy. And the laughing always turned into a sigh at the end, a shaking of the head. Then they would start to talk about der haym again, olden times backhome. The forests and the families.

He watched them shlupping hot tea from glasses or saucers, tea drizzled from the tap of a beaten brass samovar with its smoking coals. The steaming glasses with a fuzzy dollop of apricot jam at the bottom, a wedge of lemon floating. The way they lifted the hot steam to their mouths, the careful shlupping noises through the pouted lips – the longer the sound the better the satisfaction – then the great sigh, appreciating the heat of the tea into the belly. Vestige of a land where snow chilled the fingers and the blood. Where do any of these huddled attitudes come from? It's the fading place on the far side of Isaac's furthest memories. Some essence a part of him still yearns toward.

The couchers. Theirs was a poignant human warmth, and Isaac could have sat before them as before a fireplace in winter the whole day long if not for Mame. He knew his father felt the same warmth. So much better than working alone, all alone, with only the cold tickticking of irrevocable time for company.

Down the alley they are moving. A mother, a boy, and a dog. Night has dropped like a sudden curtain: African night. A wind brings mine dust on it, to coat the laundry on the bobbing lines, to make them blink and wipe at their faces, to scratch and hiss on the iron roofs of Doornfontein. The white dog drags on the string behind him so that he has to yank it every now and then. It's easier for him not to look back. They plod all the way down to the railway bridge. The bruise on his back aches.

His mother doesn't say anything. She's looking toward the other side while they wait and he watches the side of her scarred face in equal silence.

It didn't just happen out of nothing; there were dark rays before.

If he was in the kitchen when she came back from the couchers with an armload of dirty plates and cups, to fetch more food for them, he would hear acid curses in her breath that puzzled him with their ferocity. Calling them parasites and lazy scum. And if she caught his eye she would stop to lecture in a hiss: what it was exactly that she meant by the word parasites, how these couchers would one day gnaw the very walls down from around them and they, the family, would have to live on the street like half-starved squatting animals, was that right? Would even one of the couchers lift a finger to help them then? Tell me, would they? Isaac would nod but really couldn't picture anyone gnawing at any walls, and when he thought of the couchers he only wanted to smile, and felt a little sad for them, for their pouchy watery eyes. Even to think of the couch just as an object made him feel good, to lie on its piled threadbare carpets, its rich smoky manly smell, the only soft thing in the workshop.

Mame would tell him how the couchers were abusing Tutte's great gifts, his talented hard work, for his father was a craftsman and a gentleman with a heart of solid gold, only he was too good, too good for this world, he couldn't see what they were doing to the family, because the golden shine of his own heart blinded him so.

When she spoke this way her eyes would narrow almost shut; the scar tissue would turn shiny, livid. This was the dangerous thing in her that was stirring. Isaac knows it's there always, like a lioness bound up in a sack. Knows it because he was in the kitchen on the day she finally had enough of the couchers, *enough*. No more polony and pickled fish and booze for the leeches, the freeloading termites! When she barged through the kitchen door that day, Isaac held it for her and watched her drop the plates and go on outside into the backyard.

—Mame?

Watched her through the open doorway moving into the sewing room so calmly and fetching out for herself the second-hand wood axe that she'd bought only that last week.

—Mame?

But her eyes were slits, as if she were dreamwalking, with the scar so brightly livid on her face. Back through the kitchen past him as if he wasn't there. From the doorway he watched her stand before the couchers. Holding the thing behind her skirt with both hands, a strangely coy gesture but her voice was so flat and dead that, even though it was very soft, Isaac's father looked up at once from the bench. He knew what he knew. Pity on them who did not. It's finished, she told them. The party is closed for good. Get out.

It didn't seem to dent their bleary joking. Shmulkin was there that day and he leaned forward to address her with a nodding forefinger, with one eye shut. Kaplan wondered where his ashtray had got to. Taysh tried to prod an empty bottle at her, meaning bring them another. Someone grepsed; someone else – Ellenbogen no doubt – broke soft wind. Their voices were all hoarse and thick with liquor and fatty food, their laughs gruff unshaven rumblings.

Don't Mame, Isaac thought. Leave them, the poor sad couchers. Don't hurt them Mame.

Even within the glowing clarity of these kindled memories there are parts of what happened next that Isaac can't remember, though at the time he stared so hard his eyes ached. He remembers his father lurching up and calling out his mother's name, plus the sense of sliding and clattering, and how loud their shouts were and how savage and quick she was with that flashing axehead with everything happening, tumbling, at once.

Hacking into that hated couch with all her power, feathers and splinters and back-flung slats of shredded carpet. The men snatching their limbs away and rolling off, breaking plates, shattering bottles.

His mother's thick arms lifting and falling and the breath grunting in her clenched face: the flash of that axe.

The men tumbling before her into the street and then she was pitching chunks of the couch out after them. Simple Fivel sitting on the dirt wailing in incomprehension like a hurt child. Neighbours came to the cries. Isaac watched her, outlined by the light in the doorway with the axe lifted and shaking in one hand, the mass of her upper arm quivering in the sleeve, her voice raw in a scream he'd never heard before. All those insults she'd long nursed in her acid muttering ripping out into the daylight then, calling them nochshleppers, kleps, kuylikers, mumzayrim and shmootsikuh shnorrers.

Clingers-on, leeches, cripples, bastards and dirty beggars.

Scum, *scum*, she said. Nothing but parasite scum. And when Isaac's father had limped up behind her with his bad foot scuffing and gently put his hands on the backs of her stout strong shoulders, she wriggled him off without looking around. Said: Not one word, Abel. Not even so much as one.

His father had hesitated for a long time, his hands still up. Then he'd slowly turned and limped back to his bench, his bad foot scuffing. As he sat again he'd seen Isaac in the kitchen door and become frozen for six beats of Isaac's smashing heart; he lifted one hand slowly and dusted the air, two quick shooing motions. Out, out. Don't look at this.

Isaac had turned and run. The men never came back and Isaac's father has worked alone at his bench ever since.

———

At the railway bridge a long time passes and then someone comes from the other side to where they are waiting, a woman with vast hips who looks like a maid, with her checkered blanket wrapped around the great belly and a blue doek tied on her head. When she gets close she says: —Mevrou Gitty, hulloh.

—Hello Mama, and how you?

—Oh medem is not so good, business time. My husband he put so bad now also. Who is? Your boy?

—Yes. His name, Yitzchok.

—Hullo, Itziok.

—Yitzchok, this lady is Mama Kelo. Say hello Mama Kelo. Isaac is shy. He looks down. —Hello.

—Mama, his mother says, today is ten shillings. No more seven and six.

—Heh?

—Ten shillings, ten shillings.

She holds up all her fingers as she is saying this. Mama Kelo seems to sway back from this. Shrinking from this squat wide figure before her, a third of her size, shaking those plump digits.

—Ow! Mama says at last. No no no.

—Yesh.

—Why put for me this? No no.

—I put, Isaac's mother says. She repeats her price. Isaac looks at her: her face is stone, scarred stone. She says, —Mama, if you like you take. Otherwise I go.

—Oh but is too too much. Why is so hard you put for me today? Why is?

His mother doesn't answer. She puts up her chin in a way that Isaac knows well, stretching the scar tissue a little where it runs to the jaw, showing the tendons in her strong neck, and what it means is that she has made up her mind and will not change it, never. —Ten shillings.

This other one huffs and sighs and shifts her huge shoulders. Finally her dark round face dips, she mumbles into her palm.

—Nu? You take or you not?

—I . . . yes.

—Veruh nice. And you have for you this present also.

—Present?

—Dis little doggie here.

— . . . Oh. Is not you boy for this one dog?

—No, no, you take him. Present.

—No medem.

—You take it. Can give it someone by where you are. Nice present. For free, I give.

— . . . I not . . .

—Take.

They look at each other. His mother so much smaller. But when she pushes her chin up and stretches her pink scar the other woman only sighs and Isaac watches her great bulk deflate, watches her fold herself that much closer to the earth. She pulls out a small purse tucked under the waist blanket. Upends it to tip out coins. Counts off two half crowns, three sixpences, three one shilling pieces, and then, slowly, all the rest in the dulled brass of pennies and little farthings. She holds these out on her palm and his mother takes them and counts them all again, then hands over the bottles. The white pup is looking at Isaac as it is dragged away. It yaps only once, maybe because the hairy string is cutting into its throat. Isaac sees Puppyman in his mind, that long leg swinging, the trembling pup on the wet brick. His mother is staring at him.

—Are you cry?

—No, no, I'm not. Not.

Listen, she says. Come walk this way.

They pass under a lamplight then another.

She says: Mama Kelo has a shebeen for them to drink over there where it's not allowed. In the Yards. She can't get brandy in the shop like us. She needs us but we don't need her. Am I a bladerfool not to charge?

Bladerfool: a serious insult of her own. He knows she got it when someone important in the news one time called someone a *bloody fool*; the words were explained to her and soon after she started bladerfooling. The most Stupid of the Stupid is what it means to her – the worst of the worst – and Isaac is already nodding.

Mame stops. Isaac faces her. She puts her warm square palm on his head. Believe me, she also will take everything from us if she could. A nice woman she can be, but give her the chance and she would take and take and leave us with nothing. That's who people are. We have to be strong.

Like the couchers, he thinks, who gnaw at the walls.

His mother hefts in a breath, lets it out slowly, looking away. Isaacluh, Isaacluh. There's a low wall in front of them and she leads him to it. —Zitz.

Sit. She helps him up and he settles before her and she bends, her face coming out of the lamplight. Looking up, it is the scar he sees first. Now her eyes, fixed. She holds his face from both sides so that he can't look away.

I want to say big things to you. It's time. You are nearly in school. But you run all day with Coloureds. You don't even know why you don't have shoes. I want you should be awake. Life is good but it is very hard. Where we are is no playground. Give a look. This is like a jail, but hard work escapes. To live one day in a house far away, quiet and nice, a house with no bond. Who can buy this house? Can you buy this house for your mame?

He opens his mouth but she shakes her head.

Rively is a girl, she'll get married. Your father is too good for this world full of miserable takes. A thousand little biters on every side. You have to be so strong against them. If someone is taking, put him away from you. Someone wants to play with you, remember it's not a game, a playground. You are young and healthy, not like your father. You are the son and what will you do? One day. Tell me.

—Zog mir.

—I will.

—Zog mir.

—Ich vel.

—*Zog mir.*

I will buy us a house, Mame. I promise you.

Yes you will. Parasites you don't let klep onto you. You don't listen to crybabies and nochshleppers. People they will try to stop you and be jealous, to trip you. But you go forward and make and do. You don't play with Coloureds and poor rubbishers.

—I won't Mame, I promise.

You don't give to takes.

—Neyn, neyn Mame.

At last she smiles. Half a mouth, half a scar. Two kinds in the world, she says to him.

The Stupids and the Clevers.

The Stupids and the Clevers. And what are you?

I'm a Clever, Mame. I'm your Clever.

—Ot uzay, meiner sheiner, meiner klooger, ot uzay. That's it, my beautiful one, my Clever, that's it . . .

And when she hugs him this time it's so tight it crushes the breath out of him, fills his head with floating and dizziness. A house for you Mame, I promise, I promise so hard. He squeezes back but his arms are so weak against the warm bulk of her loving self. The dense power of her unmovable being.

The next day when he goes out walking he stays away from those certain streets; but a few days after, he passes close to the strip of veld behind Nussbaum's. They are there. His mouth dries. He pretends he doesn't notice their waving or hear their whistles. That Charlie is bouncing up and down and smiling so hard. He turns quickly and he runs the other way, fast as he can, runs home, to his mother.

3.

THOUGH SOMEHOW HE MAKES it to high school, the way Isaac sees it, him and schools were never meant to mix. Even swotting for his barmy when he had to learn his Torah portion from that Rabbi whatsisname, Saltzenburger, up in the attic on Van Beek Street, he managed to get himself expelled. All he did was glue the old topper's beard to the desk after he'd fallen asleep snoring for, what, the tenth time already? Rabbi's getting paid – supposed to be teaching them izzen he? Ukay, maybe Isaac shouldn't have then screamed the word FIRE into his ear loud as he could. Maybe that was a bit much.

They've said the same thing in all the schools he's passed through, that he always goes too far. They called him Rabies Helger cos of that time he used a chair on Johnny Marks and Stan Allan and the name stuck (well they shouldn't have said what they said about Ma, right?) – Rabies Helger: son of that scarfaced axe lady on Buxton Street. But he didn't mind it so much, he minded more how upset Da got when they kicked him out of Jewish Government and those other two primary schools. Ma, she wasn't so worried. She knows what he is; she's always wanted him to get out and start earning.

Ma is a bit of a whizz genius when it comes to that, always pointing him in the right direction. She it was who noticed that so many boys were constantly playing pinball in the cafis and encouraged his avid researches into the phenomenon till he discovered that Wilson's XXX Strong Mints, filed down with fine sandpaper, would work on the machines just as well as pennies. She got him free envelopes from the Barclays Bank on Smit Street and, for a few weeks, he gave her daily reports on his sales of the little packages, until the Greek cafi owners got sick of finding their machines stuffed with white discs and learned to chase him away and to sniff their clientele for the telltale odour of peppermint dust.

No matter, she had a backup scheme all ready. She had heard how the Slavin boy had learned to make free telephone calls at a tickey box. Isaac bribed Slavin with a toffee apple and found out how to outwit the operator in any public telephone booth just by scratching a copper wire to emulate the sound of dropping coins. As per Mame's suggestion he started selling trunk calls around the neighbourhood, but in two weeks flat everyone knew the method and no one would pay. Then the phone company wised up and the trick wouldn't turn at all.

Her next idea was a trade in counterfeit tram tickets but before that goody could get off the ground, Abel found out what had been going on and gave them both lectures. Ma told Abel he wasn't opening his eyes: the whole world was sliding down and down with the Depression, the few customers they had weren't paying, she was having to feed the family mielie pap and thin gravy almost every night (in case you haven't noticed) which is no good for growing children and their bones, specially, and look at all the boarded-up shops on Beit Street, look at the *White* beggars now . . . This didn't seem to matter to Abel who started waiting for Isaac after school and still does, making him sit down in the kitchen with his books, counselling patience and calm attention to his homework, before limping back to the workshop and hours of tranquil absorption in his own labours. But Gitelle lets him slip out the back door when she can. His bar mitzvah present was a second-hand Raleigh bicycle with wonky wheels, which he's now too big for (what he wouldn't do for a car!) but still uses to pay visits to people who owe them money. He stands there looking sad and hungry and accusing till they give him something, or if they don't he might come back later and put a stone through a window. He shares Mame's view of people who don't pay their debts. Parasites. No-goodniks.

When he can't get out and is forced to sit in the kitchen or the classroom his mind goes out for him. For hour after hour all he'll do is fantasize about automobiles: all the models and all the makes that he doesn't own and has never driven in. A red and black '31 Pierce-Arrow; a new Chevy Roadster, all cream with the neat hood of the leather top down; a big '33 Hupmobile, jet-black with whitewall tires and that long vertical grille – just a beautiful brute of a machine. Or the opposite, a sporty lightweight GM or a racing Talbot tourer, the new '34 Talbot built for pure speed with the engine cooped in that narrow front like the fuselage of an aeroplane. Eventually these automotive cravings lead him to try start up a weekend car polishing business but such manual work doesn't pay well in a market saturated with cheap Black labour. He hangs around some garages in Braamfontein instead, where he fetches tea and they teach him – savage thrill! – how to drive, then even allow him – can you believe? – to park some of the cars.

But when Gitelle finds out he's doing this for no pay she makes him quit. He's being a Stupid. She has a better idea. In this summer heat, specially now that the convertibles have their tops down, how about offering the people exactly what they want? Be close to cars that way. She provides the start-up capital and he invests it all in col'drinks. Bottles of cola and cream soda and fizzy granadilla, Bashew's ginger beer and raspberry. He packs them in tin buckets with chipped ice from the iceman and waits for rush-hour traffic to dam up when the robots turn from green to red at the bottom of Harrow Road, wearing a bottle cap opener on a string around his neck. When the sun makes the cars hot enough to sizzle spit, his iced bottles beaded with the sweat of their own coldness begin to sell themselves even at a steep markup. Farther down are the Black boys in their rags pushing copies of the *Star* or the *Rand Daily Mail* as they always have; he's making more cash from his col'drinks in a day than they will see in a month, if that, the Stupids. He smiles at them sometimes and they smile back. He starts to think of hiring a few, of expanding . . .

The next week the police charge him for non-possession of a municipal street vendor's permit and his (and Mame's) dreams of building a col'drink empire are crushed.

That night another argument in his parents' room: Tutte saying he's too old for this nonsense, he has to be studying seriously now, high school. Mame saying not everyone is like you and can sit all day like a stone. Tutte saying if he wants a good job he better learn to.

Mame makes a guttural sound: Guch! A job! He is more than a job!

Rively shakes her head at Isaac, the two of them listening at the door, her mouth a funnel of twisting pity. She's not wrong: all during this time he's been failing his first year at Athens Boys High School out in Bez Valley (a good White government school, picked for its disciplinary reputation, full of mostly yoks, English Christians, and a few like him from emigrant backgrounds), and he started off already more than a year behind the others. But he can't change; classroom is prison. All those bluh bluh sums and bluh bluh numbers and Greek and Latin names, flower parts and bluh Shakespeare bladey blah.

Nights he sleeps as always on the same folding cot that's unfolded in the workshop at the end of every day, only now he rolls onto his belly and presses his hard prick against the canvas, grinding it there while he thinks of women's bodies. His own has matured fast into first manhood and the bush of red hair at the base of his thing is a thick clump now. If only there were girls at school – it might make it all worth it, he might have a reason more than his father to stay there, to endure.

The following year, 1935, when Isaac turns sixteen, he finds he has surprised himself by managing to scrape through to standard seven where there are a new set of teachers waiting for him. One of them is a woman. She teaches History and English and her name is Jacqueline Winterbourne. Miss not missus. She is not too tall, with black hair and glasses. Not too busty, quite flat really, and she wears a short skirt and the skin of her knees and her fine arms and upper chest is very pale, as if she's been powdered. He can make out the dark puckers of her nipples through that thin blouse, the lines of her bra. He sees too how her slender torso swells wide at the hips. How beautifully wide and full the bum is, how it jiggles a little when she writes things on the blackboard.

He sits frozen, dry-mouthed, staring. His groin throbs almost painfully. His young heart beats hard, transfixed without mercy.

In the classroom under the tinted photograph of King George V with his frosted beard and walrus moustaches, Miss Winterbourne tells them how this wonderful country, the Union of South Africa, belongs to us all. We are her citizens and her caretakers. The Almighty has entrusted us with the sacred responsibility to look after her diamonds and her gold, her giraffes and elephants, her mountains and rivers and all of her many quaint Native tribes.

Unfortunately, all through our history we have been divided into two races. The one mostly bad and the other all good. The good ones are Englishmen (like everyone here in this class), and the mostly bad ones, of course, are the Afrikaners. There was a big war at the turn of the century and we the English gave the Afrikaners a good thumping; but being English gentlemen, we let them back up to run things (don't ask me why, Miss Winterbourne's expression seems to say). We gave them votes and there's more of them than us. That is how the Afrikaner Mr. Hertzog came to be

our Prime Minister. Up till recently, Mr. Hertzog's National
Party has been in charge and has been making a right mess of the
economy, but now, touch wood, there has arrived back into power
a gentleman called Jan Christiaan Smuts.

Miss Winterbourne smiles and shows them a picture of this
Jan Smuts who is bald as an ostrich egg except for a white fringe,
has hard eyes, a sharp nose, and a long thin face. She explains how
he is one of the good Afrikaners, just a wonderful man, who
fought for Britain in the Great War and studied law at Cambridge
where he scored the highest ever in exams, being a mental genius.
He's an Afrikaner who understands that South Africa needs to be
part of the great British Empire and not, heaven forbid, against it.
Now General Smuts and Mr. Hertzog have joined up to make one
new government called the United Party and the first thing they
did was follow Smuts's sound advice and take the country off
something called the Gold Standard. Straight away, the economy
was fixed! . . . Meanwhile the bad Afrikaners have split away under
Dr. Malan, to form the *Purified* National Party . . .

Isaac is amazed to find this woman is not only gorgeous as
hell, she's dincum interesting to listen to. Despite his throbbing
crotch he can link in his mind what she's saying to what he knows
has been happening on Beit Street over the past year especially.
Nowadays there aren't so many men in crinkled suits loitering
outside Cohen's Café all day using rolled-up racing papers like
blunt swords to impress points of vigorous debate on each other;
the shop windows that were boarded have turned back into
washed glass with clean new goods stacked up behind; ladies wear
bright new hats and the beggars have all but evaporated; the wind
has no more loose rubbish to tumble. At home they eat meat and
fish again every week. The deadbeat accounts are paying up more
easily and new repair jobs are coming into the workshop for Tutte
all the time. It's been like strangulation released: that dramatic. He
never knew what was behind it before, exactly, never knew that

this Jannie Smuts was so clever as to work all that. He pictures this Gold Standard as hillocks of ingots and lines of trucks coming to fetch the glittering bricks, feeding them back into the world so that things can move again, work and breath, the flow of money and life.

In the night come other pictures: of Miss Winterbourne giving him special lessons after class. He grinds his hard shlong under him to these fancies, imagining what her behind would feel like in his hands, squeezing, spreading. This feel of want for her sometimes unbearable as thirst. He finds himself wanking all the time, even in the school bog in the daytime.

He starts to hide things in her desk. A bottle of fancy perfume. A nice brooch. Lots of different kinds of flowers that he picks from the field at the far end of the cricket pitch. One Thursday after class she stays late, busy with papers at her desk, and he takes a long time to buckle up his satchel so that he's the only one left. When he walks to the front she looks up with the line of her dark eyebrows kinked above the nose. —Isaac. He steps closer. The smell of the woman-musk off her skin dizzies him, his eyes this close drink up the liquescent colour of her thick hair, rich black curls of it that come down to the neat earlobes where they tuck behind. He can't stop trembling and his heart like a trapped madman slams the cage of the ribs.

—Ja miss.

—Have you been leaving things in my drawers here?

—Hey?

—You heard me Isaac.

He looks down. —Maybe.

When he looks up she's holding out a paper bag to him with the top angled so he can see it's full of all the stuff he put there, even the old flowers all dry and dead. —Enough funny business, she says. All right? Concentrate on your work. Swot hard. Your last test was disgraceful.

Her face looks cross but when he takes the bag his hand passes over the top of hers and, without thought, he turns it and dips his head and breathes in the fragrance of her inner wrist and kisses her there, the pale softness, the cool blue veins. She makes a sound: too breathy for a squawk, not quite a yelp. She takes her hand back – not yanking it – and holds it to her chest and stares at him. He watches, astonished, as pink and red patches colour the ivory column of her neck. She seems to try to speak; her lips tremble.

—Sorry miss, he hears himself say, hoarse. Can't help.

She stands up and the chair falls behind her. He wants to say, I found out you're only twenty-two miss. That's only six years. His mouth is so dry. He wants to say, I love you miss, love you love you.

She says, —Don't, don't do that again.

— . . . Why?

She scoops her papers and picks up her bag and walks out without looking back.

A framed portrait of a seaside scene. Pressed flowers between the pages of a fancy book. A pair of cut glass earrings. All of these items go into her desk over the next couple weeks. He watches her look into the drawer and give no sign. The way her pretty eyes flick away from him he knows that tasting her skin has made a secret pact between them, a translucent cord. She understands.

He knows her dresses, the long black skirt with the red flowers and the blue top with the long sleeves. The green one-piece, the white blouse with puffy shoulders. She always hurries out at the end of class. During her classes he asks to go to the bog and wanks in the stalls, full of her in his mind, ripe with her. When he spurts he screams the words *Miss Winterbourne* in his mind.

There is a storage closet in the space behind the blackboard. One day he writes a note for her to join him there after class and leaves it covered on the desk. He gets into the closet before the bell and waits in the dark, listening to the class come in. Her voice gives the roll call and there is the silence of his absence. Sooner or later she will read the note. He shivers in the dark. He can hear the ich-ich scratching of the chalk on the board through the wall. The blind trembling, the hidden lust; being both here and not. He can hear his breaths against the unseeable walls.

After a time he thinks if she was going to unveil him, drag him out, she would have done it when she read the note which she surely has by now, hasn't she? The class carries on. A span of time unending that feels like her silent consent. Then the bell rings and now he hears the elephantine sounds of desks grating and sliding and school shoes tramping and the voices of the class as they leave.

There's a silence after. He feels like an electric thing, his very blood must glitter.

Maybe she has left. The slow sweet torture of the unspooling moments in the dark while he trembles as if fever-struck. Then: a click that is not a school shoe but must be her long elegant heel. In his mind he sees the calf, the thigh, the stocking. Another click then another and now he knows she is standing on the other side of the door. He closes his eyes even in the dark and feels out with his ears and his nostrils and finds her breathing, her perfume. The handle of the door creaks, minutely. Stops.

The blood clots painfully between his legs; he unzips himself and prongs free. Grips it in his fist like a gift.

Now the door slowly whines and he sees brightness through his eyelids. He exhales and opens them. A bald man stands before him, shaking his head with a look of sadness and pity. It's Mr. Larkin. Principal Larkin.

He sees himself in a tram window, a schoolboy without a school. The way his big ears stand out like bat wings and the tough rumples of orange hair that won't consent to being combed, the freckles that patter his white face like mud from a passing wheel.

Mame lied to him when he was little, said they would wash off. It's the first time he connects the word *ugly* to himself. The wide lump of a nose, the small bitter mouth. Long arms on his short frame like an ape, an orangutan. Of course she ran away from you shmock, you idyat, clickety-click on those high heels as fast as she could. Straight to the principal's office. Who exactly do you think you are?

There is no way of course that he can tell anyone at home, or anywhere, why he was kicked out of school this time so he positions it as a request, he wants to stop school, to start earning. (All the school gave him was the expulsion letter; they don't telephone the immigrant parents who can't speak English, and even if they wanted to, number fifty-two Buxton Street has no telephone.) It causes a meeting in the bedroom with his parents with the door locked and Rively creaking softly in the passage outside. Mame says school has never been for him. Business is better for everyone now. Let him start to earn full-time, proper, why not.

His father is long-faced, his gloomy limping crippled father, who stands there with his long hands tucked into the pockets of his leather apron, a lanky man with socketed eyes and an Adam's apple that points like a finger when he rocks back on his good heel, disappears when the head stoops low again, the spine curled permanently from so many years bent over watches. He wants to know why now, why doesn't Isaac finish the term? He must finish the year.

—Da, he says. I hate bladey school. I don't wanna go.

His father's eyes are not the eyes of a Stupid. They narrow. What's happened? Tell us.

—Ach nothing man. He looks to his mother, gets only: Answer your tutte.

— . . . Got in some trouble.

What now?

—This one teacher, just duzzen like me hey. Wants me kicked out, like. I dunno. She's a bit nuts or summin.

His father nodding, slit-eyed now. Tomorrow we'll go see that Mr. . . . what's his name, London? You will translate what I talk.

—No man, Daddy, please. What for hey? I don't want school. School wants you.

—But it doesn't!

I say yes.

They stand close, staring. A blue vein brightens in the wrinkles of his father's left temple. Gently Gitelle takes her husband's forearm. Why not let him try in business? Can anytime go back to school later.

What kind of business? he says to Isaac, not looking at her.

Isaac shrugs.

Be with me, Isaac. Without a trade, man is lost. Work comes from God.

—Oh jeez, says Isaac.

I'm your father, look here at me. You need to learn so you can choose your work. The right work for your own soul.

Gitelle says, A soul doesn't pay any rent, Abel. Let him go in business, this is what he wants.

Abel angles at her. Him or you?

She flips her hands up, stubby fingers spangling. What is you want from him? A scholar he's not.

It's not what I want. It's what *he* wants. He pivots back to Isaac. You like cars, so let me talk to Ginzburg. Maybe you can apprentice for a mechanic. But after you finish this year.

Or a salesman, says Gitelle. Selling the cars.

Abel glotzes at her: a sullen mean-eyed stare.

What? she says.

His hands come out of the apron to sit on the hips. Gitelle—

—A mechanic is azay vi a shvartzer, she says. Dos is nit a zuch.

A mechanic is like a Black. It's not on. Let me find for him. With cars, all right. But a business he can learn.

His father points, to her, to Isaac. A long Jewish forefinger, full of warning. He finishes school, the whole year.

All right, all right, says Gitelle. She moves across between them and her look at Isaac as she nods is a sly one, with the eye over the scar crinkled down. Never mind that part, the look says, I'll organize it.

His father is limping to the door, right shoe dragging. Isaac's seen it bare, the horror stumps of the blunt mutilations in place of toes. He did it to himself, to get out of the army of the Czar backhome, when he was almost as young as Isaac is now. He knows it from the street, heard it told with glee by a son of one of the men who used to be on the couch, but he didn't believe it, except when he asked Tutte he got back only silence and a grimace – a confirmation more brutal than any weeping confession. Now a flare of bitter feeling burns in him: it's this voluntary crippleness of his father, in order not to be a soldier. But soldiers are brave and his father is – well what else is it? what else can it be called? – a coward. Look at him, taking another loss, hoodwinked again, another backing down, shuffling away with his neck curled over. There goes a man who will never get his family out of Doornfontein, too soft and kind in this world of takes. Greenburg comes and collects the rent from him like milk from that passive cow of his in backhome. He loved that cow, Baideluh, because he is one! How powerful is this feeling in Isaac then, this contempt that burns in his throat like acid, like a gargle of venom.

It's all right, Mame is saying in a whisper. It will be fine. You'll see.

4.

FROM HIS COT ON SATURDAY MORNING Isaac hears Rively sing a song of Dusat:

> Let us go / The woods and the flowers are calling / Let us go
> The smells and the birds / Will confuse our senses
> The sparkling waters / Will make us drunk
> It doesn't matter / Doesn't matter
> Let us go
> Today let us go

The back door whines opens and Mame says, Where did you learn that song?

Tutte taught me.

Mame sniffs. —Better you learning sings from Sud Afrika.

Mame, can you teach me to make ingberlach?

—Vhy?

Tutte said—

—Ach!

What's wrong Mame?

Isaac puts the pillow over his head and pretends sleep. In a while his father and Rively, already dressed in their Shabbos bests, come to rattle his cot to get him to move.

—Ach Da, why do I have to?

Why does God have to keep you alive? Is one day so much

that you can't even say a thank you to Him?

—Get up Isaac, says Rively.

—But Ma doesn't go.

His father's face tightens. —Don't cheeky you father!

—She doesn't, she *never* does, so how come I have to?

—Just get up hey Isaac, says Rively. Don't make him upset. You've caused enough this week hey. We waiting.

On the way to shul, something odd happens. Isaac sniffs fishy business and straight away takes some quick action. Nobody's ganna put anything over on him.

But before then he first got up and got dressed with Rively still nagging, his body moving slowly because of the way the idea of shul weighs down on him even more than any school ever did, the gruelling boredom in that gloomy place always like a marathon trial for his jumping nerves (if he ever prays for anything it is for an end to the service).

Then, shlumping along behind them, he got irritated with himself for doing what he doesn't want to. Old enough to find work and earn full-time now, he should be old enough to decide what to do with his Saturdays. Tutte's walking stick was stabbing ahead, his useless right foot scuffing grit behind, and the sun kept flashing off the buckles on Rively's fine shoes and was bright on the clean ribbons so blue against her frizzy hair. As always she was walking with her head up and turned to Tutte, bouncing a little on her steps as if she's small again, excited for shul. All her bright adoration concentrated in that little freckled face, watching the old man while he went on and on about the old times. Her tutte and God and His temple: it's what makes her come alive. She always does her homework so carefully, her sums and her neat underlining ruler, the goody-goody. Wants everything proper and exact, like the perfect neatness of her room. In shul they tell you how to live every bit of your life, and it makes her happy to be doing what she should be, and doing it perfectly. He pictured tripping her fancy shoes, shoving her flat down on her excited face.

Meanwhile, Tutte telling them all about ingberlach, how his mother, their late bohbee, their grandmother, rest in peace, used to make the best in Dusat, boiling up pounds of mashed ginger and sugar and leaving it to cool into hard slabs on the windowsill while outside the snow hung on the pines and the birches. That beautiful cold fresh weather that keeps a face young, not the rotting heat of this place that ages everything before its time. And how the goyim used to race their handsome horses on the lake once a year, with bells on the reins, the people dressed up to the nines (—oys geputzt). And how the cold wind off Lake Sartai would cut you like a knife (—uzay vi a mesher!) if you didn't dress yourself warmly and properly. Not like here where there are no real seasons, a little bit of frost in winter the people are complaining of, they don't know real cold . . .

Tutte always talks this way when they're away from Mame. One time he was going on about Dusat, saying to them it's our village and *your* village also *always*, because it's where you come from never forget. About how in the autumn when the trees change colour that it's such a pretty place by the lake that you will never see another if you walk for a hundred and twenty years . . . And Mame walked in and shushed him. Said to him in front of them that he mustn't talk about yesterdays to them. Said all they need to know about Dusat is how poor we were, how we suffered. And don't ever talk about the goyim, the wonderful goyim. What we only had of goyim in our lives, the poor poor Jews (—der oremer oremer Yiddin). What they did to us, what they came and they *did*, no one will ever know the suffering, no, better to be quiet about such yesterdays and let our children sleep nicely in their beds . . .

Maybe it's cos Tutte moved to the village and married Mame there that he thinks of it the way he does, running there after his own family had died in the war. Not like Mame with her sisters that she must still bring to Africa.

And now they reach Pearse Street and the fishy-odd thing is happening. No, nothing gets past Isaac. What, does Tutte think he's a Stupid all of a sudden? Because as they're walking and Tutte is going on about backhome, Tutte is also quietly crossing the street all casual, leading them as if it's the most natural path in the world. Rively doesn't even notice. Isaac keeps looking backwards to the other side. Then he sees there's a man on a cart parked there, sitting behind the reins of a piebald dray horse. (Less and less are there carts to be seen in Doornfontein; automobiles, Isaac's great passion, have almost taken over, so different when he was a barefoot kid and the manure filled the gutters.) Isaac squints: maybe he recognizes the side of the man's face, even at a distance. A block farther, they cross back. Again Rively doesn't even notice, all the while she's been in rapture to the words of their father, and now Isaac also tunes into the voice:

. . . This old man Platt, he was a very special gentleman, believe me. A tzaddik, a holy man. He was the kind who on Shavuos does not sleep but is learning Torah all through to the dawn. The kind who will close up his shop and lose business to get to shul early. Backhome in Dusat everyone must greet everyone, not like this madhouse. So when they greeted old man Platt on Milner Gass by the well, the people, they would stand still if they weren't on their way to shul, so that he would not see they weren't going, because they were ashamed. That is why it is written, A holy man is he who makes everyone else want to be holy. That is the blessing they give . . .

He turns. You hearing me Isaac?
—Ja Da.
—You hear vut I'm say, Yitchok?
—I just said I did.

—Isaac, says Rively.

—Ja, ja.

Abel starts to talk about their late bohbee's voice, what a singer she was, the birds would come out of the trees to sit on her shoulders . . .

By now they are veering left onto Seimert Road and can see the Lions Shul ahead on the right, with a bit of a crowd in the front there.

Isaac stops. —Da, Da. Riv. Sorry, I gotta go back. I forgot summin. My yarmy.

Before they can speak, he turns and runs, hears Rively's thin cry and looks back to lift his arm. —I'll catch up! Go on. I'm coming.

As soon as he's halfway down the block, he puts his hands in his pockets and makes himself saunter. Like this, he comes up to Pearse Street and sees the cart is still there, the presence on it his father avoided. Isaac studies his profile for a while, considering, confirming his suspicion, then he walks up straight behind so the driver can't see him coming. He steps round and reaches up, slaps the man's tall boot where the trousers tuck in. Looks up into his face. Ja, it's him. Same pouchy crags of unshaved stubble. Same belly only larger. No need for a saucer at your left foot when all the world's your spittoon. He's no longer smoking, apparently; no tobacco smell and he has only a toothpick wiggling in his teeth. He regards Isaac's synagogue clothes. What are you collecting for, young monarch? Palestine? Tell them don't send you out on a Shabbos. It's a sin.

Not if you go to the sinners who're working, Isaac says, smiling, glancing at the load in the back: sacks of potatoes with the red sand still clinging to their skins.

Listen, you cheeky savage, a man has to make a living. It's in the Torah, to save life's the most important, go look it up. If you have to eat, you can work on a Shabbos, but I only do what I have to. The rest kisses me in arse. So away you run with your piggish charity box.

Isaac shows his palms. I don't have any boxes, Lazer Kaplan.

—Ah vos?

You heard me, Lazer Kaplan.

The toothpick gradually becomes still; the flesh crinkles around the watching eyes. I know you?

Abel Helger's boy.

Ahhh.

You remember I used to sit on the table in the workshop, in short pants with no shoes and my feet swinging. And you and the others on that couch.

That couch. Ai, that couch. How's your dear mother?

Isaac grins. She's well.

Send my best.

Best curses don't you mean.

Hoy! Don't talk like an animal and disgrace yourself. Your own mother.

Yes, but you.

Me what?

You still think well of her?

He takes the toothpick out. Why shouldn't I? That mother of yours . . .

What?

He hunches his shoulders. The hand with the toothpick turns over and lifts as if pricking at the sky. Who could condemn?

The other hand strokes at the side of his own face, the cheek and chin, where Mame has her scar, that lightning streak of melting pink solidified. His dense eyebrows wiggle in a coded way, a meaning that seems to try to take Isaac in close like an embrace of understanding. If it's an embrace it's an illicit one, filling Isaac with confusion he tries to shake free of with a quick wiggle of his head and shoulders.

It's not *that* bad, he says. Dr. Graumann fixed her and all.

Kaplan shakes his head slowly, full of mourning. Thing like that happens to a person – *boom*. But it can't be fixed so quick. It's not like one of your father's broken watches.

For a couple seconds Isaac thinks the man is talking about Dr. Graumann's surgery, and then he sees no. For some reason his heart picks up and his mouth dries itself.

Youngster, what?

What are you saying man? A thing like what happens?

Hey hey. Don't boil, be easy. I only mean how sad it is. I'm a Dusater also. I understand, believe me.

Understand what?

Listen, all I'm saying, you can forgive anything. Yes? Anything.

Isaac stands there thinking for so long that Kaplan says, So? Youngster? Are you all right?

—I'm ukay, he says.

Now I'm sorry for bringing up such a thing. Better my mouth should be sealed. Once a word jumps out it can't be pushed back in, not even after Messiah comes.

Isaac leans in. Puts his hand on Kaplan's arm. No, you're wrong. It's good to hear. Tell me the whole story.

What?

Isaac taps his own chin with his free hand.

. . . What's the matter with you?

Tell me.

Hoy! Let go, youngster. That hurts. What's the matter with you?

You tell it to me what happened to her.

. . . You'll get this whip on your cheek you don't let go.

Maybe you'll get worse.

I'm not worried, little pisser. But from your mother is another story. Maybe that axe won't miss next time. I'm saying nothing. I see it's not my place. I'm sitting shtum.

Isaac has a moment of paralysis, of trembling. He'd come only to see who his father would avoid, and then to greet an old coucher when he recognized him. Now what is this? Some shameful concealment. All his life he's known Mame was sick before, when she wore that cloth on her face, then Dr. Graumann fixed her, that's all. But now – what's Kaplan saying? He's not talking some illness. Or is he? *Happens to a person - boom.*

Kaplan has dropped the brake and is touching the whip to the piebald mare. I have to go, youngster.

It's not fair, Isaac hears himself say. His nose is running, his eyes are moist. He draws his wrist under the nostrils.

The cart has started to roll but Kaplan eases the reins back. One hand fiddles with the crown of his hat. Why don't you take a sack potatoes. Lovely potatoes. Take it free for a present home.

—Stuff your bulbiskes, says Isaac. I don't need your bladey charity, man.

Kaplan hunches. I'm sorry, youngster. He looks down for a while, sucking his teeth. His chin twitches sideways while his eyebrows go up. Nobody's at fault. Uy-yuy. That seventeenth of April.

—Hey?

He leans over and spits, not the black jelly of the old coucher days but a pale fleck meant only to dispel some unnamed evil in the words.

Isaac frowning: —What's that what you said?

Kaplan grimaces, looks away, looks back. Listen, when you're older, you'll know.

The whip stirs. Isaac watches the cart moving down Beit Street.

The hell does it all mean? He stands there muttering the date to himself again and again.

He walks back to the Lions Shul slowly, his head down and stomach tight, a hard and tingling feeling like a poison stone in his chest. He comes up on the shul hardly noticing there is still a little crowd even though the important part of the service – bringing out the Torah – is about to start (he can tell by the chuzun's nasal chant through open windows of yellow glass). The crowd is mostly youngsters. Isaac sees Rodney Epstein and them. There's Shimmy Kahn, Noam Levinson, Big Benny Dulut. Then he sees past them that one of the two gold-painted cast iron lions by the pillars in front is down on its side. Black paint on its muzzle, its mane, black paint on the wall above showing the word *Jood* and other Afrikaans mostly filth words, and then four big twisted crosses. He stands there numb, trying to take this in with his thoughts still on his ma.

Rodney Epstein nudges. —Howzit, Rabies. You check the good news hey. They come in last night like Father Christmas. Sweet of them hey? How many Greyshirts does it take to paint one swastika? A hundred. One to draw it wrong and the other ninety-nine to blame the Jews.

—That who it was, Greyshirts?

—Well it wasn't Rabbi Kramer or my uncle Yitz. The shammos reckons they drove right up on here by the tire marks. Old Mrs. Holberg reckons she saw lights four in the morning. Check it: forget Shabbos, the shammos he's aweady went to the cop shop. Know what they tuned him? Said it's pro'lly *our kids* who did it for a laugh. Told him, Don't take it so serious.

Shimmy Kahn snorts. —So serious. Ja, watch how serious they take it if we slap some kuk upside one a their churches. Pull down pants and take a few nice Yiddish shits all over their bimah.

—I don't reckon they got bimahs in church, shmock.

—Bimah-shmimah. Whatever the eff it is in there.

Big Benny taps his palm with his fist. —What we need, set a trap. Wait round here for a Greyshirt. Make him a dead shirt.

Still half in his numb mood, Isaac says: —But why they doing it? I mean like *why*. They don't even know us.

Rodney Epstein squawks laughter. —The boy asks why. Listen, Rabies, you ever open a newspaper your whole life?

Isaac steps close. —You ever eat one?

—Oright, don't have triplets, mate. Don't catch a harry. I'm only saying.

Noam Levinson has had his spectacles off, rubbing the bridge of his nose. Now he settles them back on, says: —They got them everywhere, right. They love Hitler, ole Adolph's their god. It's like this club is spreading over the world. They got their Brownshirts in Germany, the Blackshirts in Italy and in England. Different-coloured shirts for different kinds of mumzors. Who knows what else, Blueshirts, Pinkshirts. Now we got them over here. But our chutus is so thick he can't even pick a real colour. So they just gave em grey.

Rodney Epstein: —It's getting big hey, everywhere.

—They should all stick with brown for their shirts, ay, the colour of shit. Brown*shits*, Black*shits*, Grey*shits*.

—I think just plain *shits* about covers it, Shimmy.

—These shirt kinds are all the same, Noam Levinson tells Isaac. Pure race this, pure race that. Only one blood per country. Anyone else, chuck em out. And any problems blame on the Jews.

—Hell, they getting big man, says Rodney Epstein. I heard they had like a thousand in town. They go by City Hall there.

—It's not a thousand.

—S'what I heard.

—Your ears is full of idiot wax.

Noam Levinson: —Ja, well. My old man reckons half the guvmint is in with them!

This pricks at Isaac; he turns from the fallen lion. —No, no, he tells them all. Not Jannie Smuts.

A pocket of curious silence accrues around him.

—Listen a Rabies, says Big Benny Dulut. What a you, a doctor in politics now?

The others watch him while heat fills his face. Benny's big, ja, but Rabies is Rabies, even standing right outside shul.

Noam Levinson breaks the moment: —I don't reckon Smuts can help much. All the cops and army is in with the other lot, what my old man says. Plus opposition is bladey Malan and the Nats — I mean they kissing cousins with these Greyshirts! Can turn like Germany here!

There's another silence of a different kind. Isaac looks at the wall, feels the others doing the same. He shakes his head. —Jannie Smuts won't never let it happen, he says.

Noam Levinson's tongue clicks. —Jannie Smuts, Jannie Smuts. He's not even Prime Minister, mate. He's deputy and Hertzog's in charge and Hertzog used to be a Nat, don't forget. And Jannie's not so great anyway, like he did nothing when they stuck Quota on us hey.

Big Benny: —Slice their necks. Bleed em like chickens, turn em proper grey. Slice their bladey necks open.

Isaac's squinting. —What you talking Quota?

Noam Levinson's arms wave; he has to push at his glasses to keep them from sliding. —Quota Act, Quota Act man. The law they put for no more Jews to come. Cut us right off. Don't you even know?

Blood blooms fully in Isaac's cheeks then; he shouts out, hot-faced in his lie: —Course I know! Course I do! Then, thinking furiously: —Smuts didn't put that Quota! It was . . . Wait, when was it? . . . Smuts didn't put that!

—Was years and years ago, says Rodney Epstein.

—*Exactly*, says Isaac. Was before Smuts, was Nats in charge then, isn't it? Isn't it hey?

—Ja, Professor Rabies. But now your great Smuts he *is* there and he hasn't gotten rid of Quota has he? Has he? Nooo — nothing. Ach, he's just the same. Go and look it up man, I got no time, Rabies.

Big Benny: —We make an ambush. Catch a few. Skiet them in the balls. Right in the balls.

Shimmy Kahn: —Hey Rabies, how is it in Bez Valley there, that yokish school? They make you eat a pork chop or what?

—It's oright, says Isaac.

—We shoot their kneecaps, says Big Benny. Go for the kneecaps.

—Hey Rabies, there's your old man hey.

Isaac looks up to see his father in the doorway, waving at him with the whole of his arm. Isaac goes in, his father limping off ahead of him, leading the way, anger in the stiffness of his back. Inside they find their seats in front, his father's cane hung on the pew. The women sitting in the galleries with their hats overlook all. On the bimah, the chuzen's face turns pink under his black cap, twisting out the high notes that to Isaac are a kind of wailing, a tormented wailing, as if a suffering infant is trapped inside the man's chest. This shul with its old men with hairy ears sitting in rows and muttering and watching, people whispering and holding in their farts, the shrewd widows in their black hats noting every move from above, the endless droning through hours – it's just like a schoolroom, oppressive to his jittering spirit as it always has been. Except that now he also sees the black paint, the broken lion outside, and it dawns in him what a weak place this is, a monument to victimhood, helpless.

He thinks of Kaplan, of Mame. That dark bandage on her face all through his early life, tied in his mind to Dusat. Dusat was the cause. He tries to remember back, really for the first time, to glimpses he had of her face uncovered? Something else he was told about it? . . . But of Dusat he can find only vestigial memories, as if the blinds are being drawn in that part of himself. Inside that dimming chamber he summons the houses built with wooden sides, some yellow, some dark green, and with steep-slanted roofs of tin sheets or wooden shingles or sometimes thatched straw. He breathes again the cramped human smells in the little rooms. And cow manure and woodsmoke. Muddy yards with woodpiles as tall as the houses. A stove made of large bricks inside called a pripachik, with a round hole in front and a door in the side and another door in the brick back, facing into the room behind, that opened as a heater in winter. Everything revolved around that pripachik, purveyor of hot meals and life heat. On very bad nights they blocked the chimney to a trickle to let the orange warmth of the coals throb to the walls; the best place to sleep was on the pripachik's flat top. He remembers: Stay off the lake! Its whiteness looked solid but it could swallow you. And the cathedral on the rise, that fearsome overlooking cross. An arrowhead of ducks against a white sky. A field of painted crucifixes. Playing in the bright twinkling shallows in the summer, copper pots and pans scrubbed there by the kerchiefed women, scoured with handfuls of coarse river sand white as flour. The streets in spring turning to mud glittering with melt ice, and the village inspector hanging bags of disinfectant and sprinkling powder on the turds the melting unveiled, left by those too cold in winter to make it to the outhouses, and the neighbours pointing and laughing, calling the frozen stools *treasures*. Winter: the way of that brittle sky, how the line of the snow rose smooth as a dune to the roof edge, white billows of it sweeping the rigid lake in waves of tumbling powder. Branka the Tatar woman stooping to light the pripachik for them on a cold Shabbos morning, the flame playing shadows in the wrinkled crevices of her wide kind face. Bloodhot milk squirting from the udder gripped in his tiny fist. Market days on Wednesdays filling the square with carts, and a goy peasant passed out drunk on the vegetable patch, snoring with his mouth open and he and Rively squatting fascinated, putting sticks and sand on the pale cracked tongue till Mame pulled them inside.

But of the veil that hid the bottom of his mother's face there is nothing, nothing except that it was always there, token of some sickness never spoken, a part of her.

They have entered the part of the service called the Amidah, the Standing, where everyone rises in silence to face toward holy Jerusalem, to address God in the silent chambers of their skulls, their hearts. Isaac feels like he's suffocating. Feels as if the embroidered cloth on the Holy Ark and the thick ruby carpets underfoot are being pushed down his throat. Mame, Mame – where is Mame, why is she not here? It's such an obvious question, but he's never really asked it. Suddenly he wants to ask *her*, more than anything, wants to understand. It's a question that can't wait. He turns and starts saying excuse me, edging past the seats, not looking back, knowing his father must be staring at him but also that he won't break the holy silence to call him back.

He walks home quickly, agitated. The shop has its *Closed / Gesluit* sign on the door. His hand on the door handle hesitates, he leans to the window glass to look inside. It's like that time when he was free and little, running barefoot with Skots and them. Remember Skots? What's become of that lot? He imagines Coloured faces under flat caps, workingmen now, or else loitering gangsters waiting to go to jail, sipping methylated spirits they first siphon through a loaf of bread to filter out the poison. *Auntie* Peaches probably dead of TB by now. How he came back from the Yards with that little dog, that poor little animal. She should have let me keep it, what's the bladey harm? And here he is again nervous as hell to go in, this time not with a dog but with the guilty sense of having left shul. She'll try to make me go back like she made me give that dog away. But I didn't want to give it away, and I don't have to now. I can tell her no.

He's surprised to see her seated at the front desk with her back to the door. He's never thought about what Mame does when they're all away. He expected cleaning, fixing; but here she's motionless, bent over in a posture not so far removed from that of Abel over the guts of a watch. He shifts around, gains a better angle on what she's doing. The cashbox is on the desk and it's open and the top level of it has been lifted out and set down, opening a bottom space he never knew was there. He squints at it: empty, looks like. She must be doing accounts except that the cashbook is closed and she's not writing.

He watches her for fully a quarter of an hour before she shifts and he sees her hands are folding sheets of paper, a stack of other documents beneath; she pulls another sheet, curls forward again. The way she starts to rock slightly over these papers is familiar, it's how the oldsters pray in the synagogue, as if they're on a ship riding swells. Praying: this is what she does while we are in shul. But if she prays then why must she do it alone, why doesn't she come to shul with us? And again the question so obvious, so massive he's never put it to himself till this very day: why *does* she never go to shul, not even on Yom Kippur? Why?

At that moment she lifts her right hand to her face. Paws at her eyes. Her shoulders quiver. God. He has never seen her weep before, never. The sight of it socks him under the heart. He wants to turn away then, to run; but he is also held.

He thinks of Kaplan the coucher, touching his cheek at the place, saying of Mame, *You can forgive anything.*

Mame, Mame, Isaac thinks, what is happening to you?

He walks off, a blank wildness in his mind. When he gets back, Mame is sweeping out the workshop. He opens the door and stands there with his pulses throbbing. She looks up. Big eyes, her voice tight: What's happened?

—Don't worry, everything's ukay. Everything's fine.

Where are they?

—At shul.

Then what are you doing here?

He shrugs at her, shakes his head. The questions drumming in him are impossible to release, not in front of her, this live and watching presence, this mother of his who was just weeping so that her eyes are still a little pink-rimmed and to ask her might break into her heart again and make it bleed more tears. No, he cannot. Still, he tries to force it but his mouth only opens very slightly and only silence comes. He closes it, closes his eyes. Not now, he thinks. Another time, any other time, anytime but now.

5.

TRANSPORT IS RELATED TO CARS, a good business and easy to get into since all you need to start are some wheels. Think how Mr. Jackman began with one cart, not even a horse cart, a push-cart. Yes, trenshport is good: so Mame says, flexing him into a job with Morris Brothers Packers & Movers, Pty. Ltd.

The Morrises have a compact warehouse on Jeppe Street in town and three battered Chev trucks. One brother, Sol – tall, thin, mellow – runs the warehouse. The oldest, Errol – short, wide, aggressive – rides with the biggest closed truck. The last brother, Dave, is both tall and wide and veers from aggression to calm and back; he goes with the other closed truck. What the Morris brothers are in need of when they hire Isaac is a White for the third Chev, an open flatbed, to deal with the customers and make sure, as Sol puts it, that the bladey coons don't steal us dry.

So Isaac rides with four Blacks. He is the boss and they are the boys. Silas, the driver, is a Zulu from Natal with stretched earlobes that dangle and sway like strands of overcooked spaghetti. Morgan, a different kind of Zulu, from Rhodesia, is chubby and rubs some kind of grease into his skin to make it gleam and is always smiling or reading his bible. Hosea is a Shangaan and has welts and dots on his face, clan markings. Fisu is the tallest, the quietest, and is from the mountain kingdom of Basutoland. He always comes to work with a cone-shaped woven hat, and if it's cold he drapes a bright blue blanket of silken wool over his shoulders. All four wear overalls and long duster jackets stencilled in purple on the back with the words *MORRIS BROS*. Isaac can wear whatever he wants: no more school uniforms.

During his first month, he is casual about the address that appears on his clipboard one day, a place in Orange Grove. He asks Silas about going there and Silas only shrugs, it's just another place to him, a White place. But Isaac is trembling, he's never been that far north, beyond Yeoville, up into the suburbs. Above Orange Grove there sit even richer neighbourhoods, Observatory and Sydenham, and above them, along the overlooking ridge, are the dream places, the Mr. Jackman and Mr. Joel and Mr. Rhodes places, where the masters of gold and diamonds and industries can survey their city below: Westcliff, Parktown, Houghton. Coddled mansions of highest repute. Generators of dreams and magnets of achievement. In his mind a cloud swirl guards the upward pathways into their golden realm.

Isaac shakes himself back into the now, sitting low in the truck's passenger seat, this cab of the truck redolent with the tang of Silas's sweat. Silas has beads hanging from the rearview mirror and his leopard-skin totems and family photos are tucked above the sun visor, his fighting sticks (just in case) point out from under his seat and a tuneless whistling leaks steadily through his bottom teeth like a function of his driving. The rest of them sway and jounce on the open flatbed behind. Isaac watches the brown grasses and the low red-rock quartz-glinting koppies on Observatory Ridge to the south as they turn off Harrow Road and onto Raleigh Street which turns into Rockey Street, up past the place where the tram cars turn around, then up to Louis Botha Avenue and then east and north.

New territory.

Orange Grove is absence: no shops, no pedestrian life. A silence strung between garden walls and jacaranda trees that line the road like pillars, their flowers tiny trumpets in regal purple. Their target house has a roof of overlapping clay tiles instead of sheet metal and bars against burglary at every window shaped into leaves and stems. Wealth needs bars: he hadn't imagined this detail, nor that the bars could themselves be made into decorative symbols to signify the goods they protected. He stalks around with hands on his hips, a little hunched, ferocious in his feelings so that the want in him is almost like a kind of anger. *This* is the only cure for Mame's secret tears. Forget old man Kaplan and useless buried events, papers in a cashbox. Forward, only forward.

Such workdays bleed into months that themselves stretch out and Isaac learns his job well. Talk sweetly with the wives who are the hoverers as they pack, but make sure to take very thorough notes and have them signed; it is the husbands who will ring back later to complain of damage, to make their accusations of theft. This is what is called experience. Mame is much satisfied by his growth; Tutte only wants to know – baffling – if he's enjoying himself. Such irrelevancy slides beneath his understanding and he can only shrug. Rively has taken the school's maths prize, the first girl ever.

One day in Hillbrow there is no wife but a plump divorcée. It's a flat in one of the tall blocks with Englishy names, this one called Willow House. He keeps looking at this woman in a way that she has to pretend not to notice while the boys take the boxes out and down the service elevator. When the job is done he accepts her invitation for a cup of tea even though they are running late. He comes down some forty-five minutes later feeling glazed, knowing how oddly his face must loom, afloat on the cloud of astonishment that's replaced everything below the neck.

Silas is napping stretched over both seats with a newspaper over his face and Hosea, Morgan and Fisu are smoking hand-rolled cigarettes and sitting on the curb, Morgan looking down at the open bible across his lap.

—Oright, Isaac says, gruff. Lez go. Haven't got all day.

Silas sits up. —Baasie, he says. Little boss. —Baasie, was that *tea* very nice?

They are all looking at him, expectant.

—Was it *sweet* tea? Fisu asks, holding in a grin with twitching lips.

—Maybe, Silas says, maybe my baas, he spill some.

Isaac looks down. His fly unbuttoned, bright flecks of lipstick on the shirt, half of it still untucked. When he looks up he can't stop the spread of his own grin and they all thunder into eye-watering laughter, beautiful deep African laughter, wild as rain. They clap their hands, beat their feet and shake with the glee of it. Ten minutes later Silas is still repeating the word *tea* to himself and shaking his head, wiping a fingertip under each eye as he drives, till finally Isaac has to tell him behave yourself. But he's not truly in the mood to put much vim behind the words, his mind so full of the new revelations of the flesh. That touching and licking, the undoing of the clothing in that raw tumble to the bedroom. No speaking, only animal pleas. Teeth on skin and what a woman's mouth can be, so hot and wet and savage. The furnace of it around his thing, the marine tang of her taste, and then the final soft-wet engulfment as he kept expecting her to stop him, so utterly mysterious and complete. She hooked her nails into the meat of his buttocks like some carnivore. He hunted her salty sweat with the point of his tongue in the wrinkles of her armpit. Woman. The sound she made at the end. A heat forge of desire that almost scared him, dissolving into her, draining.

Yes Da, I am enjoying myself very much at work nowadays, thank you very much for asking. I surely am.

For some months after that infamous incident he feels the eyes of his boys on him every time he chats with the lady of the house. Even though now he can look at these women in a truly knowing way there is never a repeat performance and gradually he realizes how lucky he'd been. Once or twice he thinks he is getting similar signals but he can't believe, truly, that a married woman would do such things (or that his rough looks and short wiry body would be enough to tempt her into such sin), stopping him from trying. Each time on those occasions Silas in his uncanny way is ready with a fresh comment.

—No biscuit tea time today, my baasie.

—Shut up hey will you Silas.

That big smile so bright in his square face. —Sorry sorry my baas.

—Qhuba! Isaac will say in Zulu. Drive. Clicking his tongue on his palate at the first syllable, getting the pronunciation exactly right, for he's learning more of Silas's language all the time, fascinated by the sound of it and discovering an aptitude for languages in himself out here in the practical world where words are useful things, real as tools, as opposed to the drone noise in the constraints of a brick classroom. (Also he hates it when Silas speaks to other boys and he can't understand – he doesn't want to be some Stupid getting mocked to his face like any ignorant umlungu, any other Whitey.)

Mame asks him what he's learning and when he has nothing to say, Mame has suggestions.

Don't stand still. You been nearly a year already. Time goes like water. Remember always that you're working for more, to be on your own in business. To buy a big house one day. Don't sit on your tochus too comfortable. Open your eyes.

He opens his eyes and a scheme comes to him. He shares it with Mame and she bakes him an apple strudel in honour of its brilliance.

Next day on the way back to the warehouse with the truck unloaded he tells Silas to pull over at that Native bus stop: a sign on a pole near which Blacks have patiently massed with their goods and their infants. For a tickey a head – a penny less than bus fare – he lets them pile on and taxis them into town. He splits these takings half and half with his boys; overly generous, ja, but he's becoming quite fond of the buggers.

So this taxiing becomes a regular little earner for them, a secret that binds them all.

His father has technical questions about the work. It's real work, he tells Abel, snapping a little. But inside he knows he does not do the real part of the work and can sense the judgment in his father's questions. For Abel, work belongs to the worker, like a prayer to the worshipper (to do a *properly job* is his highest English compliment). What your work produces is what you are. But Isaac mostly stands around watching his boys do the lifting and the carrying, moving endless White goods from one spacious household to another, disassembling and reassembling White lives. He knows that his mother will say the bladerfools are the ones who break their backs like donkeys day in and out, sweating for a pittance with not a chance of advancement while the Clever is the one who makes the profit and sits on a nice clean office chair. But watching how hard his boys work – how they shake with the sweat-dark canvas straps looped around their wrists and under the edges of heavy awkward things (cabinets, beds, ovens, iceboxes), slowly up and down that steep ramp off the truck all day – he feels a secret pulse of jealousy; his blood is restless, his bones feel trapped. To them belongs the dignity of expressing their strength as men. Yet always in his heart is also a kind of contempt for their Black passivity, the same way he felt it years before when he was selling col'drinks on Harrow Road and the Black boys only had their newspapers and their rags and their grins.

Meanwhile Silas goes on teaching him new things. Ubusika is winter. Izolo is yesterday. To pay is khokha and to run umjaho. Bhebha is fuck and ikhekhe is both cake and cunt. One day he learns the word for sweat. Juluka.

―――

Countless times they criss-cross Johannesburg (iGoli in the Black tongue, the place of gold), a city of mingled chaotic streets since it bloomed unplanned out of a gold rush town in the middle of nowhere, a rush that has never died because the lake of sunken gold under it has never dwindled. Isaac thinks about this as they drive, watching the blur outside. He sees the head gears on top of the mine shafts, sees the poison dunes of the mine dumps (lumpen pale hills of excavated rock crushed finely to sand once washed with cyanide to rinse out the gold). He can hear this rock dust whispering in the slipstreams, a hungry mocking sound. There are no other reasons the city is here, no big rivers, no port or coast, nothing but the buried mineral that waits beneath ever undying like some immense yellow demon, feeding on the massed life it lured with greed to squat above.

Yet they never get the call Isaac truly wants, for a job in the uppermost tier, in a place like Lower Houghton. Once they do Dunkeld and another time Saxonwold, but only for apartments, never a grand home, never one of the mansions, the pinnacle. Meanwhile he starts to grow a little blasé about the neighbourhoods like Observatory and Highlands North that at first so awed him; it's around then, as if the world is attending to him, that they get the job in Parktown, up on the high ridge.

6.

USED TO BE that access to this section of Parktown required a key to a private gate that only the residents held, now they can climb St. Sebastian Road unimpeded and at the top they branch onto Gilder Lane. Here the steep road curves between mansions of redyellow stone hewn from the ridge like carved natural extrusions. The high walls stretch between spiked gates flashing glimpses behind: he catches columns and turrets and treetall windows; a ring of gaping stone fishes watering a great bowl (the wind skims off spray to dapple urns of proteas bright as fired coals); glossy dogs spring at iron bars; once an open lawn stretches away lushly vivid as any bowling green, with a dark face slowly crossing holding out white gloves and a silver tray between. Silas keeps whistling through his bottom teeth. Uphill they reach a municipal park on their left, drab and dry and tiny by contrast, behind a simple log fence painted green, the repeating pattern of two stumps and a horizontal pole, with a small clump of willow trees in the last corner. Farther uphill on the other side is number eighteen. Silas turns in without breaking his whistle: a long steep driveway to wide garage doors of varnished wood. To the left, a wrapping stone wall rises twenty, twenty-five feet. He finds a small locked gate inset in an archway. He pulls a cord and a maid comes, leads him up a corkscrew of tiled stairs with oval hollows in the wall cradling vases of flowers like shrine offerings. At the top, a sudden airy plateau. A gardenboy in overalls is poking a pole as tall as three men through a watery skin; only sky backlights him for the land drops away in terraces, intricately gardened, down to a clay tennis court. Far beyond, the distant city unfolds in its shrunken grace, so green with clumping trees closer in, but running to khaki and grit under a smearing haze out towards the south where mine dumps glint pale as icebergs against the angled morning sun.

The soft tinkling of spoons on china makes him turn to the house. There's a couple at a patio table laden with silver tureens; the scent of coffee with butter-fried eggs and toast and sausages makes water jet under his tongue. The maid leads him again, pausing at the table to add fizz from a green bottle to tall glasses. He sees half a pineapple in crushed ice, a neatly cored pawpaw. The man and the woman both squint up. She's wearing a kind of turban, bizarre, almost like the doek that maids wear but fancier and with a bright gemstone in front and some green feathers. He gives his professional smile and she looks away, to the man. —This?

The man sighs. He is thin and fineboned, with long fingers fitting a cigarette to an ivory holder. He wears a puffy kind of scarf in place of a tie, white trousers on crossed skinny legs; a cream jacket with black stripes hangs off the back of his seat.

—We can presume the mover?

Isaac nods. —Mr. Linhurst?

The woman has been shaking her head metronomically. She covers her face with both hands. —Cecil. Come off it.

—Bupsie, says Cecil.

—This is assurance?

—Poppy, he says. Now don't.

—I'm sorry, but schoolboys.

Cecil unfolds his lanky self from the chair and stands lighting his cigarette. —You do have experience transporting glassware?

—Ja sure, says Isaac. All kinds a glass. Salad bowls, whichever.

—Oh my good God, says the woman. *Salad bowls.*

Cecil looks away. Isaac sniffs. He notices rigid streamers of

reddish meat with streaks of white fat: a mystery. He says: —
Summin wrong?

—Lalique, says the woman. Baccarat. Waterford.

Isaac studies the feathered turban, this grown woman talking
gibberish to him over the breakfast table and it hits him she's
a mental patient, an absolute loon. He begins to understand
Cecil's embarrassment; he waits for him.

—You see, Cecil says, art glass is really Bupsie's life.

—Right, says Isaac.

The woman says, —A rugger ball in a satchel, I don't think so.
I'm sorry.

—Right, says Isaac.

Cecil sighs and dips his long head sideways, the cigarette lifts.
He has fine light hair like candy floss. He walks off towards the
house and Isaac follows. They descend three flights of marble
stairs, passing seven-foot oil paintings. Make bladey sure this
man signs off: no telling with that madwoman. At the base
spreads an unadorned hall full of boxes, Cecil tips his cigarette at
them. —These ones, those ones.

Isaac says: —Wait a sec. We on the bottom level here hey.
Same as outside by the gate?

—It is.

—And those doors, they go through then hey? The garage?

Cecil doesn't seem to want to answer, his tongue makes
a shifting lump in his cheek, he nods very slightly.

—That is great stuff, says Isaac. Great stuff. We can take it
straight through the garage. I was worried–

—No, says Cecil.

—Hey?

—No.

Isaac tries for eye contact but Cecil's pupils keep flickering
side to side.

—I'm afraid not. The car is rather in the way.

—The car, says Isaac.

Cecil draws on his cigarette.

—Coulden you just move it, like?

The right corner of his mouth kinks; a smoke funnel stabs down. —No.

—Pardon?

—No.

Isaac looks at him there with his cigarette holder and his weight on one leg, one foot pointing out, slender soft-skinned fingers on the hip that would snap in half like stale Marie biscuits if they were ever to try and lift a bedroom suite or a coal stove, even a mere box of glass.

The cigarette sweeps. —Everything on this side, basically, straight to the new shop.

—Mr. Linhurst.

—Popsy's opening in Rosebank next month, all her art deco first. Thank God. Gives us some space to breathe around here again.

—Mr. Linhurst.

—What's the trouble?

—Mr. Linhurst, if we can't use the garage, where we supposed to go?

—What does *that* mean? says Cecil.

—I mean is there other stairs?

—Others?

—Not the ones I come in on.

—No, there are no other stairs.

—Mr. Linhurst, those stairs are like this wide. No landings, plus.

—Well. We all have our jobs.

Isaac feels the heat seep up into his tightening face, he looks away a moment, his lips working.

Slowly he says, —Mr. Linhurst, the stuff is already down here. Otherwise they ganna have to come up all the way two flights inside first. Plus then go back down those outside stairs there that're pure bladey killers hey, just killers, scuse my French but they are. This's glass we talking. Any little bump. It's not just the boys hey, it's putting like ten times more chance for accident.

—Let's not fret about accidents.

—But the garage.

—The garage, the garage, says Mr. Linhurst. I have just told you you may not use it. I am not having movers near the Cadillac.

—Dadsy and his Cadsy, says a voice.

Isaac turns, sees a girl on the stairs. —I'm ready, Dadsy, she says. Her voice is very high, very musical, something gentle and shimmering in it. She is a tall well-made girl in a school uniform with a round doll's face, and plump pouting lips, thick blond hair dragged back with a headband like the kind dancers wear and the hair spreads out behind the band down to the level of the collarbones. The school uniform is a green blazer over a white blouse, tartan skirt below, dark socks pulled up three-quarters of the way to the knee with parallel stripes at their tops. A coat of arms on the blazer's pocket over the soft shape that pushes it out. Isaac looks at her face, the wide cheekbones, the colourless eyebrows, and a kindliness, a blood warmth, radiating from the whole of it. A light switches on inside of him, in his chest. Strong and clear and icily flooding.

—Okay, Shookee, says Cecil.

She goes up. He can hear her school shoes on the marble. When he turns back, Mr. Linhurst is talking about the Cadillac limousine, saying that Isaac perhaps couldn't appreciate this automobile and what it means.

Isaac says: —No, I know exactly what a Cadillac is. What model you talking?

Mr. Linhurst smiles with one side of his mouth. —Do you now.

—Ja I do.

—A 1934 Fleetwood. D Series, four fifty-two.

—The V16? says Isaac. That's a monster hey. Biggest engine in the world. A hunned seventy horsepower right? What's it, a seven-litre?

The line of Mr. Linhurst's eyebrows breaks steeply, like a raising bridge, and he's no longer smiling. —Seven point four, he says slowly.

—Ja, no, I look in the car magazines hey. All the pictures . . . Unbelievable that thing, but I thought there's none in South Africa.

Now the smile stretches back, fully and slowly, like a sunning crocodile. —I've got the only one.

When they are outside again, Isaac's notes on the goods signed by Cecil and safely buttoned in his shirt pocket, he sees she is sitting at the garden table that has been cleared of breakfast, her school bag on the ground beside her and a book open on the tabletop between her elbows, her hands cradling her head and the thick hair hanging down over the wrists. The mother is still in her seat, twisting now to look over her shoulder. She asks Cecil if he explained it all properly.

—Yes, Bupsie, he says. Most thoroughly.

—But properly.

—Thoroughly, he says. Most thoroughly.

—Har har I'm sure, she says. Then to the girl: —You see what's come. When you leave things to your father.

—I'm going to be late, Dadsy, says the girl.

—*Dadsy*, says the woman. Father or Pater.

The girl goes on reading.

—I'll go and get the boys, Isaac says to Cecil.

—Where are you from young man? says Mrs. Linhurst.

—Doornfontein.

—Doornfontein. Morris. Wouldn't have said.

—Pardon?

—And how old?

—I'm twenny-two.

A silence. They all look at him in the nakedness of his lie, the girl too. He scratches his nose.

—Would you call yourself a *boy*? says Mrs. Linhurst.

—Hey?

—But they're older than you, your staff.

—My what?

—Tell me, what is your opinion of the Native Question?

—Ma, says the girl.

—Mother or Mater, she says without looking away from Isaac.

—Half past eight, says Cecil, on a Thursday morning is not the time.

—When is? says Mrs. Linhurst.

—About to take Yvonne to school, says Cecil.

—God, says the girl.

All Isaac can feel then is his heart reacting to the sound of that name. The light switching on in his chest again, so bright and icy clear. *Yvonne.*

Mrs. Linhurst gets up; her azure robes flap against her bulk. —When you get to the shop, my man Cornelius will open. Just knock, he's there. Boxes with the tan cards to the left, the blue opposite. Cornelius will indicate. Cornelius will assist.

She starts back toward the house, slippers scuffing.

—All right Shookee, let's skedaddle, says Cecil. And he's turning too, moving to the stairs.

Isaac speaks quickly: —The garage, he says. S'there really no way to go through hey? I mean really.

Cecil turns back. —Do you not want this job?

A wash of bloodheat rolls through his head. His voice croaks. —I's just asking.

—But we're taking the other car, Dadsy, says Yvonne from behind. There'll be tons of room for them.

Cecil grimaces. —Yvonne, pack up.

She lowers her head over the book, seems to become absorbed in reading.

—I'm not having them near the Cadillac, says Cecil to no one and everyone. He goes downstairs. Isaac looks to the woman, who is almost at the doors. He jogs across to her. —Mrs. Linhurst.

Up close she has white paste filling in the wrinkles of her hanging face.

—Can't you like open the garage doors for us, like later on?

—What, what are you saying to me?

—So my. The workers. So they won't have to go all up and down.

—God gave them feet, bless them.

—But all the stairs. Your glass.

She closes her eyes. Opens them slowly. Now her voice is clear and sane to him for the first time: —Just you make bloody certain not one single crack. Understand?

Isaac nods. —Ja, he says. I do.

She goes in. Below, a car starts. The girl is standing to put the book back in her school bag, now on the tabletop, not a canvas satchel like what he used to use at Athens Boys High but a stiff leather number like the one their doctor in Doornfontein, Dr. Allan, has for house calls, only hers is brown and slimmer. He gives her eye contact. She brushes arcs of hair from under her small pouted mouth. —God, she says. Sorry about them.

He puts his hands in his pockets. —It's ukay.

—No, it's not. It's shaming.

Shaming. While he turns this word over in his mind, like some found tool with a purpose unknown to him, they hear the rumble of the garage doors shutting at the base of that twisting stone staircase. Isaac moves closer to her. So fresh and bright she is in this waxing morning light. She has the book in her hand; he asks what it is. She has green eyes with a touch of yellow, limpid and bright. —Poetry.

There it is: that light inside his chest again, switched on by itself. —Like Shakespeare hey?

—Coleridge, she says. Milkwhite teeth in a balanced smile well under her control. He can feel the strength under the doll's face and the high voice. Her neck is thick and browned by the sun.

—Ops us a sec hey. Lemme check.

—I beg yours?

—Can I please see?

—You like Coleridge?

He is not altogether sure her smile is a hundred percent kind anymore. What is it with these people and their sly pricking ways, their gibberish? It starts to bring up a redness in him and he says: —Ja f'course man. Who duzzen?

She hands him the book, small with tan hard covers. A label has a name in pen. *Yvonne Linhurst, Standard 7V.* A school smell off the pages, that dull musty gloom, the onerous mass of a boredom that never ends. The words he scans make no sense, the lines are clumped up funny. It's like a code book. Down below the car hoots. He feels a teetering, a desperate feeling, and starts to read out loud, something about rocks, a river, picking out easy words then trying a long one: *half-intermitted*, and failing, stumbling on it. When he looks over the top of the book he sees she's covered her mouth.

—Here, he says, and snaps it shut at her. Take it.

She does, but slowly. —I've made you cross, she says in her musical voice.

—Why should I be cross? But he cannot believe how crushed he feels inside; a mewling crushed feeling, almost nauseating.

He has moved away but she calls him back.

—What?

—Just hang on, she says.

—I got work to do hey. I'm a working man. I run a crew. I don't have any larney school to go to, to read poem books.

—Just hang on, okay.

He looks at her, face to face now, she's not as tall as he thought she was on the stairs, but still a little taller than he is.

—I apologize, she says to him. I shouldn't have laughed.

He tries to speak but his throat is plugged. The car below hoots again. He tries to smile and feels a crooked stiffness spreading on his face and hears himself say: —Better run to Dadsy hey.

It comes out all wrong, flat and harsh instead of as the joke he meant. Her face changes, she's frowning. —I just said sorry. You don't have to be so–

He can feel his eyes getting watery. He blinks hard, he can't look at her. He makes a sound – *tsuh* – that he's picked up from Silas, an expression of harsh dismissal. He means it for himself, for his own turmoil, but she flinches from it, he feels her shrinking.

When he looks up she's walking away. No: betrayed by his mouth, his wilding heart. All the churning unfairness of not being able to use the stairs joins with this feeling, joins with the frustration of not being able to understand their off-balancing enigmatic babble, and all the muffled jealous anger he has underneath everything – all of it melds as one and mounts the column of his dry throat in one unbottled rush: —Ja you run to Dadsy! *Shookee.*

It stops her; she turns at the top of the stairs. —Jesus, she says. What's wrong with you?

He doesn't move. She keeps staring at him, something odd in her gaze. Then: —It is Yvonne, actually. And who the bloody hell are you?

—Isaac, he says, hoarse. I am Isaac Helger.

7.

SATURDAY NIGHTS HE LIKES TO GO to the bioscope, the Alhambra of course, and not the posh Apollo, and always in a sixpenny seat in one of the front rows, for farther back costs a shilling and a penny. Hot dogs and chips for two tickeys. Inside, the blue fog from the audience's cigarettes is lanced through by the projector beam as if by a lighthouse. He likes the Warner Brothers films best, the hard gangster stuff but also the African Mirror and Pathé newsreels before the main action.

The rooster cartoon and the trumpet note, then that fast-talking pukkuh-pukkuh English voice going like a Vickers machine gun. Tonight: *French might can resist any attack, so says Monsieur Georges Bonnet*, and they watch the sabre-nosed French minister reviewing ranks of Black soldiers in Tunisia. *Even a razor-sharp sword needs oiling from time to time and here the finest navy in the world is on high-alert manoeuvres in the Adriatic* and they see British destroyers with their big guns, carriers with seaplanes. *The same old story, one nation makes demands and another nation asserts her rights. It's democracy against might makes right, and we all know who'll be winners in this little dance!* They see images from Spain where Franco and the Nationalists with help from Italian-German fascists are marching on Madrid, seat of the Republican government. Pack mules loaded with heavy machine guns, men in greatcoats climbing muddy slopes. When it's South Africa's turn the cinema erupts, most noise from the cheap seats around Isaac. Whistles and claps and stomping feet. On the screen coastal guns track the clouds above Cape Town. *Anyone thinking of invading the Union had better watch out! It's the same cry here as everywhere in the Empire. Ready for action!* And too, when it's the turn of Palestine to make the news, this Doornfontein cinema turns rowdy with Jewish pride. Showing the rocky soil being spliced behind the ploughs of Jewish farmers, Jewish orange groves, Jewish buildings, modern and clean. *By the work of his hands the Jew is redeeming his ancient land, enjoying the fruits of his labour. The Jew has proved once and for all to the world that he needs only a crack at freedom to make a go of it!* Comic relief always follows the society weddings in London. Mud wrestling in Australia or a regimental charity pantomime in the Midlands. Fat women get the most laughs, double if they're falling over. *Look out old girl! We'd better pray she doesn't land on anyone's foot! You look famished. Fancy a cheesecake?* But the laughter dies to muttering when they watch President Franklin Delano Roosevelt giving a speech in someplace called Chautauqua, New York, to a loving audience, saying, *I have seen war. I have seen war on land and sea. I have seen blood running from the wounded. I have seen men coughing out their gassed lungs. I! Hate! War!* And all those Americans applauding him like mad, the President promising to shun any commitment that might *entangle us in foreign wars* and warning that he won't permit any American to send help to any side fighting overseas either. Some voices in the dark give out soft hisses then; but when the Chancellor of Germany comes on there is only utter silence. The cinema seems to grow cold around Isaac. This Herr Hitler throwing his hands and sputtering like a spastic peacock and the thousands going berserk and shrieking and baying in waves back at him, spearing up their stiff arms. Earlier in the year the Rhineland was illegally reoccupied by German forces, an act of war, but France did nothing and neither did anyone else. Probably because they hate war too. Now there's a friendship pact between Mussolini and

Hitler. The newsreel illustrates all this by showing black arrows spreading from Germany and Italy, leaching across the map like a poison. All those first pictures of the Royal Navy and the French army are very little against the ice feeling spreading around and welling inside Isaac then. The Archbishop of Canterbury appears from behind his big wooden desk to ask cinema patrons to give generously to help people who must flee from persecution in Germany, saying, *Particularly I want all to remember that amongst these poor multitudes not all are Jews, but Christian souls too are included in their number . . .*

This makes Isaac think of the Quota Act that was passed back in 1930 which he knows now cos it's about the only thing he ever read up on from his old high school textbooks since he left Athens Boys. Looked it up after that time outside the shul when the okes tried to make like he was an ignorant or something. Read how it was true how the Nat government put a block on anyone trying to come to South Africa from Lithuania and some other countries near there. The bastards saying it had nothing to do with Jews when everyone knew it was *only* Jews – that just about every Jewish family in South Africa comes from Lithuania, Kovno province. But at least there's ways round Quota, according to Mame. She told him she was sad for a time when it happened (Isaac too small to remember it, just ten or eleven) but then she realized that all you need to do is get documents showing you were from a country that's not blocked. And there are so many other countries. Mame believes it can be done. With just a little bit of money and patience and organization. Mame the optimist.

She may not be all wrong: the last item on the African Mirror newsreel tells of the recent arrival of the German liner *Stuttgart* in Cape Town. On board were over five hundred German Jewish refugees, lucky to get away from Hitler, free to come here since Germany is not a country affected by Quota. But on the night the *Stuttgart* was expected to dock, a Greyshirt protest marched down to number seven quay to let the Jews know they weren't welcome. The ship didn't show; it rained and the protesters drifted home. Next morning when the *Stuttgart* slid early into harbour there were only a few sodden bastards left to Sieg Heil at the arrivals. Still – they had marched, there had been a *thousand* of them willing to take the time to head down there against the refugees, against Jews. And still more: the government now says it's bringing in a new requirement for every refugee. From now on, cash money only. No deposit, no landing . . .

Walking home chewing licorice and smoking his Max cigarettes (MEN of the WORLD smoke MAX!) he runs into none other than Shimmy Kahn and them, heading for the tram stop. They say there's a Greyshirt rally and they're going to see what's what. Shimmy Kahn has a steel pipe stuck down his trouser leg. Says his little brother had his arm broken by some Greyshirts two weeks ago. There's families in Bertrams that had bricks thrown through their windows with swastikas drawn on. It's like getting out of hand, he says. Noam Levinson says his old man reckons it's gotten worse since the Olympics, his old man says can you believe in this modern day and age, in the year nineteen hundred and thirty-six, that the whole world would have gone to Berlin for the Olympic *Games* when everyone knows that they treating the Jews like absolute dogs over there, worse than dogs. It shows how no one truly gives one kuk about us.

When they get to the steps of the Johannesburg City Hall, Isaac sees a red flag crossed with a yellow hammer and sickle over a crowd. Some faces in there are part of the Yiddisher Arbeiter Klub in Doornfontein, he knows, the Jewish Workers' Club who are such big atheists they have their picnics on Yom Kippur. He sees some blue and white scarves on necks, emblems of the labour Zionists of Habonim, and the newer more extreme lot, the Hashomer Hatzair.

The Greyshirts are on the far side and now, as he and his mates come up, some well-known Communist Jews, the Bernstein brothers, are running back with a bloodfaced man on their shoulders, his head flopping. Mounted police ride in hard to make a wedge between the two sides. Bottles come out of the night air to pop on the street and stones rattle across it, people are everywhere hunching. Someone has a bicycle chain wrapped round his fist. He watches a baton go up and down and hears the oddly high-pitched thwacking noise when it meets a bare skull.

In the shouts from the Greyshirt side there are English voices taunting also, not just chutaysim, Afrikaners, which shocks Isaac more than a little. English Nazis – is it bladey everyone in the world who hates us? Another bottle cracks on the stairs. A blotting redness leaches into his soul. Of his friends, only he wants to get at them, the Greyshirts, truly. He rushes close enough to get a warning charge from a police horse. A baton pointed at his face. He spits. His mates pull him back, laughing. Rabies Helger. Good old Rabies. Oke is so mad in the head he needs a vet, not a doctor.

—Stuff off hey okes. Leeme go.

But they all go home unblooded, three of them singing Zionist Hebrew songs that Isaac doesn't know. That stuff is Rively's department. One of the Bernstein boys, Yankel, is on the same tram and he makes his way over, starts to huck them about the Blacks, about history, about something called imperial something, capital shmapital. They laugh at his nonsense, jeer him away. Isaac, watching him go (what a langer loksh he is, tall and skinny as a strand of egg noodle, with round spectacles under a curly mass of black hair), starts thinking: a family like them Bernsteins, of book learners and historians, they might know what April seventeenth could mean. Ever since that incident with Kaplan on the cart the question still nags at him now and then, even though he decided that he doesn't want to know – about Mame's tears, about the old country: what the hell for? He used to feel sorry for those old couchers but now he sees Mame was righter than right to chase them out of their lives like a bad smell. Forward, only forward. Forget what's behind you, or behind your family, what use is it? But still there remains that stubborn nudging part of him. The part that keeps on wanting to know.

8.

PACKING & MOVING. The rhythm of daily work that piles into months. At the end of every week he gives his pay to his mother. What is his to keep is the taxi money earned from giving Blacks a lift into town whenever they can, not an insubstantial sum. A good little side business that makes his mame smile to hear about, though she is always urging him to think ahead to the next idea. He likes to sit in the kitchen after work while she is busy making the supper and he will tell her about the different houses he has seen and been into. In Orange Grove and Observatory, in Linksfield and Highlands North. He gives his considered impressions of the neighbourhoods and where he reckons they should buy, which always makes her laugh and say, —Dat's it, dat's it my boy. You'll win them all! Sometimes they'll even get out the real estate section of *The Star* and look at the pictures, talking over the yawning gap between their dream and the real world printed so starkly in the unforgiving ink of the prices. Not all the saved money goes to the dream of a house, though; Mame lets him order them the luxury of their own telephone and a listing for *Helger Watch Repair* in the telephone book.

Meanwhile in secret he has started saving a little something himself, from the taxi business money. He doesn't tell her this – wouldn't dare – but for him buying a car should come before buying a house. Already, soon after he turned seventeen, he passed his driver's licence with a borrowed Packard on the first go, and

a few times now at work the urge to drive has been so strong in
him that he's had to stop himself from taking the wheel from
Silas; but he can't because he's the White and being a White driver
with a Black in the passenger seat would feel like committing
a crime he is half sure he could be arrested for. So instead he
names aloud the model and make and year of almost every vehicle
they pass on the road, as well as its engine capacities, and he is
rarely at a loss. When the Chev breaks down he gets underneath
it and watches and learns from his boys (Fisu and Silas the most
handy), who use their clever self-taught fingers to inflict quick
and brutally effective repairs not found in any manual. Once, at
the warehouse, inspired by his boys, he even replaces a starter
in one of the other trucks all by himself when no one else is
around, impressing Benny Morris so much that Benny goes so far
as to crack open his wallet to buy him a cold Castle Lager.

And all through these accumulating work days he finds he is
never quite alone: Yvonne Linhurst slides inevitably into his
consciousness. When he's riding in that Chev truck with Silas
driving and Hosea, Morgan and Fisu in the back, she is almost like
a phantom sixth member of the crew. It doesn't seem to matter
how long ago their meeting was, he keeps seeing fresh shimmering
images of her that stroke the nerves in his stomach as well as his
mind. He might think of her with a book of poetry, reading in her
uniform, and if he is eating his lunch of Mame-made sandwiches
(leftover white fish on challah; cheese, tomato and onion; fatty
brisket or deboned flanken on rye), such a picture will make his guts
prickle and steal away his appetite. He might see her going from
class to class at her larney private school with plants growing on the
stone walls, the rugby posts and immaculate cricket pitches, boys
calling each other *chaps* and gold buttons on their blazers. He might
imagine that one of the *chaps* is talking to her, holding her hand,
which makes his heart thud redly in him. In the nights he holds
himself, his belly all slippery inside with ideas of her. He finds

himself scheming of ways to make contact with her again, impossible
Yvonne. A practical way to do it without being . . . what was that
one word she had used, that he had to look up? . . . without being
shaming. It sickens him to imagine how little he has to offer her.

He studies the clipboard every morning at the Morris Brothers
warehouse on Jeppe Street for any address in or near Parktown.
Just this looking for it makes his blood jump in him like a trout to
the lure; but of course they have no cause to go back to the house
with steep stone walls that he thinks of now as The Castle. And
she inside is, naturally, The Princess (her mother the Mad Queen,
her father the Cruel Duke). The Princess with that golden hair.
And what is he then? In this world of castles and royalty? He is a
troll and a peasant, with jug ears and mean eyes and empty pockets
and coarse ways. If she were to send down her hair like the girl in
the fairy tale, he wouldn't climb it, he would yank her out and
down to him.

Stop thinking of her so much, he starts to tell himself almost
every day. She laughed at you, man, don't forget. Luched you
out so bad. And then what you said after she told you sorry – no
man face it, if she remembers you at all she doesn't even like you.
And she's only a little snob, she's nothing to you, and they're all
a pack of loonies anyway. Forget them. But the thoughts of her
are not under his control, they are like hummingbirds, they make
their own way into his brain to flutter and glitter there, annoying
him but also stupefying a little with their beauty if he ever pauses
to watch.

No Gilder Lane on the clipboard but one day he does see Buxton
Street, his own. That's the delivery address, the pickup is in
Booysens. The name is Oberholzer. He takes the clipboard to Sol
Morris: —Boss, this one checks a mistake hey.

Solly has a look. Goes to the office, comes back. —No you
wrong, it's a hunned percent.

—But that's a chutus name hey. There's no chutaysim on that street, believe you me.

He shrugs. —Well maybe they moving in.

Isaac laughs. —Ja, and flying pigs also.

But when they're on their way it hits him. The old lady, that widow at number forty. He checks the number, ja, it's her. A tiny shrivelled-up thing who lives so quietly by herself with a couple cats that she hardly even seems alive, no wonder he forgot her. He knew she was a yok, ja, but not a chutus, an English Christian but no Afrikaner, because her name is Smith. Maybe she's gone and sold up. He wonders who is moving in instead, what the story is, what brings Afrikaners to his Doornfontein now.

When they get to Booysens they find the home on a treeless street of identical houses, all dull yellow bricks with walls made from horizontal plank-shaped lengths of pale concrete. But it's hard to miss the right one, because there are belongings in the driveway and a man also, sitting on a lounge chair, his shirt unbuttoned to the sun.

They pull up and Isaac approaches. This man is a solid trunk of flesh: the areas of fat that hang from him are like sandbags attached to a brick stump, their drooping conveys no sense of softness. His skin has become angry in the rays, a few curls pad the middle of his exposed chest. —Hello there! Isaac says. Cheery and loud: the voice he's learned to use doing this work.

The man takes a sip from a bottle of Lion Lager, his hand so wide Isaac can't see much glass. The other hand comes up as the bottle sinks, curling a lit cigarette to the moustache.

—Uh this is one fifty-eight hey? Isaac says. We the movers.

—Nee, the man says, using Afrikaans. Dis nie hierdie plek nie. No. Not this place.

—Oo-uh. Ek's jammer meneer.

Okay then. I'm sorry mister.

—Morris, the man says. He rolls some beer in his mouth, swallows. —Morris.

—Scuse meneer?

—Is jy dan 'n Morris broer?

No, I'm not a Morris, he says, staying in Afrikaans. Not one of the brothers . . . But he's looking at the number on the garage door behind. He scratches his chin, coughs. —Maar meneer. Dit *is* hondred agt-en-vyftig.

But mister. This *is* one fifty-eight.

The man shows teeth under his moustache. He's wearing shorts from a safari suit and there are lumpy twisted varicose veins on his shins; his massive feet, crossed at the ankles, are pale and long as bread loaves. He touches his ear. —How say?

—It says there one-five-eight, right there.

—You say to me I am a liar?

—Is what it says, man.

—You chirping me? says the man. Don't you backchat to me, boy.

Isaac stands there confused: how fast this is happening. The nature of it.

—You a chirping little backchatter hey, with your long nose. Isn't it so, *Morris*?

—Hey.

—Bet you from Doornfontein and all. Isn't it. *Morris.*

—What? Whatzit you calling me?

—Magnus!

It's a shout from the gate. A woman there. Very tall, with long straight sandy hair and a face that is peculiarly narrow, like a horse or a bird, the eyes seeming almost to touch through the thin pipe of the nose.

—Hibbly bibbly tibbly, the man says to Isaac. He burps. —Hey Morris. Let us make a deal hey. Hibbly bibbly Doornfontein. Hey? Hey?

He gets up slowly, in stages, the hinged sections of his massiveness unfurling. He makes some kind of bobbing gesture.

Like an oak door swinging shut he turns and lurches off. Only then does it touch Isaac what he has just seen, a parody of the religious, the oldsters rocking as they pray in shul. He wants to shout but his voice dries in him and he just stands there, feeling the blood slowly peeling away from the back of his face.

It is the woman who comes out to make the arrangements, he doesn't see the man again. But when they are packed up and on the road, he tells Silas to pull over.

—What is, baas?

—Just ganna check something hey.

He gets out, climbs up onto the flatbed. The drawers of a desk have been removed and lashed down under a tarp. He lifts the tarp. He had noticed a glimpse of papers before. There's nothing much in the first three he looks at, just envelopes, stationery. But then he finds articles cut from copies of *Die Transvaler*, and whole folded editions of another newspaper he's never seen before. It has a bilingual title, *Die Waarheid* on the left side and *The Truth* on the right; in between is an emblem with a springbok and a kudu and between them a standard with a fat black swastika right in the middle. Under the title it reads, *Official Organ of the South African Greyshirts*. The articles are a blend of Afrikaans and English. Headlines he sees: THE JEWISH QUESTION. DIE JOODSE VRAAGSTUK. ANGLO-JEWISH-BOLSHEVIK AXIS. JEWISH WAR CRIMES. DIE JOODSE PROTOCOLS: WAT BEDOEL HULLE? There's also clippings from the *Transvaler* newspaper full of anti-Jewish stuff, cartoons of a character called Hoggenheimer, a fatty with a fat nose plus cigar and Star of David. Ja, he's looking at the very thing. He can barely believe. Man's one a them, a fucken Greyshirt: those toxic newsreel arrows leaching across the map of the world have poured into the back of his own stuffing truck.

He folds some of the papers into a pocket then straightens up and unbuttons his trousers. Hosea, Morgan and Fisu are big-eyed with interest. The passing cars can see everything but Isaac doesn't care, his pulses beat the red rage into his head. He feels the air on his dick and then he is pissing. His boys shout, they cover their mouths, they stamp the flatbed and whoop and laugh. Only Silas looks unhappy, Isaac sees him through the back window with his own face superimposed (and ja, it does have a lot of nose – what did he call me, big nose, long nose? – under the orange hair, but it's more the freckles and the widespread ears that make it what it is).

Meanwhile he is aiming his circumcised penis with great care, making sure to give all the drawer's contents a thoroughly democratic soaking. When he has no more piss to give he hawks up lumps of green snot from the back of his throat and chobs them in for extra measure, —Read that now, you Greyshirt piece a shit. Read it nice.

Back in the passenger seat, Silas has worried eyes for him.

—Cheer up hey, Isaac tells him. Happy happy.

—Can make troubles, Silas says.

—Just relax max. Let's roll.

They drop the goods at number forty on Isaac's very own street. The old lady shrivel-dried as a stick of biltong stands there holding a shawl close around herself and gives no sign that she recognizes Isaac as a neighbourhood kid. Cats ooze around her legs, peering. It turns out that, ja, she is a chutus lady after all, even with a name like Smith (it happens sometimes), and who ever imagined it? After unloading, Isaac tells the boys to head back to Jeppe Street without him since the workday is almost over and by the time he gets to the warehouse he'll just have to turn around and take the tram back into Doornfontein.

Then he walks up the street to his home, where Mame is at first suspicious as to why he's back early but then she sits him down in the kitchen and serves him a plate stacked with French toast dusted with her mixture of cinnamon and sugar. He is chewing and swallowing down this good stuff with mouthfuls of sweet milky tea when their new telephone rings. It's Sol Morris, his voice clipped, telling Isaac to come in. Isaac tries to explain that he'll just have to come back home again and that he's sorry he's knocked off a little bit early but–

—Just come in, Isaac. Now. Oright? And then he hangs up.

When Isaac gets to the warehouse all the Morris brothers are waiting and he knows his feeling of gathering dread has been justified. He reckons they've heard about what he's done so he jumps off with a pre-emptive apology, saying he is really sorry but the oke is one of the Greyshirts, for real hey, genuine scum, and what's he supposed to do, nothing? But it's not about the pissing on the customer's things in full view of the whole world. At least not only. Much worse, they've found out about the money he's been making on the side giving lifts to Blacks into town.

He goes quiet.

—Who is it that you think you are hey? says Solly. Just who the bladey hell do you think you are?

He says sorry again. Then: —I just seen how we always had this empty truck like. We going into town anyway. So why not . . . I mean it seems like a waste . . .

—Ja so why not turn it into a bladey stuffing kaffir taxi service? Make a quick buck and chup it all and not tell us a thing. So clever.

I didn't grab it *all*, Isaac wants to say. I split it with the boys. But he checks himself, not wanting to get them also in shtoch.

Errol says: —Jesus Christ. He says *why not* to us. What do you mean why not? Like what kind of people do you come from that you could even *think* why not?

—Hey. Hey hang on. Was my idea. Don't start on my–

—Ja, brilliant idea. We get caught being a taxi and we lose our whole business licence. Brilliant.

—You a real genius, Solly says. A real little operator.

A redness wells up in him, blotting. — . . . Well it's better than having no ideas like you got! Doing the same things over and over.

—Oright, we finished, says Solly. Overs kadovers.

They hand him his last pay packet. Isaac takes the envelope with a dead hand and walks out, his eyes burning. Round the side he goes. The wheels are turning in his mind and he realizes that the only way they could have found out about the taxi was from one of the boys – his boys that he tried to protect!

He waits. When he hears their voices, coming round from the back, he steps out. He sees Silas and the change in Silas's face.

—Ai wena! Indoda!

Hey man.

—Wena, it was you!

Silas backs away, the others disperse from him. Silas is their leader, the driver, Silas with his beads on the mirror and his family photos of the kraal back home in Zululand, in verdant Natal, tucked above the visor. Silas the whistler who laughed so much when Isaac came downstairs from that divorcée that time.

—No, no, he keeps saying.

Isaac mimics him. —Noh-noh. I can't believe you'd do that, man. Noh-noh. Where the hell you going?

—I never–

Silas puts up his hands but too slowly, already Isaac has punched his mouth, quicker than thought (even Isaac is a little surprised to see his quick flicking fist shoot out), splitting the top lip to the teeth. Silas balls over, covering his head with both arms. Isaac hammers, kicks, pushes him back into the brick wall and drags him up. He's so close he can smell the fear in the man's sweat, African-tanged sweat, the scent of all those hours together in the cab of that truck. He's got him by the throat. —Man, he says. How can you *do* that. I thought. Thought we were . . .

—Mr. Morris, Silas says. He gives me this job so long time. He take cares for me, my family. Now he say for me to watch on you. Say if he catch you later, I'm losing this job, good job. Mr. Morris the baas, I'm wanting loyal for him.

Isaac has his fist pulled back. Silas's nervous tongue goes across the fractured lip like a windshield wiper, clearing the blood; but more drips onto Isaac's wrist, the hot blood of this Black man, this Zulu with his stretched earlobes and his sad eyes. Something in them holds echoes of his own father, somehow, and of the couchers and the watery sadness in theirs.

For a moment Isaac's cocked fist wilts; but then another counter-instinct rears in him, hard as steel, and he squashes down the other Stupid sentiment: —And *my* job hey? he shouts into Silas's face. Is my job nothing? They just bladey fired me! Where's loyalty to me? To *me* hey? When you were happy to put in your pocket all those times what I gave you. Now I lost my job cos a you, I've *lost* it, you . . . you . . . You're a *kaffir*, man. Bulala wena!

I'll kill you.

There're shouts behind. One of the Morrises. Isaac runs. He keeps on: he is running through town and there's liquid fire in his lungs and his heart is a firing cannon in him. Only a dark flaw can draw such rotten fate, it must be. Some sickened twist of wrong in his soul. His eyes are streaming to make a blur of the world. And then he hears that question of Solly's again, and it's just like when he got expelled from high school, so clear, as if hissed directly into some innermost secret ear: Just who the bladey hell do you think you are? *Who?*

9.

HE CANNOT BEAR TO FACE what his parents' reaction will be, Mame's especially, so he pretends to go to work every morning, spending the days wandering in town. Something nameless in him holds him paralyzed, keeps him from looking for another job. Maybe it's letting down his parents, maybe it's that his work record is already tainted now and he's worried about what he might have to tell a potential employer. For sure it makes him sick to think about, so as much as he can he does not. There must be a solution and maybe it will come to him soon. Idly, he reads the Greyshirt and Nat papers he took: the Jews cause all the war, the Jews suck the nation's blood, the Jews are inciting the Blacks to destroy White civilization. It makes him tired and sad instead of angry. He doesn't even bother to burn them, just leaves them in a diner.

He goes up to Parktown on the bus and walks past the Linhurst residence at number eighteen Gilder Lane: The Castle. There is that municipal park a little way downhill, on the opposite side, and he sits on a green wooden bench there with his back against the sign saying *Whites Only / Slegs Blankes*.

He sees her once, walking up from the school bus stop. He keeps hidden behind the long fronds of the willow trees.

On impulse one afternoon he buys a half-litre of Cape brandy, like the kind the couchers used to have. It fits in his pocket and as he wanders he sips from it. It burns in the throat but banks a sweet heat into the belly; the heat dissolves into the blood and he feels better about himself. So easy, like medicine. He buys more bottles.

At the end of the week he pays his ma from the severance envelope so that she does not suspect his unemployment. At night, when everyone's gone to bed, he sips from his brandy bottle and sits on the low wall in the backyard, his eyes looking up the alleyway to the back of the Oberholzer house at number forty. That looming totem of ill luck: he moved the Greyshirt in there and the same day God took his job away. Often he will sit till it's early morning, brooding in psychic pain on number forty till his eyelids curl down with the weight of his brandied exhaustion; it suits him better than sleeping. Some nights in that evil house he can see their shadows behind the lace and hear their voices, the shouting. Everyone on Buxton Street by now knows about the new chutus couple that's moved in. How he hits her (what else do you expect from a chutus?), how the police have already been. One night Isaac witnesses it himself, or at least he hears them. The meaty slugging noises of human hands whacking human flesh. Yet she doesn't scream.

There is another reason to stare at number forty that is not all baleful: the Oberholzers have brought with them a fine vehicle of their own, a DeSoto Airflow. He admires its lines, speculates about the engine under its peaked bonnet. They keep it parked in the alley. She – the wife, the tall thinfaced one with the sandy hair – comes out around eleven, usually, and sits low down on the running board in her blue nightie and slippers to have a cigarette. Maybe she's not allowed to smoke inside, who knows. But he gets into the habit of waiting for her, watching her from his shadowed seat on the low wall. The Oberholzers' story (word in the street, that infallible word) is that they got evicted in Booysens and he doesn't have a job; the old lady is her aunt and she's putting them up.

As the third aimless week begins, Isaac sees he will soon be discovered; he is almost out of severance pay to give to his mame. She seems also to be growing suspicious, there haven't been any excited conversations about houses at the kitchen table lately, no laying out of fresh schemes for his future, he's been avoiding her by staying out late. This is when his brooding mind turns again to the cashbox and the secret that is in it, underneath the money. Papers that Mame weeps over on a Shabbos morning; prays over. One night he takes the locked box out and sits with it on his lap under the moon. He takes a bit of wire and fishes in the lock then chokes on a bone of self-disgust. Look at me. A person who would betray his own mother is the lowest scum there is. He puts the box back and the next day he goes to Gordon Court, a block of maisonettes in Bertrams where the Bernsteins live. Being Communists, lots of these Bernsteins don't work and there are always funny people at the apartment, Coloureds and such, and even, it's been rumoured, one time a Black wearing a three-piece suit. There's a big dog named Brutus and jammed bookshelves in the front hall, a smell of greasy cooking. The doormat seems saturated in mould. The old man of the house wears big square glasses and has food stains on his vest, standing there scratching his chest, telling Isaac where he can find Yankel, the one closest to Isaac in age, who approached them that night on the tram coming back from City Hall.

He goes to a shoe factory in Mayfair, enters stealthily in the back way where it's all Blacks, finds the Black toilets and has to force himself to enter the danger of this forbidden space. Yankel and another White are in there, handing out Communist literature about workers this and workers that, comrades and red stars. They can get away with it inside the Black toilets, Yankel says, cos the management would never come in here. Meanwhile the other one shows him a paper called *Umvikeli-Thebe* which he's told means *The African Defender*, has an ink-smudged cartoon inside with Mussolini and Hertzog slapping chains on a Black, and written underneath, *Tata amakantango ako. Angiwafuni!* Take away your chains, I do not want them. It has to do (Isaac's told) with Mussolini invading Ethiopia plus Hertzog's new laws for Natives that've taken away the vote from the tiny handful of rich

Blacks who still had that right, left over from the old British colony days.

Isaac sniffs, looks around at the shit-spattered tin holes, the plugged reeking urinal. He can think of better ways to spend his time. When Yankel comes out for a walk, Isaac asks him does he know anything about what the date April seventeenth can mean.
—Whatchoo mean do I know anything?
—Like in history or summin. Is it important?

Yankel stops and takes off his flat cap (not a White cap but the kind darker workers wear), scratches his wiry curls. —What the hell you asking me exactly? What's this about?

So Isaac explains what he can, it might be something big to do with his mother that no one talks about but is known to others (or else it's just the ramblings of a potato seller called Kaplan, but this he doesn't say). He can't ask his ma or his old man cos it's too sensitive, but he wants to know. He thought maybe Bernstein, who's up on all this history jazz, might know something offhand but if not, ukay, well stuff it, he'll just go right now . . .
—Hold your horses, ay. Don't be so hitzik. Tell me, where is your ma from?
—Dusat.
—I heard of it, ja.
—My da always says it's the size of a yawn.
—It's in Zarasai. Lemme ask and see if anyone knows. Fourteenth April.
—Seventeenth. Thanks a mil hey.
—Here.
—What's this?
—You coming with me to hand out.
—What, me? I'm not a bladey commie, man!
—Quid pro quo, says Yankel Bernstein. Isaac's not familiar with the words, but he gets the meaning. He spends the rest of the arvy pinching his nose with one hand and handing out banned

literature with the other in various factory shithouses. Mighty
pleased he is when those whistles go off for the end of the day. As
for Bernstein's jibber-jabber about the movement of history and
workers united, Black and White and Coloured and Indian all
together, it's mere fantasy babble to Isaac, most of which is
expressed in code words he doesn't understand, about as relevant
as the mumbled ancient Hebrew in the shul prayers. What's real
to him is the stink of Black shit and Black sweat. The filthy walls
and the puddles of piss full of mosquitoes on the cracked concrete
and the need to get the hell out of there as quick as he can.

     In the end he can't quite reckon who is more mad in the head,
Yvonne Linhurst's crazed mother babbling gibberish in The Castle
in Parktown, or Yankel Bernstein with his flat cap and round
glasses spending his days talking equally senseless kuk in literal
sewers. It's a messed-up world hey, Isaac thinks. So messed up.

He needs his brandy after a day like today and he does three-
quarters of a bottle in Joubert Park then goes home late and sits on
the wall under the fingernail moon, sipping the rest. Watching and
waiting. How pretty are the curves of that big DeSoto washed in
the pale luminescence of the lunar glow, the top of the windshield
opaque with eyebrows of settled mine dust. Mrs. Oberholzer does
not disappoint. At twelve minutes after eleven she comes out to
have her smoke, sits down on the running board next to the side-
mounted spare wheel with her long knees sticking up under her
nightie. He finishes the brandy as she finishes her cigarette. He
watches her stand up and go inside and then he drops down out of
his concealment. Sways a little on his feet. Taps the bottle on the
edge of the wall, then does it harder and it breaks with a pop and
a soft tinkle. Thickheaded, he moves down the alley to the DeSoto.
Bladey Greyshirt shit, mamzor chuleriuh: bastard cholera carrier.
A geshvir af dir in zeit: a tumour in your side, you piggish pustule.
May you be hanged in fire. Drowned in ice. Three times over.

He reaches the blue automobile with its long handsome box shape, the swoop of the curved mudguards and the round headlights like peering eyes low on the front, the criss-crossed spindles of the wheels, and he puts one hand on its smooth steely loveliness and lets his palm taste its coolness. The madwomen get Castles and the Greyshirts get beautiful cars and what do I get but fired. Not even egg noodles to my name. Eff him, this chutus, he deserves nothing.

He bends and slashes at the closest tire with the stub of the bottle; but the jagged edges only break off against the tough rubber. He curses some more, then starts stabbing. This too is ineffective: the thin glass keeps snapping. He drops it and is looking around for something else sharp and harder to use, some stone or nail, swaying from the brandy mist behind his eyes, bent over, when the back door behind him smacks against the side of the house with a heavy clap and a force like a great wind rushes into him. He's lifted before he can even turn. He slams into the car, is pinned without breath. It's Oberholzer who's grunting in his ear, that moustache. Isaac wriggles sideways and kicks loose and goes for the balls on instinct, with a knee. He gets hit so hard in the side of his face that everything explodes the way a firework rocket blooms into arcing tendrils of falling stars. He can only see again as he bounces from the brick wall. Oberholzer there, massive. Isaac pretends to slump then jumps to one side, sets himself, aiming, and punches for the white pillar of the throat in the dimness below that wide head.

This Oberholzer for all his size moves neatly and precisely: he slaps Isaac's arm aside and grips the side of Isaac's neck in the same smooth movement, with the same hand. So close now that Isaac can see he is smiling. Smiling. He's taken cunning hold of the muscle that joins Isaac's neck to his body and his thumb is in the notch of the windpipe and he is squeezing and twisting and the motion feels very precise and very practised. He knows exactly what he's doing and he is incredibly strong: the grip paralyzes Isaac as it chokes him. The huge hand feels non-biological, like a piece of industrial equipment, a vise of iron.

The blotting red rage comes up but it is no good. For the first time in his life Isaac can do nothing against an assault. He is choked down to his knees. All the time Oberholzer talks in a soft voice full of soft meanness. Bad Afrikaans words against the Jews that he digs into Isaac with a great bulking pleasure that Isaac can feel behind them. The white teeth in the smirk under his moustache. Words against Isaac's family, his mother, terrible injurious words that at last make Isaac's eyes stream in his paralyzed face. He blacks away, a mercy. He comes back to himself and he is in his own yard. He feels wetness on his face. Blood? He touches it, sniffs. No, it's pungent. Piss. He rinses off with shaking hands at the outside tap in the yard, goes inside.

In the morning he is stiff in his cot. His father runs to summon Mame. She wails over him. He gets to a mirror and sees the empurpled eye, the swollen forehead. He makes up a story about Blacks trying to rob him on his way home. They got his pay packet this week; Morris gave it to them early. He tried his very best to fight them off.

They want to telephone the police and Dr. Allan. They want to telephone the Morrises to let them know. Absolutely not, he says. No no no. You'll make it worse, promise me you won't tell anyone. They want to know why not. Because I'm ashamed, Isaac tells them. He'll talk to the Morrises himself, ukay, don't worry about the Morrises.

He pretends to phone work, speaking into a dead receiver, telling the phantom Morris brother on the end of the line that he had his pay stolen and that he won't be coming in for a while. A bit ill at the moment, you see, going to need some time to recuperate. The Morris brother is exceedingly sympathetic, tells him to take as much time as he needs.

—Vot a gentlyman, says Isaac's father.

Mame's arms are folded and her scarred face is stern. Tutte goes back to work, stooped and limping. Rively is at school, underlining things with neatness and precision.

10.

HE CONVALESCES IN THE DAYTIME in his sister's bed. The wounds on his face, his head, are nothing – a bruised eye socket (it's doubtful Oberholzer even made a fist, just an open-handed swat, probably the way he smacks his wife), plus a scabbed scrape on the forehead where there's a bump like a cue ball, and a thick rope of purple lower down that his collar can hide – but he is badly hurt inside, under the skin, in his heart and in his mind, his spirit. He lies there with the curtains drawn. In the next room his father works, tiny clocks tick like toiling beetles. Customers wander through the front door with its jingling bell. Mame brings him thick barley soups but he has little appetite.

What am I waiting for? He realizes it's for the redness, he's waiting for the rage to spark and fire up in him. How the Coloured boys used to sometimes call him Crazy Izey. Later on it was Rabies Helger. That temper that always got him through every scrape, biting and scratching. But this time the brute mass of his enemy, the elemental power in that grip – there was nothing, nothing that he had against it.

He tells himself to get up now and go and get a cricket bat or half a brick and get this bastard back. That's what you need to do.

He lies there and makes dreams of this in his mind but his body knows they are just lies, baby lies. The fact of that tidal force has broken something in him, maybe something more vital than any bone in his body.

To be choked like that, like a dog in a sack in the lake. To be made to hear those words, so intimate, like some obscene parody of a lover. To have the sour taste of piss on your tongue. No place more loathsome to fall, none lower. Nobody must ever know.

Get up and fetch a brick, Isaac, a knife.

He lies there and he turns to the wall. He hears the jingling of the front door. He lets the bowls of soup cool on the floor beside the bed. When he closes his eyes it does not stop the tears. These tears have a viscous quality, they're not surface water, they come up from the broken thing deep in him, they seep up like translucent gel to slowly wet the pillow where he lies on his side.

Choked down, pissed on. Loathsome little worthless thing.

He asks God what he, Isaac, has done to Him, the Almighty, to so deserve His wrath; was it quitting shul? He hears no divine whispers in response: he is not his father.

Mame brings him chunks of ice for the bruising and he holds them diligently against the empurpled tissues and, after a few weekdays plus a weekend, the vivid colour softens, the swelling eases. But not the tainted feeling.

He lies in bed and craves brandy. There's no brandy. Too wounded to even pretend he can get up and walk to the bottle shop. Dr. Allan comes to visit, against his wishes. Allan glances at the bruises, doesn't even need to touch, he shrugs and leaves some aspirins. Look in my guts, Isaac thinks. Look down my throat, in my heart and my guts where it's all smashed in. Gimme pills for that.

He takes a cracked hand mirror from Mame's items in the sewing room and looks at his face in the outhouse. What makes him vomit is not the black eye and the bumped forehead, the bruise around his throat, it's not how he has bat-wing ears and carrot hair and a shapeless mass of a nose and cheeks spattered with freckles, no, none of that, it's the dullness that he sees in his eyes, weakling eyes. Outside he feels the presence of that other house, number forty, the very structure like a stranger always watching him; he can feel it at his back when he's crossing the yard, hurrying to the safety of his sister's bed.

Get a rock, get a baton. Get your revenge.

But all that he gets is more fearful, more sick. He can see the real worry in Mame's face when she comes over to sit on the bed now, in Tutte's also when he leans over behind her. *You'll be all right, my love, my rainbow.* I know, Mame. *No evil eye – you're so strong you can kill a bull.* Yes Mame. *You'll win them all!* She brings him the newspaper, the real estate section. He drops it next to the cold soup in the bowls, unread, unreadable. Soon she will find out what a little fraud he is, pretending to still have that job. All her pride in him will wither. How he begins to loathe himself then.

One day Yankel Bernstein shows up. Isaac is having a dream in which Yvonne calls and he tries to jump the wall at number eighteen Gilder Lane but he floats off like a balloon, The Castle becomes small, just a gem glinting in a sea of golden liquid, he's full of dizzy sadness, everything below keeps getting smaller . . .

When he opens his eyes Mame's warm palm is pushing down gently on his chest. She steps back and he sees Yankel at the door. Your friend comes to visit, very nice, she says. Talmud teaches, when you visit a sick one you take away one-sixtieth of the sickness.

—One-sixtieth! says Yankel. So precise hey, that Talmud, ha ha. Those mathematicians!

Gitelle grunts. The Talmud knows, she says, not like the nonsense in other books. And she gives the smudged manifestos tucked under Yankel's right arm a hard look on her way out.

Yankel closes the door, brings a chair to the bed. —So how you keeping, my mate?

—Had happier days thanks. He sits up, asks Yankel to pass him his cigarettes. They both light up.

Yankel: —So what happened exactly? Your ma tuned me you got robbed.

—Jumped, four of the bastards. Your lovely shvartzer friends.

—Genuine? Where was this?

Isaac turns aside to blow smoke into the wall. —I'd rather not chit-chat about it. I'm tryna forget it happened, like.

Not till he says this aloud does he realize that that is exactly what he should be doing. Let go of it. Stop with the revenge. This idea of revenge, it's his drowning stone. Let go and swim up, back to the light.

—Isaac?

—Hey?

—I said these crimes.

—Ja?

—They wouldn't exist if there was no property, right? Hey? It's all completely solvable, right. Take away the property, take away the crime. One day soon this capitalist economy's ganna croak off, then you'll check how crime just disappears so fast, cos there won't be any need hey. Right? It's obvious. It'll just melt away hey, like hailstones when the sun comes.

—Like hailstones.

—You like that one.

—Ja, you a real Conridge you are.

—Who?

—Poet, whatever. Pretty little hailstones.

—Cynicism, that's what you got. Look at history, how it's moving.

—Whichever. All I knows is what I know.

—What's that?

—If there is hailstones around, people will probably chuck them at each other, full-stick.

—Why would they do that?

—Man, they'll aim for the children. They like to hear them cry.

Yankel studies him. —You in a bad way, my mate. You need this. Brain medicine. Listen to Uncle Yankeluh. He has pulled a blue pamphlet out. He leans over into the creaking chair and puts it on the nightstand, taps it three times and leaves it there.

—Better not let my old lady catch that or she'll bell the cops on you like a shot.

—Give a look when you get a chance.

—I can't wait. Just let me get my cap on and my reading glasses warmed up.

Yankel doesn't seem to catch this one, he's stubbed out his filtered Max in the ashtray on the bed and he's rubbing his palms together. Now he leans in and lowers his voice.

—Look hey, I wanted a let you know that thing we were talking on.

—Ja.

—April the seventeenth.

—Ja.

—You know Blumenthal?

—The chemist?

—No, the laundry.

—Uh yuh.

—Well, he's from Dusat, like your people.

—Like *me*, what you talking?

—Oh ja?

—Ja, I's born there.

—That a fact hey?

—My sis too. This is her room.

He looks around, a little dazed-seeming.

—Ja, in case you wondering why I got a teddy bear and that. I'm not running queer on anyone.

Yankel reaches over to the bureau where there's framed photos of Mame and of Rively with Tutte. —She's pretty.

—Shut up hey, that's my sister.

—Just saying.

—Ja well I spose all the pretty went to her and the rest they chucked on me.

Yankel puts the photo down. —Anyway, what I wanna tell you, this Blumenthal, I asked him, April seventeenth–

—Shhh, hey. Down a bit.

He nods, leans closer to whisper: —Asked him April seventeenth, Dusat. Does it mean something? He had to think on it but then he comes back to me, says oh ja, ja, absolutely. Wants to know was I talking about the bad one.

—Bad one?

—He says that was a day long ago. They had a pogrom in Dusat, a right proper pogrom hey, like they hadn't had for years and years. Talking a vicious one. People killed and all.

—Pogrom.

—You know what that is, right?

—What you think, I'm a Stupid or summin?

Yankel shrugs.

—When was this?

—Was before the war. He wasn't sure, nineteen and six or five.

—Was he there?

—Right *there* man. Saw it his own eyes.

Isaac smokes for a while, not looking at Yankel, not really thinking either, just letting the fact of it sit there.

—Does it help you hey?

—Ja, says Isaac. I'm sure that it probably does.

—You wanna talk to him, Blumenthal? I can get him to.

—I dunno, says Isaac. That I dunno.

Soon after Yankel's visit there comes a moment he has to face. Either he must admit to himself that he has been beaten and he will go away, he will seek no redress, no revenge, or else he will only get sicker because he knows that there is nothing he can do against this force, this Greyshirt chutus, he is simply too strong, so take your beating and move on. Put it behind you. Go on and limp down the road with humiliation on your head, and piss in your hair, and smile about it . . . smile . . . How like his father he's becoming!

But all the same he does it, he makes the vital decision that he will not brood on vengeance, not live with the weight of such a drowning stone around his neck.

Soon as this is done the fatigue starts to lift. A little appetite returns and he mops the last of the soup from the bowl with a chunk of Mame's good sitnise bread. Another day in bed, he thinks, and I'll be ready to get up and tell them the truth about the job.

Next morning a powerful laugh makes him spy into the workshop where he sees a fat man in a blue suit. A salesman. Great round head like a watermelon. Belly fat packed low in the bladder under the belt. His smile is permanent, the suit shimmers, the feel of his presence holds a kindling warmth. The tip of a banknote edges from the slit of the cashbox; Mame is out and Tutte – skilful elongated fingers – fishes it free, pays the man for a set of leather cloths that he does not need. Isaac steps out without thinking and the man bobs the great dome of his head at him, thin brown hair side parted and lacquered over the scalp. Even from across the room the smell of cologne is strong.

Tutte flinches around: that way of his stooped alarm. Uh! My son, he says.

Such red hair, says the man. He looks a monarch. Another King David.

Isaac feels heat in his face not for himself but his father, the needy hovering in the weak smile.

What's the matter? asks the salesman. Don't you speak mother's tongue?

He speaks it beautiful, says Abel. It's his first language. Say hello Isaac.

The salesman has already crossed the room, chubby hand levelled at Isaac's forehead. —And this?

Isaac shrugs.

The animals they are, these Blacks, says Abel. Stole from him last week. Home sick in bed ever since.

The salesman has blue eyes; not the shimmering blue of the suit but a thinner shade, pale and strange in the ruddy marsh of the face. His hand has settled on Isaac's shoulder. A squeeze, the feeling of enclosing warmth. —It's absolutely nothing hey, tiger, he says. Little knock. Tell you something free worth a million. Whatever happens, shiny side up. Shiny side to the world. Always. Don't ever let the bastards see nothing else. Whatever happens. Remember that, tiger.

When he leaves, Tutte says: —Loverly man that vos.

Isaac is examining the shammies. —Can get these half the price cheaper at Zimmerman's.

His father's arms flap. —I got work to do here, Yitzchok.

—Better not tell Ma.

—Never mind what I say to who. You get back in bed.

—You know she'll count the cashbox hey. Better stick something back . . .

—Go vay, I say. Go!

Instead of bed, Isaac dresses fast. A block down Beit Street, he catches the glassy blue mass of the salesman swaying out of Levinson's. —Hey Mr. Shammy.

He turns with his grin untroubled.

—My father wants his money back.

—Does he?

—Ja, he sent me. Changed his mind.

—Highest quality. Tell your father he's going to be a very happy man. Best coupla pounds he ever spent in his life. Tell him.

The salesman goes on. Isaac keeps pace. —I'm telling *you*, we want our money back.

—Highest quality.

—Man, they nothing special.

—Takes an eye, says the salesman. Takes an educated eye. He'll be well happy. Was my own father I couldn't make a better. Excuse me.

He passes into old lady Meltzer's vegetable shop. Through the lettered glass Isaac watches him talking, lifting his hat, igniting smiles with the charged beam of his own. After ten minutes even the old lady buys a shammy set, following three of her customers. Mame's always said to dredge a living from the good folk of Doornfontein needs miracles and prophecies, but here this salesman is the proving exception. And watch the ease.

When he comes out he points that hardy grin into Isaac's face like a gun barrel. —Shine up hey tiger. You look like a bad Monday morning. Nobody likes a Monday morning.

—I want that money back.

—Thought it was your father.

—You not so clever like you think.

—We all have our limitations. Scuse us there.

He steps past.

—Hey man, he's a cripple you know. You took advantage.

The salesman stops. He looks at Isaac's shoes then up to his face. —Quite the boychik, aren't you. Quite the tiger.

—I know what I know. Those shammies is nothing special.

—Who says it's shammies I'm selling?

He goes into Eckler the barber. Isaac watches him from outside again, moving down the chairs, handling shoulders. The creamed faces show teeth and twist in their tall seats; their laughter carries through the glass. Eight minutes. Isaac counts two sales.

When he comes out and sees Isaac, he puts his hands in his blue pockets and huffs a long breath.

—What you mean you not selling shammies?

—Listen here. If your father sent you, show me the goods.

—He didn't give them to me.

—That so. How interesting. Why don't you go home already?

—Why don't you give us our bladey money.

—Go home and ask your tutte if he's happy. That'll answer your question.

When the salesman moves on towards Rudolph the accountant, Isaac catches up. —I'm ganna come in with you. Tell everyone go to Zimmerman's and get the same thing half price.

—No you won't.

—Wanna bet me?

Again the fat man scans from shoes to face, pausing at mid level where Isaac's hands twitch. —No sir, he says. I do not believe I'll take those odds. Don't believe so at all.

He reaches to his breast pocket for his handkerchief, puts a foot up on a rail and bends over the heavy pack of his belly to stroke the dust from his oxford brogues. Hanky matching socks. When he puts it away he sweeps out a coin in the same motion. Isaac snaps it from the air: a half-crown.

The salesman's thumb is pointing. Across the street stands the Imperial Ice Cream Emporium, Purveyor of Fine Teas & Confections.

—So you can buy me a cup.

Isaac looks at him. —Bladey cheek.

He has a slanted way of grinning. —Best you'll get out of me, tiger, that I promise. But I got something else you might be interested, such a sharp boychik as yourself. Worth a whole helluva lot more than any couplea shammies, that I can guarantee.

Inside, what he does at once is split four scones and coat them with clotted cream and apricot jam. Slides one to Isaac while eating three. Then mops crumbs from his mouth while leaning back with his cup, grepsing softly against his fingers to ask, —So what's your story now?

Isaac shakes his head, irritated.

—Never hide your shine, tiger. What are you, shy? Need formals? Herewa. Shake a paw.

He leans over and Isaac takes the hand. Not soft, not hard, very warm.

—Mr. Helger. Yitz was it?

—Isaac.

—Just testing. Me, I'm Hugo. Hugo Bleznik, Esquire. Freelance travelling sales representative. Now we shaken proper, you tell me, young master Helger, tell me what's your story.

He sinks back and Isaac looks into the eyes, the soft blue. He says nothing for a long time. Hugo waits. When Isaac starts to talk he has the feeling that it is not himself who is talking but some detached other. This other relates the full truth. It tells in a flat voice how it was that he lost his job and how it is that he is still hiding this fact from his parents, and how he was not robbed at all but beaten up by the Greyshirt neighbour, how he is sick in his soul over it, and how he believes there is something wrong with him because everything he does always seems to end up so messed.

Hugo nods all the time: this is normal, says the nodding, banal even. He orders cheese sandwiches and braided honey-fried koeksisters and more tea. When it comes he pours a funnel of sugar into his cup for five beats of Isaac's pulsing heart. And cream. He eats nimbly, making little noise. Now and then he tells Isaac to tuck in; Isaac doesn't move. Finished, Hugo says: —I reckon what's best for you, tiger, in all honesty, is to have for yourself a change of the scenery. Fresh wind in your sails, if you get me.

—Wind.

—Absolutely.

Hugo clears a wide space on the tablecloth, the centre. He reaches back to the side pocket of the bright jacket on the back of his chair, brings out a bundled cloth. A sense of grave care in his slow-motion setting down of the bundle, its soft and silken ruffles, its purple most sumptuous against the white cloth.

Isaac watches it while Hugo cleans off his hands with a fresh serviette, smears down his side-parted hair with a flattening palm it does not need. Dips one pinky fingertip into ice water and touches it to one eyebrow. Cleans his hands again. Then he grows very still, his eyes on the bundle.

Time passes. Hugo clears his throat. In a new voice, without looking up: —Sometimes a man gets lucky enough to meet his future.

Then silence.

Then he says: —His fortune.

Silence.

He says: —Ja, but then he has to be clever enough to see it when it comes. Could be a little thing. Tiny thing.

Very slowly he moves one of his plump hands toward the purple bundle.

Isaac finds his mouth has parched itself.

—A fortune, says Hugo Bleznik.

He takes hold of the lush cloth and gradually parts it and lays it flat and there on its velvety softness is a round object with a missing centre. Isaac leans forward. A little wheel of an odd green colour. Like the rounds of sticky tape in Mr. Weiner's stationery shop. When Isaac looks up Hugo's eyes press into his.

—This, says Hugo Bleznik, is Miracle Glow.

Isaac looks again. A little wheel, dull green.

—Miracle Glow, says Hugo. Shines in the dark. Forever. No electric, no battery. Same stuff what they painting now on the hands on special watches like your father I'm sure would know, bless him. This green stuff, it eats sunlight. Then at night it shines it back. Miracle Glow, latest from America, and I am telling you it is a killer. A stone killer.

Isaac looks up and almost pulls back from the feeling in the blue eyes, the ruddy crinkling flesh around them.

—A killer, says Hugo. Think on the savings. Whatever needs a light. A coupla strips of Miracle Glow instead. Think, where is it there is no light ? You realize, not here, the city. No. *Out there.*

Isaac looks at the wall Hugo has lashed at. —There?

—The platteland. The open bladey country, man. Home on the bladey range. Where you breathe proper. Where our good Afrikaner friends is grafting day and night to feed this nation, bless their busy little hearts and hands.

—Hey?

—Stay with me, tiger. Think a farm, any farm. Fences, wheelbarrows, chop machines.

—Chop what?

—Ach, whichever. The point is no *electricity.*

The bill comes. Isaac presents his half-crown. Is refused by Hugo Bleznik, Esquire. —Absolutely no ways. But I want you to listen to this. Tiger.

—Ukay.

—Serious business. A proposition.

Isaac looks down at the dull green wheel on the lush cloth.

—Serious business, says Hugo Bleznik.

II.

IT'S FATE, IT'S A MIRACLE. Reap a fortune from Miracle Glow. There are historic opportunities and your son, he has blundered into one: the luck of youth, how it is to be envied. Without Hugo behind these words, Isaac knows his life would have collapsed; but Hugo is there in the night to do all the talking to both parents, to win them to his entrepreneurial cause. It's like when Isaac was expelled from high school, which his parents still don't know: he tells them he's left Morris Brothers voluntarily and, as with school, his mother is all for the move, the risk, the new venture, but his father is long-faced and calls a conference in the shut bedroom. Only Rively deviates from the pattern, not hovering in the passage; she's in the kitchen laughing aloud to Hugo's stories with an open packet of Marie biscuits between them.

His father with his long hands tucked into the front of his work apron, his Adam's apple bobbing with every swallow: You were supposed to be learning the trenshport, that business, something with cars, your favourite. You only just got going there at Morris.

Mame: Didn't you hear the man? Once in a life can get such a chance.

God gives chances, not sales reps.

You're the one who bought from him. How many pounds for a few few little piggish cloths!

Ach!

Don't ach. If he learns anything, Isaac can learn how to do *that*.

That's not a trade for Isaac.

Who is to say? Let him learn how to sell.

Isaac watches his father turn to him.—Nu? Yitzchok? Vos daynks du?

—I wanna go, Da. Wanna learn.

And what happened with cars, which I know how much you love? I can still talk to Ginzburg, to be a mechanic.

Mame asks no one why it is that Abel wants so badly for his son to be a shvitzer, an arbeiter, all his life. A sweater. A labourer. A Stupid (maybe even a bladerfool) is the final designation she does not have to say aloud.

Let him have this chance for something else, she says.

Is it really what you want, Isaac? This? This bit of nonsense? The roll of tape is in his hands, being turned, shaken like an accused. Earlier, Hugo had given a demonstration of Miracle Glow, switching off all the lights at number fifty-two Buxton Street, telling them in the dark to watch, watch now as he unveils the truly miraculous, a sight their eyes will neither believe nor ever be able to forget.

In truth Isaac has to admit to himself that he was not quite as overwhelmed as he'd expected to be. When Hugo, muttering in the darkness like some pagan wizard issuing incantations over an unholy ritual, had removed the dishcloth covering the strips of Miracle Glow he'd applied to the kitchen table, what was revealed was not so much a glow per se but a rather meagre smear of luminescence, certainly nothing like the burning bars of molten lime that had lived in Isaac's imagination till that moment. But it seemed that Hugo's personality had made up in glow what the product seemed to lack; Mame seemed satisfied when the lights came back on, and even Tutte had been slowly nodding with his eyebrows lifted. Not bad, he'd said. A good idea.

But in the closed room afterwards, the good idea has become nonsense and pech, a shtik drek, a piece of crap, this puny roll of tape in his long fingers, not something that his son should dedicate himself to purveying to Afrikaner farmers, what is the point?

Mame shakes her head. Even a blinder can see the point. This can become a big business.

And if your eyes are too big, Abel says, sometimes you miss what's in front of you. Then with a sigh he limps out of the room while Mame gives Isaac his victor's hug. Looking over her shoulder at the blank wall, bound inside her strong arms, Isaac is thinking how sorry he is, how one day she will find out about this new lie he's told about leaving Morris Brothers. But then again, Mame has her own secrets, doesn't she? Probably everyone has.

Just five days after the teahouse meeting, Isaac is on the road with Hugo Bleznik, Esquire, cruising the northern Transvaal in Hugo's big black Opel P4. The boot of the Opel so full that it hangs its dragging steel arse, unscrolling red dust from the unpaved rural tracks they take to tinroof farmhouses where often a leathern old matriarch squats on the stoep rocking chair, shotgun close to hand. In their stiff new black suits (collected gratis from an Indian tailor on Fourteenth Street who owed Hugo a favour), they pay visits to Boers on horseback in the mielie fields, overlooking the toiling Blacks in their rags and broken sandals. These horseback farmers have leopard-skin hatbands and the thumbs they use to prop up the brims are hardly smaller than the heads of ball-peen hammers. And Hugo knows how to talk to them all. He has some guiding sense that is a mystery to Isaac. How he catches the right mood at once, the right word. Isaac is silent – the magician's assistant. He carries boxes and he holds the lightproof camera blanket that they use as part of their act, getting the potential buyers to put their heads under to witness the Miracle Glow, to see the Miracle of its Glowing with their own two eyes. No kerosene, no battery, no electricity – forever. A one-time investment. The savings unimaginable. Put it on fence rails, put it on gates. On vehicles. Along roadsides so you won't go off in some bladey ditch and bust your neck. Hell, stick some stripes on the backs of your kaffirs to keep tabs on them in the night ha ha ha.

They make their individual sales on the farms and sleep over in the dorps, the tiny country towns, where they always visit the local gazette, if there is one, to win some free press for their product. Also, at the local general store, almost always run by a fellow Jew, they make sure to drop off a box of Miracle Glow on consignment, to collect on the way back.

Isaac's Afrikaans improves through necessity. Ja, there are Greyshirt bastards like Oberholzer, but he is also amazed by the hospitality they are accorded here in the Afrikaner heartland. These pious chutaysim are steeped in the Old Testament and Jews often hold a fascination for them bordering on awe. Hugo genially exploits this phenomenon without hesitation, muttering Hebrew prayers or even on occasion producing a set of tefillin, invoking cryptic benedictions of good luck on one arid stretch of farmland after another, in this time of the drought that obsesses every conversation. The dry air, the dry sky, the desiccated crops.

New experiences accrue. Isaac learns the taste and crunch of morning bacon with his eggs (so this is what those strange banners of reddish meat were on the laden table at The Castle that morning). Once, he kisses a bucktoothed farm girl he bumps into on the way to the outhouse. She feels sorry for him, touching the grey bruise still rimming his eye socket. The bucktoothed girl is blond and tall and smells of the earth; it makes him think of Yvonne The Princess, and his heart dims a bit in him, that she is so far away and not merely in distance.

Another time he watches Hugo sell a box of Miracle Glow to a family who are eating boiled potatoes and salt and sitting on upturned pails around a table made of crates covered by newspaper. The wind is musical in holes rusted through the corrugated iron walls, the cracked glass shudders in the windowpanes. Hugo makes the rolls of Miracle Glow seem like powerful totems of good fortune, summoners of God's very grace. To pay them, the woman of the house scrounges last coins from a tiny purse so weathered it's beginning to crumble. Afterwards, Isaac murmurs his bad feelings about the transaction. Hugo wrenches the Opel over to a stop. —We are grown people and so are they grown people. Human beings and adults. Who are you, God? Let the people make up their own minds. This is business. This is life.

Isaac looks away. It's the first time he's seen any anger in his travelling companion. He doesn't say anything, but when they go on he's thinking of the way that Hugo charmed them, amazed them. Thinking they didn't really have a chance at all. Ja, but what does that mean? Aren't they grown people and humans just like us? Who have mouths and can say no – can't they? Then he thinks of the Linhursts, the Mad Queen and her husband the Cruel Duke, standing there with his ivory cigarette holder and telling Isaac no, because the Cadillac is more important. Now *those* are people who know how to refuse. Take away the fancy liberal words and underneath they're ruthless as blades. Then he thinks maybe that is the defining difference between them. The ones who live in the shacks on boiled potatoes with salt and the other ones in their Castles. The Clevers and the Stupids. The little word *no* is all that separates them. Or at least the will to use it.

That night in his bed at the inn, Isaac dreams that pieces of watches spew out of his mouth when he tries to talk. Springs and cogs, the taste of copper. Unloading boxes of Miracle Glow in the morning he sees a strip of paper flutter loose. It's an invoice from a factory in Durban. American product my arse. But he says nothing to Hugo. Good old Hugo, jolly as a party balloon.

—Hey Hugo, hows about you let me drive for a change?

—Boychik, no ways no how.

Now and then, in this dorp or that, Hugo disappears. Isaac
doesn't need to ask him about these gaps: the floral whiff of perfume and the lipstick on his rumpled collar the next morning
over breakfast is always enough. In his chatter Isaac detects
Hugo has assembled extensive data on the married ladies of this
region which he's passed through before more than once in his
time; this data set includes useful knowledge of when certain
husbands are or are not around. Isaac requests no specifics of
these adventures, but he does seek more general advice, not going
so far as to tell him Yvonne Linhurst's name but describing her
pretty well nonetheless.

—The female, says Hugo, sighing back with a toothpick.
Tiger, I could write an encyclopedia on the female and maybe
one day I will. Be a bestseller but they'll have to lock me up in
chookie and throw away the key. No one's ready for the truth on
the female. All I can advise you, go the opposite.

—The opposite.

—Don't drool yourself on their feet like a stick from a dog.
That's number one and number ten. But you can be nice. Spend on
the good wine. Best time to make that first move is six a clock.
Never the lips, go for the neck right here. Slow and easy. And
never forget the female is like a bus, there's always another one
coming round that corner.

Like a bus. Somehow Isaac thinks not. Lonesome country
wives are one thing but a rare and shimmering Parktown bird like
Yvonne Linhurst is a different species entirely. Nothing that Hugo
says could possibly apply except for the admonition that if he
wants something to happen he's going to have to *do something*.
That part is true. Make a move or you're not even in the game. But
to make a move could also only serve to prove that you've never

had a chance in the first place . . . that he's not even a forgotten blip
to her by now.

They are travelling eastward and despite the drought the farther
they move the more green the land becomes, even accumulating
a veneer of tropicality that starts to feel slightly alien to Isaac.
There are woods on the koppies and not just anthills and cacti like
he's used to; a moist heat seems to seep up off this land in the angle
of the waning sun.

It's getting close to four and Hugo is driving very fast and
muttering. Isaac knows what he wants: a telephone. That morning
he got hold of a new racing paper and now he needs to ring Joburg
and lay down some bets before it's too late. A familiar fever. Hugo
gets edgy if he doesn't put down some money now and then.

—Slow down, hey Hugo. You ganna prang us in another sec
man.

—Speaks the expert.

—I'd rather drive than talk.

—There's a shock.

They pass a sign too fast to read and Hugo mutters. Isaac says,
—You know Hugo I's thinking maybe you should let me have the
takings hey. I'll stick em in envelopes and whatnot for us.

Hugo doesn't answer.

—I mean like I gotta be straight hey. It's like if my ma saw
how you just sticks it all in your pockets, and we don't even write
nothing down, man she'd have a bladey cadenza on the spot.

—Boychik, be quiet. You starting to grate just a tiny bit.
Believe me, I know exactly down to tuppence what is what. And I
don't need your mother in my head this second oright.

Isaac looks out the window thinking, Ja, cos you all twitchy to
get your bets down, that's why. They come around the next corner
too fast to track their lane and the Opel drifts out. There's
oncoming traffic, luckily a slow truck with the black muzzles of

doomed sheep pointing out the sides, but Hugo overcompensates getting back over and they mount the shoulder and cross it and bounce and judder over rocks. They flatten a fence post and the bonnet flips up, blinding them. Stones bang steel. They flail in their seats and the Opel slews up short in a wash of gritty dust.

They get out to find not that much visible damage, surprisingly, aside from the dented fender that popped the bonnet. But when Hugo tries to start up there's a dead click. Isaac has a look: stones and little rocks kicked up by their tires have gotten into the engine compartment. A battery wire's been severed, but what's more seriously wrong is the rock jammed against the pulley behind the radiator and the missing fan belt. Isaac cups a hand over his eyes and scans the road, a hundred yards back he sees shredded parts of the belt.

—You know what's the matter?

—We could start it but the battery would run down. That's if the engine doesn't start melting first.

—We hitch, says Bleznik. Already getting his jacket from the back.

—Just calm hey, says Isaac. Lemme think.

—I gotta–

—I know. Get to a telephone. Believe me, I know.

—Whatta you tryna say?

—I'm not trying nothing. I don't have to.

Hugo waves a finger at him. —Hey, junior. Don't forget who is who.

—Man, look at you. Hopping like your undies is on fire. Christ, it's only a horse race.

—Only a . . . ? . . . Gach!

Hugo starts marching, his jacket over his shoulder, his shadow a slimmer longer form he never quite manages to stomp with those bear-swaying strides. Isaac calls after him but Hugo just flaps the jacket like an angered tail.

Isaac comes back to the engine in the fading light. He uses a tire iron to lever the rock out. Needs something to get that fan belt working. He stands there chewing his knuckle then he makes a search of the Opel and finds silk stockings on the floor in the back, no doubt property of some most well-satisfied Transvaal house-wife, kissed on the neck at six p.m. after half a bottle of the good stuff. Twisted, the stockings make a strong and flexible line and he loops it round the pulleys and knots it tight. The severed battery wire is an easy fix by rebraiding the copper and sealing it with a loop of Miracle Glow. When he starts up it seems to hold fine. He picks Hugo up half a mile down the lonely road. Not a single vehicle has passed them. When Isaac pulls over and Hugo reaches for the door, Isaac eases the Opel away. Hugo stands there in his shirt sleeves with one fist on his washtub waist.

Isaac leans across to the window. —I drive from now on hey.

Hugo glares for a solid minute. —You got some chutzpah, junior.

—Oright then. Meet you in Vekklesdorp. Best a luck.

Hugo shakes his head and advances; again Isaac lets the car trickle away. This happens twice more before Hugo says, —Oright, oright, you little shit. You can be driver.

—Ten fingers on your Jewish Torah?

—Nine and a half.

—I'm serious.

—Oright, oright.

—Say it.

—Little shit. Fine. Ten fingers on the Torah I promise you can drive.

—Tank you, tank you, my baas.

Once he's in the passenger seat he starts laughing. What a little chuleriuh, he says. What a cholera, crafty and fatal as a germ. What an operator. He laughs harder when Isaac explains what he's used for the temporary repair. The female is a giver of many gifts. He wants to know how come Isaac knows how to do such things and Isaac tells him about Silas and Morgan and Fisu in the Morris Brothers days, how he learned from watching them and their dexterous means of repair on that aged Chev truck, adapting whatever they had.

They make it in time to Vekklesdorp but by then the engine is making freshly problematic noises. Hugo gets his phone call in and that night he holds a light for Isaac while Isaac works on the Opel with borrowed tools. In the field behind the bed and breakfast there are a number of wrecks – rusted vehicles on bricks or crumpled on the raw earth. Isaac's seen similar everywhere in this countryside. Now they sneak across and Isaac strips some motor parts: a crankshaft pulley and a functional fan belt. Again Hugo holds the light while Isaac like some surgeon of rust transplants the belt and pulley into the Opel. A little past midnight the engine runs smoothly as it ever had.

Hugo pulls out a bottle of Bell's Scotch and they sit on the back steps and pass it back and forth with grease-blackened fingers; they light cigarettes under a sky so festering with southern stars it seems gummy in places with their globbed radiance.

—Listen, Hugo, I know it's none a my business hey, but wanna ask you something. You're an oke can sell anyone on anything right. So how comes it that you and me are shifting little lots of shiny tape to farmers in the middle of the bladey platteland?

Hugo palms the bottle, examines his heels on the step below. —My friend, you hit on the question of my life. I been close, Tiger. I've repped some top lines. Industrials. Real estate. But there always comes the twist.

—The twist.

—Ja, the twist. The bladey twist. Hugo shakes his vast head methodically.

—Right.

—Maybe I did play with money I shouldn't have. A little bit.

Maybe old Blezzy shoulda saved some more here and there. But you can see how I am now.

—How you are now.

—I mean, a little bit of the ponies, nothing.

—Right.

—But I been up, Tiger, don't you worry. I've had so much it'd take me a week to count. But people, they don't always appreciate. People can be blind sometimes, you know. Then always comes that twist.

—The twist, Isaac says.

—Ja, the twist. Again shakes the watermelon of Hugo's lugubrious head. Infinities of sadness in the motions. —The bladey twist gets in the works. They like to cut me at the knees just when I get going, the bastards. But old Blezzy always fall shiny side up hey. Old Blezzy's like those stars.

He points with the top of the bottle. —No, you can't put Blezzy's shine out, and you can't pull him down. Blezzy always shoots up to the tops. And now, Tiger, I can tell you I am finished with repping other people's lines. I want my own operation, the toes to the nose. This is what I'm looking for with our Miracle Glow.

—Oh ja, you've got a piece of this firm?

His hand wiggles. —You could say.

—Right.

—Our own operation, Hugo tells him, and cradles the back of Isaac's neck with his warm palm. Hey boyki? Hey? All the way.

—All the way, says Isaac, taking the bottle back.

Early next day they hit the general store, a certain Mr. Shapiro. Then they do an interview at the *Vekklesdorp Weekblad* and gun off into the dry countryside. They find their true momentum by mid-morning and Hugo seems high as a wheeling kite, closing deal after deal like a pool shark sinking balls.

It's shaping to be their biggest day yet when they join a farmer for commiseration over the killing drought and a field lunch of fat links of boerewors piled on mielie pap – the fluffy maize meal boiled up like mashed potatoes and covered in grease and onions. Hugo asks the Boer about the old cars and rusted trucks parked behind the barn. The Boer says it's too much trouble and expense to have them towed, the nearest scrap dealer is miles off.

When they're back on the road with Isaac driving and loving the feel of the Opel's steering wheel in his right hand, the breeze smoothing his left elbow out the window tangy with the nip of farm dung off the bright sun-washed fields, Hugo says: —There could be something hey. Could be something.

—What?

—All these old skedonks hey, these junkers you see every-where. They are full a parts you can use, like we did last night.

—Oh ja.

—There's bladey good chop in the motor game. You could buy up those kaputniks for nothing. Pull out the good parts, sell off the scrap. Make hell of a good chop.

—What you talking the motor game? says Isaac. *This* is our operation, isn't it? Miracle Glow.

Hugo pokes his lip out with the tip of his tongue. —Ja man, sure. Absolutely.

For a second there Isaac wants to ask about the order slip he saw, some address in Durban. But he lets the second pass.

—Ja, but the motor game, says Hugo. It's something hey. Something.

Late afternoon in the semi-tropical hills they turn off onto a farm road. A tinroof house with silos behind. They have to hold hand-kerchiefs to their faces to combat waves of stench.

In the farmhouse sleeps an aged Boer in his chair with a bottle in his lap, his cheeks so deeply lined they resemble the marrows of bones split open and left to dry in wind and sun. Intestines and organs fill a basin under flies. More guts overslop buckets. Staring pig heads wait on the table for some nameless fate. Pig corpses dangle from chains. Blood has dried on the walls. Hugo tries to wake the man but gets only snores. A wind outside grows sharp and brings with it more of the fetid rotstink of manure plus the faintest sounds of penned animals squealing. The room grows dark and cool and Hugo grimaces and swears with much fervour.

Isaac says through his hanky: —Whatzit man?

Hugo runs out and Isaac follows, happy to flee the deathmeat horror. Crows flap from a coming storm front. Hugo stands panting by the Opel. As Isaac comes up, Hugo gapes at the blackening sky, the rushing clouds. Yells: —Fu–uuuuck!

Isaac looks: just Lowveld clouds, fat-bellied with the weight of the water they bear, black as deep bruises. The wind is strong enough to pry loose even some strands of Hugo's plastered hair and they beat and flail from his round skull like broken wires. He appears now to try to whip at the stomachs of the black clouds with the hat in one hand and a pudgy fist formed out of the other.

—What's wrong? Isaac shouts into the lifting wind.

—What kind of a bladey stuffing drought is this?

—Hey?

—It's not supposed to be this way!

Isaac squints upwards. —What's a matter, is it the lightning hey? You afraid of–

—Just get in the bladey stuffing car, man.

Isaac doesn't even try to argue over driving rights: Hugo bangs his head jumping in behind the wheel. They bounce hard back to the main road. Isaac reminds him that he's already laid off his bets today, at that railway station after lunch. No need to hurry. But it's not the bets, not this time; something else has gripped Hugo Bleznik. He has turned them in the wrong direction, heading back to Vekklesdorp. Accelerator flat.

—You'll kill us this time, Isaac says calmly. And then a bit later: —What happened to shining up hey? Where's all the shine gone, tigerman?

Hugo is grim and rocking behind the wheel, both hands squeezing hard. He has the window down and more than once he sticks his head out, looking straight up.

—We ganna die, says Isaac. We so ganna die.

The only thing he sees that he can do is grab at the wheel, but that would not be wise. Strange sounds are wheezing out of Hugo, like he's on a toilet at war with constipation. Now and then he hisses the same phrase: *Always the twist, always the bladey stuffing twist.* The rear window shows a sky overtaken by the blotting thunderheads, mute and massive as mountains suspended.

It's well past dark when they tear into Vekklesdorp. Hugo guns straight for the general store. —Might still catch the bladey bugger, he says, still bowed forward over the wheel, clenched on it like a monkey to a lifebuoy in a flood. Might still be in there locking up and counting all his bladey boodle.

But the shop is dark, closed. The sign above the door says SHAPIRO TRADING LTD. FOR THE SHARPEST DEALS IN TOWN!! It's like before when they were here, but now all the letters have been taped over with Miracle Glow and so they shine with a soft swamp-gas green.

—Oh wow, Isaac says. That is *nice*.

—Fuck *shit*, shouts Hugo. He dredges a canting, squealing U-turn out of the Opel. There's a man in a railways uniform at the station; Hugo gets out and runs to him. Isaac watches them talk, the railway man pointing as plump drops of rain start to burst on the dusted windshield.

—Jee*zus* man Hugo, Isaac says when he gets back. Have you gone mental for real or what?

But Hugo isn't answering, Hugo is driving, swerving them

through the little town and hunting for a street it seems by process of rapid elimination. They find it soon enough – not too many streets in Vekklesdorp – and then the right number. A wide bungalow with a big lawn and a garage in front. Hugo runs over the rubbish bin on the driveway and parks on the lawn. When they get out the droplets are coming faster and Hugo swears with much viciousness. Isaac runs after him up the path to the front door where Hugo bangs hard with the flat of his fist.

Lights come on; a dog woofs.

—Hey man, Isaac says, panting. You ganna get us shot dead here man.

—Never mind.

—Never *mind*?

An unfriendly male voice behind the door desires to know who the bladey hell it is and who the bladey stuffing hell they think that they are.

—It's Bleznik, Shapiro. I put goods on consignment. Open up. We in a hurry.

—Hey who? Hey? What? Who? The rep?

—Ja, Hugo Bleznik. Ja the rep. Consignment. Open up.

—What the hell you doing here the house past eleven a clock the stuffing night, you mad?

Yes, Isaac thinks. Fair questions.

—Open up, says Bleznik. Open up, you gunif. You tryna swindle us our goods.

—Jesus, Hugo, Isaac says.

—What? says the voice. What you says to me?

—Open up is what. I says open up.

The door moves back, a chain stretched across a crack of light. Half of Shapiro's face hovers, worried. —Ach, what you people want here? You mad in your heads or something? You drunk?

—We want the money for our goods, Shapiro. That's what, finished and klaar. Over and out.

—That shiny tape?

—Miracle Glow!

—Okay, so come to the shop tomorrow, meshugena.

—No, Shapiro. Now. We on the move. And you not ganna rook us, Shapiro. I know your game.

—Hey?

—Give us our money!

—Bladey hell, Shapiro says, looking to Isaac. What's a matter with your da? Has he gone sick?

—He's not my da, Isaac says. We *partners*.

Shapiro's one showing eyeball rolls. —Partners. Listen to this pisher here.

—Show him the consignment book, Hugo says. He wants to try and argue us, show him the book. Then to Shapiro: —We got a receipt, gunif! Right here! Don't even try think you can rook us.

—Now look hey, Shapiro tells them. This's the second time I heard you call me a gunif to my face, my own house. I dunno what's going on here but you try tell me I'm a crook and call me gunif again and I have to open this door – man, I was Eastern Transvaal wrestling champion and I'll snap the bladey necks on the both of you.

—So if you not a gunif, Hugo smoothly says, then give us our money. We seen how much tape you already used up on your shop sign there alone.

— . . . Awww so that's what it's about. The shop. Oright, I will give you your boodle, ukay. Look, it's nice stuff what you got, this miracle watchmacallit. But that doesn't mean you can come banging on a man's house calling him gunif . . .

Hugo for once says nothing. Hugo is looking to the sky. Raindrops are hitting the lawn, getting faster. Hugo makes that wheezing constipated noise from deep in his throat. Shapiro closes the door and they hear the chain coming off. Hugo shifts feet.

Door opens. Hugo rushes, Isaac follows. Shapiro is to one side, bathrobed, wild-haired. —Tell your da he's too hitzik hey. Give himself a coronary heart attack just now.

—He's not my da.

The rain drums the roof, taps the windows. Hugo paces in the kitchen where Shapiro leaves them. Mrs. Shapiro comes in, blue curlers under a creamed face. She makes tea. Then Shapiro comes with the chequebook, shaking his head. Hugo says, —No, it's cash. Cash latkes only.

Shapiro's thick neck trembles. —The chutzpah on this bladey oke!

His wife starts to hum over the tea things.

—You dincum are meshuga, says Shapiro. You genuine are.

—That's how we want it, Hugo says, so unlike himself, closed off and insistent and unsmiling and jittery. No sign of any shining up. Isaac is inclined to side with Shapiro in his snap evaluation of Hugo's sanity. Where is the melting beam of an easy smile, the cobra charm in the blue eyes? Something seems connected with the rain. The drumming on the roof seems to have invaded the brain under that great dome. A rain-a-phobic, Isaac thinks. He always suspected there must be something big time wrong.

—Bladey insult, Shapiro says. My cheques are gold!

The two of them lock stares. Hugo wheezes softly; one eye twitches. Slowly, Shapiro shakes his head. —Oright, oright, meshugena . . . I haven't sold the whole lot, but it's starting to move. I think you got something here. How can I reorder?

—No problem. Here's my card.

Mrs. Shapiro hums, pours the tea looking out the window, remarking to no one that it is really coming down outside.

—*It's supposed to be a drought!* Hugo tells them, his voice hurting eardrums. Everyone stares at him. A dog in another room begins to bark. Mrs. Shapiro has spilled. Hugo snaps at Isaac: —Nu, make out the invoice already.

He hands him a carbon paper cashbook that Isaac's never seen before. A blank book. Isaac fills in the top invoice, tears it off, gives it to Shapiro. Shapiro goes out and comes back with cash which Hugo snatches. —Bye.

—So fast? Not even a cup?

—We got things to do.

—It's nearly bladey midnight.

—Let's go, Isaac.

Hugo is out of the room when Shapiro touches Isaac's arm. —Tell your old man he should slow down, he says, not unadmiringly. I tell you, he's heading for a coronary heart attack.

—Thanks, Isaac says. Bye.

Outside, he runs with Hugo bent over against the drumming rain. Once they are driving off, Isaac strokes the rainwater from his eyes, says, —Hugo, I think you better listen to me hey. I reckon those dead pigs gave you a shock in your brain or summin hey. Cos–

—This would never happen in the motor game!

Isaac blinks. —Hey?

—Supposed to be a drought! A bladey stuffing drought! It's the flippen bladey *dry season*!

Isaac shuts his mouth. Turns his attention to the side window. Main street splashing past as they hurl out of town. The hard rain has turned it into a shallow brown river. He regrets he didn't snag a finger biscuit from that tray Mrs. Shapiro had, at least. Finger biscuits are so lekker, he likes them so much better than Marie biscuits or those ginger things. He watches Shapiro's shop coming up ahead.

The green glow of the miracle tape shows through the falling water; he leans close to the glass, squinting. As they pass the shop Isaac reads only four letters: *SH O G*. As he watches, the green *S* slowly disintegrates in the rain, running and running, washing away to nothing. Looking backwards, the last he sees of Shapiro's sign is the word *H O G*. This green too begins to run and fade even as he stares, but for the moment it speaks purely to Isaac of that reeking farmstead, that blooded abode of porcine doom.

12.

NINE MONTHS AFTER MIRACLE GLOW, Isaac is back home working as a salesman in a shoe shop in town. Mame found him this job, through Mr. Altman from down the road whose wife was married to a third cousin of Mr. Gibblers from Troyeville who has the best cabbages and the job connection to the proprietor, a Mr. Pivnik. Here at the shop they are importing Italian shoes and Mame says being a shoe salesman will train him in the foot-wear business. Footwear is good, even as good as transport. Every time someone takes a step, they are also taking a step towards their next pair of shoes, think about it.

A wonderful business, maybe, but Isaac is battling, barely making his sales quotas. He likes handling the feet of the ladies, though, squeezing the sensitive flesh in his strong hands and three times he takes different ones for private fittings of another kind, in the stockroom. Hugo Bleznik's advice on the female was not all wrong, it seems; but these encounters do little to quench the gilded images of Yvonne Linhurst that continue to twine through his dreams, awake or asleep. Yvonne in The Castle, how is she, what is she doing? That bright and distant mirage.

Certain interested ladies aside, Isaac is not able to establish much rapport with his clients. He tries to copy how Hugo was, but the act never lasts. What is it, is he too ugly, too rough? One day Miss Jacqueline Winterbourne, his old history teacher, walks into the shop and he runs to the stockroom before she can see him.

He stands there in the dark smelling the shoe leather and only then does he remember that time when he stood in the closet behind the blackboard with his rigid shlong in his fist, Christ. That Principal Larkin opening the door, shaking his head. Isaac the poor little humper. His scalp shrivels in the dark. He has to have a smoke break after he spies out that she's gone, and his fingers tremble so badly he needs three matches for his light.

When he goes home that night he is low. Turned eighteen already at the beginning of the year – real manhood – and now 1937 is three-quarters over and what's he achieved? How far has he come since getting kicked out of school? He's been fired, been beaten up by a Greyshirt chutus, failed as a travelling rep (he limped home early and with nothing from that disastrous washout of a road trip but his tail between his legs and a rueful admission to Mame that Tutte was right, the tape was useless drek), and now he's still hiding away ashamed in a cupboard, slowly crashing as shoe boy (the same way that Hindenburg airship slowly sank and crumpled and buckled in a cocoon of its own devouring flames over there in the USA as shown on the Universal Pictures newsreel). A shoe boy: he can't even make the grade as an effing *shoe boy*.

At the supper table Mame asks what he's learned about the business today, and when there's no enthusiasm in his one-syllable answer his father starts up about finding a good trade. Mame bangs with the knife and fork, bunts him under the table (with her new shoe, a free perk of the job). Isaac's not going to be any sweating tradesman with dirty hands, not her Isaac. He's going to be a big maker in the footwear industry, he's on his way, he'll be buying a big house for them in no time, isn't so, Isaac?

A beautiful house for us in Orange Grove, in Observatory. Isn't so Isaac?

Isaac says yes. It is so.

With a garden. Quiet. With no more Greenburg.

His father mutters and saws harshly at his kosher lamb chop, as if the meat still needs murdering.

Meanwhile Rively excuses herself early. She has started learning how to be a legal clerk at a tech college in town but most of her spare time she goes to Hashomer Hatzair meetings with Yankel Bernstein. Bernstein, like the shrewdie he is, started calling on her the minute Isaac was away. Since then it's evolved into a habit that Isaac can't do a thing about but be sharply irritated. Politically, it seems Rively has gradually influenced Yankel enough to stop being a universal Communist and start being a Zionist-Communist (or at least pretend); while he's got her to stop being so Orthodox religious and start being more Zionistic. But she shouldn't be associated with those Hashomer girls at all, Isaac reckons; all the neighbourhood okes nowadays call them Hashomer Hatsitskes – Hashomer The Tits – cos so many of them with their progressive ideas don't even wear bras under their uniform shirts and therefore must be loose as anything.

He looks up then and advises her to go wait for Yankel outside.

Rively: —What's your problem hey?

—I don't wanna see that bladey Red in here. Bad enough he comes for my sister like a vulture.

Isaac, says Abel.

—Sorry hey Da, but it's true.

He goes into the backyard and bounces a rotting cricket ball on the outhouse door. The real reason he doesn't want to see Yankel is because Yankel reminds him of what maybe happened to Mame on April seventeenth in that faraway country of his birth. If he sees Yankel he has to think about such things and that makes him irritated with unease, so better not to see him at all. Rively tells him that Yankel always asks after him. —Tell him I went to Russia, Isaac has answered. Tell him I changed my name to Hotshki-Shotski or summin, I got a moustache and a private shithouse in the Kremlin now.

His father steps out. Isaac, come here, I want to talk.

They go into his mother's sewing room, the shiksa's hut: all these years and they've never had a shiksa girl at all. It strikes Isaac that this fact makes his mame less of a capitalist-whatever than any commie that he knows, especially the Bernsteins who keep a Black in the back of Gordon Court same as the rest of the residents, the bladey hypocrites.

Abel puts his hand on Isaac's shoulder. I arranged for you with Ginzburg.

Isaac thinks about this, blinking. —What, a mechanic?

No, says his father. Some other kind, an apprentice to work on cars. Cars you love.

Isaac folds his arms, watching the toe edge of his shoe as it starts to chip at the ground.

I have eyes, Isaacluh. You look unhappy. Never mind your mother, you don't have to say to her. Here.

He takes a card from his apron and pokes it across. Go and see the man. Say that Ginzburg sent you.

The next day, a Friday, Isaac gets a surprise – shock – phone call at the shoe shop. Hugo Bleznik. Hugo sniffed out his work number from Mame at home; he had to pretend to be someone else but he got it (since the Miracle debacle, Hugo's name has been more or less unmentionable to Mame, categorized with blader-fools and couch parasites). There's old Hugo, ever resourceful. Right now, for Isaac's information, he is calling from the Hotel Polana in Lourenço Marques, Mozambique. Lourenço Marques, where the rich and the big shots, the movie and radio stars, go to jol on holidays. Hugo starts painting word pictures for Isaac. How beautiful the white facade of the Hotel Polana is, with the palm trees and the swimming pool in front, the view of the Indian Ocean. Charcoal-grilled prawns big as your hand dipped in piri piri sauce and dewy bottles of Laurentina beer a foot tall.

—And you never seen the females with the skin and the eyes like this hey, Tiger. Loverly smooth brown skin and bright green eyes they got. Never seen such hoors.

For some reason (green eyes?) these words open a seam of yearning in Isaac: thoughts of Yvonne Linhurst slip wavering through him, it's a sadness to do with the feeling that no hoor could ever switch on that cold bright light inside his chest the way she did. He's had some other women now, but never that, never even close. That was only from The Princess. Even now it's still the first thing there when he opens his eyes on his cot, in that oil-reeking workshop that is his home and the trap that has secured his father the way fences keep pigs penned in for their slaughter. This is why he has resisted Abel all this time: to follow Abel's advice means to become *like* him. He'll only grow into the shape of a stooped-over man, a blue-collar, a rent-payer, just another one of the world's many Stupids.

Meanwhile in his ear Hugo Bleznik, talking, talking, is coming back to the word *contacts*. — . . . rounding up these *contacts* hey, like you won't *believe*, these heavy *connections*, these motor-game boys. Getting numbers down and all. I am telling you, when you work it out on paper . . .

Isaac thinks of working on cars with his hands. He looks at the card his father gave him. Maybe what scares him the most is how he knows his father senses the strength of it in him, knows it's there, the call of the automobiles–

—Hey! You listening here hey boyki? Hey?

—What, sorry?

—Hey Tiger. Shine yourself up man. Shine up! I am talking pounds not pennies here man. I am talking your life.

—What is it?

—I'm working on these boys. I am getting the capital up, man, it's a finished deal, almost. This plan is gold. I wanna know, are you in?

—What you talking exactly?

—What I been saying! *The motor game.* I'm coming to Joburg to start up in the motor game. Got one helluva good idea. I'm sitting here tryna bladey get this through to you.

—It's funny.

—What?

—I've just been thinking of maybe going for a job, mechanic like. Apprentice.

There's a silence. —Now why the hell would you go and do that? Aren't you listening what I'm just talking?

— . . . I dunno, says Isaac.

—Man, I've seen you at work. You fixed us up with a stocking for Christ sake. A stocking! You can probably teach *them*.

—Who's them?

—Wherever you thinking of going for this idyat apprentice idea, Tiger. You don't need it man. Listen, what you *need* is to get out a that chuzzesuh shoe shop you in.

—Ja?

—Absolutely! I'm coming to Joeys soon and I want you available and ready for service, man. We are ganna be milking the cream, boyki. Milking the absolute cream. I guarantee. So you go on and you quit that kuk job. Don't you worry. Old Blezzy's your backstop now. Don't you hassle it one second.

After the call Isaac smokes three cigarettes in a row, walking up and down in the alley. You might as well do it. Just get it over with. He goes to Mr. Pivnik's office with a knocking heart and resigns from the shoe shop. Pivnik doesn't seem surprised. Isaac gets a couple weeks' pay in his pocket and goes home and doesn't say anything when Mame starts the usual jolly interrogation. But he has to force the food down, the way this fresh betrayal of his mother makes him want to be sick. His father gives him an odd look over his gefilte fish dotted with purple chrayn.

After supper, Rively goes out to meet Yankel Bernstein and
Isaac puts on his one suit, the stiff black three-piece with the black
tie that was the only asset he ever did see out of Miracle Glow, and
he polishes his shoes nicely before stepping out. How you look to
the world, how you *shine*, is all that matters, according to old
Bleznik. No, but Isaac inside himself knows that he'll never be
a Hugo. A backslapper. A shmoozer. A salesman. He is a different
kind. He'll never kiss an arse; he'll rather rip the balls out from
under it and kick it out the way. The tough black suit hangs funny
on his wiry sinews, his hard narrow bones and pointy shoulders.
His mood is sour and harsh. He walks past number forty slowly
and sees lights on in the Greyshirt house, the Greyshirt who never
has to walk anywhere because he has that beautiful DeSoto
Airflow parked in the back.

He goes into Hillbrow, heading for a larney supper club on
Claim Street. There's four or five of these posh spots he's been
nipping into and out of now and then, stabbing his nose into that
rarefied milieu to sniff a waft of what he one time breathed so fully
up on the ridge in The Castle's golden airs. This front door is
below street level; tobacco clouds and brass sounds come up to
meet his descent. A doorman squints then sways aside. Heat press
of bodies, the sudden rush of enveloping jazz. One wall is brick,
the other painted red. A packed crowd between a three-sided bar
at the far end, some tables to its right set in little nooks of half
walls that project from the brick. On a little stage to the far left,
five musicians play swing, the trumpeter in a fuchsia zoot suit
with a long watch chain and a neck that toadishly swells over the
collar with every rising note.

With alternating shoulders Isaac digs through the crowd to
the bar. He grips an overpriced Scotch and soda, feels himself
sweating under the suit, watching the band, the heads of the
dancers jitting up and down all the way to the tiny stage. People
are pretending to be having fun when it's all just blare and squash

and too-expensive watered-down crooking drinks. How much is this bar clearing? Three hundred in here, about. Each one paying a bob for a drink and having at least two, that's just a tanner short of half a crown per head at minimum, that's–

But he stops his calculations because he is seeing something from the side of his eye that it takes a moment for the rest of him to catch up to. He turns slowly and it's with a feeling almost like uncovering some horrific wound that he thinks, Yes it's her, it is, this time it really is.

It's easy to track her through the crowd, her hair not held by a dancer's band but falling in a loose thick splash like a halo about that round face with the pouting mouth. He notices other men watching. He feels for his cigarettes in his pocket but then he doesn't take the pack out. She's being led through in a party. He tracks them as they pass him, swivelling to watch them settle finally in one of the nook tables that's been kept reserved with a little wooden triangle in the middle that the waiter now takes away. The group of them sink slowly, taking their time, all of them smart in their smart clothes and the boys moving the chairs back for the girls. She's wearing a black dress with a half cardigan over the shoulders and when she sits the cardigan comes off and he can see her good firm arms. He remembers the strength under the high voice, the thickness of her neck, but also the warmth.

It takes him almost an hour, drinking steadily, before he finds himself standing at the table, leaning back on the little half wall behind. He is looking down at the back and side of her face. He was curious in himself to see what being next to her would do to him; he didn't believe that he would feel what he felt but he is wrong. Right here and now in the blare of this dim room with its smoke and heat and motion, he feels the white flooding light switch on in his chest. The silent cold purity of it. There is no shying away from this inner reality. It is there and it is true.

So he stands with his lit-up chest and he is ignored for perhaps
a quarter of an hour and he cannot speak. The longer he stands the
harder it becomes to break his silence, the silence congealing,
hardening like a shell. Inside it's just stubborn pain, a wilding; his
face is a blood-hot flame. His hand mechanically makes him
drink from a drink that's long gone and it's only the dissolving ice
cubes that keep tapping on his teeth. He looks past his shoulder
for a time, to the stage: at least try to seem to be enjoying the noise,
but then why is he standing, just standing?

Then the band breaks and in the quiet like a suction around
him he clears his throat and says hello, then coughs and repeats,
aiming it louder, right into the centre of their bright chatter.
Nothing happens. He leans forward stiffly. —Yvonne.

She turns her head and her face opens, startled.

—Howzit, he says, breathless. How you Yvonne? Remember
me hey?

The bright chatter pauses. The fellow beside Yvonne – the one
who has glanced up from his seat at Isaac the most, who wears
a bow tie and ivory-rim glasses – squints up and says, —Who is
this chap, Badge?

Isaac's never seen a boy wearing a bow tie before. A plump
one next to him has on some manner of scarf. Another one is
smoking from a cigarette holder. The girls all have hats, gloves.
Yvonne had on a little black sailor cap with netting; it's on the
table now. Dry in the mouth, Isaac swings his gaze over the faces.
His breaths pant in him. From a distance they might look grown-up
but in close the faces are too smooth, too much puppy fat. Isaac
looks at them and sees that they are becoming their parents,
jumping ahead already to win the game before it's even started.
(A picture of her father Cecil then, in The Castle, so clear: him too
with his scarf thing and his ivory cigarette holder.)

—I, he tells them. I'm Isaac.

—Well, salutations. Inebriations.

—Tra la.

—Here's to Isaac, and Abraham and Moses too.

Isaac lifts his empty glass at their full ones. Forces a grin at them, feeling like he's peeling flesh up off his skull.

—Acquaintance of yours, Badge? the plump one is saying to Yvonne.

Bowtie is touching Isaac's jacket, fingering the point of it. —I say. I do say. Where *did* you get this?

—Chappie's enormously friendly, a dark-haired girl says. For a waiter. Enormously friendly.

—But Wayne said he *knows* Yvonne.

—I did not, says Wayne. Certainly did not.

—Waiter chappie knows Badge.

—Who *is* he, Badge?

He tries to croak her name again but she's not looking at him and in any case nothing oozes from his bone-dry throat.

—Are you sure? Bowtie says, squinting up. Are you certain that you're not an undertaker, hah?

The black-haired girl shrieks, going backwards in her chair. Drinks are poured. Isaac moves from foot to foot. Sweat caterpillaring both temples. Again he tries to speak: a rasp comes out.

—Oh shame, oh shame, says another girl. Look at him, shame. Don't all be so beastly. You're all starting to be beastly again, like that other time.

—Does he want a drink?

—He's a hovering kind of chappie isn't he?

—Look how he looks.

—Uriah Heep, says Wayne loudly.

The longest round of sputtering laughter yet.

—Uriah Heep, oh God. Perfect.

—The hair. The nose.

—The everything.

—Not the *height*.

Only Yvonne hasn't laughed, stirring her drink, with her cheek on her palm.

—Oh he's blocking the light, says Wayne, louder than all. Go way, already. *Go*. This Wayne is flapping his hand, the back of his hand, towards Isaac now, not even looking around. Isaac takes out a yellow box of Lion matches. He shifts over to lean down close behind him.

Wayne making a show of yawning now. Wayne holding up an empty glass without looking around, as if Isaac should take it away like a waiter. —Badge, he says, singsonging. So bo-ring. So tee-dee-us.

Isaac says into Wayne's ear: —Something important.

—Everyone quiet, Wayne tells the table. Uriah has news.

—You see, says Isaac.

—Yes?

—It's your head. It's on fire.

He straightens up. A second later Wayne jerks forward, his hands shooting to his hair, glasses spilling. Then he rises volcanically: dishes breaking, table kicking, bottles dropping. The girls scream and the boys are saying what and the band starts up again. Now hands are beating at the smoking head. Someone pours something over it.

In all this Isaac has gone straight for her, clamped her shoulder. —Yvonne. So close into her ear: —You. You did this.

Chairs are falling over backwards, faces are being deformed in the same way: an open-mouthed vertical stretching, disbelief and outrage mingled. Their cries are so loud that even over the music people are turning back to watch, those at the next table have stood up. The last Isaac sees of her is a hurt going right deep through the backs of her green eyes, then he's crashing through the crowd, tromping on shoes, using his elbows. As he gets to the bottom of the stairs someone punches him in the back of the head. He keeps going. At the top the heavy doorman is coming down. —He's by the bar, Isaac tells him. Someone crazymad's got a knife.

The doorman shoves him aside, rushes down. Isaac runs then walks for an hour through town, waiting for his thoughts to settle while a knot lifts on the back of his skull. He only sees now why they said undertaker and Italian waiter, it's because of his suit. Hugo got black ones cos he said the Boers wouldn't trust any other kind. He puzzles over some other words, they called him uri or uri heed, something, but he can't make sense of it, just another one of their incomprehensible posh little jabs. Eff them. His ribs are still damp with sweat.

13.

MONDAY MORNING ISAAC GOES ACROSS TOWN, to the address on the card his father gave him. It's on the far side of City and Suburban, a district like so many in Joburg named after one of the mines that dot the whole sweep of the land on which this tangled city rests, the mines like giant pins sunk down to pierce the reefs locked in the rock below, thin strata dappled with the soft yellow metal that men had always killed and died for and probably always would. Isaac finds the section of Marshall Street he seeks to have flat-topped buildings behind chainlink fences. Cars in lots, garages. He stops outside a white cinderblock unit. Gold Reef Panel Beating Pty. Ltd.

He walks up and down outside for fifteen minutes, thinking of Hugo and his new idea, Hugo warning him not to take any garage job. The sky is overcast, the breeze is warm. He tugs on his lip, he doesn't have to take the job even if it's offered, right. Right? He can just have a look, nothing more. Another five minutes pass. Then he swears aloud and goes in.

There's a room with steel mesh walls with labelled keys hung up, and bathing costume girls with tzitzkes the size of ripe watermelons are advertising Vico Motor Oil and London Aluminium (experts in ferrous and non-ferrous metals and ANODISING). The noise from the shop visible beyond is a clang clang clanging and men shouting and the shrieking sparking whine of angle grinders cutting steel and the shrill gupping rip of hydraulic screw

guns sucking out bolts (he knows these tools from his time as a kid
in other garages in Braamfontein). But a bright clanging is strange
and new, loudest and continuous: like a waterfall of knives and
forks coming down over sharp rocks all the time.

Isaac goes to the open doorway for a better look at the shop,
stands with nostrils prickling at the industrial odours of lead
vapour, burnt steel, sweetish faintly garlic-like acetylene, fresh
paint and petrol, sweat and rubber. He sees one of the cars is up on
the steel trunk of a hydraulic lifter. A closer one is on the ground
and a man in overalls cocks his head and feels its dented body with
one hand then taps with a tool Isaac has never seen, a kind of
wedge like a steel lollipop on the end of a long handle. While Isaac
stares, a man approaches from the side. —Help you?

—Ja, sorry. I'm Isaac.

—Hey?

—Isaac Helger. Ginzburg said I should come here.

—How's zat?

—Ginzburg. About a job.

The man's chin goes up, bobs. —Oh ja, Ginzy. Ja, oright. Just
wait over there the office.

Isaac goes where he's been pointed, passing on his way a section
of the workshop closed off with tin walls. From inside comes a
buzz and hiss, the stark chemical stink of paint fumes strong as
a gas. In the office he sits on a wonky chair before a cigarette-
burned desk. In time the same man comes back, closing the door to
shrink the clanging as if by the twist of a volume knob on a wireless.

—I'm Franzie Labuschagne. I run the shop.

Isaac stands to shake the man's hand. His arms are long and
hairy and there's ropy simian power in the grip. Big hands like meat
plates. Hair cut straight across as if trimmed from the lip of a bowl.
Not very tall, his eye level only slightly higher than Isaac's own, or
big (like most chutaysim in Isaac's experience), but Isaac reckons
that he would not want to ever mess with this oke all the same.

—This other ou was supposed be here this week, he says, his chutus accent very thick. Some pork-and-cheeser, Da Silva or something.

—I don't know about that.

—You ever work on cars before?

—Ach, not for pay or nothing, but.

—What?

—Ach, nothing.

—No, what?

Isaac feels himself flushing. —No but just I love cars hey.

Labuschagne gives him an angled grin. —Fok love, he says. This a fokken business hey. He jerks his head and Isaac follows back out onto the shop floor, Labuschagne saying, —We got place from Industrial Council for one more apprentice. What we gots is a dozen journeymen panel beaters in this shop. One class A apprentice. One mechanic, which is me, and I's the shop boss also, which no one better bladey ever forget. Here we got Bliksy on parts and Rustas golden hands for glass, Eddie Tops on upholstery. Also, nother dozen or so Bleck staff for the kaffir work.

He turns, his voice loud and a little hoarse over the clanging now. —You got any clue how a panel beating operation works?

Isaac shakes his head. Hard not to stare at the working men all around them, to lose himself in drifting contemplation of these various cars being operated on in the grease and the smells and the noise and the dim light where the work lamps aren't shining.

— . . . show you in a back, Labuschagne's now saying. Where't all starts when they bring in a job uhkay . . .

There are garage doors in the rear wall, one halfway open, and Labuschagne ducks under. In the back under the white open sky there are damaged cars in lines on raw stamped earth, a chainlink fence around them.

—Not one is the same, Labuschagne says. That's the thing

about accidents hey. Factories make nice cars all exact. Real life makes accidents every one completely different. This why it's custom work, panel beating.

He rubs his own chest then his chin. —Like a art, he says. Ja, art. For real.

Isaac asks how the broken cars all get there. Labuschagne tells him there are two tow trucks that are out now on jobs.

—They come straight from accidents?

—Ja-no, sometimes. But mostly from the police yards. Or from where it's towed by the insurance first fore we get it. Sometimes another firm's truck brings it in. Uhkay, so how it works, the assessor he come from the insurance and we make a quote together, ja. Like this one here . . .

He crosses to a Buick coupe with a crushed side.

— . . . Smacked by a Nels dairy truck on Rissik Street. See what we got here is front grille, let's say eight. Side panel, fifteen. Door, uhhh, seven. Uhkay . . .

As he speaks he circles, mimes writing on a form with a finger on one of his platesize palms. Mimes signing off. — . . . so you rock up, all in, lez calls it forty-five. Now the assessor, he has to write what he wants to pay or not. If he say uhkay then we gets our job, if not they pay out their client cash and it goes to scrapyard . . .

He laughs then, for Isaac has recoiled a little from peering in through the buckled door's empty window around which a few translucent fangs of broken glass still cling. There's blood dried in clumps on the steering wheel and pieces of scalp with bits of matter still attached lying on the seat, like chunks of cracked coconut, hair and dried tissue.

—Ja that's something you get use to't. One time this ou, his head was sliced right off, hey, and no one could find it. But right *off*. In the end it rocked up in the dickey seat! How could it got there? Hell, but you should have check our boy catch the skrik of his life when he check in there hey. He run away screaming like a girl. You know a kaffir, he will never touch a dead. Never ever, you know that?

Isaac shakes his head.

—Cos a kaffir does reckon if he touch a dead his spirit get dirty and he catch bad luck or summin off it. They scared of eating fish too hey, know that? No, genuine, fish is like snake to them and a snake is also serious bad luck for the spirit.

Isaac nods, thinking of fear in the eyes of Silas, thinking of Fisu, Morgan, Hosea. Those Zulu words and work songs, the sweat they shed under his gaze each day. Silas cost him that job, ja, but it's not rage he feels towards him anymore, no, it's a kind of nostalgia.

They've gone back inside. Labuschagne is again shouting to rise over the clang clanging. —Now you see once a job is got, it has to come in and gets its own bay. Uhkay. There's a job. There's a job. This is Jan Veld here. That's a job there see, Keith Chambers working. George Kazy got that Packard in the corner. See how every panel beater has his own bay? See?

Isaac sees cars set on trestles, but for that one in the air, and each vehicle beside a small bench covered with tools. The Whites wear bright tan overalls; their Black assistants, who pass tools or run to fetch, have dirty blue ones.

—A art hey, Labuschagne says. Like I told you, a art. Like what they make in museums and that. Don't smile. I'm for serious hey. In comes this smashed ugly dead thing and if a panel beater is good, when he is finish it you can't tell if it had one scratch ever. Think about that. You take three weeks, a month, on one job. Every day a full shift. One little tiny dent at a time. Straighten the frame. Everything has to line perfect. A door won't shut proper if the line isn't perfect, a window won't roll up. The new windshield won't fit. Has to be exact. A art. Lemme tell you, there's not so many good ones neither can do

it well. Now Rustas golden hands who does our glass . . .
Howzit! Rustas!

He waves to a man who lifts his cap.

— . . . Now him's an artist hey . . . and that there is Malcolmson . . .

—The thing he's using, whatzit?

—That? Lemme show you . . .

At the nearest bench tools are laid out cleanly as on a surgeon's
table. —This one what you mean? He touches the steel lollipop
thing.

—Ja.

—This a spoon dolly with a handle. This one here is just
a dolly, same thing but no handle. This one here is a sack of ball
bearings, feel. Also, it's another kind of dolly. You use a dolly all
the same way, to flatten out, to finish. You put the dolly on one
side to brace, ja, and then you tap the other side, flatten nice.
Understand? This is called a toe dolly. This one is a heel dolly . . .

He is handing knobs of bright clean steel to Isaac, some like
the heads of golf clubs, some shaped like fat blunt knife blades or
solid horseshoes. He demonstrates using a piece of tin in a vise,
showing how a dolly is held at the back side of the dented panel,
then he takes a slender hammer with its long handle and raps
against the tin, drumming. Isaac sees how the dent can be flattened,
eliminated. A glimpse of the intricate patience and control and
sensitivity that the work will require. It's not just smashing, it's
not all grob, all rough and clumsy. Labuschagne lets him try and
suddenly, grasping the tools, he feels in himself a rush of agreeable
feeling. As if he's gripping hands with a long-lost friend, someone
somehow forgotten or missed all of his life.

Labuschagne touches him. Isaac looks up, startled. —Sorry?

Labuschagne is slit-eyed. —Ginzy sent you hey.

—Ja.

—What, from his shop?

—No, my da, he's a watchmaker. He asked for a job for me.

Labuschagne takes out a pack of Van Riebeecks. —And that's what you want hey, to work on cars?

There's no hesitation in Isaac: it rushes in him, spark to flame. —Ja, yes, absolutely I do.

Labuschagne lights his brown cigarillo. —What? You think I'll blow us all up in here or summin?

—I diden say nothing.

—Didn't have to, with your eyes going like mad. Check here.

Isaac follows him to a bucket, Labuschagne saying, —This isn't bioscope hey, some movie. He points with his chin into the bucket and Isaac peers over at the dark liquid within. Petrol. Labuschagne flicks in the lit cigarillo. Isaac flinches but it only goes out with a soft hiss mostly lost in the clanging. Labuschagne laughs. —Can never burn like that, he says. Never ever. Has to be a gas vapour to catch, that is why every engine has a carb in it hey, to spritz the petrol into the heads.

He straightens up: —But doesn't mean that *you* can smoke in here. That's *if* we takes you on. No one can smoke but me. I'm shop boss. I'm mechanic.

He looks away, sniffs, looks back. —So Ginzy sent you. Your folks is what knows him.

—Ja.

—And you wanna be apprentice.

—Yes I do.

—I can see.

—Yes, really.

His head wiggles one way then the other. —Ach, ja, oright.

—Ja?

—You look uhkay hey. Come to the office and I sort the papers and that, get you started.

—Really?

—Ja really.

—Jesus, Meneer Labuschagne. Thanks so much hey.

—Franzie. It's Franzie. He scratches the back of his head, puffs his top lip with his tongue. —Hey listen. You also, I spose . . . I mean, like Ginzy.

—Hey?

—What say your name was again?

—Isaac.

—No, last.

Isaac feels the familiar curdling, the sick feeling in the belly that hardens the spine.

—What I mean, says Labuschagne, is you also some kinda Jewboy or what hey?

— . . . Ja, Isaac says slowly. Ja, I'm a Jew. Summin wrong? He puts his hand on one of the hammer handles on the bench to his right. Slips it toward himself and holds it there against his thigh, casual. Labuschagne's eyes don't even flick down for a second.

—You not a Communis hey?

Isaac jerks. —A what?

—You bladey heard me. A Communis.

—Ach shit, Isaac says. I can't even spell that.

Labuschagne opens his mouth like a hungry ostrich and laughs hoarsely so that Isaac sees his pink tonsils wiggling and gets a wash of tobacco breath. Then he says, —Ah fok it, fok it. I likes you, little ou. You a bit of a spark plug hey. You got some guts, ja. Come.

He takes a step but then frowns, turns again. —But hey.

Isaac watches, tense.

—You not some kind of a kaffir boetie now, is you?

Isaac blinks, rocking back. The thought of him being a kaffir brother, a lover of Blacks, Jesus.

Labuschagne sees it in him, nods. —Uhkay, good ja. Oright.

He starts off then stops, turns back again. —One other thing.

—Ja?

His plate hand flashes, casual. Chops Isaac's arm just under the elbow. It's like being slogged by a lead bat. His forearm numbs; the hammer rings on the concrete. —Jus don't you ever do that again, kerel, or I kill you, uhkay. I kill you.

And he smiles his bentdown smile.

14.

IN HIS THIRD MONTH at Gold Reef Panel Beating, Isaac takes a bus to Parktown, a day of thin sun and palehazed sky. Over his tan overalls he is wearing a second-hand jacket with leather elbow patches, and he has done his best to wash the grease from his rawskinned hands and to comb down the rebel springiness in his wild orange hair.

On Gilder Lane, he watches from the park, pacing. He expects that the school bus won't come on time then is surprised by the tearing noise of its gears and the whine of the big Leyland diesel engine, almost ten minutes early. He settles behind the green curtain of willow fronds in the scent of grass and mildewed bark, a little tent to enclose his nervous shivering. He thinks, She won't be on that bus.

He watches the bus with its school colours painted on the sides. It stops at the base of the street; when it moves on there's a group of girls left behind, all of whom but one walk off downhill. The one climbs. Closer, he sees what he already knows, that it's her. Skirt and stockings. It makes him tremble. She's got the doctorish leather briefcase in one hand, the other pushed deep into the pocket of her green blazer. What the hell: a feeling of self-abandonment and lunacy as he steps out from behind his green cover and into the selfsame daylight that ignites the smooth skin of her cheeks, the swoop of yellow hair that gleams like golden oil.

He crosses the street and the sense with him is not good as he goes. It's like when he's shooting pool and the second he hits the shot, even before that second, he knows it's going wrong, it's off, just off. And now he has walked across to her, he is here, feeling hot in the face and cold in the chest.

—Yvonne.

She glances back, then jerks. —Christ!

He puts up one hand, one open palm, then the other. —It's oright, he says. I just want. Just wanna tell you sorry, oright?

Her face goes through some quick changes. It sets on a sour locked expression of real fear rimmed with . . . what? Outrage, anger? —Where'd *you* come from?

—I–

—What, you following me?

He hears himself saying the word no, his palms still up. —It's okay, he says. It's okay.

—It's *what*? She says this with a voice so high pitched it's almost a squawk. —Don't tell *me* okay.

—No. I mean. Yvonne. I just.

—Leave me alone. I don't even *know* you.

He is thinking now that she might start to cry. She hurries uphill, away from him. He doesn't follow. He lifts his voice: —I wanted just to tell you sorry. S'all, hey. For the. I mean. Is he oright, like? That oke. In the club. Your friend, whatsisname.

She stops, pivots. —Wayne!

—Ja, that Wayne.

—You could have darned well killed him. Seriously.

—I'm sorry, he says, walking up a bit. The sturdy well-made length of her throws down a pole of shadow between them, standing there with the good breasts and the strong neck and fine legs, the thick hair like a sheaf of new wheat. In daylight, she is a lot older than that first time he saw her and there's even more of that strong calm feeling about her; but what is most lovely is still the contrast between the handsome strength in the body and the soft delicacy in the face, and also the warmth, the special warmth that she radiates. He feels the light come on inside of him.

—You're sorry! she says. You think it matters? She's shaking her head but she's still standing there, not moving away, that's the main thing. Be so careful, he says in himself. Don't drop this moment, made of the thinnest crystal.

—You told me sorry, he says. He can hear the trembling in his voice.

—What?

—Remember, up in your house, outside . . . He moves his shoulders. —It's like that time, that's all. Sometimes you have to say sorry.

She's shaking her head, her eyes scrunched. As if she's trying to focus on him through a storm he cannot see. —You're a little bit mad, she says, aren't you. I mean truly.

He nods. —Ja, I know I am.

—And you told me it's my fault.

It takes a while to realize she's talking about the jazz club again. Did he really say that to her? He remembers getting punched. He says: —This is exactly what I come here for. To tell you the apology, all that. I got like carried away.

—You don't say.

— . . . But it was also a little bit mean hey, how you were to me. And your friends and that. Going on. Laughing me out. I only come up to the table to say hello how you.

—Ja, so try and kill them, she says.

He goes on, dogged. —And you were like ignoring me.

She lifts her forearm to her mouth.

—You were. I think you were like embarrassed.

—I wasn't *embarrassed*.

He shrugs. —Embarrassed of me. I don't know. I just wanted to say hello. And now I come this time all this way, to tell you sorry.

She looks past, then looks up the street. —You drove here, your truck?

—No, the bus.

—Bus?

—Ja. They let me take my lunch late today, I asked. I get an hour and a half on lunch.

—From what's it called again, the packers and movers, Morris?

—No, uh uh. Got a new job. A really lekker one. I really really like it hey.

—What is it?

Isaac grins. —Panel beater, he says. You know what that is, a panel beater? I'm a apprentice class A panel beater now.

He doesn't know whether it's her curiosity that does it but without saying anything she allows him to walk with her up to the driveway of The Castle. He holds his hands behind his back and keeps his distance. Tells himself not to say anything dumb and feels that badshot pool feeling slowly fade as they step together. She asks him about panel beating and he tells her. It's hard for him to keep the excitement that is in him now all the time for his new work from filling his throat and rounding out his voice, making his hands move, his words come tripping in their rush. Trying to relate to her what it is, what he gets from it, this wondrous phenomenon that has the name of panel beating, the whole grand thing of it, a world within the world. The words and the practices and the people. And most of all his hands on crumpled damaged steel, learning to mould it, heal it. How it is both so rough-hewn – the banging, the dirt, the cuts and bruises and scratches – but also at the same time so full of refined concentration, a sensitive feeling, delicacy almost. It is true what Labuschagne said at the beginning and he repeats it now: It's an art.

That makes her smile and the cold light inside his chest gets brighter, his words fade. At last he says, —Ja, I know I'm going on . . . I just . . . It's like I can feel I'm good at this, you know, I can do this . . . and I want to get as good as I can . . .

—You starting to sound like Father when he talks about his Cadillac. Dadsy and his Cadsy. What is it with boys and cars?

—No, he says. No. It's not just cos it's cars.

They walk for a while quietly and then the need to try to put it across to her wells up in him again, another wave of tumbling words: —This job, it's not even a job, like. How can I explain? Like the money, it isn't a lot. But honestly, sometimes I don't even care about the boodle that much. What it is, it's like you see this smashed-up thing come in, and then you see it going out and it's all brannew. What it is, it feels like we almost making, I know this sounds mad hey, you ganna think I am even more mad, but it is, it's like we making *time* go backwards in there. It only takes one second to smash something to shit, scuse my French hey, but it does hey, it's true. Just one second. But then it's a whole long month of this hard work, all patient, all careful, to turn it back like it was. Like in the movies when they play things backwards sometimes you know? An oke jumps out a window then he comes flying back up with his feet first. We doing that in the shop, only in slow motion. See what I mean?

And he stops. A sick realization. She's looking at him, maybe puzzled. It's the realization of how much like his father this all sounds. Because what his father does, it's not that separate from panel beating is it? Both repairing damage. He fixes accidents and sets the clocks back; his father moves stalled timepieces again into functional ticking, both are ways to close the same circle and return a fallen object into the ceaseless flow of the now. Death back to life: repairing the world. What scares him is that maybe for the first time he understands why his father does it, and it's not to get out of Doornfontein. It's the feeling that such labour gives to you, your life and your self.

Her laugh brings him back.

—Can I come too? she says.

—Hey?

—You dreaming of it, aren't you, actually dreaming of being at work, you lost boy.

He snorts at himself.

—You make it sound like so much fun, she says. I wanna come.

—No ways. Girls not allowed in the shop.

—Then you shouldn't tell me how exciting it is.

Exciting. He sees how he was waving his arms before, hitting his palm with his fist, the motions of panel beating. Something else there, an idea, is spreading in his mind, but when he reaches to bring it into words, it slips away.

—Isaac.

—What? Sorry.

—Look at you. You're in love.

He stares. Blood rushes from his heart, all his vessels seem to flood open; even his mouth hangs.

—You love this job so much, she says.

—Oh, he says, tight-throated. Ja, I do, I spose. I do . . . love it. He studies her. The flowers of a bougainvillea are on the stone wall behind, wavering in the dry air, the browned petals crackly as roasted chicken skin. Her face is so pretty, her eyes so liquescent and alive, there in front of him, after all those nights and days full of mere gliding images. The green in them lighter than he remembers, rimmed with a tawny yellow; and the high cheekbones below, the ripe plum of the small pouting mouth. Beauty: it hits him in the heart, this, her. Makes his blood fat with the need to stay near her.

—He's in love, she says, mocking.

Love: a plunging space between heartbeats.

Then she nods a little bit to herself. —No, Isaac. It's good. To find something you really like. That's really good. Something real.

She seems almost wistful saying this last part, then turns to go and he tells her: —So you know that I'm sorry. For . . . what happened.

She stops. —Maybe you should tell poor Wayne. He had to go to the hospital. Second-degree burns. They shaved off what hair there was left. They don't even know if all of it will grow back. He still comes to school with a huge bandage on. They call him Rajah and Mr. Towelhead and things. It's really quite horrible.

Isaac chews on his lips to keep his glee in. Soberly he says: —You want me to go to your school, wait for him and tell him an apology?

—Do I? That's up to you, what's it got to do with me?

He looks at her levelly. The fattened blood rising to his eyeballs. —Everything, he says. Everything that happened is all about you.

15.

ALL THROUGH THESE EARLY MONTHS of his apprenticeship his mother has been gloomy, withdrawn. She takes the meagre pay that he can give her but she is not happy. It's more than just seeing the end of the footwear dreams; more than just losing Isaac to the blue-collar world; he senses there is something secretive to do with the family in backhome that is possessing her moods. She gets letters from over there, of course, he always knew this, but they disappear into her, she never reads from them or even acknowledges their existence. Now Isaac begins to wonder, are such letters the same papers that she keeps hidden in the cashbox? Those lines that she used to rock over, praying out her grief, when everyone else was at shul? And are they connected to her new mood? This sense of grief and anguish that seems to encloud her presence almost all the time nowadays.

Think of the seventeenth day of April. Try to feel and see the word pogrom. He sounds it out in his mind. Thirty, thirty-five years in the past. A scar on his mother's face and inside her secrets bound to papers. *Pogrom*: it has the tang of Russian savagery to his ear. At night he slips into the room in his mind where the shutters are drawn and he concentrates hard and forces those shutters back for the first time in so many years. Sees again in the straining light of his attention his most distant memories: pictures of Lake Sartai, the flat water past the twisted trees (summertime, and dust from the road has settled on the trunks; winter, and patches of snow cling like hives); flocks of kept geese down by the water, the streaks of their green-white dung and their croaking and gabbling. Who were the Russians in the village? Not the farmers who came to the market every Wednesday, those were Lithuanians, Catholics. The Russians had been the owners of the country before the war, the soldiers and Cossacks with a different cross. And there were also Tatars, who lived on the far side of the bridge past the cathedral, the other side of the river Šventoji that flowed into the lake. Those Tatars with their high slanted cheekbones and how lots of them spoke Jewish and he remembered Tatar boys urinating in the river and how their cocks were trimmed like his own, so they were almost a kind of Jew to him. Of course there was also Branka the old Tatar charwoman; she used to pick him up and she was soft and had yellow teeth.

Pogrom. Russian word, but he could find no fear attached to the Russians. There were a few Jewish families from over there, the Russian east: with funny dangling sidelocks and odd hats and their own synagogue, a half shack in the muddy earth at the waterfront, exuding strangely lilting melodies. These few Jews were called Chassidim, and were suspect, he remembers that now, Rabbi Kapelushnik telling how it was written that a Chassid was not a proper Jew, for they had wandered off into strange practices, unspeakable beliefs most blasphemous.

But the pogrom. Think of what it could have been. If not Russians then it must have been the Catholic poyers, the peasants, the Lithuanians. All he could summon of them were the carts full of produce they would bring into town on market days, to trade with the Jewish shops around the big market square. Their long-limbed bodies and fair hair. How they would get drunk at Yeshi's inn, and that one who fell asleep snoring in the patch of the kitchen garden in front of their house. The Lithuanians with a social place lower than the Russians, still left over from when the Czar was everyone's king, the poyers still closest to the dirt where they made it grow. Names with an *s* on the end like Paulauskas, Kazlauskas, Markunas, Boggus. If there had been a pogrom, was it them? And why? And where was his mother when it happened? Long before she'd even met Abel.

His mind turns back to Yankel Bernstein, who visits Rively now. Yankel who had said that Blumenthal the laundryman, he knew.

But in the morning he goes to work and he does not think about any laundryman or old times backhome. The shutters in his mind are closed again, as they should be, the memory chamber dimmed: he thinks now only about the manifold satisfactions of the job.

Now the days add up as they never have before in his life. For the first time a job bolts him into a routine as hard as the steel he works: it forces him to grow as upright and as unbending as a young sapling held by the traction of a gardener's wires. From eight to five every weekday he watches and learns and tries. Gradually he feels the cumulative beauty of an appetite, a talent, recognized and growing and nourished within. He is apprenticed to a man named Jack Miller who is not much of a talker, with a squashed loose-fleshed face and fishlike way of opening his mouth so that his chin presses down into the puddled skin of his throat. At first Isaac thought Miller was always annoyed with him, because of the silences and the grim expressions. But later he finds out that is wrong, that Miller is good inside, and patient. He is also one of the best panel beaters in the shop, humourless and stolid-seeming though he may be (he even eats his home-packed lunch with the same lugubrious care he uses to turn screws or measure a gap with his steel dividers and precision ruler). He never whistles to the tunes of the Boswell Sisters or Benny Goodman's band on the nearby wireless. Doesn't even smoke. At the end of each shift he takes time to clean off and carefully oil each of his tools; he won't let a Black do it, even if it's late after a tiring day. Always the same: steady and calm. What he teaches Isaac through example is how to slow down, to concentrate, to think. Not to rush in and start hammering away but to spend the time to plan and feel each step before taking it.

For before a dent can be reversed it has to be understood. Sanding a dented panel unveils a map of high points and hollows that Miller shows him how to read. Hitting a bulge on the underside of a dent too directly can make worse damage; it has to be hammered at slyly, carefully, from the edges, because every bulge has a humped rim on the top side that also has to be coaxed down with the same blows. Miller shows him how to use the whole of his hand to feel the surface of the steel map, understanding that the true size of any dent is not just what is seen.

So, under Miller's supervision, he practises how to bounce the right panel hammer sensitively and rhythmically against a dent braced underneath by the right-shaped dolly, sometimes if lucky popping the dent out flush, most often working it carefully by angled degrees towards its former contour. He learns how to use the big tanks of oxygen and acetylene, adjusting the mixture to refine a flame to a shade of clear yellow or opaque winking blue, according to its purpose. The flame can be used to heat a panel to render it more malleable or it can melt lead to use as filler or it can burn out bolts that are rusted and crushed into their threads; flames can be licked lightly over a part to make it expand so that once fitted it will shrink to maximal tightness, or they can be centred to that hard dancing blue like a needle that can bore tiny holes or cut clean crackling lines through steel plate. He learns to use hydraulic bars to straighten crumpled pillars. Learns to use frame hammers and suction cups, alignment bars and forty-five-degree hammers for door panels and ones with picks for bumpers. Most of all he learns to value precision, and not to care when the sweat and rust flakes and caked dirt get into his eyes and make them burn, into the cuts on his toughening hands, his arms shuddering deep in the tendons with the ache of hard labour.

On occasional Wednesdays he takes the bus and gets off in Parktown to wait at the municipal park on Gilder Lane. Yvonne Linhurst comes straight home on Wednesdays, her early days: no last period, no netball practice, no standard nine dance committee meetings. When he comes – maybe only about once every three weeks or so at first – he'll bring her a slab of Aero chocolate (her fave) and she lets him carry her briefcase from the bus stop to the driveway.

At every visit he is always careful to keep a respectful distance and he listens to her words as if they are lobbed eggs he has to catch and cradle to himself, not allowing himself to miss even the silences between them. She tells him in her soft high voice about her fears of not being picked to be a prefect. About this one girl, Amanda, whom all the others hate, because this Mandy spreads these gruesome rumours that are *such* lies. About idiot Mr. Williams who gives her Bs on essays that deserve A-pluses, minimum. About her parents and how crazy they are, no one has any idea (Isaac thinking, Yes I do).

Gradually the Wednesday visits become more than occasional; they turn weekly, fixed, he is always there, waiting, and she always expects him.

One time she tells him, —It's all so serious for you isn't it hey?

—What you mean?

—Life, I mean, for you. Serious business. And she mimes his expression, going sombre (Isaac thinking, Is that me? For real?), hunching her shoulders as if protecting her chin.

He fights not to let himself get cross, to snap at her, the protected silliness of such an opinion. —Ja, but the thing is, it *is*. Maybe you just don't know yet.

She looks at him, her cute snub nose wrinkling, disagreement akin to distaste.

He says, —When I's little maybe I thought not, thought it was all different.

—Like how?

—Easy, like. All nice.

She goes quiet then, till they reach the driveway. —So what, do you reckon that I'm all . . .

—What?

Now her eyes have that other look, calm and thoughtful. He has so many of these looks of hers now in him, sometimes at night he'll go over them, one picture after another, as if sorting through a box of irreplaceable photographs.

—But I'm not, she says.

—Whatchoo mean?

—Spoiled.

—Who said spoiled?

—I know what you're thinking.

He smiles. —Nah, you not spoiled, you perfect.

She blows air out of her pout: ridiculousness. —Don't even think that.

—I think it's true.

—There's nothing perfect, Isaac. I'm just a girl. And I can be bloody cruel.

—No.

—Seriously. Don't say those things.

—Ukay, ukay. You just a girl. Here. He hands her briefcase across. She holds on to it, looking down.

—Hey, she says . . . Want to come in for a bit?

16.

EVERY APPRENTICE HAS A SIX-MONTH period of probation
and Isaac now nears the end of his own. As if in anticipation of it,
Labuschagne hands him and Jack Miller a challenge in the form of
a badly rear-ended Willys sedan.

For weeks they painstakingly uncrumple mashed steel. Like
used tissue balled up it must be carefully stretched and smoothed
without tearing. With this wreck, Isaac has the feeling of
undergoing a final exam. He gives his all to the work and at the
end of every day is filled with a happy drained sensation. After
work he walks over with the other men to the Great Britain Hotel
to drink whisky and talk meaninglessly in the tobacco haze.
Rugby, cricket, war, money, women. Jolly abuse slurred at
Ricardo the diminutive Portuguese bartender with his small hairy
hands and dapper cufflinks.

At home over supper it's his father now who has the questions
about the work and nods at his answers, encouraging, it's Mame
who mutters and interrupts with comments about the meagre pay
and the long hours and what *else* does he have on the go?

—Loz em, says Abel. Leave him. Isaac is happy learning his trade.

A trade, says Mame. Tradesmen don't live in nice big houses
in Orange Grove.

But I *am* happy, Isaac thinks, floating in the steaming zinc tub
in the backyard afterwards. My father is right. The water cools
around him, turning black, and he reads comics in *Radio Fun* and

feels the good tired feeling of the heat through the marrows of his bones, of having worked hard and well all day, and smokes his Max cigarettes, one after the other, and sometimes nods off to be awakened by the wet touch of the surface on his chin.

During this period he also finds himself getting called to the phone at home sometimes, for a Mr. Shmear, a Mr. Kidneystone, a Mr. R.J. Pickles. When he picks up the receiver he tells Hugo: —You're going to run out of voices.

—When are you coming out Brakpan way, Tiger, give a look at the place at least?

—When you ganna stop asking me?

—I shouldn't, you don't deserve the opportunity. But what can I say, I got a gold hand when it comes to picking people, you the right lad for the job.

All Isaac can do is sigh. —Hugo, what can I tell you my mate. I'm happy panel beating.

—Happy? What's that? You know what's happy?

—Ja ja ja.

—A pig lying in its own runny stinking shice is what is happy. Duzzen know better. There were pigs on that hell farm by Vekklesdorp, remember? Chop chop chop.

—I gotta go now Hugo.

—Happy is one a *those*.

On Thursday nights when they get their pay packets they open the yellow envelopes and take out a few of the notes according to a fixed percentage and give them to Labuschagne for the kitty. The kitty is kept in an old Quality Street sweets tin that only Labuschagne handles. Every fifteenth of the month the kitty goes to one of them as a cash bonus. Each one of the staff, of the Whites, gets a turn and everyone must contribute. Handing over his cash, Isaac feels he is almost fully one of them; once he's passed his probation, he'll be up to collect the kitty too: drawing a man's full pay for a man's work.

Now comes the day when the panels are back on the Willys and only an unsightly dimpling covers the parts of them that were crushed the most, like the cellulite under the skin of an old lady's legs. For this final planishing work Miller forgoes the use of filler, calling it a cheat, and instead uses a custom-bent file as a slapstick. He shows Isaac how, braced with a comma dolly, even the smallest bubbles can be patiently tapped flat by the broad file – his work guided in part by the just-right tinking sound of a correct impact – and then afterwards sanded almost smooth as new steel.

The frames too have been exactly realigned under Miller's patient hands so that all the doors open and close with factory-perfect thunking. Now Blacks take hold of the wheeled jack by its long handle and others cluster behind; pushing and heaving and singing together, they manoeuvre it to the glass station where Rustas fits new windows and windshields. Isaac has been permitted to follow the Willys on, to watch and learn. Again the Blacks sing as they move the sedan to the paint shop-within-a-shop, Mornay Pienaar's kingdom. The new glass is covered over with newspapers, all edges taped down (not with Miracle Glow, mind, but standard masking tape, and Isaac understands now why it's called masking tape at all, for it masks what you don't want painted). The Blacks move in and sand away any paint still left on the fixed bodywork, smoothing down to raw steel. Then primer is applied, the bodywork turning terracotta. They smear black putty on any uneven patches, let it dry and sand it flush. Then Pienaar mixes lacquer paints – another, separate art, Isaac is told and sees is true – till the new matches the old so perfectly it is impossible to tell where it begins and the factory coat ends. Pienaar fills the electric spray gun, aims and pulls the trigger and the gun buzzes and hisses; he works the beam of lacquer back and forth evenly over the healed rear so that when the newspaper and masking tape is peeled off, the car is one and new and whole again.

The Blacks then move it on its jack to the upholstery station where the trimmer, Eddie Tops, crawls inside. He had earlier stripped out all the seats and interior linings, to repair them at his cutting table with its heavy sewing machine. Now, on his knees on the bare steel, he wires the new-stitched hood lining into the roof, then lights up a Primus stove and sets a can of water to boil. A length of rubber hose rises from the can to coil through a gap in the roof edge. Steam fills the narrow space above the lining, and the leather gradually loses its creases and fills out like a tightening drumskin, beautiful. Eddie puts back the interior panels, the carpets, the seats.

Then Labuschagne the shop mechanic – first in, last out – comes to put the wheels back on, to replace the battery removed before, to retune the engine, gunning it, making sure. That afternoon they wait for the owner, who arrives to pay his insurance deductible, and sign the clearance certificate, and then Labuschagne gives him the keys and the man can legally drive away. His Willys sedan resurrected.

Labuschagne turns and grins at Isaac and waves him into the office. While he fetches something down from the top of a filing cabinet Isaac stands there with a swollen heart, chewing his lips to keep his feelings in. Then Labuschagne shakes his hand and welcomes him to Gold Reef Panel Beating and presents him with a new set of tools of his own. His own hammers, his own shining set of dollies. It will come out of his pay, of course, but they are his. Earned. He runs his fingers over the clean smooth steel, the polished wood. Labuschagne touches his shoulder. —You done real nice, he says. I can see it. You keep on.

The shining tools fit into moulded grooves in a flat box of red-painted steel. Isaac pastes a label on the box, writes ISAAC HELGER in careful letters. The tools are ordinarily stored in the shop but he takes the box home with him that first soaring night, lays the box on the kitchen table and opens it to show his father. Abel picks them up with his long fine fingers, one at a time, gravely gentle. He goes to the closet and fetches down the brandy and two glasses. My boy. This. This is a real thing. To life.

—L'chaim, Daddy.

They are clinking glasses – to doing a *properly job* – when the door opens and Mame looks in. His father says something that Isaac doesn't register because he is staring at her. Her face has gone hard and her eyes are like glinting breaks in the stone of it, the skin all grey but for the scar that throbs livid. —Ach come on, Ma, he says.

She lifts her chin, stretching the scar. A space hollows out behind Isaac's loins. His throat crowds with tears.

She turns away and the door shuts. When he goes after her, Abel touches him. —You drink with me first. Never mind it your mame. Your mame is oykay.

Isaac drinks, picks up his cap, walks out the backyard into the alley then the street. Goes on walking without thinking – quick angry steps – until after half an hour he finds that he is stopped outside the laundry shop.

17.

MRS. BLUMENTHAL AT THE COUNTER: a woman with a side-parted fringe that slants across a white brow, hair black as wet coal. Isaac asks to speak to her husband. She squints at his face. What's the trouble?

Something important. I want to ask.

Important? The man's resting. What kind of important?

Important is important.

He waits and she squints at him then mutters and goes up to convey his request and seems surprised when she comes down that he has agreed, yes her husband will see him, the Helger boy. Isaac climbs the spindly staircase to the apartment over the shop, the woman muttering in her teeth and watching him from underneath. When he knocks the loose door creaks in. From the hallway he sees Mr. Blumenthal washing his face at the sink. He presses his nose into a towel, tells Isaac to come in and sit. Isaac settles behind the kitchen table. Blumenthal, a man with wide wrists and a face underslung by a heavy jawbone, fetches down a chess set. You play?

Not really.

He sets up the board. You see, he says. Just like this country. Black against White.

I'm white, says Isaac.

Yes. You go first but I can promise you I know who will get the last move. And he laughs.

Isaac waits. You know what I came for.

I know. Make your move.

Isaac advances his king pawn. Blumenthal mirrors the attack. A kettle is murmuring on the stove. Around the fourth move, Blumenthal starts to talk. When the kettle boils he gets up and fetches tea in glasses with lumps of Cape apricot jam, actions that do not interfere with his narrative. He talks simply, without emotion. But there are long groping pauses as he tries to find the words, the right sequence of sounds to unlock that blotted day.

This was ten years before the war. A fire had chewed at the village of Dusat around Easter time and the Jews knew it was the Christians who had done it to put the blame on them and the Christians knew it was the Jews who were the devil's spawn (after all) and one and the same as the tormenting killers of their Lord in Jerusalem most high, spitting and howling as the nails sunk through the flesh of his holy palms.

Pay attention: The brothers Felder had been building a new brick house, one of the only brick structures in that wooden village, an emblem of new wealth. Baruch, Tuvya, Feivish. They were smugglers and forest wardens, legal owners of a shotgun.

Now on the day a brave girl Hanna Seft who had goyisher looks under blond hair went like a spy into the cathedral and came back with a report that sent the Jews running and hiding, away from the shops with the houses above, all around Maskevitcher Gass, the market square. But the brothers Felder resolved to defend their brick house, the labour of years in that time before such things as insurance policies.

Blumenthal hid in the woods called Silvitzke's Grove down the path that passed Rabbi Kapelushnik's house. He climbed a tall pine and huddled there for hours and saw the Christians coming along Unter-Dem-Brik Gass, down from the church that rose before the bridge over the Šventoji River. The men were in front and they had hoes and flays and rakes and scythes and rifles and they were drinking from bottles and their women came behind with the children and they had flowers in their hair and were holding hands and singing. When they came into the market square and found no one there, there was anger: the men broke windows and smashed in doors and dragged the goods out and threw them into dust and the women carried them away and the men went into the shops with their axes and climbed to the deserted apartments above and smashed and broke all the insides and then there were flames and smoke. They came to the brick house at the corner of the square opposite the well and the brothers Felder were standing on the roof and Blumenthal could see it all as clearly as if he was down almost with the crowd at the base. He saw Baruch yelling down, warning them off, saw him fire the shotgun over their heads, saw a shot from below clip his side, the shotgun tumbling first as he spun and then fell into the crowd. They caught him and held him spreadeagled while an old woman took a scissors and stabbed his eyes one at a time and twisted the scissors in them and dug the jellied orbs out, then she cut off his clothes and Blumenthal saw her cut off his penis with the scissors, Baruch Felder still alive and fighting and shrieking all through, and she cut open the scrotum and took out his balls and held them to her breast like snatched jewels, muttering warding curses. They used the axes on his fingers then, and his feet, then his limbs, taking their time, passing the implements around so that all who wished might have their turn, their bottles marked with bloodfinger smears. Above, his brothers smashed the chimney with kicks and dug out bricks with broken fingernails and threw them down to try to drive them off Baruch but others brought up straw and they packed the bottom floor and set fire to it. By then all that was left of Baruch was a torso-thing that yet writhed and squelched in the red mud of its own making. Flames rushed up and first Tuvya Felder jumped and then Feivish Felder. He saw

Tuvya landing on a leg that snapped and the jagged white bone flashed and jutted from his torn thigh and they dragged him clear and stood on his arms and stuffed severed parts of his brother into his mouth until he choked to death and meanwhile Feivish who lay broken was picked up and thrown alive into the flames where his screams were the loudest of any so far and his shape somehow rose again then warped as the heat melted him and he crumpled and was silent. Children mimicked the zigzag slump of his melting collapse. Men were drinking and men were pissing and men were vomiting and men had their arms over each other's shoulders and some children picked up pieces of Jew and ran away with them. Women were carrying flapping chickens upside down and bolts of cloth on their shoulders and sides of beef and inverted chairs and dragging tables behind them. Young ones threw down barrels from top floors from the shops not yet burning and the barrels bounced or they burst into showers of nails or horseshoes or erupted great spurts of dark molasses and everywhere goose feathers wafted on the smoky air from all the gutted pillows.

Checkmate, says Blumenthal. Those were the same ones who used to smile at our faces and come to our shops. The very same ones. Never forget what's behind a goyisher smile.

Isaac lifts his eyes. Did you know my mother?

Of course I knew Gitelle.

Where was she when all this was going on?

I don't know. Probably she hid with others.

Where?

Some in the mikveh, some in woods. There were also cellars underground where food was stored in the winter.

My mother's scar, her mouth.

This is between you and me.

Yes.

I never said a thing.

No.

What happened to your mother, yes, it happened that day.

What was it? Didn't she get away?

He shakes his head.

What?

Afterwards she always wore a veil, and she couldn't speak properly.

I know *that.*

He shrugs, leans back. That is what happened on April seventeenth, in Dusat. What I saw.

But not everything.

He shrugs again. Enough, I think. Not every evil needs to be dignified with words.

Isaac nods. And how did it end?

Some of us got word to the Cossacks in Rokishik. They came later that day and the peasants ran away, but some of them were too drunk and got arrested. I think one was killed when he tried to stab a Cossack. I think another one drowned trying to swim away. Later, some did go to jail for the murders.

Isaac waits. Is that all?

Isn't that enough?

Afterwards, at the door on his way out, he looks back. In English: —She musta been different hey?

—Uh vos?

—Meine mame. Before the . . . what happened, she must have been a different person.

Blumenthal pauses, maybe thinking about it. She was always strong, a powerful soul. But I remember the rabbi used to go to your grandfather's house – he was the butcher, yes? – and Rabbi Kapelushnik used to go and go, trying to talk to her, but after that day she wouldn't even see him.

The rabbi?

Yes of course. Wanting to get her back.

Back?

To shul . . . Didn't you know?

He stares at Blumenthal, watching his hesitation, then that shrug: Your mother – she was a frummer, she was *thee* frummer. The most religious girl in Dusat. Morning till night. They used to call her The Saint.

No.

Yes, your mother. She made the pious ones look like sinners did Gitelle Helger. That shul was more her home than your grandfather's house ever was.

18.

EARLY IN THE YEAR 1938, Isaac Helger passes through his nineteenth birthday and into his twentieth year alive with no ripples, no fuss. There are times when he wants to talk to Mame, to tell her about all that he knows now, but he can't. Still, the need is there, to unburden, and that's what he takes with him on the bus at lunch breaks on Wednesday afternoons.

Since the fated day Yvonne Linhurst first let him into her house, it has become their habit: she goes through the gate ahead of him then opens the garage door from the inside. They sit together in the storeroom behind the garage, talking softly, never touching. But now she starts to sneak him upstairs, avoiding the maids. She shows him the upper lounges with their views and soft couches, patterns of paisley and camel. The library with a ladder that slides on a brass rail. The wireless room with a beautifully contoured EKCO set, the newest model in a custom walnut stand. The billiards room downstairs with its ivory balls that shine his face upside down back at him from across the soft carpet while men in red coats hunt foxes on wall prints.

It comes to him that maybe she wants to show him all of this so that the house will not be something over him, another way of saying, *I am not spoiled, it's not my fault I'm from here.* A kind of grand joke in the way she throws open doors for him, in the ironical sweep of her arm. Once or twice she even makes it verbally, exultantly: —It's only a bloody house! What is the meaning under these words that he cradles into himself like tossed eggs? Is she saying the house is not me? But that would be a lie: this is where she is from, this is what she is. And then she wouldn't have to do it at all if he wasn't from Doornfontein, would she; so it's not because he is Isaac, it's because of where he's from, in truth. But he's not complaining.

Instead he laughs with her. Just a bloody house! The whole of number fifty-two Buxton, backyard included, could well fit inside The Castle's master bedroom ensuite, an ivory-cool chamber with a hallowed feel like a place of worship that they take their glimpses of from the shelter of the doorway. Her own room has white walls, wooden floorboards, rugs from Persia. Green curtains undulate by glass doors opening onto a tiny balcony that she calls a Juliet, overlooking the terraced gardens, the swimming pool, the tennis court and the neat rose bushes and cacti stands tended by the gardenboys in their overalls.

He washes his hands in the bathroom and his eyes never leave the eyes in the mirror. Tough and pinched, freckled centre and orange bush above. Don't ask yourself what are you doing here. You belong. Life has chosen you and you are here. You could have been one of those poor bastards backhome getting cut up and burned, instead you're here. But the face in the glass is furtive where he would will ease. It looks ready to bite when he tries to smile.

In her room he likes to sit on the thickest carpet with his back to the white doors of the closet. She sits on the chair by the rolltop writing desk or sometimes on the bed with her legs straight out in front of her, her back to the wall. He listens so very hard to her. The more he does this, the more she confides. He can feel there is no one – no friend, no teacher, certainly no parent – who listens to her as deeply, totally and acceptingly as he. Sometimes he doesn't believe that he will ever touch her and is not shocked when this doesn't worry him. Just to be here is miracle enough. Once a week she is as close to him as an arm's length, sitting there on her bed with her silk cushions, but there might as well be an electrified fence between them. The more he listens to her with this total craving intensity, the more there is a feeling of trust and the more it seems that to move physically to her would be a kind of betrayal. The strangeness of it is how it doesn't seem to matter to him.

Afterwards he always goes back to work happy and full. As if her voice and presence has added to some essence inside of him, made him denser, older. And he always works better for having seen her, on through those gilded Wednesday afternoons. He is calmer and surer with his tools, more patient and even lighter of touch in his work.

So the time accumulates: how he and the world together pass into the cool season towards the mid-year when the Highveld sunlight thins and the sky meanly pales. The unfurling of his young life starts to feel as smooth and sure to him as a long drive on a straight and empty highway. In May there's a general election which Isaac doesn't bother to vote in and which doesn't change anything, except that the Nats get more seats than last time. The fusion government of the United Party is still in charge, Hertzog still Prime Minister, Smuts his deputy.

Yvonne, seventeen, is too young to vote (though women are allowed to now), but that doesn't stop her from bringing up politics in the bright room upstairs. One time they're arguing about the big fuss in the papers over the national anthem: should it be the Afrikaans *Die Stem* or the English *God Save The King*. He makes a joke about why don't they just have a bladey Zulu one ha ha. She goes silent.

—What? he says.

—Where you work. There're African men there.

—Ja, f'course.

—What's it like there, I mean for them?

—Oh, he says, like anywhere. We all do our jobs.

—But not the same ones.

—Hey?

—Africans and Whites don't do the same jobs.

Baffling him. —F'course not. We all got our different ones.

—Yes, but you're an apprentice.

—Class A, ja. Absolutely. And a good one too.

—There's no African class A apprentices are there?

—Hey wachoo mean? He laughs. She's joking. No, watching him, serious. —Na, na, he tells her. F'course not, no.

—What do Africans do?

He shrugs. Why is she so serious? —Well, like, they, you know . . . Suddenly he sees where she is going. So he says, —Well it's like around here hey, in this castle of yours. They do those kinds of jobs. Same as here, ja.

—Don't say that.

—Princess, he says, trying to make her smile.

—No.

—Princess in The Castle.

—I really wish you wouldn't.

— . . . ukay. Sorry.

—I'm just asking a serious question. About this.

—What do you mean serious?

—It is serious, she says, folding her arms.

There she is in the cool room with the green curtains, sitting on her bed, her ankles crossed now. Look at the green and yellow in the eyes over those cheekbones, the perfect prettiness of her doll face, the way a curl of blond arcs up to the chin, the buttery mass of the rest of the hair above raked back by her dancer's headband.

He tries a joke again. —Serious in your mother's head hey, hu hu.

She'll be with him on this, the craziness of the mother, she's said as much before. But no: he gets instead a hard, hurt look.

—I diden mean it, he says.

—*I'm* being serious, she says.

—Ach. Ukay. Serious? You want serious. What's it you trying to get at?

—Just answer me that question. African apprentices, why not?

He feels his body twitching, his eyes roam, his feet kick. —Because it's a joke, man. You talking about some coonboys in the shop. What? They are what they are. And you want me to be all . . . It's like every shop, every place. Like here, like I said. Who cooks, who sweeps hey? Who does the roses and your lovely swimming pool?

She's looking away completely now. Not good.

—Am I saying anything wrong? I'm just saying what's true.

— . . . I wish you wouldn't have used that word.

—Which, about your ma? I said sorry.

—You don't even know.

— . . . hey?

—It's so ugly.

—What? What'd I say?

She only shakes her head.

— . . . Coons? . . . Jeez hey, it's just a word.

—It's ugly. It's horrid.

—Oright, ukay. Africans. Blacks. Is that a better one? If we used a different word is it all oright like? All of a sudden.

— . . . It just makes it sound like they are . . . like they're complete animals or something. Animals. Not even people.

He shrugs. Feels the weight of even where to start with this rich girl from this rich dizzying place, how it is, how life is. She just doesn't have the first clue, her head full of the craziness from the mad mother running around with her crazed towel on her

meshugena head. —Listen, he says. I dunno all about this word
stuff, *Africans*. But lemme tell you, they are them and we are us.
They have their words for us too, you know hey. I can speak with
them a little bit in their own language.

—They are *people*, she says.

—They different, he says. I can speak with their language even,
can you? Can you hey?

—Oh, come *on*, she says.

—What?

—They're human bloody beings, Isaac, like me and like you.
That alarms him. He sits up: —You don't know! You don't
know how it is.

She hugs herself, hiding her eyes from his.

—Oright, he says. You call them humans whatever, fine. Well
and good. People say shvartzers. Shochedikah. Or kaffirs or coons
or floppies. Moonts, whichever.

—Don't *say* that, she says. Don't!

—No, but I'm saying. It's just words.

—How would you like it if I said—

—What?

—Nothing.

—What?

She whispers three words. Bloody Jews and then he doesn't
quite hear all of the last one but he sees her mouth and it's like
being slapped, he goes breathless and a pang shrivels his scalp.
—You don't know, he says. You don't know nothing. You don't
know what happened to us, what was *done* to us, or you wouldn't
open a dirty filthy jaw like that.

—I thought they were just words.

—How could you say that to me? His lips are twitching and
he gnaws on them to keep them still. To think of Greyshirts and
pogroms is not in the head, it's in the guts, a sucking death. How
he was lifted and slammed, pissed on. How the crooked crosses

leach their black toxins over European maps and onto the walls of
the shul in Doornfontein. And three Jewish brothers standing on
a brick house aflame. The screaming when they cut their *balls* off,
Jesus she has no clue. And his mother was somewhere there at the
same time, huddled, shivering.

Moisture gets into his eyes then. He can feel her looking at
him. —Isaac.

—...

—Isaac, can you look at me?

—...

—Isaac, I didn't mean it, it was just to show . . .

—Show what? He comes up angry, the redness is better for
him than crying, it always has been. —One has got exactly nought
to do with the other.

—Oh Isaac.

—It doesn't! One is just all those lies. I mean what we are is
what we are and what they are is a different thing.

—And what would that be?

—Hey?

—What do you think they are that's so different?

—You know. You know exactly what I'm saying.

—No, Isaac. I actually don't.

He takes an unsteady breath, scrubs at his nostrils with one
knuckle. —Come on. He is what he is, a Black. Everyone knows.
How it is that they look, how they smell. How they sound with
their language. How they move like this. The way they do with
their girls and that. How they dance around. Different, *different*.
You can't compare with a Jew. A Jew like me is a White. We
Whites. You can't say any White is anywhere near the same.
Maybe you can say it if you live here in Parktown all the time
and it's only the maid and the gardenboy you ever see, but even
then – please. The Black is completely different to the White.
Everyone knows what the Black is.

—Don't lecture to me, Isaac, saying how things are and I don't know anything. I am quite aware as well as you are that African people appear to be different. What I am saying is that those differences are actually superficial.

Her accent has gone even more larney, getting almost prim. Using these hard posh words that she knows he isn't very sure of. It seizes him with irritation. He writhes, his heels knocking.
—Ach why are we even jawing on all about this hey? What for?

—I don't know, she says, looking off again. The long green curtains swelling and easing from the breath of the sky through the open panes.

— . . . You were asking about work, what they do . . .

She doesn't move or say anything but he can tell she's become attentive. Whenever he talks about his work she listens like this. She cares because he cares: the sincere love of the labour that he has entraps her. It links with what his father was always trying to get across to him, the special gravity that having a real trade can bestow. But think how bladey messed up that is, in a way. Girls will only care about an oke if he doesn't care about them the way he cares about his work. Like they want to be off to the side a bit. They want to be there while you go for it but off to the side; it can't be *them* that you go for. Yasis, but that's messed. Girls are so messed.

She is looking at him again, pressing with the green eyes.

—At work, he says, they bring us things. Bring you tools and that. They clean them too except for the okes like me and my journeyman who don't let no one else touch our stuff. They jack up the cars for us. They push them and that. They do all the cleaning out, all the prepping up and that.

—But not what you do. They don't do that.

—Hu-uh. No ways. That is skilled labouring. They can't touch a panel hammer, not unless they passing it or cleaning it for us.

—A White you mean.

—Ja man, well who'd you reckon invented panel beating the

first place? It's ours. It's in the Industrial Council regulations and all hey. Strict. We got our jobs and we give them jobs too – their jobs.

—And you've got your pay.

— . . . What's that supposed to mean? You know how hard I work? I deserve.

—Yes, but if there was an African who could do what you do? Why can't they have a chance to make the same?

—Ach don't be all silly. You know what you sound like?

—What?

—I won't even say it. You think I haven't heard communistic stuff before.

She blinks at him.

—Oh ja, he says. I know commies. I even gave out commie papers the one time.

He's got her now, he doesn't know exactly why but he's knocked the words right out of her. —Ja you see, he says. I been around hey. You listen to me and don't talk about what you don't know. What I do, it has got thinking in it, oright? You might just scheme it's nothing but bashing and banging and whatnot, but I promise you, it's your brain hey. That's why you need a White.

—Because only a White has a brain.

—Well ja, he says. One big enough.

—That's such rubbish!

—No it's not. It's scientifical. It's proved. Listen. Who do you think made the business, the shop, in the first place? Not one a them, I guarantee.

—Cos they not allowed to!

—Oh sure, ja. And when the first Whites ever got here they found a big city full of cars and streets and buildings, ja. They found fancy schools all like yours. Beautiful *castles*.

—Stop saying that.

—More words I'm not allowed.

—I don't believe you that you gave out any Communist papers. Not if you talk such absolute–

—Ach I never read that kuk, I just did it for a favour one time.

—Well maybe you should have. Maybe you would have got we are all the same. All just people.

—Then how come they live in huts made of cow shit when we have aeroplanes? Hey? How do you explain that one?

—I don't know, I hadn't thought–

—Exactly!

She gives him a long bad look. —I was going to say I hadn't thought about it all like that, aeroplanes and huts. Whatever that has to do with it. I just know that they are people too, people like us.

—No. They different. I told you, it's proven. Their head is thicker with more bone.

She gapes. — . . . And where exactly'd you learn that bit of *scientific* knowledge? Which school exactly?

That pumps heat into his face. —Well not everyone gets sent to lord-whatever private school for pukkuh-pukkuh yoks from bladey Parktown. But I can read hey. I can think.

—Of course you can. You have such a big White brain.

He is not sure what to make of that one. Getting mocked in some way. Later on, at work, he finds the conversation has stuck with him. Not just because it's disturbed things between him and Yvonne and he's scared of losing her, the ritual every week of entering The Castle together that has become such a vital portal to all of his yearnings, such a stoker of his finest ambitions, like confirmation from the world that his path is true at last, but also in the way he's started to observe the Blacks at the shop. What does she know? Ja, they are jolly and that. A good one can make you want to smile like nothing else. When they sing and dance it can make your skin go all prickly. It's like a happy kid or something. But she doesn't see through to the truth that he does with his burning angered gaze: how they also got no human feeling. How a shoch will take a goat and just stab it as casual as nothing. Stab each other. Fuck each other anywhere, anytime. How they kick puppies to death and live there in filth. Remember Silas and how he told on Solly Morris that time because Solly was the baas, Silas too simple to juggle a little bit of action on the side. Remember them in the country with Hugo, the way they live there, which is their true natural way. Squatting in the dirt and the shice. Well, it is a kind of animal isn't it, what else? When you get down to it. How wrong she is. It's also there in the Bible somewhere, he's sure. But you only have to look and see. Look at that one, Johannes, and tell me that that is not a gorilla nose, a gorilla face. So bladey obvious. How can a person not see the obvious! A little kid sees it and smells it, but she has to be taught to lie about her own senses by that insane mother. Isaac sees the mother again in his mind, with that jewelled cloth wrapped around her head, saying in that pukkuh accent like she is sucking a plum, saying, *the Nay-tive Question*. Ooh, the Native Question. Hell, come down here to Marshall Street, Mrs. Linhurst. Come down here and learn all about the *Native Question* in the back with the boys. You'll get your rich puss pounded, they'll native-question your bladey arsehole if they ever get a hold of you, Mrs. Queen from her Castle up on the Parktown ridge . . .

One afternoon Labuschagne needs a frame hammer. The boy he works with is an older Shangaan called Pieters. Instead of a frame hammer he brings the slide hammer built into a puller. Labuschagne shouts at him. Pieters is one of these proud boys, Isaac knows, so he watches. Pieters answers back. Labuschagne stares at him. Here it comes: but there's no blow, instead Labuschagne snags the hat off Pieter's head. This is another thing about Blacks that Isaac knows that Yvonne would not, how much a hat means to them, cos of how they need to cover up that chunky springy stuff they

have instead of normal hair. Now Labuschagne has dropped the
hat on the ground, telling Pieters stay where you are. Labuschagne
picking up an oxyacetylene torch, Pieters standing very stiffly.
Other Blacks watching, Whites too. Pieters takes a half step and
Labuschagne tells him no, lights the torch. Pieters is holding himself very stiffly all over, but then the bottom of his mouth starts to
twitch. Labuschagne flicks the hat over with his foot. The sweated
inner leather smoothed to a shine with wear, the brim almost worn
through in places with pieces of newspaper pasted around inside
the crown to make it last longer. Something very sad about that to
watching Isaac, the pasting of the newspaper over the thinning
leather. When the blue flame touches there's a corkscrew of smoke,
a peculiar stink. A shout jumps out of Pieters – a bellow of raw
pain as if it's being ripped out of him with a hook.

He drops on his knees, his quick hands snatching back the hat.
Already it's burning. He shakes it hard, slapping the flames out on
himself. There is laughter and whistling and clapping from the
Whites. Labuschagne adds a slogging kick to Pieter's backside to
punctuate his shame. Back to work everyone. But Isaac is doing
something he would not have before: looking at the other Blacks,
their silence and their watching. There is no laughter in them, only
hooded eyes. Crouched back in the shadow spaces like a single
presence they are, brooded and hurting. It makes him uneasy.

He's nervous as hell the next week, waiting for Yvonne Linhurst
in the park on Gilder Lane. She half ignores him, folding her arms.
He walks with her in unconnected silence, uphill from the bus
stop. It is good that he has his speech prepared, not the words
exactly but the ideas: that it's not his fault, he didn't get her education but he's trying, he's looking at the Blacks at work differently
now (true, but not in the way she imagines). The more he says
these easy lies salted with a few granules of the truth, the more all
of them start to taste in his mouth exactly like the salt of truth so

that by the time they reach the driveway he feels he is making a blood confession. He could almost cry.

She does let him in.

In her room they talk about the Native Question and there's a feeling of breaking through, the current becomes different between them, and for the first time he kisses her. She holds him, her fingers in his coarse orange hair. His mouth talks more flat lies about how much he is changing while his hand plots a course to her left breast. What brought him this far is the Native Question. More of this Native Question is needed. The Native Question is pure magic.

They are talking for a while when a fresh idea moves through him like a wave of physical pleasure, so brilliant and natural it is: to combine the parents with the Native Question. He shivers a little, and murmurs at first so softly he has to say it again for her to hear. Wasn't it sad how the mother changed that day. *What do you mean?* How her mother spoke so big about the Natives and that but then would not let him, let his – he almost says boys here, but catches himself – workers go through the garage. And Jesus did they have to battle to get all that bladey stuff, that fancy glassware, down down those narrow killing stairs, how they suffered. Didn't she remember that? She doesn't at first, then, *Yes, yes I do, yes.* This is what I mean about some people, he says. See, I know I'm rough, but I call a spade a spade. I don't say one thing when I think another thing. (Hu hu, his inner self laughs, what a little lying bastard you are; but don't you dare stop, so soft and warm she is, don't you dare stop, the smell of her, those swelling ripe firm tits so close to your face, don't you dare stop you brilliant lying bastard you.) *Oh God, I know, I know. That's what really gets to me about them also.* I have to be honest, he tells her, have to be honest. The hypocrisy. Ja, that is the word I wanted to say. I am sorry, but ja. Hypocrites. His throat all fat with trembling blood and need so that the murmur is squeezed almost to hoarseness. Hypocrites. One thing what I hate, I'm sorry hey, but it's a hypocrite.

Now they have this new thing between them, whenever she lets him in and up to her room. Close together, kissing and touching. They use this criticism of her parents like a stimulant. Because what she is doing with him is a rebellion against them, he knows, the rebellion exciting her and in turn bringing him in closer. The bad words she uses aloud against her own parents to her are like physical acts. Whispering to him as he touches her through her school dress. All slows down for him, existence pivoting round the slow movements of a heart enlarged, words like a salivary glimmer between them, a strand chaining their mouths, so corrupt and sweet. He spasms against her. In the toilets at work afterwards he finds his cock stuck to his underpants with dried seed.

He has this little trick he does where he'll walk behind you when you're sitting down and gives you a tap with his hand, like this, on the back of the neck. It's supposed to be friendly or funny or something. You have to laugh. But it's really kind of nasty, it's a crack. I've seen him crack her like that hard enough to make her head go back. It shuts her up. Yes, when we're all alone it shuts her up beautifully. But then when there are guests there she uses her mouth to get him back. Oh she uses that mouth so viciously. She cuts and she cuts with those words. People try to laugh but she only goes on. They start looking down at their drinks or in their plates. And he's only sitting there, looking sick with this mousy idiot smile pasted on. As if he's bilious. The pasted-on smile about to vomit. He turns grey. I swear, actual grey. But then when we are alone he gets her back. With the crack on the neck and other little things. God, you know I hate him sometimes. I actually hate the man's guts. He can't deal with her and anything straight on. Everything has to be from the edges with him. He has to come in sideways, sly, like a crook, like a crooking crab, scuttling. Has to pretend he's not doing what he is. And she's the same. She waits for other people to be there to treat him like a dog . . . but when we're alone she pretends like it's all fine. Darling and darling. I'm darling and he's darling. Everybody's darling . . .

He feels intense claustrophobia sometimes, holding her, listening so hard. She might live in a Castle but she has less open space in her family than he does, even with his mother posed so watchfully, fiercely, over him, because she's the only child of mad parents. And she is mixed in with them in a way he's not with his. With her and her parents, they're a threesome. He is separated from his because they belong to backhome, another language and place. But her – he can see her role even if she can't. When she says how close they were when she was small, he understands when she elaborates that she really means she had no brothers or sisters to take the parental attention off her, nowhere to hide, and that her father and mother used her as a thing to distract themselves from each other, as if she was and is a living excuse for their marriage.

It's strange for Isaac to understand another person this well. Because he has never listened to anyone like this before. Neither would he ever have but for the hunger he has for her, Yvonne, her exquisite dollish blond beauty, honey for his tasting eyes, and her firm strong goyish body, spike of fire for the blood and dagger for the loins, but also for her world, the world of high castles in the dreamish air. Fantasies pump richly through him now, really for the first time in his life, visions so dense they seem alive. He sees their wedding, the creamy white veil and the tuxedo, the flung rice on the silver Rolls-Royce. And long afterwards, with their Anglo-Saxon fortune secured in a private vault, he sits in a deck chair by the tennis courts, Yvonne's cool hand under his, the both of them taking lime cordials through straws and wearing white hats and tennis togs, dark gold-rimmed glasses against the sun and the rose bushes gently fragrant nearby.

Everything that they say is a lying. They call each other love and that is a lie. She is always saying darling but she doesn't mean darling what she means is something so bad there's no other word bad enough to contain it. It's like she is onstage all the time, but she is such a grotesquely bad actress. I think maybe she knows what she is but instead of stopping the pretending it makes her pretend even more, to run away from it. She should be ordinary. She should stop the pretending. But she wants to be grand so she acts all the time and I think she's been doing it for so long there's nothing else left, she can't go back. She'll never be able to admit that she's only ordinary. That she's not special. Not really clever or beautiful or glamorous, just a plain-Jane average middle-aged woman whose face has dropped long ago. And he. He's too much of a coward to try and make her see this, he'll just go along with her theatrics but then do tiny nasty things to sabotage her, to snipe at her, vicious tiny things, because he's such a small coward inside. I almost hate him more, I swear, than her for his cowardice. I truly do.

—You have such an honest life, she says to him another time.

He doesn't feel guilty. He feels satisfied she doesn't suspect.

—Why? he asks.

—I don't know. Everything is clear. You have to work hard. Your parents, they can't even speak much English or write it. So your family, it's so straightforward. You don't have time for anything else.

—Maybe, he says, considering. Then: —Well, if you rich you can do whatever you want, ja. So then whatever you decide to do is all, like, your fault hey. If you know what I'm saying.

— . . . Responsible, she says. Yes I know exactly. My parents could do so much. But all they do is talk instead, they use words to make us feel better. The *Native Question*. But we have all these servants, you're right. She won't do without her servants for a morning, never mind a whole day. But all she yaks about is the Native Question. And him. Jesus. They don't *do* anything.

Listening hard to her like this is tiring, it physically saps him. It's as if he knows her one way as a young woman in the world but now he is building her again, taking bits of her and implanting them within, the way a painter's brush darts from the colours on the palette to the canvas, gradually vivifying her truer self inside his being. And becoming another.

19.

IN THE BIOSCOPES the newsreels flicker-flicker and Isaac smokes his Max cigarettes and takes in more news of strutting Hitler. All this year Germany's been gobbling and puffing itself bigger. In March they swallowed Austria, a new act of war that nobody did a thing about, not Britain, not France, not Russia, and definitely not Mr. Roosevelt in Washington who just gets more and more vociferous about keeping America neutral. Nice word that, *neutral*, Isaac reckons, thinking of a gearbox, a coasting car. The trouble is if you don't put it in gear you can't move if you have to.

He watches now, late in the year, as Hitler starts demanding a fat strip of Czechoslovakia and all the British Prime Minister can do in response is talk about talking some more. When Isaac looks at that Neville Chamberlain's sad and leathery face up on the screen, with his white temples and his high Victorian collar, he can't help but think of him as a butler in a farce, bowing and scraping. He's scared. That's all it is. Scared of the shrieking maniac who is kicking in the front door, here to steal the silverware. So Isaac's not surprised when nobody does anything as German forces guzzle up the swath of Czechoslovakian territory that they want, with all of its mountains and fortifications, leaving the rest of the country helpless. On the newsreels Chamberlain holds up a sheet of paper. Peace in our time, is what he says at the airport after flying back from a meeting with the Nazis in Munich.

Everyone cheers him, because Hitler will be satisfied now, with
what they've let him have (and Isaac can't help but think of all
those new Jews under Nazi control). The glutton has been stuffed
to satisfaction. Right. People are such bladerfools, even Prime
Ministers. They see what they want to see.

In November the African Mirror newsreels go on flicker-
flickering and show a night when all over Germany and Austria
the Nazis burn shuls and smash Jewish shops and break Jewish
bones. What is odd is how detached he feels from it, where it
used to set his blood bubbling and his legs twitching, making him
want to go out and fight. Now the images of the British soldiers
loading Bren guns, the sailors drenched in salt spray, the pilots
firing up the engines of the Hurricanes and the new Spitfires,
hardly stir him. Nor do the rows of French tanks (France has the
strongest army in the world plus the impregnable Maginot Line
and therefore there is nothing for them to fear from even ten
Hitlers). No, Isaac's body is calm and unjittering, full of the
good calming work he does, and his mind and feelings are aglow
with Yvonne Linhurst and the beauty of his own unfolding fate.
Sometimes these things do happen to a person, they truly do,
and it's his turn, it's his luck coming round, Isaac Helger. Truly
he does kiss her in her bedroom in The Castle. Plainly he is going
to marry her. Him. Isaac Helger from number fifty-two Buxton
Street in Doornfontein, apprentice panel beater class A. With big
ears and wadded orange hair and spattered freckles and crimped
cynical mouth, not even a high school education. Ja but look at
me, look at me now, all you bustuds. Stuff you all. It's happening.
Like when God in the Torah says something and lo, or whatever,
there it is: kaboom. What they call a miracle. Saying the words *it
is happening* to himself gives a spark to his guts. I'm the one that
kisses her and holds her in her bedroom, I'm the one who has felt
her crying hot tears on my cheek, I'm the one who is closest to
her in the whole wide world and nobody else. I've *got* her.

And how fine his work is now, how talented he is. Everyone in the shop has started to notice. Everything is clear and inevitable. And all this soldier play, this war stuff, seems like a child's fantasy. He runs into Stu Finkel and Big Benny Dulut, part of the gang that went out to City Hall that time, and all they want to talk about is Greyshirt this and Greyshirt that and war this and war that, worried about what will happen if Britain and Germany go to war, because South Africa is supposed to join in for Britain but there is no way Prime Minister Hertzog will do that. It could be a civil war here, between Afrikaans and English again. Maybe Dr. Malan and the Nats and the Greyshirts will get control and want to fight with Hitler's help, like that Franco in Spain – who the hell knows? So the okes are even talking about saving up for tickets to go to Britain and volunteer if needed. But then what about Palestine? If we fight for Britain we'll be fighting against our own who are suffocating under the British in the Holy Land. Isaac doesn't offer anything to these febrile street discussions. They can't believe that Rabies Helger isn't more jazzed. That he's not first in line in whatever line is getting ready to kill some scumsucking fascists dead. What can he tell them? Rabid no longer, he shrugs off their admonitions with a sly blank smile. An old saying of his mother's floats up: Zollen zey brechen zeyere kep. Let *them* go break their heads.

But when he tells her this, she doesn't smile. There's a wan faded quality to her being lately, her posture is more bent, her skin more ashen and with mushroom grooves of purple under each eye, maybe she's been losing weight even. Mame, he says. What is it, Mame? And when she shakes her head and moves away he finds the newspaper, the real estate section, and goes to sit with her. — Look here Mame, give a look at this beauty. On a quarter of an acre lot, in Observatory. Seeing her try to smile hurts him more than any tears. She touches his hair. —Mame, don't worry so much, when I'm qualified I can have my own shop one day. You know—

Her warm palm on his cheek, her thumb quieting his lips, and again he's eight years old, the feeling of that old time ripples through him, how she sat him on a wall to tell him all about life. She says, You'll be all right, Isaacluh. For you I'm not so worried.

What can that mean? Her scar is so close to him, that signifier of a hidden world. Once she was The Saint of Dusat, now she won't set foot in a synagogue. Why? The urge to tell her what he's learned from Blumenthal rushes crazily to his tongue and almost beyond. —What's it, Ma, tell me, what are you so worried for?

There's a half a minute or so there where he doesn't move and she stares at a space on the floor unblinking. As if now she will speak her secrets. As if she is hefting their mighty weight within, deciding at last whether or not to pitch them out into the world. Into her son. Do it, he thinks. Do it Ma, tell me, Ma, what it is that's eating you alive.

When she speaks, he starts in his chair. Isaacluh, go and fetch for me the albums.

So he goes into his parents' room and comes back to the kitchen table and they sit as he once did when he was little and again her wide fingertip moves under the faces on the photographs, turns the stiff cardboard of each freighted page.

Name them. Tell me their names.

That one and that one. Who is that one?

Trudel-Sora. Dvora. Rochel-Dor.

Orli and Friedke.

Afterwards she takes the albums into the bedroom and shuts the door: her afternoon lie-down, something new. Never before had she been enervated during the day, napping would have been a lazy disgrace. A question stabs him: is she well? Is that the secret that he senses, the inching progress of some dread disease? His mind bleeds horror pictures. He's still sitting, gripped by this dark meditation, when Rively comes home, carrying her satchel full of textbooks for her paralegal courses in town. (Mame doesn't understand why she's trying to do men's work instead of settling down proper to start a family, when she's so young and pretty and she can have any man, why must she wait to get married old like Mame was? But Rively has a nice way of laughing her off, loves telling Mame about how a modern girl is capable of achieving anything a boy can. Women can even vote now like any White man, since 1930 already. He remembers one time Mame retorted: Look at that Amelia Earhart in the news, with her hair cut short like a boy, trying to fly air machines, and what happened? She disappears into nothing. If you look for crazy trouble, trouble will find you right back.)

But Mame doesn't even try to argue with Rively so much these days, down, down in her new mood of dark morosity. Now when Rively drops off her books and heads out to her night job as a waitress at The Tulip Café and Restaurant in Hillbrow, Isaac follows her into the yard. Low-voiced he asks her if she's noticed the change in Mame.

—Honestly, she says, I reckon it's that new law hey. She asked me about it like four times and I had to explain it to her every time.

—What law?

She grimaces and clacks her tongue, impatient with his ignorance. But she tells about the Aliens Act that came in just last year. Something he's completely missed in the bliss of his work and his Yvonne, the detached sense of indifference to the larger world that is generally his attitude now. Rively saying there were too many Jews leaking in from Germany and Austria, so now the government put this anti-aliens law in that anyone wants to come here has to apply before a special board. They didn't use the word Jew in the law (even though Malan's Nats pushed for it), but everyone knows no more Jews are going to get in anymore, from anywhere. What Rively doesn't see is why Mame would be so fussed now. Lithuanian Jews have been cut off for eight years so why would this make any difference?

—You don't understand nothing, Isaac says. Nothing.

She takes a step back, her face screwing. —Unlike mighty

brain here. Who never heard of Aliens Act and couldn't even spell it if his life depended.

But Isaac only half hears, his cigarette hand digging at his sternum. —What about Smuts?

—What about him?

—Smuts wouldn't agree on a law like this.

—Course he would! He *has*. He did it for the election, you think he was ganna lose that for a few thousand Jews? And if he tried to stand up for us, his whole party would've kicked him out like a dog. The voters don't want us, full stop.

Isaac stands there shaking his head.

—Feel bad? Knife in the back? Imagine you're a German Jew and stop moaning. Those double-crossers in London won't let those poor people into Palestine neither, when they can see how desperate, and after they signed and promised us back in . . . Where you going? Hey – wanna do something useful, come to a meeting with me and Yankel, hey Isaac I am *talking* to you.

Alone, Isaac smokes, his thoughts still with his mother, those black-and-white faces. Name her. Name him. The other night there was some shouting from her room and he woke up and went to have a look what was wrong but his father said it's nothing, just a dream she had. He knows that Mame remembers the Great War, Tutte too; they were married during the war time and neither one will ever talk about it. War: ja, maybe it's coming again now. Maybe.

Name this face, name that one.

Three brothers chopped up alive, thrown into flames. Pieces of their Jewish bodies in the hands of children.

The shutters are drawn on a far-gone place inside. The here is the here. What does everyone want from him?

I've got Yvonne, he thinks. I've got Yvonne.

He smokes down four cigarettes, grinding each most carefully into a saucer.

20.

AT THE CASTLE when Yvonne lets him into the garage he catches her by the waist before she can pull down the garage doors. The concrete floor is pale and immaculate in its empty brightness; left of centre rises the long bulk of a sheepskin cover. He walks her into it, kisses her. When she sways back he lets her go. —Where are you going, perfect?

—You know you not supposed to say that.

—Why not, perfect?

—Do you want to sound like Dadsy?

—No, I'm trying for Momsy.

—Like Dadsy when he's on about the dear love of his life.

Isaac smiles, puts one hand on the soft pad of the sheepskin. —Is it really the dearest love?

—The very dearest.

—Not Momsy?

—It's Mother or Mater.

—I think Mater is his trade-in.

She smiles. —Yes. Mater has skin and blood and Dadsy prefers steel and petrol.

—American steel. He says the word Cadillac in three syllables. Like a spell off the tongue, a summoning. —I wanna have a look.

She laughs. —No–o.

—You know I've got to see it. I'm tired of pictures.

—Don't even.

—I'm going to.

For the moment he can feel she still thinks he's joking, while he sinks to his knee, looking up at her. Then his hand hooks under the bottom lip of the sheepskin and her head slants, her hands go onto her hips. —Don't. He'll know.

—How's he ganna?

—Bet you he puts things. Hairs. Measures with a ruler. Powder.

—I'm a professional, he says. For a while he waits for the permission; she bends her lips in over her teeth. Looking at her, he lifts the edge of the cover. He stands to turn it back over the bonnet. He puts his fingertips to the smooth cool cream of the steel.

—Oh God, you'll make fingerprints.

He turns more back, up to the base of the windshield, whistles.

—What?

—Steering wheel's the wrong side.

—Ja, he's got a special thing on his licence for it.

He moves around and takes a double grip lower down.

—Isaac.

—Relax max.

He starts to jerk it up. A voice: —Joh!

As he spins he is looking for a weapon. Everyone knows how Blacks can go bushy. You see it in the papers: the gardenboy or the butler one day, they take a pair of shears from the shed or a golf club or a kitchen hatchet and they spatter the lounge red with White blood.

There is a man in overalls crouched low; behind him is the workbench against the wall.

Isaac looks at the man's hands on his thighs. He hisses at Yvonne to get back but Yvonne is already walking to him, saying, —What's wrong?

—Oh sorree sorree, says the man. I too sorree, medem.

—What is it, Moses?

—I come for to get . . . He twists, awkward in his squat, to point back to the bench. —When I see for you, small medem, I scare, I wait.

She tells him it's all right, he just didn't want to disturb them, she understands. But Isaac is thinking, He could have said something, over there watching us frenching, the stuffing *gardenboy*. With his big purple knob getting all stiff pro'lly, the cheeky bastard. Should bladey whack him, I should. Can you believe.

Moses says, —I sorry to you, baas. Then goes on saying it so many times that Isaac finally coughs: —Ja, oright. Oright hey. S'enough.

—I can show for. I must to do for you . . .

He crosses to the Cadillac, reaches under. Isaac bends to see: there's a strap underneath, stitched into the sheepskin. Isaac fingers it. Ja, his matadorian yank would have ripped it, no question.

—Can make like this, Moses is saying.

He unbuckles with grave correctness then turns the cover back by brisk quarter folds. She looks at Isaac and Isaac shakes his head. She says, —That's fine, Moses, put it back now please.

—Yes medem.

—And Moses?

—Medem?

—Mustn't tell anyone. Please.

—Tell?

— . . . About my friend here, Isaac.

—Don't tell my *name*, shit.

She flogs her hand at him: quiet. —Even to Momsy and Dadsy, anyone.

Moses is a small man with a tight-skinned face like a dark plum; one eye has a thick lid. His mouth opens and shuts and the thick eye trembles. —No, never, I never . . . I . . . wait . . .

He works very quickly and very cleanly to finish the cover.

He goes to the door and leans through. Hooks his arm for them to follow.

—Ach, for Chrissake.

—Don't, she says. Do not be nasty hey.

—Me! *I'm* the nasty one!

—Shhh.

She is following and Isaac goes after her. Ahead Moses checks the way, whistles a soft all-clear. At the next turn Isaac pulls her elbow. —Hell's he doing? She plucks loose and shushes him and they go on. Moses scouts them up through the pantry adjacent to the kitchen, through the laundry room and out the back unseen.

In one wall of the courtyard there is a low basement window inset in the bricks, with burglar bars in front and a deep windowsill at the bottom. Moses shows them they can sit back on the ledge as if it's a bench, into the hollow space of the window with the burglar bars against their backs. In here they are out of the sightlines of the windows above and screened by the fig trees to the front. In the dust under the ledge are the marks of many feet and the pinched butts of many a hand-rolled cigarette.

—Gosh I never even knew this was here! says Yvonne.

—He did, says Isaac, scuffing at a butt.

—If someone coming, I will say for you, says Moses, then leaves.

—Oh my gosh, says Yvonne. Oh my gosh this is so nice. So *nice* of him. Isn't it? Oh my gosh isn't he so *sweet*.

She has slipped into the hollow and is patting the hard ledge beside her. Isaac paws the dust with his foot for a while. —Izey wizey, she says. He sits and she pulls his arm across and works in close against him. —We've never been together all snuggly outside have we. We always go upstairs.

—What's so wrong with that?

—We don't always have to do the same thing.

—Right, says Isaac. Thinking: Yes we bladey do, all day forever and ever, the same thing on the soft bed, over and over. Only that.

—This is exciting hey. This is nice?

—Ja, lovely.

But he doesn't like sitting back in the shadow with the windowsill cold under his arse, the cold iron window bars hard against his spine.

He tries to kiss her ear but she wriggles. —Don't pretend.

—Ay?

—Pretend.

—Ach, do me a favour.

—You don't like it here do you.

—I do.

She leans away.

—What?

—No.

—What?

—I loathe it, pretending.

—I'm not pretending.

—I thought you never pretend. That's what I thought of you.

—I don't. You know I don't.

She looks away. He makes a gentle fist with the thumb on top. He looks at the thumb, then he fits the edge of the thumbnail between his front teeth.

She says, —People always want things, it gets me so despondent.

—Ja, Isaac says. Me too. *So* dependent. He clips off a little piece of nail, turns his head and spits at the butts.

She slides away. —Don't.

—So–rry. Jeez.

—I mean pretending. Don't give me pretend words. My whole

life is full of enough pretend words. My *friends*. Well, you've seen them. And Momsy and Dadsy . . .

He leans forward, elbows onto thighs. Another silence. He is looking down at the red dust under his heels, he rubs his palms together carefully, drily. —Oright. Oright.

What he feels now that makes it hard to look at her, to feel her without shying off, is that old sense of her claustrophobia: how it presses on him, like a heavy oilcloth over the mouth and nose, pressing.

—I'm serious, she says.

—I hear you.

—Do you?

He nods to himself. —Oright, you want honestly? Ukay, honestly I'd rather be in your room where it's soft and warm. And I don't like this gardenboy of yours knowing about us and it makes me want to coch up my lunch to think on how he was over there in the corner watching us.

She laughs. His head jerks.

He studies her, but the laughter is real and bright, a new mood just like that. This strangeness of girls, it's like clouds that keep shifting.

—Serious Ize, serious Isaac, she says, rubbing his back. So grumpy and wumpy. So dead serious about life. Deacon Isaac.

—Hey watch it, I'm a Jew.

—A Jewy poo. Deacon Ize the Jewy poo.

He wriggles against her. —You tell me you want honest then you laugh me out.

She opens her mouth like a clown. —She does what?

He just shakes his head while she giggles. —You want more truth, I can tell you my arse hurts on this thing. My nutsack is ganna freeze and snap off like a ice cream stick.

She snorts, breaking the giggle. —This? Mate, this doesn't even define as cool, never mind actual cold. You should go to Switzerland in ski season.

—I should hey. Ja well maybe next season when there's a special on.

—Oh Isaac.

— . . . You really been to Switzerland?

She nods.

—I can't even try imagine.

—Verbier is one of Da's faves, it's near Montreux on Lake Geneva. Momsy adores Montreux. And it *is* divine. There's this castle where Lord Byron signed his name on the wall and you can touch it. And the mountains are right on the lake with snow on top and mist around and they give you hot chocolate in these big bowls, with cream that floats. The cold makes your nose feel—

Isaac's looking past her, to the side: it's Moses jogging back. What now?

—Hulloh hulloh, sorry sorry. He has a blanket; inside it is wrapped a bottle and an opener.

—Oh my gosh how lovely, how lovely and thoughtful, Moses. But where did you get this? His smile shows big white teeth and very pink gums with wide gaps at the back. —Is from me, my room.

—You shouldn't have!

But he's already moving off, bobbing his head low. —Because me, I'm too sorry, he says. Now I keep my eye for you.

—Look at this! she says to Isaac.

He takes the bottle, watching Moses disappear, then looks at it in his hand, the label. —It's milk stout, he says. S'like kaffir beer. They love this stuff hey, but they not allowed to buy it. I seen okes at the bottle shop get it for them.

She takes it back. —I don't care what, it's sweet of him, oh it's so *sweet*.

—He probably all scared what'll happen if we tell on him, spying on us all sick like. He's caught such a skrik he reckons the cops ganna come arrest his arse.

— . . . God but you say some horrible things.

He looks quickly at her and the full mouth has compressed to a tight point. The female has changed. The female cloud is a new shape. She hates you now but don't panic, just be still and it'll pass like any cloud shadow does. Gently he lifts the bottle and the opener from her, levers off the tin cap. Her curiosity brings her face down to sniff the sweet yeasty tang. He nudges the bottle neck at her mouth; she won't take any so he has a swallow. He groans, shuts his eyes. —Ah so good, nothing like it.

—I thought you said it was just for Africans.

—And for Jews too, did I forget to say. Commie ones specially.

—Haw haw.

But she takes the bottle and has a nip. They pass it back and forth. The bittersweet taste of the dark milk stout makes a warmth in his belly and chest. After a while she keeps it from his hand. —No more for you, working man.

He smiles. The female has shifted. The female has changed her shape and mood again. They spread the blanket on the windowsill and sit on its warm padding. He decides it best not to say that he is glad it is not a blanket of Moses's, full of fleas and lice and whatnot, no, it's a nice White blanket that he's brought them from the proper linens cupboard in the house, fresh and clean. Now comes a feeling of warmth from the blanket and the heat from their young bodies close against one another while around them the shade is cool and a soft breeze brushes at their faces. As he sits he feels the light come on inside his chest, white and piercing, filling him.

—Yvesy.

—Yes.

—Why am *I* secret?

—Secret?

—You talk about pretending but why can't anyone see us together? Your people.

She makes a guttural noise that to him means, Don't be insane. She says: —Oh you want to bring a young man into the house with you after school? Certainly darling, no problem there at all. Take him up to your room. Absolutely.

She's giggling hard.

— . . .Yvesy.

—What?

—I mean you not embarrassed of me, are you?

—Don't talk silly.

—Really?

She puts her cheek on his shoulder. —Don't talk silly, silly Isaac. Deacon Isaac. Deacon worrypot Isaac silly talker.

So strange this is real, he thinks as he feels her shift against him like a cat. How afterwards it'll just be like a dream he's had, he'll be back at work in the clanging and the shrilling. You can't hold on to anything. —Don't pretend, he hears himself say. Don't you pretend with me.

—Never ever, she says softly into his neck.

—Then how about I come to the front door one of these days hey? Proper. No pretending. No sneaker.

— . . .

—Hey?

—No more sneaker.

—That's right, he says. Only straight and proper.

—You want to come to the front door, ding dong.

—Straight and proper.

Her breath is hot on his skin. He closes his eyes.

—Yvonne Linhurst, he says. Will you go on a date with me? A real date.

He feels her eyelashes brushing his skin, then she moves against him and her lips touch his ear. —Yes I'll go, she says. I'll go with Isaac, I will. Straight and proper on a real date.

—Ding dong.

From around the corner of their blanketed nook there comes a low soft whistle, pitched sharp: their warning. Giggling, juggling the blanket and the bottle of stout, they hurry to get inside and upstairs.

21.

NIGHTFALL COMES SO LATE NOW, Blacks have time to stand on hot Doornfontein corners after work, trading loud voices, gambling with worn cards, laughing. The air smells of cooking. Isaac Helger stops at Fleishman's to buy flowers.

From the buckets full of long stems he chooses roses and then he discards the non-perfect one by one. He doesn't need to ask prices because his pocket is full of cash; it was his name that came up at work for the kitty this month. He chooses the most expensive – proteas – and then discards the proteas and then decides to get the proteas after all, with lots of strelitzias and daisies and then, what the hell, white and pink roses also. Lovely. He doesn't like the pattern of the fancy paper. He makes Fleishman get another kind from the back. These are the first flowers he has ever bought, this gift for his mother. The outcome of a struggle between offending her sense of economy – because flowers are frivolous, useless – and doing something nice with his bonus to try to break this dragging mood of hers, for it is beginning to alarm him, no, is alarming him already, even more than he can admit to himself. Walking up Buxton Street, he burps whisky fumes into his left fist, his right hand holding the cone of pretty flowers out before him like a torch, perfectly upright and never squeezing too hard.

A sound makes him start to look and there's a shape in the door at number forty at the edge of his eye: the male bulk of it, the cruel watching. He keeps walking. Behind him reverberates the long rasping note of a big man hawking up dark slime from deep inside then the plop of it spat hard onto asphalt. There's a word spoken that he does not hear. It's possible to muscle your ears shut, a feeling like holding your breath.

Friday evening means Abel and Rively have left for shul already and it's also the reason he came home early, leaving the okes at the Great Britain Hotel to argue over the social acceptability of sideburns. When he steps in through the front door he finds his mother coming toward him wearing her good dress, the white one, with her dark ginger hair wetted and combed and clipped flat. He holds out the flowers. Both hands. —For you, Mame. Then he waits.

She only nods and motions, moves back to the kitchen.

Behind her he hears himself saying in Jewish, Don't you like them Mame? The upright cone is still in his hands and he despises the high pitch of the question.

Hugo Bleznik is sitting at the kitchen table. Hugo in his white shirt sleeves and starched collar, with a fat yellow tie knotted under his overlapping chins.

The Sabbath table is laid with the silver candlesticks and the wine goblets; the good smell of the fresh-baked loaf of kitka lifts from under the embroidered cloth.

—You shouldn't have hey Tiger. They beauties, but am I really worth it?

—Aw Christ.

—Ha ha. How're tricks, boychik?

—Tricks are your department.

—Nice one. He's a sharpie your boyki hey Mrs. Helger?

Mame has gone to the other side of the room to fold her arms and watch Isaac. Sit, she tells him.

He looks down at the flowers, wondering what to say. At last she takes them from him. Not even a kiss. The exchange feels soiled with Hugo watching. Hugo and his giant head, his fleshy face that settles in a rubberized grin as its natural posture, his quick easy blue eyes that watch everything, like some form of lizard life they seem to need no blinking.

Sit with Hugo, Mame says, turning to the sink.

But Hugo Bleznik is already rising, saying that it's okay, lifting his jacket, tan cashmere with ivory buttons, off the back of the chair, he wants to have a cigar anyway and they'll get out of her hair while she makes her delicious supper. Isaac, reluctant, goes with him only after his mame makes nudging eyes over her shoulder.

In the night air: —You got some chutzpah coming here.

—Why's that?

—After that Miracle Glow shit, I'm surprised Ma didn't kick your tochus into the street.

Hugo bites off the back of his cigar with that ferocious grin. He lights up, runs a palm over the hairs plastered to his skull. —Boyki, what exactly is it you are tryna incite about me?

Isaac picks up a stone and throws it hard; it chips off the outhouse. —What are you doing here man?

Hugo gnaws the cigar. —Such aggro. You won't listen on the telephone, what else is the option?

—You the one who won't listen. I've told you clear as a bell I dunno how many times.

—Tiger, you haven't even heard the proposition.

—I'm not interested, Hugo. My days are chockablock.

—Listen to this little grease monkey now.

—What did you say?

—All right, get off your high horse, Mr. Not Interested.

—I don't need you, Hugo.

— . . . Don't talk down on me, junior. I've had more in my change pocket than you've seen your whole life.

—Ja, and wherezit now?

—Woo boy.

—And what do you know about the motor game anyhow?

Hugo pulls the cigar from his mouth. —Oh shit, he says. Oh shit, I see it now.

—What?

—Something's happened. Tell me I'm wrong.

—Nothing's *happened*.

The cigar hovers like a pointing finger. Isaac pushes it down.

—The female, Hugo says. That's the bladey twist here. The female has gotten hold of him. Tell me I'm wrong.

—Hugo, says Isaac, go and get stuffed. He walks to the door. Behind him Hugo rumbles: the bass chuckle of a very knowing man.

The plan gets outlined on the Sabbath table. How many fingertips formed like birds' beaks have thumped tables over such proposals in the life of a man like Hugo Bleznik? The decimated plates of sweet herring and chopped liver sprinkled with powdered egg pushed aside, the last balls of gefilte fish and the bones of the roast chicken gone cold with pumpkin mash. The candles have burned to stubs that will soon expire. Abel and Rively have sung the grace after meals. The bronze samovar smokes and steams and Mame pours out more glasses in silver holders of amber tea with the seedy jam that sinks to the bottom. Even Rively has been held by Hugo, by his impending Great Idea. Only Isaac leans back with folded arms.

Hugo tips salt onto his fleshy palm. A fat man in shirt sleeves with the sleeves folded up, hairless fatman forearms. That giant globe of a skull with the side part plastered down. He blows on the salt to show its cheapness. —But say, he says, say there's no more salt in the world. Then every grain becomes a gold nugget. He picks up the shaker. What is it that will transmute the pale grains of salt into shining gold? It is war. Hugo thinks there will be a war.

Isaac hisses at him, looking quickly at Mame – but her face is calm.

This war will not be quick, Hugo is saying, it will be longer than the last one and it will be fought with bigger machines, enormous machines. The last one will be a tea party compared to this.

—That's bull, Isaac says. Such bull. You don't know. They signed for peace!

Mame shushes him.

Hugo chuckles. Now he comes back to how it started with Isaac. Isaac's really the one. Isaac stands at the root of this transmuting dream: he showed how all those rusted scrap vehicles that they saw on the farms in the platteland, those corpses of steel and glass, were truly repositories of hidden value. They are full of working parts and they are made of scrap metal. When this war gets rolling, Hugo says, I bet that there will be no new metal and no new parts – all of it will go into the fighting machines. Now the scrap vehicles are salt; tomorrow, soon, they will be gold.

Mame says, But those farmers, they can also sell for more then.

Hugo rubs his hands. The objection like a dessert dish placed before him. His tongue moistens the wide grin. Mrs. Helger, I'm so very happy that you asked that.

From his jacket he brings out folded documents. Contracts in a rich sheaf. Just a sample of many hundreds (he says). What he has done (he says) is gotten the farmers and other country gentlemen to sign with him for the removal of their junked vehicles from their said properties. —Best part is that I got *them* to pay *me*.

No.

Yes. Listen: Hugo tells them how these farmers would love to get the wrecks off their land, only towing costs too much. So he offered to do it for a price they couldn't say no to.

—A loss leader, he says. I reckon they were laughing behind their hands. They caught a Jew! But I'm the one who's getting a little something to cover my supply costs. And a contract isn't enforceable less money changes hand, and I got down payments on them all! You see how there's the best part. I've taken these contracts to the finance firms and I factored them for my capital. Enough for a down payment on a plot with a building in the East Rand and to put for the trucks on hire purchase. Man, I'm ready to move on this thing!

His excitement has come in a rush of English that Rively has to explain to Abel and Mame while Isaac toys with a fork, watching his fingers.

Yes, Hugo has capital assembled. He has his property organized, his trucks. He is shining up. And here he has come to offer the opportunity to shine up with him.

Rively is the first one to rise, she's late for the political meeting, Yankel will be worried. Isaac glances at her, her voice has changed. —Mr. Bleznik, I'm sure you'll do very well out of it if it comes war, God forbid. While other men go fighting to keep you safe.

Hugo's smile escapes blemish. —Why, thank you, my dear.

Abel is next. He limps around behind Hugo, curves one of his long-fingered hands over Hugo's shoulder. I want to wish you a good Sabbath and much success, but for an *investhment*, I'm sorry to say—

—Neyn, Mr. Helger, ich zooch nit fur kayn investment.

I'm not looking for an investment.

—Ah vos?

He doesn't want our money, says Mame. He wants Isaac to come work for him.

Not for, Hugo says in Jewish. *With*. He looks at Isaac. —I'm offering a piece of the business. A share. A partnership.

Partnership. Mame knows the word.

Abel's mouth bends down, his chin sways. —I don't shinks so. Vot you shinks, Yitzchok?

Isaac has been making that fork cartwheel over and back.
—Hu uh, he says. I am an apprentice, class A. And I don't like all
this jawing about war. Not ganna be any war.

—Dat's it. Dat's it, my boy. A champion.

Mame's face doesn't twitch; it hardens like plaster. The scar
turns slowly livid. Abel says good night, he is tired and will be at
shul early in the morning, hard praying to be done. He limps away
and Isaac doesn't look up from the busy fork, not once.

In the night, summer rain eases onto the corrugated iron roof of
number fifty-two Buxton and a droplet worms through one of the
rusted scabs in the roof and falls onto the cheek of Isaac Helger
asleep on his canvas cot. He lies there in the sweet weakness of
a black sleep still clinging and he listens to the whispering of the
rain. It will be bad with his mother in the morning. There are
certain lines of tension that have been pulling for a long time in
her and in him and there will be a break in the morning, he knows
this as surely as he knows by the feel of his tapping hammer when
a dent in the steel curve of a broken vehicle is about to pop out
clean. He slides under into the dreams again and is dreaming of
working on a car in the clanging shop when it turns so loud that it
forces him out of his dream and he opens his eyes to find the workshop brimming with pale first light and the roof and the walls and
the windows rattling and thudding and scratch-noising with countless little impacts like the scurrying feet of some pestilent invasion.

He goes to the front door and opens it and feels a rush of cool
air in the sudden staccato blare of louder noise. The white hailstones
are hitting the street and the other roofs like juggler balls. African
hail the size of golf balls, the white balls bouncing off the asphalt
and veering off the cars and appearing to dance on the rooftops as
if the rooftops are vibrating. A man runs with a newspaper spread
over his head. In the gutters the collected hailstones drift like paint
chips and heap up on the drains. He puts out his hand and gets his

palm stung then catches one and puts it into his mouth, presses its cold hardness to his palate. The water has a chemical taste. Gold mine water, he thinks.

Later in the kitchen he cups a hot mug of tea to his lips and says goodbye to Abel and Rively off to shul. It's him and Mame now, her in her slippers and her nightgown keeping her back to him. He has a vague need for a cigarette that he quashes. He puts down the mug and walks to the counter and back, one hand rubbing the back of his neck. —Ma. I wanna ask you summin.

She doesn't answer. He opens his mouth to say, Ma, can you look at me please, can you just do that? Then he sees through the window over the sink down into the open rubbish bin outside. On top of the old tins and the potato skins and dappled over with the white nuggets of the hailstones are fanned out the broken stems of the strelitzias. The rest takes a moment to recognize: the maroon pollen fluff of the shredded proteas, the scraps of the wilted almost black petals of the ruined daisies, the rose petals torn to bits. Just throwing them out wasn't good enough; had to be ripped on top of it. He looks at it and he feels it in the belly, low down. He sees his wide-eared face in the glass looking down on the floral carnage, the reeking farshtunkene rubbish, looking through himself at it. Oright. Don't give her any bladey satisfaction. Don't you let her see a thing in your face.

She's finished with the sink and starts to leave the room. He moves past her and closes the door and stands in front of it. She lifts her chin at him: the stretched scar turning livid. Then she turns around and heads for the backyard door.

—Where you going? Fetch your chopper?

That stops her.

In Jewish: Get your axe and come and get my hands.

She looks at him and he holds up his right hand and chops at it with the edge of his left. Then it won't be able to do my *job*.

You like to hurt your mother, she says.

—Ja, that's me. Stupid me. I'm king of the bladey fools.

What's happened to you Isaac?

—No Ma, it's you.

She shakes her head. Touches the buried pouches under her eyes, sad eyes now. Isaac, my little Isaac.

I'm not little anymore, Mame.

Then why do you talk like a baby child? You get an offer from Bleznik and no, like a child you want to better play with your hammers instead.

—I'm going out.

Yes, go. The truth is hard.

He stands hunched in the doorway, his neck shivering. Just cos you don't understand doesn't mean I'm not proud of what I do. All you care about is what you want.

She snorts. Is that what you think?

Ma—

Is that what you think, it's for me?

A house, a house, a house. Yes for you! You and your piggish house!

He shouldn't have said it. Now he has to stand and watch while his mother who is shorter than him, his squat scar-faced little mother, standing there in her nightgown, his mother who never cries, slowly gets moisture in the eyes above her mutilated cheek.

He bites his lip and hits the door jamb with the heel of his palm hard enough to jar him to the shoulder. Then he goes towards her but she holds out her own palm.

—I'm sorry, Ma. I shouldn't have.

His mother presses a dishcloth to her face. There is only one thing that I live for, Isaac. Our family.

—I know, Ma. I'm sorry.

We are here but where are my sisters, Isaac, your uncles and nephews and nieces?

Isaac gnaws on his lips, swallows. It helps a little but still he has to bring the crook of his arm to the bridge of his nose, blotting.

They are my dreams if I manage sleep. More than your hammers. To bring them safe. You don't know what war is. We need money for this, real money. And with Bleznik comes a chance.

—No, Mame, not true. Can't be done anymore. There's a law now, the Aliens, you know it.

She gives him a quick knife-sharp look. You let me worry about that! Here you have a chance for real money we can use!

Isaac shakes his head, touching his eyes, looking down. —Bleznik. Come on. Remember last time, pushing that Miracle drek. I came back without a penny.

Yes, that didn't work. So? You don't think *this* idea is good?

He grimaces, his head see-sawing, conceding. But he keeps on not following her into the language of backhome, keeping the aural distance that marks the division of this country between them, how he belongs to it in a way she never could: —Maybe it is, ja. But Ma, I don't want you to get your hopes all up.

Don't worry about me! *You* should try. You! You can only try. That's all that I am asking. You want to go back to your job after, then go. But now is this chance from God.

He keeps shaking his head.

For your family.

He goes into the other room and she follows. He turns: —You didn't have to throw them out in the rubbish.

—Ah vos?

—I bought you them for a present. For you, Ma. For you.

Her face crimps, a bitter look. Ach, better keep such little presents for your girlfriend.

His turn now to be stopped, at the front of the workshop. —My what?

Yes, yes, and it's true it's a goyisher girl isn't it. A fancy one.

—Who told you this?

Nobody has to say. You going round like a dreamwalker. You think this goyish girl will fix everything but you don't know the goyim. What they do to us in the end. Never trust anyone but your own, Isaac. Family.

—Ma.

You have forgotten what you promised me all your life.

He starts to pace, hands on his hips, like someone walking off pain. —Who told you about her? Was it him, was it Bleznik?

She shrugs.

—I'll skop him in his fat belly, says Isaac.

It doesn't matter who.

—It's a secret, he says, his voice twisting. Another bladey secret. I'm sick a your bladey secrets!

He picks up the cashbox and shakes it at her.

What are you doing?

Now he has the box in a headlock with one hand and he's stabbing it with the forefinger of his other, his voice lifting and at last thrusting back into the intimacy of Yiddish. In here, in here, isn't it, all your secrets that you won't tell anyone. Uh? True? Do I lie? You heard about a goyish girlfriend, well I heard about *this*, yes!

And his hand, his angered demon hand, jumps of its own will to his chin and pokes there.

Mame makes a noise – *oosh* – that is the sound of someone being elbowed in the belly. She sags against a workbench.

He drops the cashbox back. There, it's done now.

When he looks up her face is like chalk, her face too has sagged. He watches her move slowly away, hears the door of her room close, softly but solidly.

He goes out and walks in the washed streets where steam is already beginning to lift as the sky clears. He needs a drink. He still needs a cigarette. It gives him pain to ignore these needs and the pain is good. He feels it would be good and satisfying to drive a steel nail into his gum or to scratch flesh from his forearm with a wire brush till it runs.

At home, Mame's door is still shut but he can hear her shifting around inside, thumping. He knocks very gently. He expects the door to open a crack and to see half of her chalk face, her sad eye. He must apologize from his heart, he must explain everything.

The door swings wide and Mame is there in a clean pressed skirt and a good blouse, with her hair clipped down. Her handbag dangles from the crook of her left arm and in her other hand she is holding the cashbox by the handle.

Can you borrow a car from your work? Otherwise I want you to go to the Altmans' and ask them for their Austin.

Mame?

Me and you – we're going for a trip.

What about Tutte and Rively?

I left for him a note, don't you worry. We'll be back by tonight. Tomorrow morning latest. Go and get the car.

Mame?

Hurry quickly now. It's time for this. Past time.

PART TWO

Lion's Rock

22.

AFTERWARDS, PARKED IN FRONT of the Standard Bank, nine o'clock in the morning with a little dew still evaporating at the bottom of the windshield, and yellow-beaked birds peeping and cawing in a nearby palm tree, Mame asks him if he understands, and he can only shake his head. She has the cashbox on her lap and she unlocks it and lifts out the cash tray. He watches her put the bank savings book back into an envelope, down amongst the secret papers. Five minutes ago he was with her inside the Standard Bank with its cool marble floor deserted, the two of them the earliest customers already waiting as the manager unlocked the door. He watched Mame use her bankbook from the cashbox to obtain eighty-five pounds, two shillings and three-pence in cash, the lady behind the wicket counting it out twice because Mame wasn't happy with the first time. Draining the bankbook account of every penny so that they can be on their way, except that Isaac still has no idea where to.

Now Mame – calmly, slowly – is showing him the secret papers. There are letters, many letters (his old suspicions are right about that); there are her and Abel's immigration documents from years ago; there are copies of title deeds; copies of Lithuanian citizenship documents; of birth certificates for her family in der haym; of all their passports.

It's their lives all here. Everything. Now you understand?

Yes.

Did you steal a look into my things here?

I would never do that, Mame. How could you even ask?

She doesn't answer, bends around to put the cashbox in the back as it was before, under a blanket. He looks forward while she works at this, grunting a little. Then she says, So you talk about me behind my back. Gossip. Your own mother.

He starts to say I didn't, but there's no point. She's sitting back level in her seat now, neither of them looking at each other. After a time she says, Tell me what it is you think that you know about your mother.

I've got a big mouth, he says.

What does that mean?

I said what I shouldn't have. I don't know anything.

I'm not one of your car cronies. Talk straight to your mother.

He inhales slowly and deeply.

Isaac. What is it you think that you know?

I'll tell you.

Good. I want this to be a cleaning out, right now and here. Everything. Before you start to drive. It needs to be cleaned out between us.

Cleaned out.

She makes a gesture toward the back. I've shown you what is in there. Now you tell me what is in here, hidden. And she presses warm fingertips to his temple.

He takes another heavy breath. That box, he says. One day I looked in the front window and I saw you crying with it. Then someone on the street said you weren't sick.

Sick?

I always thought your face, the thing you wore to cover it, was a sickness.

Did I ever tell you sick? Did Tutte?

No. I don't know. But Dr. Graumann . . .

And this someone on the street said what?

Said something bad happened. I asked some questions. They said a pogrom. I found out about . . .

Yes, about?

It's good that they are sitting facing forward because he couldn't have done this facing her, her eyes, across a table or on their feet. Never. He speaks the date.

She sighs, sighs again: weary sounds filling the interior. People make grannystories, Isaac. I'm surprised you a grown-up man now doesn't know this.

It's not true?

They make grannystories. Tell me what.

Isaac's shoulders lift and fall. Bad things happened and one of those bad things happened to you. That's all. Nobody said more to me.

—Yitzchok.

—Ja Ma?

Are you lying to me?

Surprised, Isaac blinks. No.

Here and now. Is this all that you know?

Yes.

Everything?

Yes.

Good. I will tell what happened. First you promise – no more questions behind your mame's back. No more grannystories on her. I am the only one that knows the truth of me.

—Ja, Ma.

Yes?

Yes Mame.

You swear to your mother.

He glances at her and she's staring at him now. Serious as a wall of iron. I do, he says.

She doesn't speak, he waits motionless. Then: It was an accident, Isaac. I was riding with a cart to get away. The cart fell over. No, not sick, but hurt. That's all.

A kind of dizzy cloud moves behind his eyes.

The dead look backwards. There's never a good reason for the living to.

I know.

Do you?

I feel scared, Mame.

Don't be.

Why did you take all that money out? I never knew you had so much.

Don't worry, it's only mine, not yours or Tutte's. It's my hard work for a long time. Don't be scared. You'll see.

He thinks of all the brandy bottles, the sewing, the broken furniture repaired; the sum is more than he can earn in a year as an apprentice. He turns to her and tries a smile but feels its crookedness on his face. Only forward, he says.

That's right, she says. My love. My Clever.

Her hand cups the nape of his neck and he lets his head be tilted in to her, feels the kiss on his brow, the harsh scar tissue on one side of it. Are you ready now to go forward with me, my love?

Yes Mame.

Good. Good. Then start up the car.

23.

SIX HOURS THEY DRIVE in the borrowed Austin, stopping once for petrol. First through the west Rand outside of Johannesburg and then into veld, brown grasses and mielie fields made haggard by drought. Little dorps with names like Black Hole and Death River. Beehive huts or shanty cubes of the Black villages. It's like the Miracle Glow trip only going the opposite way.

They stop for final directions in Lichtenburg; he has to ask for Bakerville. The men he talks to call it Bakers. The flat land on both sides of the road has been grassed till now, but now when they go on the country changes. Paved road turns to rutted track that splits off to paths like veins into veins. The dry grasses have been ripped away and the red and bonewhite soil exposed and dug down into to make deep potholes and shallower pits like so many graves abandoned between piled mounds of gravel. Crumbled edges of plots abandoned are strewn with rotting claim sticks and wires laid flat or snarled in their rusting. Flagpoles flutter rags. They have to keep the windows up against the dust. Mame is telling him all about this place when they see the first workers, distant lonely forms in the heat ripples. These parts are called the diggings because years before there was a diamond rush, men running from everywhere in the world for a chance to find a diamond like the one a farmer turned up while digging a trench to dip cattle. Turned out there were plenty: diamonds lying everywhere on the surface or just under like ordinary stones. It was too early for Isaac to have remembered but Mame does. A fortune in bright stones was lifted, but the findings ran down and now only a few diehards still cling on, those labourers like tethered smoke. Closer, the vapours harden into shirtless Blacks with hats and suspenders, the long crescents of their picks lifting and dipping or shovels stabbing low. By a long table, some Whites work with big squares of wire, shaking them hard over water barrels. Mame says some of the diamonds once found here were stones too big for the crowns of European princes, picked up by hand sitting on the dirt like so many bird eggs under the naked sky.

Bakers is a tin town. Raw streets. Rust and boards. A man on a horse with a hanky tied over the bottom of his face. A stripped-down Ford flatbed hoo-hawing at him to move over more in the narrow track. Faint piano notes plink from a corner tavern and men with hands in their pockets stand in front and watch them, a blank unshaven dirtcollared watching. From the windows above women with bright faces dangle cleavage.

Mame says, You will have to stop and to ask.

Yes.

A Mr. Suttner.

—Suttner, whozat?

Go ask.

He watches her for a span then pulls over and reaches down with his left to the T-bar of the handbrake and cranks it back and gets out and walks across the street, stiff down his back and into both legs from all the day's driving. No relief of coolness in this tin-beaten place, this treeless reservoir of hot wind from the great desert to the northwest.

He tries some lizard-eyed men on the corner; when he says he wants Suttner they move around him. A knife comes out, lifts. Without thought he pushes it away and someone punches him in the cheekbone with brass knuckles: a drilling pain that makes his eyes water. They press him to a tin wall. Someone runs out and

waves both arms and when Isaac looks down the street there's
a tan Nash LaFayette coming up very slowly, the wheels crunching
on the grit. He sees a Black behind the wheel and on the passenger
side a long arm hanging out that sways like a great pendulum.
Two faces in the back.

A nervous feeling from the men around him as the Nash pulls
up. Isaac looks at the passenger: a tough face and Asiatic eyes, flat
nose and milk-coffee skin. He lifts a thumb to prod up his hat
brim, a homburg. —You bleeding, jong, he says to Isaac. An
accent and slang word for lad that confirms he's a Coloured. And
there's Hottentot blood there also, Isaac thinks, looking at the
slant of the eyes. Maybe even a touch of Bushman.

Meanwhile he presses his cheek, examines red fingertips.

The knifer bends to the window. —Andre, he looking for
chief he says. Says it to me all cocky.

—What you got? says this Andre to Isaac. What you want?

Isaac eyes the faces in the back of the Nash; one of them has
one of those little moustaches sharp on both sides and a mouse
face over a bow tie.

—Who you? says Isaac.

—See, see, says knifer. Cocky little bustud.

The door opens and Andre comes down over the running
board like spilled quicksilver, a very lean tall gentleman with the
collar loose around his weathered neck. Wearing a green tie and
grey suit with the homburg. —Who is it you are looking for here?

—Mr. Suttner, says Isaac. He glances past the Nash and down
the road to the Austin with Mame in it facing the other way and
Andre's eyes follow the motion. Andre whistles a quick cutting
note. —Hai! he gestures to the ones in the back then circles his
hand in the air and they slip out and swing up onto the running
boards and stand looking back toward the Austin as the Nash revs
and moves off.

—Put your hands out to your sides.

—What?

—Like this.

Isaac lifts his arms, watching the Nash U-turn and drive out to the Austin. —Hey man, where they going?

—Don't move.

This Andre patting his sides, feeling his waist, bending down to touch his ankles even.

—It's my ma there man, what they doing?

—Your who?

—My ma. My *mother*, man, that's all. What the hell they doing? Who're you?

The quick patting hands – knowing touch of an expert – have done with his shanks, he can let his arms down and Andre looks back up the road where the car is beside the Austin. Now one of the men is leaning into the window. He climbs back onto the board and gives an easy wave. Andre lifts up his own thumb, turns back to Isaac. While he's been faced away a number of the men have left, first backing up then spinning and jogging.

—What you people want with Mr. Suttner?

Looking at the Austin, Isaac says: —S'a family thing.

—What you mean family?

—My ma, she would like to see him.

—Who's your ma?

Isaac shrugs. —Family thing. We the Helgers. We come all the way from Joburg. I promise you, ask her.

Isaac watches this sinking into Andre, Andre nodding. Meanwhile more of the men have skittered off; but when the knifer starts to go Andre looks up and clicks his tongue. —Uh uh, he says. And he points for him to stand over there.

A pulsing grimace has taken hold of the knifer's face. He drops the blade like a hot iron. He starts to speak then wheezes.

— . . . Andre . . .

—Be quiet.

The wheezing sounds like a hole in working bellows.
— . . . diden know, Andre . . .

The Nash has U-turned again and its thin needling nose with
the narrow radiator has started back toward them. The new model,
Isaac thinks. A hundred horsepower from six cylinders and a
clever new kind of heater that sucks in air from outside. Andre
looks at the knife on the dust. —That yours?

The knifer says no five times, shaking his head, criss-crossing
his hands with spread fingers so quickly that they blur.

—Pick it up, says Andre. Then he looks at Isaac. —Sorry
about this hey.

—It's oright, says Isaac.

The car is almost back. —Pick it up, says Andre.

—No no, says the knife man.

—Not ganna say again.

Another man steps forward. —Get it, he tells the knifer.

—You can shut up, says Andre. The man looks down.

The knifer stoops for his weapon. This Andre makes a short
motion with his left hand, as if he's waving a fly off the back of the
bent neck, stepping out and back to the bowed man with a long-
legged stride easy as a dance step. He's next to Isaac and he's over
there and he's back: the whole of it at once without strain and the
knife man falls on his face and lies still, snoring heavily in the dust.
His hand is awkward on the hilt of the blade, twisted under the
wrist angled up. Andre puts his dancer's foot on it and makes a
quick swivel; certain small bones drily crackle.

Andre moves to the car and opens the passenger door. When
Isaac steps up to get in he glances down from the running board and
sees the stocks of rifles on the floor at the feet of the men in the back,
and pickaxe handles and one or two pangas. He sits on the passenger
seat and Andre shuts the door and stays on the running board. As
they pull off Isaac sees him point his hand shaped like a gun, making
it shoot, pow, and the man standing there that he told to shut up

tries to grin but sits down slowly in the dust as if plugged truly through the belly. When Isaac looks at Andre he can see up in the armpit under the jacket that he is wearing a real pistol, a flat black semi-automatic like the guns in the Warner movies that he's watched in the Alhambra on Friday and Saturday nights. This is not good. What is this? A numbness. How nothing else can be done.

When they reach the Austin, Andre gives him a hanky. —Better maybe if you don't tell your old lady how it happened, keep it calm.

Isaac nods, pressing cloth to cheek.

In the side mirror he sees this Andre get into the Austin then the Austin passes them and he sees Mame looking at him through the windshield and he waves but she doesn't wave back. The Austin goes in front and they follow after. When the bleeding has stopped he uses the hanky to clean the dust off both shoes.

They are taken across to a better side of town, brick buildings and one of them with a sign, Orange River Trading Co., Proprietor Abraham J. Suttner Esq. Inside is a big clean shop full of miner's wares and above is an office with a lawyer named Papendropolous. Waiting for this man, Mame wants to know how Isaac hurt his cheek; he says he caught it on the car door. The lawyer proves to be short and rotund, bald on top, with a spaniel nose and olive skin. Mame refuses to believe he is not a Jew, keeps talking only in Jewish to him.

—I regret I can't understand you, madam.

Says Mame: —Ret mameloshen, chulleriuh!

Speak mother's tongue, you cholera.

The lawyer looks at Isaac.

—She says she's pleased to meet you.

Mame says, You tell him, this crook, tell him we are family of Mr. Suttner.

Family, says Isaac. What the hell Mame? I don't know any Suttner.

Just tell *him*.

Papendropolous coughs, asks who exactly they are.

Why should I answer him? says Mame. Who does he think he is to ask me – God? Look at him so arrogant.

He works for Mr. Suttner, Ma.

She grimaces, huffs. Avrom Suttner is my nephew.

Mame?

My nephew. I am his auntie. We have come to see him all the way from Joburg and no one here has even offered a cup of tea, a piece of a rusk, nothing – disgust on them all. Scandal and disgust.

Auntie? *What?*

Isaac. Clean your ears.

—Jesus Christ, Ma.

Don't say Yoshka to your own mother. And she leans over to mock-spit with force onto the soft carpet. A gesture that causes Papendropolous to angle slightly forward and peer over the edge of his desk; but when Ma whips her eyes onto him again he leans back with a slow creak.

Ma, what are you talking nephew all of a sudden?

By my brother Hershel.

What brother, what Hershel? I never. You're joking.

Do I look like a clown?

No one ever told me a Hershel. You never showed me any picture.

You don't know. You don't know the whole long scroll of a story and there's no time now to start into it. Just tell this man auntie. Tell him I want to see my nephew.

—This lady, my ma, she's the auntie of this Mr. Suttner hey.

—I see.

—Mr. Suttner's her nephew, like. That's why we drove in all the way from Joeys. To meet him, see.

—There's an appointment.

—Ja, there's it, ay.

The corners of the lawyer's mouth twitch once very slightly.

24.

ISAAC IS BEHIND THE WHEEL of the Austin again, this time following the Nash with Andre and his blank-faced friends in it. Following them to The Farm, which it seems is the home of Mr. Suttner who has agreed by telephone to see them but only after a very long and very tense wait where Mame made it clear that they *were* going to this farm to see her nephew, that's what they had come all the way from Joburg for, and no one and nothing was going to persuade her otherwise.

Isaac has held his tongue, is concentrating on the driving. He will wait for her to tell about his cousin, this mystery nephew of hers, this mystery brother Hershel; it's beneath him to have to ask, for a part of him feels badly hurt that he's been left in such ignorance all this time. But Mame doesn't speak either.

An hour and a half passes. Around a long curve there appears a line of eucalyptus trees with their pale twisted trunks and leaves like paper streamers, the line of them stretching off. They drive parallel with the trees and turn in at an arched gateway beyond which a paved road bends. A timber board over the gate hangs down from chains with the name *Leeuklip* burned into it – Lion's Rock. In the lead car the driver is out and opening the gate while Andre is on the running board, his face turning as he scans a circle.

They drive on for another half an hour, sometimes passing through openings in low wire fences, over cattle grids that judder the Austin's suspension. The land is rolling and grassed, with distant clumps of browsing cattle, their long necks dipping and lifting.

The house they reach is large and white on a rise. In the slanted light that hits greenish on the wild grass the house looks like a painting Isaac has maybe seen before, the clean lines and whitewashed walls, the Cape Dutch curve on the top in the front shaped like buffalo horns with the thatch roof behind very dark and then in the distance the line of hills humped low back from the block shadows of the falling day.

Closer, there's an oval full of flowers in front that the driveway loops around.

Mame squeezes Isaac's thigh. Stop here. Stop it here.

—Ma—

Here!

So he parks the Austin on the far side of the flowers while the Nash drops Andre off, then drives on around the back of the house. Mame talks urgently to him while Andre looks back at them from the stoep with its red tile floor and a maid on her knees with a bucket, scrubbing.

She tells him to wait here, to sit in the car, not to come out until she comes and gets him, will he promise her.

—Ja, oright.

She wants him to swear to it.

—Aw Christ, he says, another swear? How many bladey swears do you want from me in a day, Ma?

But he does nod, he swears to wait. Mame gets out and walks around the flower bed to Andre on the stoep. The maid sits back on her heels and shades her eyes to look up as the two of them pass inside. The engine ticks in its cooling. He watches the maid resume, working her slow knee-shuffling way across the big stoep with brush and bucket. Cicadas pulse the dry scentless air. He fidgets against the stickying heat, probes at his tender cheekbone, picks a fleck of crust from the inside of one nostril. The maid has gone in.

When Ma appears he restrains himself from jumping out; he crosses to the porch with hands in his pockets. Up out of the evening light and across the polished tiles, into a hallway cool and dark: his eyes grope out the shape of a tasselled lamp on a sideboard, the head of a kudu with beads for corneas. Mame's face looms, stern as plaster. A form deeper in glides forward on the rug. Isaac takes in the khaki safari shorts, the rolled-up sleeves of a white shirt with collar unbuttoned. Sandals. A slanted ruler of light from the doorway slides up his chest to show a round face with heavy cheeks, the skin with the gnawed look of pimples long ago healed around small dark eyes. Not an old man – thirty-five, thirty-seven – but the hair stroked back from the wide brow is thinning and frosted. What is it that makes the animal presence of another human? There's a moment where they all three stand and inhale whatever it is that they are. Isaac wondering if he should embrace this fleshblood of his. His heart drums and he looks to Mame, who inclines her head so very slightly. He crosses to the man.

They are sitting at a long and gleaming stinkwood table, the coffee urn and the teapot radiate heat through skins of polished silver, there are sandwiches without crusts on china platters, there are two cakes, one round, one square. But Isaac can't stop looking at his mother's hand, how it rubs at the varnished wood in a nervous motion he has never seen before from her as she's telling him about her much older brother Hershel whom she hardly remembers, hardly knew. This Hershel was a vilderchuyu, a wilding animal of a boy; still young he ran to the far-off city of great Vilna with its red castles and cobblestone streets. Who can say why, what it was that got into him, only God, or more likely the Evil One. Mame telling of the scandal of how he then had a baby with a woman he did not marry, this child was Avrom and her name was Suttner, which he took for himself, and so here he is, Avrom Suttner, a man across the table. He is my nephew and he is your cousin.

My blood, Isaac thinks, trying not to stare. I'm tied in to this place. He asks about Hershel, where he is today.

Mame says he passed away young. Very sad. Isaac gives in to examining the bulldog face that watches him back and makes no comment, Isaac trying to find resemblances there, perhaps in the nose, the shape of the jaw? But the flesh yields nothing. He settles on a certain feeling of congealed will within, an iron core: some gravity of inner resolve that this cousin and his mother both have and exude.

He's an only child, says Mame. His mother raised him up herself, in Skopishok. She too, rest in peace, passed away. Then he came by himself to Africa.

Avrom clears his pipes with a deep cough. He sits solidly in his seat, well back from the table with his hands on wide-parted thighs, both sandals flat, he would not be easy to lift or push over. —You're the oldest.

—No, says Isaac. My sister, Rively, she's a year ahead.

Mame says: You would know this if you'd read. You don't even know their ages. She has lifted her handbag onto the tabletop and she opens it, takes out bundled envelopes tied in a string. You can ask my son, she says, how I cry over letters, like a baby. He has seen me himself. And these you sent me back every single one. Not even opened.

When I saw you last time, says Avrom, I wasn't even ten. Auntie. I remember you had a cloth on your face, covering.

Mame tells him about Dr. Graumann, the pain she went through.

Avrom looks at Isaac. —Maybe it's better you go outside. Wait while we discuss.

Stay here, says Mame.

The bulldog face doesn't change, with stocky fingers he pinches at the loose skin of his elbow.

She says, And if I telephone here, still no, nothing. Until we have to drive through half the country.

Avrom: —Must really want to see me. And there is hollowness in the eyes over the parody of a small smile: this sombre globular face full of something like a sneer, only harsher.

What does that mean?

Means what it means.

Say what you want to say.

If I was living under a bridge, says Avrom.

What?

A silence.

Of course I would still come, says Mame. *Especially* I would come.

—Really.

The squat cynicism in that English word, the way he hunkers behind his small eyes. Isaac has the feeling of the man's self-encasement in the pocked shell of that skin. So much interior distance from the world that nothing can reach into him.

Because you are family.

—Oh is that so, he says softly. Then: —How's your English, Gitelle?

—Can say veruh well tank you.

—Good. Then let me put this another way. How much?

—Ah vos?

—How much do you want?

Mame elongates herself in the chair, her head rising to the top of a stiffening back. You think I need from you charity? That I come for myself?

—No, worse. You brought your son for it too.

She hisses. That is a vile vile thing to say to me. Yes I brought him. Yes, you must remember that people are alive and not just a word on paper.

His chin moves a little to the left; there's no other motion. I told you send him out, does he understand us?

You stay exactly here Isaac. I want you to see the man that your cousin is.

Avrom folds in his left arm and puts the right elbow on the left wrist and starts to stroke at his face with his fingers, tracing the pockmarks there.

A vile thing, she says.

Vile, he says. I never begged in my life. Begging to me is vile. Does he see that?

Mame hisses again in her next breath, louder, as if she's burned herself.

Avrom creaks in the chair, looks at Isaac. I was much smaller than you when I came by myself. Not one soul, not one penny. The sky for a roof and hunger for an only friend. The debt for my ticket on my back. I shovelled out the crap of ostriches. I was filthy down in a mine with the Blacks. I shlepped skins in an abattoir, my one finger still has no feeling. That debt almost broke me into tiny pieces.

He looks back to Gitelle, dead-eyed. Funny, nobody lined up to help. Nobody knew me then, nobody tried to find me. Now when I get a beautiful letter from Skopishok or Dusat, from New York, London, Doornfontein, I know it will call me *dearest* Avrom. Lots of love. And by the way, send a few thousand quick.

She blinks in silence. Then: Do you think I come here for myself?

By the way, he says, the dead hollowness floating in his eyes.

We are family, she says.

I sweated my blood, Gitelle, I paid off my debt. Other people can pay their own.

Mame waits, then speaks in a voice that makes Isaac's skin prickle. For me, you could burn your money, I don't care. If you had read what I wrote a hundred times already, if you would've taken one telephone call, you would know. I come to you for them. For *them*.

Oh yes, says Avrom.

You must know what I'm saying. How bad backhome is now, Avrom. Not like before the war. So much worse for the Jews than even the Czar ever was. Everyone so scared. Another war can come any minute. Hitler and Stalin and tiny Lithuania in between, God knows what can happen. How they feel it there, the pressure, the problems – you must know this also! And I must tell you I had a man I was going to send my money who could help to bring them, first to other places, then here. But now the piggish cholera bastards of the government have closed every door and nailed it shut. Avrom – you listening?.

He shrugs. So the doors are closed, you say yourself.

Yes, but with enough grease, everything moves. You of all know this. And not just money. You know people. Big people that respect you. I was never going to ask like this, Avrom, I'm a proud person. But there is nowhere else to go and no more time now. I'm at the end.

Isaac thrums with shock: she's at the end, she says, and she means him, that she's even lost hope in *him*, her own son.

Meanwhile Avrom strokes at the craters in the bulldog cheek.

Avrom, says Mame. Avrom!

I heard you.

I'm talking about Trudel-Sora, Avrom. Orli and Friedke. This is who I speak for. I don't know if you've helped anyone else, maybe . . . I mean of your . . . Skopishok people . . . if there's others . . .

He makes a horizontal cutting gesture. No, he says. No. You're no different.

Mame is almost panting, as if she's trying to push a heavy weight up a steep hill. She swallows hard and goes on quietly. Listen to me. We have to bring them out.

—Do we.

What's a few pounds to you? Some telephone calls. For family, for life.

He smiles: that tiny parody of good cheer. Isaac gets a sense of the mass of perfect cynicism that is embodied in this Avrom, perfect and impervious as a stone, like the name of this farm. —Ah por foont, he says.

A few pounds.

And when I needed someone, he says. Didn't seem like *a few pounds* then. There was no *we* then.

Past is past, says Gitelle.

—Really.

—*Ree–lee*, she says, mimicking the English. She slaps the table hard enough to make the cups quiver in their saucers; Isaac jerks. We have to be serious now, Avrom. This is war and death. This is family. They are screaming and crying for the help.

He shifts in his chair a little, presses down on his thighs, taking in an expanse of air, letting it out very slowly. What are pleas against such a toughened and weary sound? It's like the desert wind. This is a man who's heard all the pleas that there are, Isaac thinks. And his heart dips for his mother, how sad this doomed little mission is now that he can see what it is.

—So we're back to your question, says Avrom. The only question.

—Oon vos iz dos?

—How. Much.

His mother stands. All blood has leached away from the skin of her face save for the livid scar. It's a look that strikes deep in Isaac. Her eyes are fixed on Avrom, the scar glows. It's the look of the day of the couchers. When she came in with that wood axe behind her skirt.

He finds himself standing up but doesn't remember rising. Her right hand is in the handbag, buried to the wrist, groping in there. Time has become very slow, very sticky. He knows she will bring out a gun, a small revolver. She will make this Avrom give what he must or she will fire into his head. It's the couchers all over again, it's that total commitment of her decision.

He reaches out for the wrist; but he is moving so slowly in this sticky time. Her hand comes out of the handbag holding what he takes on the instant to be a pack of cards then no, of course not, it's a wad of folded notes, it's the cash. He falters, freezes. He watches her hand rock back behind her shoulder. She aims it like a stone and throws hard. The notes flutter apart like fleeing sparrows, spreading over the table, the tea things. A few make the other side and settle on Avrom's lap, around his feet. He looks down at them.

—The hell is this?

—Finf oon achtsik foont, she says. Eighty-five pounds.

Are you mad?

I told you I'm not here for myself. This is my sweat also and my blood, you're not the only one.

In my house, he says.

She grabs Isaac's arm, her handbag in the other hand. We're going.

Throw money in my face. In my house. Where you going?

I scraped and saved one penny at a time. It's yours now. Put with it what you can and use it for the right thing. For family. May The Name help you.

She starts pulling Isaac to the door and he moves with her without looking back, not till he hears the chair fall. Avrom standing, finally a little emotion in the bulldog face, some twisting force has trickled in. I am not responsible, Gitelle!

She is in the doorway but stops, pivots back. And if you step on broken glass and cut your foot?

—What?

So tell your foot too bad. Family, Avrom. Blood.

She goes on, gripping Isaac's shirt, and he moves with her and this time there are no noises behind.

The sun still clears the rooftop but only by a distance of its own diameter. His mother slams her door so hard the Austin rocks. Isaac tries to start but the engine only clicks.

Go, Isaac, already.

—Can't Ma. I think maybe the battery.

A long shadow and a tall man: through the windshield Isaac watches Andre's approach: he doesn't seem to have come out of the house. He leans against Isaac's door, prods up the brim of his homburg and taps his knuckles on the glass. Isaac rolls down a crack. —Mr. Suttner say you forget this.

He starts to slot the wad of notes at the gap but Mame is quicker, lunging across and rolling up the window with two quick jerks. Andre taps again. Mame checks the door is locked. —You don't oypen for nobody.

—It won't start, Ma.

She sits back in her seat, looking forward, her handbag on her lap. Isaac looks up at Andre and shrugs. There's more tapping which he ignores. Andre goes back to the house. Ten minutes pass in a hot silence. He doesn't even try to look at her, it's crunching steps outside that make him turn his eyes, and this time it's Avrom coming to them, over a gravel path through the flowers, his sandals angled a little outward and his knees a little bowed over each step. He has a pressing belly packed against the belt of his khaki shorts, his bulldog face impassive.

He stops on Mame's side. Still she looks forward. Isaac tries the engine again: useless.

—Open up, says Avrom. Open up the door.

Mame doesn't move.

Avrom switches to Afrikaans, language of orders: Make open. *Make open.*

—Go tzoo hell, Mame tells the window.

It's evening and the sun is waning, yes, but the car is still so hot and suffocating now with all the windows tightshut; Isaac feels sweat already itching on his scalp and starting to slide over his ribs.

—My boys will check the car, says Avrom. Come and sit inside.

She doesn't answer. They sit still in the throttling air. Avrom uses the flat of his fist on the hot roof. Mame says, You go out, Isaacluh. He can fix the car with me in it. When it's ready, we'll go the same minute.

—Ma, what you ganna do?

I stay by here. I don't move. You tell him.

—I'm not going. I'll stay with you.

—Go.

—Uh uh.

She stretches her chin up, looks at him. —I shay go.

He nods slowly and gets out, slams quick and walks round to Avrom, Avrom with the wad of cash in his hand. They stand looking at one another for a while. Isaac says, —She won't–

Avrom jerks his head backwards, turns and walks to the house. Isaac tries to get his mother's eye but she stares only at the windshield, so he turns and follows Avrom, seeing the bulk in the shoulders, the way the calf muscles shift and ripple. How is it possible that he has never been a black-and-white face in the albums of photographs at number fifty-two Buxton? How is it his name was never once a word in his mother's mouth, his mother who dreams of family, thrashing and shouting in the night? A runaway brother called Hershel. This secret cousin. Unreality is the sensation of trying to reconcile life with a parallel dream: Doornfontein over there and this farmhouse here but all the time the two as entwined as the wax of a Havdalah candle. It's a knowledge that refuses to dwell in his body, refuses to take on the rooted feel of a certainty. Who is this man? Who?

Through the hallway window Isaac watches the parked Austin outside, the silhouette of his mother's profile motionless, enduring. Avrom wants to know how old he is, then asks him if he's in school.

—I'm a panel beater, apprentice class A.

—You like that?

—Absolutely.

Avrom grimaces and picks up a bush hat; Isaac follows. He looks at a staircase and wonders for the first time if there is a woman above, a wife; but the bare lean furniture, the undecorated walls, lines clean and spartan, speak against it. They pass through the big airy rooms and out the back where a path leads downhill to stables with a garage at the back and living quarters on top.

On a balcony men are playing cards or lying down in the mellow evening sun. They have their hats on and their pleated trousers but their torsos are bare. When they see Avrom below they all get up and some of them start buttoning on shirts. There's a smell of cooking here, mingled with horse dung. Laundry hangs on a line in the brick courtyard. Isaac recognizes one of the men by his odd moustache, he was in the back of the Nash before. Avrom makes a cutting movement with his raised hand and they settle back. In the garage he and Isaac climb into an old Ford truck.

—Your mother, he says. Head made from stone.

—I know, says Isaac.

—From stone.

They drive and the road dips and rises in the furrows and humps of low hills at first, but farther out it stretches into a plain towards the bigger range in the distance. The sun has slid to their right, blinding and orange, closing on the cold black line of the horizon where it will douse itself like a suicide. Off to the left the light has that greenish shine on the dry grasses and some thin long clouds in the deep blue dome above seem like sifting banks of windswept beach sand. In the middle distance are the cattle in three separate herds and the tall shapes of horsemen in back of them, cutting across like shark fins.

—I can't actually believe this.

—Believe vot?

—Is it really all yours?

—Someone say, The only rich is land rich. I don't know.

—How many watchmacallit is it?

He shrugs one shoulder. —Few hectares, few tousand.

—Jesus, and all I ever wanted was a house in Orange Grove.

Avrom leans forward and brings up a bottle from under his seat, pulls the cork with his teeth and has a drink, hands the bottle across. Isaac wipes the top on his sleeve, sniffs. —Whatzit?

—Is good bloody mampoer is what.

Isaac laughs.

—What?

The bulldog face is not a laughing one. Isaac muscles his lips into good behaviour. —No, man. Just like I thought you'd be having twelve-year Scotch or summin. Mampoer.

Avrom's shoulder hitches again. —That fancy I don't need.

Isaac swallows the harsh homemade spirits, product of some Boer's hidden still. It rasps his digestive tract like a swallowed rattlesnake then curls up in his belly to throb its venom heat. Avrom steers with his thighs and rolls a cigarette from a pouch of tobacco. —I like to drive, he says. I think good when I drive. Then he asks about Isaac's pay, as a panel beater, is it enough for this house that he wants?

—Maybe in a few years if I save up, for a down payment. Maybe I'll be able to afford a freehold bond. Pay it off thirty years.

Avrom snorts. —Debt. That's all a job can ever get. Jobs are for kuylikers.

Isaac passes the bottle back. Kuylikers: cripples. A stinging word. He presses down an uncomfortable rush of images to do with his father.

—You want that house?

—Yes.

—Then why go on job? You can do what any man can. When I buy this farm, I paid cash. Told the man, he asked me about a bond, told him, Mister, I *give* bonds, I don't take them. Should have given a look at his face.

He drinks without removing the cigarette, the sweetness of that memory (no doubt) making his eyelids hood with pleasure.

Isaac says, —What did you do? When you came here like?

—Furshtayste mameloshen?

Isaac nods, though this must be the third time he's been asked if he speaks mother's tongue, as if cousin Avrom doesn't quite believe he's a real Jewisher. Avrom starts talking about coming to the diggings here in '27. Men were leaving their families and selling their homes then, from all over the world they came for the diamonds. Depending on luck. From the start, Avrom says, he didn't waste time trying to stumble on such lucky stones. He made business with other businesses. Buying into those who equipped the prospectors. When he needed premises he went into construction; when he needed transport he took up trucking. Restaurants he was in needed beef so he got into butcheries also. And then cattle. And there're other ways to get diamonds than by mining. The stones have to be valued and sold, and those are businesses also. Money is a business too, a commodity.

Very simple, he says. Always get your percent. Make sure and get your percent. On everything. Always.

When they spin around there's a vehicle, that tan Nash LaFayette, a ways behind them and it pulls off the track to let them pass and when they do Isaac has a glimpse of Andre's narrow-necked shape, his thumb touching his homburg. Avrom seems not to have noticed him. When Isaac looks at the mirror he sees the Nash falling into their trail.

There's a pressure in him now. *Kuyliker.* He looks out his window. It's the grandeur of this other life and how miserable and distant it seems to him to be crawling under cars in the grease and the shmootz. What's wrong with him? *You can do what any man can.* Then why has he chosen to be like his limping father with his tiny clocks in his tiny workshop? Instead of *this*: vastness, space, power, ease. Men with weapons, a lawyer in big offices. Respect. Where even his mother comes to ask for favours. The pressure – it's a feeling like wrongness, like guilt. It makes him want to shake himself as if he's been in a dangerous dream, been sleepwalking. What he's been counting on is Yvonne, yes, that's the truth, marrying Yvonne Linhurst, getting her to let him into The Castle. But what kind of a man does that? Waiting passively for her approval, kissing her tochus and shlupping up to her so that she might bestow gifts on his life – is that the way he wants to be? What has happened to him? He's stopped listening to Mame, but all this time she's been so right! She's been trying to wake him up out of his satisfied trance, the drug of his labours. There is so much more. You can do what any man can. And he remembers Hugo Bleznik looking disgusted, saying to him in the backyard that he could see it in his face how he had lost something because of the female, the bladey female . . .

He says, his thoughts coming out through his mouth in their unfolding: – But it's also good to do a good job, like for yourself?

Avrom snorts. – Kid, he says. There's an unanswerable weight of cynical finality in that word. A whole world in that word.

Isaac looks at him. He has grey hair and a paunch but he is not that old in years, they're on opposite sides of their twenties, that's all. Avrom says, – I'm going to show you something. Between you and me only, not your mother. Nobody.

– Okay, says Isaac. I understand.

In the hilly country behind the farmhouse Avrom steers them off the track, downhill over rough veld then down the side of a shallow donga – a dried riverbed – amongst these prickly yellowstone hillocks, these koppies. The sand along the donga is salt white and gritty. The riverbed twists and the rocky sides grow higher. This is an intruding finger of the desert country they are close to. In time they reach a wide curve and Avrom parks the truck. No sign of the Nash behind. In front, slanted sheet rock with undulant tan and ochre bands in its grain faces them, its gradient mild enough that they walk up and over the top as if climbing some gigantic clamshell. Then the land swoops away before them: there's a kind of open crater below and strange rocks rise from its slopes. The rocks are thin and tall, as if they've been whittled by the wind. They stand apart like stone trees in a kind of scattered orchard, so stark and rooted on the sloping land in the red dust.

At the bottom on the flat of the crater is a singular mass of rock, a different colour to the others, huddled and massive, more yellow in colour where they are rust-reddish and burnt orange. They climb down towards it, wordless, down past the stone trunks and their long shadows. Bird wings clap above but when Isaac looks up he sees no moving shapes, only spilled fire in the sky's last quarter. He feels thirsty, dizzy. The mampoer is to blame. Must be. There is some kind of buzzing in his centre and he shakes his head as if that might clear it. He becomes aware of his own thoughts in his head like a separate voice. Hears himself: *This is the most important thing that has ever happened to me in my life.*

At the bottom Avrom steps to the rock and puts his palm against it. It's only a rock but Isaac has a dread of approaching, of even being here while Avrom is, as if he's seeing something he should not. Avrom turns, beckons. It's Isaac's chance to touch. He uses both hands. The day's saturated heat eases from the rough surface. The last of the sun is flush against one face of it, this rock that is shaped in two ungainly humps like mating elephants, with a great forked split down the middle.

Avrom sits down with his back to the rock, takes off his hat and closes his eyes in his sunflushed face. Isaac sits at his shoulder. Keeping his eyes open would be his choice but the glare is so strong he closes them too and in the warm darkness hears his cousin say, —I want to tell you what happened to me.

—Yes.

He waits, feeling the unmoving mass of this earth rock against his spine.

Now Avrom's voice dips into Jewish, dips deep: vibrations: the melancholy body music of their shared tribe, belly and heart and throat, the juicy-mouthed winding rhythms of family, words of womb and kitchen. He grasps in this blind moment why Avrom kept asking if he understood Jewish – because he didn't mean literally, he'd meant did he *understand*, did he *feel*, truly and fully; and he thinks, Of course I do, this is mother's tongue, home soil, heart's blood. It's the wind off Lake Sartai where he was born, snatching plumes of woodsmoke from the chimneys over the thatched roofs, the slanted timbers. That is his forestland also, his frozen rivers. Six, seven centuries of Jewish bones rest in that village soil over there, no matter what else he might try to tell himself . . . Avrom saying, It was a few years after the war when I was still just a boy that I started dreaming about Africa for the first time, about the lions of Africa . . .

Yes, says Isaac, listening with all of his being.

25.

PEOPLE IN SKOPISHOK HAD SEEN aeroplanes during the war years before, but those had passed over like insects crawling the high blue dome of the sky. So when a flying machine swooped and growled low enough over the village that the faces of the pilots could be read under caps of leather with their earflaps and their goggles, there was a panic. Women grabbed for the children. Howling dogs ran with tails curled under. Men fetched sticks.

Avrom Suttner was fifteen years old and was first at the dock to watch the long-winged machine with the taut X-shapes of the wires between the wings slowly lower itself onto Lake Mituva, the waddling fuselage breasting the waters. By the time it had drifted in, a crowd was behind him. On the biplane, a man climbed over the windshield to balance on the nose, kneeling with a rope. Nearing, he flicked it underhand. It was Avrom who tied it up while the vessel bumped the dock fenders and the crowd helped the man across. He stripped his gloves first, not hurrying, then the leather cap, the goggles last. The skin of the face was suntanned and healthy. His moustache was rich, his eyebrows thick. He stuffed his gloves and goggles into the cap, handed them to Avrom:
—Nu, ingeler, vos daynks du?

What do you think, young one?

The sound of Jewish out of his mouth turned Avrom into a dumb pillar. He took the cap as the Jews on the dock pressed in, shouting. Avrom heard the pilot's name then: Tannenbaum. Oyzer Tannenbaum. Hands flapped against him, as if needing to contact the dubious reality of his form. Men shouting to others at the back, all the voices coalescing to a sudden cheer. Oyzer, Oyzer Tannenbaum. He's back!

They wanted to lift him up onto their shoulders but he made them clear a path for there was another pilot climbing over the windshield. They watched him crawl forward and stand up on the nose, balancing well, long thin legs wearing khaki trousers and the same leather greatcoat as Oyzer. On the dock Nachman Kaplan shouted: —Nu, Oyzer, ver iz?

So Oyzer? Who's this now?

There were other shouts but then as if quashed like a snuffed candle, all voices ceased. Oyzer was grinning. The man on the machine had removed his cap. As he shook his head long caramel layers kept spilling out and lapping down over the shoulders. Now the man shook again, becoming a woman with beautiful eyes. *A woman in trousers.* The shock of it like a double slap that stung then heated the cheeks. Mrs. Katzenellenbogen grabbed her boy, Mendele, and tried to cover his eyes. Oyzer had out his hand and the woman took it and he helped her across onto the dock.

When the crowd started moving off with the two aviators, Avrom called to Oyzer, lifting the cap. What should I do? Oyzer shouted back: Look after for me.

—Ich vell, said Avrom. I will.

At their return two hours later Avrom was still there, breathing hard through a bloodied nose, his left eye fat and purple, his shirt torn. He came forward to Oyzer, took the cap and goggles out of his pocket, returned them to their owner's hand.

I looked after it for you like I said. No one touched. Not one finger.

———

Inside Tzvi's Inn only three people were allowed to sit at the big
corner table while Tzvi pushed the rest back, the open windows
full of craning faces. At the table were Oyzer and the trousers
woman, Oyzer telling Avrom how he had grown up in this tiny
place and gone away before the war, to Africa. The woman was
not his wife. She was tanned and had big hands and those glisten-
ing eyes and all that hair and she spoke no Jewish. She was from
Africa too; her name was Coleen. There were beautiful women
over there and there were human beings with skin as black as
coal dust who walked around with leopard skins and spears,
there was an animal called a giraffe that had a neck as long as
a tree and a heart as big as a suitcase in order to pump the blood
up that long neck to its tiny eyes and brain. Oyzer had made
a fortune there in that mystic country in only a few years, and
claimed he would make a second when he went back. In that part
of the world (he said winking), it rained gold and it hailed diamonds. All you needed was a bucket and a will. Oyzer's own
fortune was rooted in the ostrich, a giant bird whose expensive
plumage made hats and other accoutrements of beauty for the
women of the world's richest countries. This was a bird that
could kill you with one kick. A bird that did not fly (unlike
Oyzer!) but was ridden by men like a horse, the riders tucking
their legs under the stubby wings. He had so much land that to
survey it all he had learned to fly and had purchased a flying
machine (not a Lohner like this one outside on the lake, but a De
Havilland Tiger Moth). He also owned six automobiles and a
stable full of Arabian horses. He had one house on a beach and
another on a mountain. The air in Africa was pure and dry, never
cold or damp, and it made you strong in your body and healthy
in your thoughts. When you hear about America, New York or
Buenos Aires, throw that idea in the rubbish, young one. London,
New York, these are not places for a human being, they are
giant kennels full of wild starving dogs in human skins all biting

one another. In Africa there is limitless space and freedom and a
Jew is not a Jew, a Jew is a White man. And in Africa the White
man is king. Labour is cheap and the country is rich. What more
could you want but to go to Africa?

He made Avrom so excited that it was hard for him to sit still
at the table. His knees jiggled. He wanted to get up and pace, to
run. It was like an itching fever.

Oyzer said: I like you, I see my own younger face in yours.
He gave Coleen a kiss and a squeeze that made Avrom's cheeks
hotter still. Oyzer dropped into a whisper: Women like her are
there for the taking. Gold and land.

Oyzer had been drinking Tzvi's brandy, he too was flushed.
This day was a triumph of which he had dreamed for a long time,
his return to Skopishok. And he had *swooped from the sky.* Had
delivered enough money to rebuild the synagogue, refurbish the
school, open a new poorhouse for the needy. His funds would pay
the living expenses of travelling yeshiva students who'd do nothing
but study Torah in his name, day and night, for years to come,
accruing good deeds for his immortal soul. His name would be
engraved on copper placards, would be called out in shul whenever
the Torah was read. Generations yet unborn would sing of him, his
portion of paradise in the world-to-come secured beyond question.

He leaned forward, banging his glass. Avrom, he said, you
come to Africa and I will give you a job, I guarantee.

Truly?

I'll write it down!

He took out a card with English written and scribbled on the
back, signed it.

He said: I will take you hunting lions.

Lions!

Yes my friend, lions. Not like King David who used that sling
when he was a boy, but with proper rifles. The big Winchester
like that President Roosevelt. The Remington three seventy-five.

And he told how they would ride horses in the veld looking for the lions to flush: not hard to find, for though the dry country was huge, the lions were numerous upon it. And lions are proud and do not run away. You get off the horse and you walk in. If you wound him, he will hide in the brush and wait for you and charge when you come. When they charge their ears are out and their mane is flared and the tail is straight and stiff and whips like a cane. Their claws rip dust as they come out of a sandstorm of their own making like some errant shard of heat lightning. A lion will break your neck with one swat, crunch your skull like an eggshell. Hundreds of pounds of muscle packed on a frame of bones like steel – the god of big cats. But they have dead yellow eyes. Eyes that Oyzer has looked right into, Oyzer saying they were so fast they would cover the distance to you in the space between heartbeats. You have one shot. You miss, you die. It happened one time, he said, that I shot him so close in the brain I could smell his hot breath and feel his spit on my face, and he died but still knocked me flying.

Avrom laughed, Oyzer cocked his head. You don't believe?

I do I do.

Look at this. He unbuttoned and dipped a hand into his shirt, brought out a pale curved shape like a stone on the end of a leather necklace. Avrom was allowed to touch: not a stone but just as hard yet smoother. Slowly he recognized it as a claw.

That's him, said Oyzer.

It was the same as a house cat's, differing only in scale and not substance, like a needle compared to a chisel. Handling it, the raw force and size of the beast was imprinted in Avrom's chest, his guts. His blood was charged and he knew he wouldn't sleep that night. Africa, he thought. *Africa!*

. . . After a time, Avrom's voice in the sundrenched dark, eyelids lit by the orange solar fire, asking Isaac this question: What is it that makes men do things?

Isaac mumbles. Don't know. Money.

Not money, not land, not women, not children, not anything outside. What makes a man want something is a picture inside of himself.

A picture?

A picture so clear in your mind. That's what I had after Oyzer Tannenbaum left the village. Pictures. A picture of the lion hunting. A picture of the flying machine, and me as the pilot. A picture of a woman with big tanned hands and a wild laugh. Those I had, plus a signed guarantee in my pocket; but I didn't know it was worth less than toilet paper because once I got here I couldn't even wipe my arse with it. It was that worthless.

He didn't—

Didn't even want to know me when I landed, he had sudden deafness and sudden weak memory. Avrom who? What? The piggish crook. I think Oyzer Tannenbaum is dead now. I hope so. I heard a story he died in an aeroplane crash. If there's some lesson in that I'm too thick to learn it. Lessons. When I got here I found no such a thing as a diamond rain; no easy ways at all. Nobody called me a king, White, Black or Coloured. But before I came it was that picture in my head that had me like a fever. A picture of a lion, a charging monarch of a lion. But that was not how he looked, my first one, when I finally put my eyes on him. It was like the end of a dream, but it was also the start of another one, different . . .

Avrom telling how when he started out at the diggings all he had was a half-blind mare and a cart to smouse with, to go around selling varied goods to the prospectors. One night he got lost, ran out of water. Thirst swelled his tongue. He rode past a great rock, had a feeling like a voice inside. He stopped and looked into a crack in the rock and there found a hollow full of rainwater. So he made camp. In the night as he sat by his fire a shadow untouched by moonwash moved on the rock, moving slowly down, and his mare began to snort and pull against her tether. Then he heard it: that forced groaning that climbed to a barking cough, and the trickling noise in its heavy breathing between each roar, a sound like a stick being dragged across the hollow rails of an iron fence.

When it came to the level of the firelight he saw it was an old tom with the heavy black mane of a desert lion. He favoured one of his back legs and Avrom could see his ribs and knew he was injured and alone and hungry. He could smell the rotmeat stench the lion gave off, his wound and the carrion in his fangs that he must have been surviving on, and the wave of it was so potent it brought the acid gorge of Avrom's fear to the back of his throat.

I had a decision to make (Avrom says): get away and leave my horse for the lion to make his supper or to try and stop him. I didn't have a rifle, not even a good sharp knife. But there was a long branch of firewood on the ground and I picked it up. This lion was watching me with gold eyes. Never will I forget his eyes in the firelight. I lifted the branch and I put it to my shoulder, here, like a rifle. You see, I knew old lions know men and their rifles, and what rifles can do. So I aimed that wood at him and I went forward. He looked at me and he roared again. I could have run but I kept on. Found something deep in me to do it. I even started roaring back. Listen. A lion takes what he wants. Nobody gives a thing in this world. Be a lion or be a mare – it comes down to our decision. The rest is commentary. Understand?

Isaac digests this, silent. Then: What happened?

I went up to him. A few feet. Shouting, roaring. Last second, he flinched. He jumped away and went running back up over the rock. I stayed up all night by the fire but he never came back. In the morning when I looked at the rock I said one day I will

own this place, this land. I was different from then on. And here
it is.

This?

This rock. This is where it happened, where I changed. This is
Lion's Rock.

When they climb back out of the crater there's a clink of steel and
Isaac looks up and across to catch the flare of a cigarette lighter,
Andre's face under the homburg blooms. Isaac lifts his hand but
the flame dies and Andre is gone, even the cigarette tip concealed,
his bulk abutting a rock tree as indivisible as any other night
shadow against the vast screen of massed stars behind.

They drive back in silence. At the house it is told that the
Austin has been repaired and is ready to go; Mame is still out there
grimly behind the dashboard. In the front hallway Isaac says, —
What was it, distributor cap?

—Ay?

—One of your okes did something to that Austin. I know that
engine was fine cos I checked it fore we left. You didn't want us
going nowhere.

Avrom shrugs.

—Why do they have guns, cousin? What do they do here?

—What guns? There's no guns.

—Those okes of yours. That Andre.

—It's nothing to do with me if they do. There's bad people
also in town. They just my staff, that's all. Business.

Isaac tugs his nose. —Listen, cousin, tell me. What was
Hershel like?

Avrom squints at him. Who?

The puzzlement seems so real. —Your father, Isaac says.

Avrom shakes his head. —Never mind.

—Do you have a photo?

—I told you never mind.

—It's just. He's my uncle, but I never even seen a picture. Ma's got all the others—

Avrom walks off. When he comes back he says: —Don't worry yourself with uncles-shmunkles. He pulls out a folded wad of cash. —You know what is?

— ... Is it Ma's?

—Yes. Now you take.

—She won't take it back.

—That's right. She will never take it. She will rather die, I know your mother.

Isaac shrugs. —That's how it is, then.

—Nineteen years old, Avrom says. You are the one who needs this.

There's a dropping feeling in Isaac, his guts sag in on it, a sinkhole dragging silence into his throat.

—Don't show her. Don't tell her. Take this and put in your pocket. I added a few extra. Use it for your future. Do you want that house?

Isaac has a feeling that is akin to standing up on the top of a high and narrow wall, looking down through his toes.

—Take it and put in your pocket.

There's a croak his words have to push through. —I can't, cousin. It's hers.

—No. It's mine. She gave it and she won't take back. Now I offer you. Tell me yes or tell me no.

—No. No.

His other hand suddenly rings Isaac's upper arm, digging. —Are you a lion or are you a sheep? Better decide it right now. For your life. Right now.

The feeling of teetering, the feeling of terrible height. His pulses chip at both eardrums.

—You decide how you want it, your one life. But decide now. This is it, you won't see this again. If you can't find the lion inside here now, then you don't deserve your chance.

Isaac bites one dry lip and starts to shake his head. No. Say no. But as the breath rises to his vocal chords another thought breaks into his mind. He hears her, her voice, her lesson:

Two kinds of people in the world.

The Stupids and the Clevers.

And what are you? Which one are you?

26.

HIS FIRST SATURDAY BACK from Lion's Rock he takes an early morning train out to the East Rand. Walks the last three miles on a dirt road with trash scattered on both sides in the brown grasses and the charred streaks from old fires. In the treeless distance lies a squatter camp where the Afs hunker in their tin kingdom with the dust and the sewage. Beyond them rise the lift heads of the gold mines and the chimney stacks of factories. Close in, a tributary of some forlorn mine reservoir winds through a dry trench gouged by flood waters, the water no more than a rusty trickle over rocks.

His destination is unmistakable for it stands alone on the desolate plain: a wall of stone with a stubby gruesome hedge of jagged glass cemented along its top. There is no front gate, instead what seems to be an old railway car crusted in rust plugs the gap in the wall, a crude way hacked through it by welding torches and filled with barbed wire. Isaac puts two fingers in his mouth and whistles shrill notes for three minutes before an albino watchman comes to move the wire and let him in. These albinos, they're double cursed. White as milk but still a Black inside; but then other Blacks cross the road when they see them coming. Nature's cruel: it's how it is.

There's a big patch of open ground, of sunbaked soil stone hard. The building is made of concrete blocks with boards for windows and cracked front steps that Hugo Bleznik comes down as they approach. Hugo in a cream suit with two-tone shoes and powder-blue hatband bearing a single red carnation. —Tiger! Shake a paw.

Isaac nods, takes the hand. He's looking back around. — What's that sposed to be?

There's a flatbed truck with a winch parked against the wall beside the railway car.

—I'm just fine, thanks for asking. S'matter with you, man? What you so tense? Sounded same way on the telephone.

—I'm asking does that truck work?

—F'course it works, man. Pride and joy. Can haul five wrecks on that beauty.

—Then what's it sitting there for?

—Ach man, that's our gate. Truck pulls the train out the way when we need to open.

Isaac shakes his head.

—You don't know. We need it, ay. Those squatters, they steal anything they can wrap their thieving fingers round. Cops can do kuk-all. They stripped all the ironwork, the whole gate. Any face brick they could chisel out, any wiring, any piping. First thing I did was stick in a new gate and next day was gone, boy, hinges and all. So this what we got now. Plus a night watchman, and maybe we'll be getting some dogs.

Isaac is grimacing, scanning up at the building now.

—Deal of the century, Hugo tells him.

—That so.

—Used to be a reformatory for bad boys. The guts've been ripped out of it long ago. They say a few lighties croaked themselves here, was so bad.

—Jesus.

—No man it's sweet. Nobody wants to touch the place with a ten-foot barge pole. They scared of ghosts and kuk. The agent was only too happy to kiss my tochus for whatever I offered on a lease. Deal of the century. It's *huge* man. You'll see. Come in feast your eyes.

The interior with its boarded windows is gloomy and has a floor of damp soil specked with rodent feces, but the ceiling seems twenty feet high and the stone pillars are widely spaced. A portion of the back wall has been smashed out to give a view of the yard and exterior wall with it gouging semi-bottles against the desolate sky. About half the floor space is packed with wrecks, stacked up three high and maybe forty deep.

Isaac nods. —Where's this workshop, upstairs or not?

—What kinda question is that?

Isaac looks at him. —One that I'm asking you.

—Christ, what you so bladey aggro for all a sudden, what's happened a you? Why'nt you looking what we got here already man! And I haven't even started telling all the contracts I got. Tip a the iceberg man, tip a the ice. And here you being such a misery. Can't you even shine up a tiny bit?

—The workshop, says Isaac.

—It's sorted. Hundred and twenty percent. Don't you worry.

But when they get upstairs after Isaac has been made to look at the wrecks up close in the gloom, he finds only more empty space, more rat droppings save for one corner where a desk has a view through a cracked board of the dribbling river on the burned plain. Pinned to the board is a calendar, each square full of scribbles.

Isaac strokes some dust from the desktop. There's a few screwdrivers and one hammer with a cracked handle. —Equipment hey.

—Don't irritate me, junior. There's no twist here. Everything's going so fluent. Everything's capitalizing.

—Looks that way.

—Once I get renovations done you won't recognize the place. Main thing is there's no neighbours and we zoned industrial. Main thing the capitalizing is going so fluent.

Isaac is studying the calendar. The scribbles are names: finance companies, individuals with amounts due. *For Chev truck* 8, he reads. *Jan Pienaar* 310s 5d. *Cohen* 7.

—Oh boy, he says.

—You wouldn't understand that, says Hugo.

—I know juggling balls when I see em.

—Listen to the big shot. Let me tell you something, most people would kill for your opportunity. You a lucky kid. Our own operation, man. Toes to the nose.

—Is that right.

—Boyki, boyki, don't you know sarcasm causes failure? Shiny side up if you want to shine. There's the only way.

Hugo falls into a chair, produces a bottle. Isaac dusts the desktop and sits. They pass the bottle and Isaac observes some swell-chested pigeons roosting in the steel beams above, the beams caked in a white crust of guano.

—Tell me summin, honestly, what's going on with you?

Isaac shakes his head.

—The female?

—No, it's not that.

Hugo puts his foot up on an open drawer. —And your people? How're they?

—My people.

—What?

—Nothing. They ukay. Old lady's a bit low. Actually very low. This war talk and that. Worried about her family back over there.

—Ja, it's too bad about that, says Hugo. On the bright side, a war's ganna make a lotta people a helluva lotta gelt. Might as well be us hey. I knew you'd click on sooner or later. Now you see the big picture, you don't wanna do shoch work for bupkas for the rest a your life. But I don't hold it against you that it took you a while to see it. You young—

—Hugo—

—Listen. The other two trucks are on the road, they'll be back tonight with a fresh load. You can start in straightaways. Put down on a paper what equipment we ganna need—

—Wait, Hugo.

—You can have a look in the back, we do got some other tools there to sort—

—Hugo, I didn't say I'm chucking in with you that way.

—Hey?

—I haven't told you what I came here for.

Hugo's foot comes down hard, puffing dust. —Well shit! What the hell you doing here then? Waste my time.

—Listen. I gotta proposal.

—Proposal! Eff that, Tiger, I'm not the marrying kind, case you diden notice. I don't need proposals.

—What I been thinking is I come work here every weekend and every night in the week—

—Forget it. You insulting me.

—That way I still keep getting my panel beater's ticket. If this starts taking off, then—

—Boyki, let me be polite as I can. You can take that part-time half-an-arse horseshit and stick it deep where the sun never shines, pardon my parlee voo. You either in or you out. Otherwise you just stuffing me around.

—Such a big macher.

—Ja, well, this isn't fish and chips we dealing in. Alls I can say is you'll be sorry in three years' time, be blubbing away while you bang out dents with your fellow African colleagues. Too late, she cried. And cried.

—I can do a lot on weekends, Hugo. And every night. Probably the same in hours as I put in at Gold Reef.

—I don't wanna part-timer ukay. You just not worth it.

—You sure?

—Tiger, if I want part-time I'll hire part-time. I'm offering a share for a partner. You put in the graft now, you a rich man later.

Isaac scratches his temple. —See the thing is, I reckon you got a slight problem here hey Hugo.

—What's that?

—You accumulating a lotta wrecks now and that's costing, but you got nothing coming in. What I can see, you're all stretched out. You're borrowing one to pay the next. And you've gotta wait till the market kicks up before you can start making back. *If* it kicks up. *If* there's a war.

—Don't you worry–

—I don't have to worry, Hugo. It's your business and it's constipated. Blocked solid.

—Do I look like I need your medical opinion?

—I doubt you can afford wages for a real mechanic for long. Meanwhile you got your three trucks going on hire purchase. Then there's the Blacks' wages. There's rent on this bladey chuloopuh of a property, this monstrosity the middle a nowhere – I hope not much, like you say, but still you gotta pay it.

—He's got it all worked out. Never you mind what I gotta pay. I'm capitalizing so fluent.

—That's right, I do have it worked out.

—Well not so well as you think you cocky little pisher, cos I'm not interested in any part-time shit. And I don't think, being honest, that I like this new whatever this attitude of yours is at all. All pushy and whatnot all a sudden.

Isaac stands and sticks his hand into his pocket. Hugo's blinkless blue eyes follow the gesture.

—You get my free labour. I know which parts to get out first and how to do it fast and what we can do to sell em. And I'll also skip in cash from my wages. Been giving to my ma to save but she won't mind for a business.

—Chhh. Your *wages*. Listen to him. What's that ganna buy us hey, bubble gum and pencils?

—I think maybe a little more than that, says Isaac. His hand comes out with a wallet. He opens it up and thumbs cash latkes onto the desk, twenty-pound notes included. —Plus this, he says. Take it or leave it.

When he looks up he takes the time to remember Hugo's expression, the drooping chin under the slackened face: like a man in need of smelling salts and a soft place to land.

An hour later they have the basics of their agreement written out on the back of an old circular advertising Miracle Glow (*latest wonder product from America, no electricity required – ever!*). Isaac gets one-third of the enterprise and Hugo, the founder, takes the rest. Hugo fills a bottle cap with a shot and Isaac gets the bottle.

—Wait, says Isaac. We missing the last thing.

—What?

—The name.

—It's Bleznik Motors. That's what it is.

—No. That's what it's *been*. We change it now. Write down this: Lion Motors.

—Lion Motors?

—That's right.

Bleznik opens his mouth but Isaac makes a fist. —I'm not debating here man. That's the name.

—Jeez, *what* has crawled up your arse lately? I seriously wanna know the answer.

—That's the name, says Isaac. Ukay? *Lion*. Lion Motors.

Hugo rubs his chin, tilts his eyes to the ceiling, makes a humming noise. —You know, actually, it's not all that bad . . . Lion Motors . . . Our prices *roar* the loudest.

—Right, says Isaac.

—Lion Motors. King of the automotive jungle . . . Lion Motors. We take quote a whole pride of pride in our work unquote. You get it? Whole lotta *pride*.

—Ja, oright, Hugo. Calm yourself.

Hugo lifts the brimming cap. —Here's to an operation that's all our own.

—To Lion Motors.

—L'chaim, you little shit.

—L'chaim, you old bastard.

That night Isaac drives back home in a Citroën organized for him by Hugo. He rushes to Newtown before closing where he picks up a suit, getting nine and a half percent off the sale price from Hugo's man, a tailor called Katz, for a shiny double-breasted number, a beauty worthy of Bogart. At home he spit-shines his pinching shul shoes and smears down his springy orange locks with Vitalis hair tonic. The cut on his cheek has healed to a scratch, nothing. He makes it to The Castle only forty-five minutes late, which is a miracle considering all the work he got done out at the Reformatory that day. (In truth he could have gone on working right through to Sunday morning yet would hardly have begun to dent the monstrous task ahead, this business already starting to loom now in his mind like some granite mountain that has to be dug out of their way with a pick and shovel, one swing at a time and by him alone.)

The Castle at night: it pricks with fortress lights. At the top, moths quiver in the scented garden. A submerged light makes the swimming pool into a lapping ultramarine gem and there are other lights that make emerald caves in the great trees down in the terraced spaces. The Cruel Duke comes to the doors with a brandy snifter and a bow tie. Isaac is led to a lounge he must pretend never to have seen before.

The Mad Queen waits, the crags of her face smeared full of

white paste, her painted lips like strings of raw meat. Yet her odd posture seems to invite perusal of a beauty that is absent if it ever was there at all, the way she lifts her chin and gives her profile, the wrinkled folds of her neck shifting, her loose-skinned arms stretching out as her bracelets chime. Isaac sits opposite and is offered a brandy. While he's accepting the drink, Queen asks him if he's really sure he wants to take Yvonne out. —She's a most temperamental girl.

Duke asks where they're going, what he's driving. They ask him about being a mechanic. Queen comes back to Yvonne, saying she was a mercurial child, whatever the word means, probably not good. Saying she goes through phases, changes her mind easily as the wind. Now she's interested in boys from Doornfontein. After she says this she lifts up her painted-on eyebrows.

Isaac looks at her. —What does that mean? he says to her slowly. Jewish boys? Is that what you're saying, Jewish? He keeps looking at her until she looks away. He can sense Duke is about to say something but is hesitating, and then there are quick footsteps in the corridor and Isaac swallows his drink and stands tall.

Her smell fills the car. Jasmine and lemon and whatever it is underneath that is the fresh young smell of her clean soft skin. It's hard to drive when all he wants to do is look at her. She's wearing a dark blue satiny dress with a half-circle at the top that shows her collarbones. He takes them to Hillbrow and makes her close her eyes. She has to hold his arm on the street and even tottering downstairs into the music she must still not open. He's got the same table reserved for them and only once they're sitting there does he allow her to look around.

He waits to see if he has made a mistake. For about a minute it seems it could go either way, and then she shakes her head and slaps his shoulder and he knows it'll be all right. —Wicked! she says.

—Give me a kiss, he says.

So they dine in the very spot where Isaac burned poor Wayne's hair off, what a shame that was (ha ha) and then they dance to the jazz, Isaac doing his best not to stomp on her pretty high-heeled shoes, coming up on his toes now and then so he doesn't look too much shorter than her.

Afterwards over drinks he tells her, —Member how you all treated me like the bladey waiter?

—We weren't *that* bad.

—Yes you were. You know you were.

She giggles. They've had a lot to drink. —Was I terrible?

—You're bad, you're bad.

—I need improving don't I, Izey.

—Yes you need improving. Give me your mouth and let me improve it. Give it to me. There's it, you're better now, you're almost a good girl . . .

He leaves a big tip when they go. Nobody could ever mistake him for a waiter now. Nobody ever will again. Men are looking at her. Let them look. She's my jewel. All mine.

27.

SO ISAAC FALLS INTO THE RHYTHM and intensity of the new working days. He spends the mornings and afternoons of every weekday under the patient tutelage of Jack Miller at Gold Reef Panel Beating and then, skipping drinks at the Great Britain Hotel afterwards, he rushes to the Reformatory where he'll put in another four or five hours. On weekends he's up early to be at the Reformatory before sunrise and often he'll stay over there through Saturday night and go on working Sunday on six hours' sleep. Meanwhile Hugo attends to the paperwork and the creditors, endlessly daydreaming new ideas, some inventive, some plain insane, and it's on Isaac to vet them for practicality, to talk him back down to cool earth when he gets too hot in his airy excitements. It starts to make him better understand why Hugo needs him: Hugo has charm and energy but lacks tenacity; Isaac has the blunt force of will and manual talents to see things through. He senses how Hugo gains peace of mind by his stabilizing presence. With things at the Reformatory solidly anchored, the nitty-gritty taken care of and no bothering questions to niggle at him, Hugo is freed up for the road, the easy dealings that reel in the contracts. A good partnership, then, as is the one with Jack Miller at the workshop where Isaac's metalworking skills are every day becoming further refined. If he starts in the morning with his body stiff and reluctant, he finds that so long as he keeps his mind on his task like a wrench tight around a nut then a trick will gradually be worked and the tiredness will crack and fall away and comes instead a lightness and a soaring inside. Hard work of the right kind seems to give him more vitality, not less; though at the end of the day when he sinks into the hot bath full of Epsom salts that Mame always has ready for him, his muscles dissolve like liquid off his bones, and later on his cot he falls without pause into black and dreamless slumbers that seem to eclipse barely a minute before the morning light is nudging him awake.

Seeing Yvonne also refreshes him. He sleeps in a storage shed through most of every lunch break at the panel beating shop, save for Wednesdays when he visits Yvonne at The Castle (illicitly), returning again on one or two Saturday nights a month (licitly) in the borrowed Citroën that has become his own de facto automobile, to pick her up perhaps not exactly with parental blessing, yet undeniably in their full and unimpeding regard. He takes her to bioscopes and to dance halls. Takes her for walks and buys her ice cream and good suppers. He, Isaac Helger, owner of dense orange hair and bat ears, freckles and crimped lips – he's the one who takes her, no other. Out there in public where she holds his arm. They kiss and talk and touch. This is now to him an official courtship and the sweet knowledge of it clings to him like strands of honey all the time.

One of his first acts at the Reformatory is to have a professional sign put up – simple and large, black and white: LION MOTORS – and also to see that a proper gate is put in place. Hugo is skeptical – they're just ganna rip them off – but Isaac insists on using their new electrical hookup for bright spotlights he positions above the gates. Thinking (as he so often does) of his cousin Avrom he buys a shotgun that he takes to firing off from the rooftop each night, in the direction of the squatter camp. He leaves this shotgun with the albino watchman, with instructions to blast at anything, animal or mineral, that wanders into the bright lights. It seems to work until the albino disappears along with the weapon, never to be heard from again. Meanwhile one of the trucks has been stolen (by the driver, they learn) and another driver gets into a post-prandial accident and is so drunk that he can barely slur his own name when the police show up.

—Hugo, says Isaac. We got some staffing issues, man.

—What you talking, we a hundred and ten percent.

—What happened to a hundred twenty?

—Never mind the staff, junior.

—Hugo, wherejoo find these people, prison? They a bunch of tsotsis and gunovim, man. And there's too many. I'm taking over staffing.

Hugo grumbles but not very seriously; they both know Isaac understands the boys better, he can speak their language and he's worked with them ever since his first job at Morris Brothers, which is exactly where he drives that same evening. He parks down the street from the warehouse and gets out when he sees Silas leaving. Silas who cost him his job, ja, but only because he was loyal to his boss, a loyalty that Isaac as a boss now himself has come to appreciate. Ja, solid reliable Silas whom the others respect and look up to, who puts the interests of the owners first.

Silas looks ready to bolt when he sees Isaac waiting for him, but Isaac calms him, apologizes for what happened with that punch last time, then makes a straightforward offer of cash and lots more to come. When Silas hesitates Isaac drives him out to the Reformatory to have a look around, then he turns Hugo and his charm loose on him. Afterwards, Isaac promises Silas he won't be just a driver or mechanic, he'll also be the yard boss over all the others. In fact, he'll be the one who helps Isaac find new staff.

Silas touches one of his long dangling earlobes; he hawks and spits on the dirt.

—The baas, he is good for offer me. But why for you wanting?

—I trust you, Silas. Then he shakes a fist, grins. —And cos you know and I know what will happen if you ever try to stuff me around.

Silas nods gravely, fingering the other lobe.

The next week Silas Mabuza joins Lion Motors and Isaac fires the remainder of those hired by Hugo. Silas brings with him some of the old faces from Morris, including Fisu and Hosea, plus a half-ton flatbed bakkie full of relatives from Zululand. These Zulus arrive with a more than generous supply of fighting sticks, shields and knobkerries, and some of them quickly form a corps of watch-men under the command of Silas's second cousin Nangi. They deal most effectively with the squatter camp marauders on their first night. They turn off the spotlights and wait in a ditch. Isaac stays around to observe. The lights come on as they spring their ambush in classical Zulu style, an enveloping charge resembling the horns of a bull. Shields, yells, walloping sticks. It nets them a half-dozen prisoners too slow to escape shrilling into the night. Nangi brings them into the yard where they must, in his words, *get lots and lots of good medicines.* These dosages raise a chorus of howls and after-wards the would-be marauders limp slowly off homeward, taking word of the new order at the Reformatory, so that Isaac becomes fairly confident that Lion Motors will be pilfered no more.

A bisel oon a bisel vert a foler shisel: Little bits fill the bowl, a favourite saying of Mame's that rings in him like a striking panel hammer through these burgeoning months of 1939. The wrecks flow into the building then overflow into the yard, piling up in stacks on the baked earth. Wrecks start to arrive by rail, testament to the stretch of Hugo's wandering ambition. With the others, Silas and Isaac work hard to strip the parts from the scrap and to keep the trucks running on schedule. This bond of labour bolts a trust so implicit between them that he gives Silas all of the wages in cash to distribute each week. Upstairs the floor space disappears under engines, generators, starters, radiators, differentials, gearboxes, brake drums, tires, batteries, doors and on and on. The spread of this is a stimulant to his mind: for once the fresh idea jumps out of his mouth and not Hugo's. Grudgingly, Hugo accedes. They empty the big room to cleanse and paint it, to install panes in the windows. On their return, parts are grouped like to like and Hugo's desk is made a cash counter as an ad goes into the *Star*. The next weekend they open for retail business and the size of the crowd shocks them both. Counting the takings at the end of that first day, Hugo shakes his great head. —Nice, but if we sat on these parts, in a year's time they'd be worth double, triple.

—If there's a war.

—Oh, there'll be a war. I can smell it.

Isaac grunts, torquing his face to ugliness. —Ja, we'll see about that. Anyway, we got the contracts right? There's plenny more where those came from and meanwhile you can keep our creditors happy for another week.

It goes on that way: if the business was constipated before Isaac joined it, these weekend sales become a regular dose of laxative, loosing the cash flow for Hugo to keep his little numbers juggling on his calendar. But they also are careful to store a portion of the stripped parts away for future sales. While outside, the wrecks continue to pile. Tires make a dark pyramid as high as the second floor. Isaac starts to talk about renting a crusher so that they can squeeze the scrap metal into steel cubes for storage.

One Saturday evening after the showroom is closed he is scrubbing the black grease from his hands and forearms, bent shirtless over an oil drum full of green water, when Hugo comes down and puts his foot up on an engine block. He wedges a cigar and a cigarette in his lips, lights them both then pokes the ciggy into Isaac's mouth. —Know what? We just busted the sales record.

Isaac puffs, one watering eye half shut to the curl of smoke, drying his arms with a rag. —Know what? I turned twenny last week and didn't even notice.

—What you want from me, birthday smooch?

—Ganna get that from Yvesy. She's taking me to concert tonight.

—How sweet. Listen, I reckon it was your boss, that Labuschagne, he was in here also today.

Isaac shrugs. It's a possibility they'd talked about, one of the reasons he doesn't show his face in the showroom (an apprentice panel beater running a business on the side in the same industry would probably not go down well). Hugo says he knows Labuschagne from having visited the garages on Marshall Street to spread the word on their sales.

—Funny thing, says Hugo. He asked me do I know of a mechanic.

—*He's* the mechanic.

—Ja, but he's looking to hire another one. Business is up for everyone, looks like. Nowadays can't find a good mechanic for love or money.

Isaac reaches for his shirt.

—Gotta hurry hurry hey, says Hugo. Mustn't keep the female waiting.

—Stuff you.

Hugo winks and dips in his pocket for the bottle. Isaac has a flash of a racing paper folded in there.

Late in the night after he drops off Yvonne he drives home with the taste of her still in his mouth and the lemony smell of her hair in his clothes, the drugged feeling of her spirit and presence still so strong in him that it lives like a sweet heaviness in his blood, beats a soft echo behind his every pulse. He doesn't even notice the Studebaker on Buxton Street till it flashes its lights at him as he walks towards his house from where he's parked. He hesitates. An arm comes out, scoops at him.

When he leans down, a voice says: —Isaac, sit with me.

He squints at the dark profile. An overhead light comes on. —Bladey hell.

—Please.

—Christ. The hell *you* doing here?

The attorney Papendropolous puts a briefcase on his lap once Isaac's next to him in the back, and the driver – wide-necked, stocky – steps out of the vehicle and shuts the door. Papendropolous asks Isaac to roll up the window.

—You been waiting here all night, what?

—I've brought a message from our mutual friend.

—Our who?

Papendropolous cants his spaniel nose, his thick eyebrows lift very slightly.

—Ukay . . .

—He's heard good things about you. He wants you to know this. To encourage you.

—He does? Av–

Lips snap on the lawyer's even teeth. —Don't say a name. No need for it.

Isaac watches him. —What you mean he's *heard*?

—He hears many things, our friend. He has ears all around the city. Eyes.

Isaac thinks about this.

—He has also had second thoughts about . . . what transpired.

—Trans what?

—Your mother's request.

Isaac blinks.

—You understand?

—What, you saying he changed his mind?

—Yes.

—Why?

The eyebrows ripple, a kind of shrug for the face.

—What, cos a me?

A pause. —He's been impressed by what he's heard. Beyond that I can't say.

—Well what did *he* say exactly?

Papendropolous stretches his neck against his bracing hand, apparent irritation that raises the same in Isaac who tells him, —Look hey, what is this now? Back of car the middle of the bladey night. Why dint he just give us a bell like a normal? Why couldn't he come and see us and come in and speak to Ma himself? Ma, she is the one hey. Not me. He is her–

Papendropolous has his hand up; his lips snap again. —Isaac. Understand this first. You may not make contact. He doesn't want contact under any circumstances. Don't ever even refer to him in connection, got it?

—Why, is he not well?

—He's fine. What I'd like from you – acknowledge my terms. Otherwise this is all off. Acknowledge.

—I don't even know what this *is*.

—No contact. Don't even *try*. Else we say good night and I'll go back right now and you'll never hear from me.

—Jee-zus. Hold your hormones, man.

—I've waited hours to speak alone. I go now and no one's the wiser. You dreamed me up.

Isaac watches him, the blunt shadows unmoving in the crannies of his downlit face. —You a tough little bastard aren't you.

—I represent our friend, that's all. I'm talking to you as inter-locutor with your mother.

—The what now?

He arches his neck, grimaces. —The language barrier. So I'm dealing with you and you deal with her.

Isaac grins. —Ach, you just scared a her, isn't it. Don't blame you.

Papendropolous doesn't return any glint of humour. —I'll deal with you, he says flatly.

Isaac nods. —He'll deal. The wheeler-dealer. Well what *is* this bladey deal then? I won't try contact no one.

Papendropolous nods, opens the briefcase. His head ducks under the light, an ostrich egg of leathern flesh ringed at its peak with black hair. It's his nose that seems to edge first into the papers, as if to sniff out the most pungent document for the hirsute groping fingers.

He lifts out a foolscap envelope, yellow, the flap tied with red string. Unwinding, he says: —These forms need to be filled out. One form per family. This means the man plus wife and dependants, defined age fourteen and under. Signature lines leave blank, of course.

—Wait a sec now. What is this?

—What what is this? This is our friend.

Isaac thinks hard, his temples knocking with heartbeats. —Ukay, listen, what happened over there, I dunno if you know. What happened, she gave *him* money hey. Told him put what he could with that and then–

The sheets are neatly stacked on the shut briefcase across his lap now; his stubby fingers tap. —This is how he wants it.

—What you saying?

—He provides the funds, but your mother must direct them.

—Direct?

—See this?

He lifts a sheet. Isaac squints in the weak light; concentration is also difficult, so many other churning thoughts want their place in the front of his mind. It's a South African immigration document. Names, ages, address. —But this all checks like something *they* have to do, ay. I mean on their end.

—As I said, leave blank the signatures. But you *must* fill in the rest. They'll be sent on to the British consulate in Lithuania. Then all they will need to do is sign them to get their visas and travel tickets.

—Everything, tickets also? Paid for?

—Correct.

The paper is back on the pile; the fingernails tap.

—How's that ganna happen?

—It doesn't matter.

—Yes it does.

—Not to you.

—I wanna know.

He grimaces. —It's complicated.

—I've got a right.

Papendropolous closes his eyes for four seconds. —There is a senior individual in immigration who'll take care of this. But it has to be coordinated with others. It may take some time.

—Hey, and what about Aliens hey? What about that emigration board?

For the first time, a look of surprise: the lawyer blinks in a quick flurry. —It'll be arranged. Exemptions.

—It will?

—It is.

Isaac looks down at the forms. —For a price, right.

—Indeed. Every completed family application needs a payment of five hundred.

—Five hundred what?

—Pounds. In cash.

—Jesus fucken Christ.

—Indeed.

—Pardon my French, but seriously, man, a half a grand *each*? They mad in the head?

—Each family.

—Mad in the head.

—You said it already yourself, how immigration policy's not friendly to Lithuanian nationals. Believe me, it's difficult even for this price. Might not be possible at all.

Isaac thinks about this, looking away, lapping once around his mouth with a dry tongue, swallowing. The cost of a life, a price for everything.

—So we fill in these forms and then what? Send em back to you?

Another grimace, this one making like Isaac is a Stupid. —No, he says. I've said that and meant it. No circumstances does our friend want his name tied to this. Same goes for the recipient. This is why this is a cash deal. This is why I'm talking to you in the back of a car. The recipient's not accepting funds even from a representative like me, right? He wants it from your mother only.

—Why would he want that?

—Isaac.

—Doesn't make sense.

Papendropolous sighs. —I don't know. There's ever an inquiry, he can plead genuine compassion as a mitigating factor. Cites a personal meeting and appeal from your mother, et cetera. That's one reason I can think of. Also, that it had *nothing* to do with our mutual friend. But, Isaac, this part doesn't concern you.

—It fucken does, Isaac tells this snot-nosed attorney, his voice lifting. And I don't understand what you just said properly, man, so just talk bladey straight English to me will you.

Papendropolous goes narrow in the eyes.

—What? says Isaac.

He shakes his head, a tiny movement. —It's got to be clean hands for dirty money. Your mother has to take these forms with the cash personally to the man. She and only she, with you of course as translator. Those are the terms. Clear now? Good. So – you want this or not? I need an answer.

Isaac looks at the forms, the briefcase. —You telling me now you sitting next to me here with, what, *thousands* of pounds right there?

—Sadly not. He digs out another envelope, shaped like an ordinary letter only longer, and unsealed. He removes two pages of heavy paper folded in three sections. Isaac sees a letterhead, fancy lines under three names. Vance, Johnson and Smythe, Attorneys at Law.

—A letter of release for the funds. When the time comes you and your mother take it to their offices on Diagonal Street. The funds are held in blind trust in the safe there. Your mother must sign for the release. Then you two go to the meeting with the recipient. It will happen quickly when it happens.

—So what, we just bell them up, let them know we coming?

—There're three direct phone numbers in that letter which ring through to Mr. Vance. When the time comes he will be expecting your call.

—When is that?

—You fill out the forms quick as you can. Be ready, that's important. But you also may have to be patient. What'll happen, sometime in the near future – could be next week, could be six, seven months, most likely somewhere in the middle – I'll contact you with details. Date, time, place.

Isaac says nothing.

—Understand me? Way it works, there'll be this short time when the right people're in place to see your relatives through. That's when you'll hear from me. You'll take your mother, go and get the money from Vance, go and pay it with these forms at the meeting. Got it?

—Ja, I get you man. What you think, I'm a Stupid?

—Then your answer is what?

—Hang on. Lemme think a sec.

There's a silence in which Isaac gnaws on the top of his fist. —Ukay, why don't we just get the money right now? Keep it all ready with them forms.

—It's there for safekeeping, says Papendropolous flatly. Keeps the source of the funds legally secret and separate. And if things don't pan out, the money goes back to our friend. Obviously.

Isaac nods. —Ja, cos he doesn't trust us hey.

Papendropolous snaps his lips. —Look, I'm here to tell you how this is going to be done, Isaac. That's all.

—Oright, man, I hear you. Go over it again one time.

A measured inhalation: —I give you these forms. You fill them in. When things come together, I'll instruct Vance to expect your call, to release the funds. The exact date of the meeting with the recipient is going to be last-minute, that's the nature of how he wants it plus other factors that aren't your concern. You – both of you – be ready to move fast when you hear from me. First you go to Vance for the money, then to the recipient. When you see the recipient, don't say anything to him. Just let your mother hand him the package. Answer his questions if there are. Nothing else. Is that clear enough now?

—So now we fill these out and we wait.

—Correct.

—Cos you still waiting to hear from this oke in the guvmint?

—Basically, yes.

—So what if we fill em out and you don't hear from him, or like he cancels?

—That is a very real possibility. There's no guarantees here at all. But don't delay. It's also possible this could happen in the next couple weeks.

—Or not, says Isaac.

—That's right. Look – you want to proceed or no?

— . . . Ukay, give.

Papendropolous shifts the pile across. There's two joined pages that make a cover around a single page, Isaac finds, and two more of these covers with pages in them under the first. He looks through them: all are identical. —Wait a second.

—What?

—There's only three of these here.

—Three sets, yes.

—I don't understand.

—What now?

—You said each one is for a family.

Papendropolous cocks his head. —That's right.

—But she's got five sisters, man. There's *five* a them.

Papendropolous pinches his lips together with thumb and forefinger; his cheeks slightly puff.

—Hey? It's only here for three here. Izen it?

—Correct. Three.

—This is bullshit. You can't—you saying she has to pick three? Only three?

—Isaac, this is how it is.

—It's ganna twist her guts to hell man. And top of it, you say they can cancel? What you tryna do to her? The woman could die man. You don't know. She could actually die.

A silence for words but not for Isaac's hard breathing.

—I see, says Papendropolous.

—No you don't *see*. Sitting there fancy suit. You playing roller coasters with her, shmock! It's not right. I don't wanna put her through that. I mean, why's he making her choose? I mean it is *sick* hey. She got five – *he* knows. Five–

Papendropolous puffs air, checks his watch. —Isaac, this is the deal. This is what's on offer to you. Is what you telling me a no? Is no what you want? You want me to leave?

— . . . I dunno.

—Well, find a way to know.

—Oright. Calm your berries. Just hang on, I gotta think.

—This is a generous offer, believe me. A person has to work with what can be done, with realistic options. I was you, I wouldn't stare too long down the mouth of a gift horse. The thing might gallop away. Isaac, you have to be a grown-up.

Watching the forms, Isaac nods slowly.

—Just remember, says Papendropolous.

He looks up. Papendropolous brings a vertical forefinger to his fleshy lips.

Tiredly, Isaac nods again.

He listens at his parents' door, his sister's. Deep night breaths in the dark house. Silent but for the submarine knocking of his own heart in the liquid blackness of his chest. He lifts the cashbox and takes it with the papers out into the yard. In the outhouse he uses two paper clips on the lock – old trick of his barefoot days – one clip to keep pressure and the other to ease back the tumblers inside. He opens the box, sets down the cash tray at his ankle. Insects coat the single bulb on the long wire above. He turns over the copies of the passports, the government forms, the personal letters. He reads. Reads again what Papendropolous gave him. An hour evaporates like a minute in the glare of his time-burning attention.

Five Moskevitch sisters: Orli, Friedke, Dvora, Trudel-Sora, Rochel-Dor. Four husbands for them: Pinchus Snyman, Shlayma Kirtzbacher, Yossel Melkin, Benzil Kreb. And then all of their children. Then a yellowed letter in the trove draws his contemplations sideways, to his father. The document dates back to April 1911, seems to be a ministry notice, with a coat of arms and words in Russian, must be. Above them in a tiny hand someone has written in Hebrew characters, translating it, surely. The lines call on Abel Levitz Helger to report to the police station in Kovno within ten days, for service in the First Cavalry Regiment in Syzran (here the handwritten words have an additional slant above – *hundreds of miles east of Moscow!*, it says). His term of service is twenty-one years. Twenty-*one*, Isaac thinks. His father would have been, what, seventeen years of age? It says he will receive five rubles if he brings his own boots (*nice of them!* add more slanted words above); eleven kopecks for earmuffs. It floods Isaac with hot shame to remember how he has thought of his father as a coward for dealing with this as he did. No money to grease an official to lose his file; no other way to get away. He must have gone off alone to do it. Isaac imagines the woods in springtime, the white lilies in bloom, the smell of moss and mushrooms. Birdsong. Maybe carrying this very letter in one pocket, maybe in his other he had a hammer and a chisel or just a sharp heavy blade, and he must have had matches to make a fire to heat a brand for the cauterizing. Christ, Tutte. He would have prayed, ja, would have spoken the Shmah for sure: The Lord is the God of Israel. The Lord is One.

But the Moskevitch sisters are still waiting when his attention swings back, their words and images staring up. His thighs have gone numb. There is enough information here to fill out the forms by himself; but information is not the problem, deciding is. Orli lives in Dusat still, so do Friedke and Trudel-Sora. Orli is single, but Friedke has Pinchus and five children, Zalman, Shayna, Tuvya, Mensil and Koppel. Only Koppel is fourteen, the rest older. Trudel-Sora and Yossel have four – Dina, Midya, Dassa and Offir-Gan – and all minors but for one. She seems an easy choice because she has three youngsters who can be included. Friedke has more kids but to choose her would be to split her family; what, would they leave their four oldest behind? Then there's Orli, single Orli – she would have no chance in his calculations but for the fact that these three sisters are still together in Dusat and maybe should stay together? No. Let Orli remain to help the older nephews and nieces who must stay behind. Then there's Dvora, married to Shlayma Kirtzbacher and living in Rokishik with two, Shimmy and Chaya. And then there's Benzil and Rochel-Dor who suffered miscarriages and lost not one but two children to some unnamed and un-understood illness and finally have only one little girl, Ilana, and live in Ponevez. To choose to get the maxium number of human beings out or to make some other kind of determination? One thing the letters make clear, there is no possibility that any one of them would turn down the chance to leave. It's bad over there.

Mame was a kind of mother to her sisters after their real one died. God, which ones to pick, how to decide? He feels weak, sick. His thighs tingle electrically. Sitting on the shitbox with the lives of his relatives under his hands like some devil king on a reeking throne. But he's becoming sure: he will not bring Mame into this torturous business, not now, not until some good is absolutely assured. No, he's not like any devil, let alone a king; just a son with a good heart, shielding his mame from needless suffering. He nods to himself five times, decided.

28.

IN TOWN HE BUYS a brannew Philco wireless set, Empire Automatic model. The wireless they used to have died a sad death, fading and crackling to silence some time ago and he gives this one as a gift to Mame to replace it. She doesn't want to take it – a waste of money – but she does because she needs to hear the news from overseas on the SABC. The Philco has excellent reception and a good strong volume so she can hear every word clearly, and she puts it in the workshop where she sits close beside it whenever it's news time, with a pad and a pencil, writing down whatever she thinks she doesn't properly understand so she can ask him or Rively about it later.

The wireless doesn't do any of the things that he hoped it would when he bought it. Doesn't help him feel better about the secret any. Doesn't please her as a gift should, but only makes her worse because of the bad news it pipes into the house like a poison trumpet blowing ill-making fumes all day long.

March is very bad because she listens to how Hitler demands possession of the city and region of Klaipėda, which is in Lithuania. Lithuania! Of all stuffing places it has to be Lithuania. The Lithuanians buckle under German ultimatums and never mind bladey Chamberlain, the Stupid, and all his peace-in-our-time kuk. After Germans seize the port they rename it Memel and Hitler himself sails there on the battleship *Deutschland*, gives a victory speech while thousands of Jewish refugees stream out, beaten by fascists along the way.

She was in a bad-enough way after the trip to Avrom but now her afternoon naps, once unthinkable, have turned into hour-long lie-downs that involve no sleep. He knows this from Abel, who tells him in a whisper how worried he's becoming, how when he checks on her he finds her lying on her back with her eyes wide open and runnels of tears tracing down both sides to the ears. She who never cries. Isaac thinks of that time after he was beaten, when he lay and oozed tears from his cracked soul. He can see that Avrom's refusal to help plus the terror of the bad news is doing to his mother's spirit what the beating did to his: it's the helplessness of being utterly overmatched. It makes you give up. But unlike his thoughts of revenge, she can't just jettison her fears for her sisters backhome.

She has bad dreams, his father says. Bad feelings. She lies there sometimes with the photo albums hugged to her chest. That picture of her hurts Isaac very badly so that he wishes Abel had never shared it with him. To think of her lying like that, all her slender hopes on the little bit of money that she gave to her nephew – it devastates him. She has no idea the money's already long gone, already been spent by Isaac on the business.

At times these thoughts make him want to rush to her and tell her the secret of the immigration forms he has filled out and hidden in the corner of the sewing room, to give her *some* hope at least. But hope for only three of the families would be a fresh torture; and it's hope that might turn to nothing at all. The fall from it would kill her. No, he has no doubt he's doing right – let him be strong as a lion and take this on himself. Avrom's refusal has done enough damage to her as it is. But the secret is very hard to keep. In May the booming wireless for weeks follows the drama of an ocean liner called the *St. Louis*, a German vessel with about a thousand Jewish refugees limping around the world's oceans looking for a place to land. But no one wants Jews, South Africa included. In the end they go back to Europe, four countries reluctantly agreeing to take a few Jews each.

Mame goes around with crying eyes, even if there're no tears. He understands: reading their words in the night in the sewing room, doing his secret filling-in of the forms, there were moments he also cried, so hard sometimes he had to take care not to drip on the letters and leave clues of his spying. Reading them he saw what Mame saw through their sentences, flashes in himself from that long ago, sometimes the faces of the photo albums fluidly moving to life again. Remembering Auntie Dvora giving him the wooden bucket stained with berry juices to carry while she lifted him onto her hip. Remembering Auntie Trudel-Sora doing tricks with her plump fingertips brushing her lips, going *brim-brom-broomdubu! brim-brom-broomdubu!*, making him dizzy with giggling. There was much in the Yiddish text slanted in longhand Hebrew characters without vowels that escaped him, his knowledge of the written language not enough to extract the deepest sense of what these documents carry, and maybe that was for the better, for the news is perpetually bad. Another anti-Semitic incident or measure taken, another one killed by sickness, another financial hardship, another lucky one able to leave for Africa or Argentina or America and bless The Name this and bless The Name that, as if the harder their lives the more they must profess their love to the deity that wields their groaning fate.

But nowhere in his scanning did he ever find the name of Hershel or Suttner or Avrom. Not once.

At the Reformatory he drives himself savagely, working late and rarely breaking. And when he's with Yvonne he kisses her and caresses her with a new ferocity, like she's prey in his lion claws, like he's devouring her down to the toes with the force of his love, and sometimes she'll turn away from him with a kind of fright in her green eyes and then he'll hold her and whisper to her, tell her it's all right, whatever she's worried about, whatever it is, it's nothing to them, nothing can affect *them* when they're together like this, nothing . . .

He finds himself telling some of this to Hugo, over mugs of sweet tea laced with whisky, dipping rusks into the brews between sips and mouthfuls; but his feelings knot up his tongue and ball in his chest so that his hesitant words trail off and he shakes his head.

—Boyki, I can see there's only one cure for you left. Dr. Bleznik's seen this disease too many times.

—You're an arse, Hugo.

—No, genuine, you ganna like this. Leave to me.

Soon after, Hugo takes him to a sunny spot and brings something out of his pocket that he holds to the light. —See how it sparks. That's the carbons. Nothing else on earth like it.

Isaac swears.

—Can thank me anytime boyki.

—No. This a real one? No.

—Diamond is as diamond does, my friend. And sterling silver. Put that on her pretty little finger and you got yourself an official engagement. Most times Dr. Bleznik will try and save the patient, but I can see you too far gone. You a terminal case.

Isaac blinks at the bright tiny stone. —Wait. Are we paying for this?

—Relax yourself boyki. Not exactly the crown jewel is it? Anyway it's not costing us tuppence. S'a favour of a favour from an ou I know down Kimberley way. From me to you. So take it and smile. You ganna need all the smiles you can get.

Isaac picks it off the plump palm. —Holy shit man, Hugo. I dunno what to say.

—Say thank you Dr. Bleznik. And if – I mean when – she says yes, try and edge me in to see the father-in-law hey. Couldn't hurt to let him in on investment of a lifetime, why not.

Isaac answers this with a long stare. Hugo looks away. —Oright, oright. Sorry.

—You better be.

He takes the ring to Chertkov the jeweller and has him engrave *Isaac & Yvonne Forever* on the silver. It's in his pocket when he picks her up the following Saturday but his plans for a nice romantic supper don't unfold as she's dying to see a new American flick called *The Wizard of Oz*, some fairy-tale nonsense starring a girl called Judy Garland. They're having a one-night-only early screening at the Metro Theatre, biggest and most larney in town, and it won't be back for months for general release, so Isaac shelves his plans and drives to the Metro instead to buy them overpriced tickets and make Yvonne happy. In the dark his work-tired body grows slack. He was nervous before about the ring, what he would say exactly when he took it out, and as the nervousness fades his eyelids sag. He falls asleep before the end of the newsreel. Yvonne's elbow wakes him up at the credits. —Now *that* was what I call a bladey good film, he says.

She wrinkles her face. Her eyes turn green as the house lights come on. That other light comes on in his chest, clean and cold and bright. He shivers and kisses her, thinking of the first time he saw her that day at The Castle, moving her mother's art glass, Yvonne (Shookee) on the stairs by the boxes, and then at the garden table with her book of poetry. What a great distance he has covered, ready to propose; but not tonight, next time, at the right moment, almost there.

This feeling of a miraculous achievement is still with him as they kiss and grope afterwards in the dark Citroën. She lets him cover her between the legs with his hand under the skirt over the panties, caressing the soft mound till she starts to shudder and he can feel the wet of it. He slips one fingertip under the edge of the panties and feels the hair and the outer lips of her innermost flesh and her body jerks. She puts her hand over his but she lets him touch her for the longest time yet before slowly easing his arm away.

As he drives back to Doornfontein he is shouting along with the radio in his tone-deaf way, music still meaning little to him but somehow, tonight, it feels good to pretend that it does, like he's a character in a film. This kind of luck only happens to bioscope characters.

He runs into a police roadblock coming down Harrow Road. They wave him through but he slows anyway, to ask what's going on. They don't tell him, wave him into Currey Street with the rest of the diverted traffic. As he turns he sees in his rearview a convoy of trucks coming up. He slows to watch it pass, turning ahead. He sees the heads of people in the back, and bags and suitcases heaped up. Truck after truck goes up, the dark heads nodding in the open air. Farther east past Ellis Park there are more roadblocks. Again the cops won't say why but one makes a crack about sanitation duty. When the clouds shift and the moonlight floods down it shows a scrawl of dust or smoke over the rooftops out toward the railway line. There's a scent of ash.

Later, as he turns into the alleyway he sees a woman on the pavement. After he's parked he walks back around to have another look, make sure she's not a troublemaker. An old Black woman with vast hips, bent over and talking to what he thinks is herself at first but then sees as she comes up is a tall white dog, tied to her wrist with a string. She has bags in a knotted blanket around her, bags in her hands. She's breathing heavily and some blood shines on her face, the back of one hand. Her shoulders work over her hobbled steps, dipping and lifting in the ponderous see-saw manner of the obese. The pale dog watches her, her voice seems angry, the Black words making her tongue knock and click in her working mouth. Another mad shvartzer; Isaac turns away.

In the kitchen he opens a beer and studies the ring. A noise outside makes him step into the yard where he finds the Black woman resting her bundle on their low wall, taking heavy slow breaths and whining slightly between each. The streetlamp shine here shows the blood on her face is from marks like scratches. Above the titanic labouring bust her dress is torn.

He asks her what she's doing here. She lifts her head slowly. He goes toward the gateway in the low wall and the lanky dog steps through it, around from behind the wall, its hairs prickling up over the shoulders, the length of it going stiff as it points its muzzle with the black lips shrivelling from the teeth.

—He's growling at me. You get him out of my yard.

When she doesn't move, he tells her he's serious. —I don't wanna skop your dog hey, but I will if he comes for me.

—You not kicking who is your friend, she says.

—Hey? What you say?

—You mummy. Fetch for her. Can talk.

—Hey?

She lumbers along the wall till she gets to the gateway and she props herself there and bends, touching the dog between his pointed ears. One of these street mutts with no proper collar, wirethin and fearless, its teeth still showing: they don't waste energy barking or even growling much. They carry disease. —He is *your* friend, she says.

Something stops him then. A nameless feeling. —Who are you?

—I want speak you mummy.

—Oh shit, he says. Oh jeez.

—Ja. Ja, is me, she says. Can have some water.

He finds Mame already up, standing in the kitchen with her hand squeezing her nightgown under her throat, as if summoned from sleep by the call of this trundling phantom, this revenant with its canine familiar attached by a string. She's looking through the glass into the moonwashed yard and doesn't even glance at Isaac. Then he thinks that she wasn't asleep at all. Eyes sunken in caverns of bruise, her face around the scar is so tired it's as if the bones behind it have shrunk, new wrinkles have spread like devouring veins. It's been so long since he's taken the time to really look at her that he feels the shock of the change. Mame.

He follows her into the yard, hears her say, —Yes. And vhy you come?

—They brek for us, says this woman whose name, Isaac remembers now, is Mama Kelo.

—Brik?

—Break for our houses. Finish, all finish. So bad.

—Who brik?

—The police, she break.

—Nu? Vot can I do?

—Can put for me. She swallows, pants, the thin dog looking up at her. —Can put for me. Letter.

—Letter?

—Writing say I work for you. Here. Otherwise must go already far. No.

Isaac doesn't need to look at his mother to see the head shaking; he can read it plain in her moonshadow.

—Say I work for you, for maid.

—I don't vunt maid.

—Is okay. Only put for letter to put. I'm go. I'm not stay here. Only letter. Have my son here, in Fietas, otherwise must go so far other place. Nothing there. Bad place.

—And where can you stay here? There's no room.

—Only put for letter. I go. Letter, for show.

— . . . No, his mother says. No.

They are looking at one another, eyes to eyes. Isaac looks at his mame. It's just as it was, years mean nothing. She lifts her chin, stretching the web of scar tissue. Just as it was over there by the rail bridge when she made her take the puppy, like a little lamb it was, now look at it, hard as the streets, all teeth and bristles. She had to pay the brandy price then and she'll have to go now without her letter. When Mame lifts her chin there is no other way.

—I make for you business, says Mama Kelo. Years.

—Is finish. You go now.

—What I do for you, too many years. Only one letter.

—I say no.

She takes Isaac by the arm and draws him back inside. He thinks, But I didn't give her water. Through the kitchen window he watches Mama Kelo slowly gathering up her parcels off the wall, her great bulk. She moves off bent with the weight of her things, the dog with its nose and tail pointing down, moving behind her. She pauses. Looks back at the house and starts to shout. Her strong sudden voice penetrating the walls. Mame rushes through the back door. —I call police for you! You go!

Isaac goes down after her, stops behind his mother in time to see Mama Kelo put down a bag and raise her arm with fingers widespread. She spits deliberate words in another language, the one that is hers, the tongue of this land, seethed up from its red soil, its glinting rocks, ancient. Her eyes swell in her skull, seem to protrude. Her hand passes across his mother, the house, then himself. He feels a heat in his chest and his mouth dries. He waits for his mother to shout, to smash this moment. The heat in his chest becomes choking. Slowly the dark arm falls. She moves off. It is Isaac who ends up taking his mother's elbow this time. Inside, he wants to say it's over. Wants to hug her and break back through to what was before, when he was little and she was there with him; but in silence she turns her back and closes her door.

On his way to work early, seeing the police roadblocks are gone, he takes a detour through the empty Sunday streets. At the end of the road of compacted dirt he finds that the Yards are no longer. All is flat, a field of scattered sheets of corrugated iron, their rusted backs strewn like monstrous autumn leaves. White children are picking over things, charred rubbish piles still smoulder, a few adults stand looking.

He parks and gets out, trying to remember if this is where he played as a boy. No, the Coloured Yards are farther south. Skots, Nixie, Charlie and Davey – where might they be now? Auntie Peaches and Auntie Marie and Auntie Sooki. He thinks of those trucks the night before. Thinks of Mama Kelo and feels the choking heat beginning in his chest again and muscles it down.

There's a pair of oldster Jewishers nearby, a round fat one he thinks works at Rippleman's hardware and a tall thin one with a hairy wart on his chin. He wanders up to them. —Shit hey, he says. All gone.

Like a storm came, says tall.

The time was passed years ago already, says fat.

What do you mean? Isaac says, switching languages to theirs.

Fat has a smug and oily smile. What blinder man couldn't see it was coming for how many years. These kaffirs and half-breeds and coolies and all their drek should have been gone long ago.

—*Geven menschen!* shouts a voice behind. These were people. These were human beings.

Isaac turns and sees three of the Bernstein boys, Yankel in back of his two brothers. Yankel half lifts a hand as if ashamed to be greeting. The older Bernstein is pale and his lips twitch.

Human beings? says fat. He spreads out upturned palms. What is he making speeches about human beings, the madman. Those who shit in their living room, they should have houses like Whites? Give them yours.

Leave them, says thin. Can't talk to Communists.

But fat seems inclined to lecture: his arms lift, along with his volume. Listen, you Red know-alls, council's been trying how many years with this. It needed cleaning.

But the grease, says thin.

Who was greasing? Isaac asks.

Who? says the older Bernstein. Exactly! Our own, our own. Bastard landlords squeezing misery for profits.

Lies, lies! says fat. Not us!

No, says thin. He's not so wrong. That Weisser was one. And Greenburg.

What are you, commie in the cupboard also? A man can't be allowed to make a living? They were only too grateful to live here, you think they wanted to leave? Ha! The police had to *drag* them out, and you tell me was so bad. Then why were they crying? They can always go live in the bush like they always did . . .

The Bernsteins start shouting. Arms flail and spittle flies. Yankel steps around and shakes Isaac's hand. They walk off, the argument getting louder behind them: four Jews, nine thousand opinions.

—How you keeping? says Yankel. I never see you.

—I'm working a lot.

—Ja, Rively says you got a business going on and all now.

—Ja, but keep that under the hat, ay. I don't reckon my boss would be too happy if he knew.

—Hey, joo ever talk to old man Blumenthal? About that Dusat thing?

—No, says Isaac.

—I could organize for you if you like.

—No.

Yankel looks at him for a moment, then stops and turns to the field of wreckage. —They'll stick up new buildings, be like this never happened.

—You know where they took them all?

—Down south, I heard. That township there, the locations getting so huge, they stick em all in and pretend they don't exist.

Isaac nods. —Oright, well, I gotta go to work.

—Hang on a sec.

—What?

—I just wanted to say . . . tell you . . .

—Whatzit?

Slowly, two mysterious pink blotches materialize, one on his cheek, the other on his neck.

—What is it man?

—Like about your sister, I want you to know, I'm like serious about it hey.

It takes a few seconds for Isaac to understand, then he half laughs, half snorts. —That's your indaba, mate. Don't get me all shlepped in. Long as you treat her good.

The blotches keep spreading, as if groping to meld with one another. He makes an odd sideways ducking motion of the head. —Ja that's what I'm tryna say. It's what I want . . .

—It's oright, says Isaac. I get it.

He says goodbye and walks off, looks back once to see Yankel scampering back to his brothers. Another poor shmock in love. Join the bladey club, my mate. Look at him go. We don't have a chance, once they get hold of your kishkes with those feelings we might as well sign surrender with the female right here and now. Overs-kadovers.

29.

FOR THE FIRST TIME, it's hard for him to concentrate on what Yvonne's saying to him, up in her room; inside he's vibrating with his proposal plans. She won't be around this weekend but they make a date for the following, the last of the month.

His head is so full of how he's going to break the question to her that when he stops at the Permanent Building Society to draw money he doesn't at first understand why the teller keeps saying sorry. He needs the money to give to Silas for the wages.

—Sir, this account, it's been closed.

—Whatchoo mean?

She checks the file. —Mr. Bleznik closed it out last Friday, the fourteenth.

—He what?

He drives fast out towards Brakpan, the East Rand. Hugo's not around at the Reformatory and when he finds Silas he has to apologize. The money's coming, he tells him. Silas does not have to say what is in his eyes, the slight tremor there is enough. This is a man who left his former job – *I have so loyal for Mr. Morris* – because Isaac persuaded him to, and now after a few months things are already looking shaky. He'll never be able to go back to work at Morris Brothers again, that's certain, and good jobs are rare and he has five children and two wives depending on him back home in Natal.

Isaac works with his jaw clenched that night, tearing into the wrecks as if they are the guts of an enemy. On the way home, near midnight, he stops at a tickey box and calls Bleznik, wakes him. —What the bladey hell's going on man? And where were you tonight?

—Don't catch a nappy rash, says Hugo. It's under the control. There's no twist here. We sailing apples, boy. I just made a few consolidations for our capital. Had to kite a few cheques around, that's all. Close up a few accounts here and there. Everything's fluent. We capitalized.

—Why didn't you bladey tell me? I had wages to give today.

—It's minor doings, Tiger. You leave it to Blezzy. Minor doings. I'll sort it with Silas this week.

—Tomorrow. First fuckun thing, oright.

—Calm yourself, Tiger, leave it to Blezzy. Matter of fact, you can relax on this for the next week also. Better let me sort the wages with Silas direct till end of the month.

—Why?

—That's when we get our new accounts all opened and that. August.

—Fine.

—Ukay?

—*Fine.*

—Good then.

Just as Isaac is about to hang up, Bleznik says, —Hey boyki, one other thing, I need a little flavour from you.

—Whatzit?

—Listen, that Citroën, I'm ganna need it back hey.

—Need it *back*.

—That's right.

—Why?

—Boychik, you knew it was always temporary. Had to go back sometime. That's now.

—Can't you organize me another one?

—Ja, f'course, f'course. Just not right away hey.

Isaac doesn't say a thing, scrubbing with his knuckles at his cheekbone. Then: —Hugo, man, what is going on?

—What you mean going on?

—You telling me wages. Now the Citroën too.

—Tiger, slow down. One's got nothing to do the other. The Citroën was always ganna come due. I'll get you a better car, nil worries. Anyway what kind a questioning is this? Getting all hitzik with me. Listen, tomorrow just leave the keys on my desk. Ukay?

Isaac squeezes the receiver hard.

—Ukay?

—Ja. Sure.

—By the by, how'd it go with the ring?

Isaac sniffs. —I haven't yet.

—No worries, Tiger, she's ganna love it. You shine up hey. Have a little patience. Know what they say, be patient or you ganna turn into one.

So his idea for the marriage proposal comes to him at first out of necessity. Since he won't have a car he'll take her on a nice long walk instead. Go to The Wilds, which is a big fancy park out Houghton way, newly opened to the public, full of ponds and waterfalls, lots of rocks and koppies to sit on and watch the sunset. Even though it's still July the winter weather in the daytime hasn't been overly cool, they can have a comfortable late afternoon picnic, a bottle of champagne, a nice soft blanket under their arses. Makes him think of how it was that time with cousin Avrom, the warm feeling from the rock and the feeling of opening possibilities that Avrom's words gave to him. Same thing for them as a couple and their future together.

He's only ever seen one wedding that he can remember, at the big domed shul on Wolmarans Street. The man wore a top hat and the women all had giant floppy hats angled at forty-five degrees.

They tied cans to the back of the car. It makes him nervous to think of a wedding with her people: all that formality too much for him to even contemplate. But take it one step at a time hey, just get engaged for now. Put this ring on her finger. Plenty of time after to get ready for the wedding and she'll help you with all that larney jazz . . .

These are the vibrating thoughts he has to keep to himself when he takes the bus out to Parktown to see Yvonne Linhurst on the Wednesday, wondering if the special excitement in his heart shows as some kind of unnatural glow on his skin. Led by her, they sneak down to the servants' quarters and she gets Isaac to whistle that special way. There's an answering flutter and they sneak back to their place in the small courtyard in the back, their private window bench. When Moses comes to keep guard, hurrying, there is something small in his hand. He asks them if everything is all right. Yvonne talks to him as if he is a White, trying to chat; it makes Isaac feel suddenly sad, for he can see the worry in the gardenboy's face. Her talk makes him think he's done something wrong, he doesn't understand what they want from him, he keeps saying he will bring them beer. Christ, she should just let him be the servant that he is, she's upsetting him with this matey-matey business, what is she trying to do with it?

—We don't need anything, it's okay Moses, she is saying. Just want to ask, are you having a happy day?

—Happi day? His smile so rigid. His eyes keep going to Isaac and back to her.

—I hope so, she says. You should be happy every day. Everyone should be.

—If the good Lord wants it, medem, he says, so will be.

There's an awkward lull. Then Yvonne says, —What's that you're busy with there, Moses?

He has his hands behind his back and shakes his head.

—Leave him, says Isaac.

But she's curious. —No, what is it? What's that?

Finally he shows them his palm. It's fixings for a cigarette he had been rolling when they came for him, but it's not with tobacco, he's got finely chopped-up green leaves instead, bits of stem and seed in it. Yvonne dips her head, wrinkles her nose. —Ohh what is it?

—It's duchu, says Isaac.

—No! She looks at Moses. Is it? Is it really, Moses?

Moses nods. —Yuh, yuh. Is good one.

She asks him to roll the cigarette and he lights it. The vegetable tang makes her nose wrinkle. He smokes some and his eyes glaze with moist pleasure. He offers it to Isaac, who shakes his head, annoyed by the cheekiness of the gesture, as if he'd ever put kaffir spit in his mouth.

—Ja this is the stuff, he tells Yvonne again, trying to sound like an expert though he's never smoked any, he's just familiar with the scent from here and there, places like the Yards (what were the Yards), certain street corners, Blacks sitting in a circle on the concrete at work.

She wants to know isn't it true that it makes you crazy in the head.

Moses shakes his head emphatically. Then she is looking at Isaac, saying to Moses can he give them some so that they can try it, together, there in the garden?

—Yvonne, don't.

But Moses is already excited, jumping back, telling them to wait, he will get, he will buy a whole bag. They must just wait for him there, sitting nice. Yvonne stops him, insists that they have to pay. Isaac gives him a pound note, which he says is too-too much, but Isaac doesn't have any change.

After he runs off, Isaac tells her he isn't going to smoke that stuff.

—Why not?

—Ach no man, it's–

—What?

—Nothing.

—Don't be a scaredy.

He sits on the ledge, hitching his pants up higher on his thighs, sitting back with crossed arms. He was going to say that duchu is low stuff, for Blacks and Coloureds, but he's learned not to go there, to set her off for no reason. He thinks he'll puff but won't inhale, make her feel better; and after she has some, who knows, maybe it will relax her to the point that his hand can swim freely under those panties. Out here in this open air maybe he'll be able to show her his thing, let her have a careful look at its hard length, maybe touch it or pop it in her sweet wet mouth, Jesus, imagine . . . Such pictures give him a pleasant stiffy hidden under the folds of his work pants as he sits back lazily on the ledge. When she sits down next to him he kisses her with a lunging leonine hunger that makes her squeak.

At first she feels a little rigid against him but he keeps on kissing and she starts to melt, to shudder. Cloud shadows move over their skins; bird calls dapple the still air. Sometimes he opens his eyes and other times they are shut and the feeling of kissing her is like driving very fast over a rising and dipping road in some country space of light and wind. Tasting into each other, the wetheat of entwinement, obliteration.

By unthinking degrees he pulls her over him to straddle one thigh and they grind together and he squeezes her hard then harder, his hands dipping low on her sturdy frame to cup the firm buttocks and then to scoop under the skirt. He can feel the hot pad of her sex where the thighs split and how it works small circles against his leg. He moves the panties aside and strokes till she gasps. One finger finds her and gently curls. She freezes but does nothing to stop him. He waits, then goes on slowly, into the mysterious unfolding, the budded resistance opening with such exquisite reluctance for the first time. He waits again, feeling her start to move against him, then he begins to love her with his hand, in determined patience,

kissing and loving, until there comes a moment where he feels her
breaths jerking in her, hoarse and shallow, and she starts to shake
and a sweet drenching graces his palm. She has buried her face in
his shoulder and she bucks against him, but at the very last she
grips his wrist and pulls his hand and sits up and stops, gripping
hard, keeping him still while her trembling subsides.

—What is it?

—No. I.

She sinks back and he wants to kiss her but she tells him no,
just hold me. So he contents himself and pulls her in close, his
hands stroking her back. —Why'd you stop?

—I don't know.

—No why? Tell me.

—Scared.

—Scared?

—I've never . . .

He laughs softly into her thick hair, the scent of her citrus
shampoo and of her beneath, much richer. He loves the way the
flesh puddles just a tiny little bit under the line of her jaw, and he
nips at it now. —You will, he says. You will with me.

—I don't know. It was. I don't know if I could.

—Of course you will, he says. It's nature.

She doesn't say anything for a while and he thinks about why
she would be scared, what's to be scared of? Maybe it's because she
doesn't want to give in to him all the way, to lose herself with him
doing it to her, in control of her. Then she jerks away.

—What? Whatzit?

—Oh my God, what happened to Moses?

—Moses?

She stands up and starts pulling her skirt down into place,
telling him to look away while she performs certain other
adjustments. He'd forgotten all about the duchu and the pound
note he gave him. Now it comes to him maybe the randy devil was

watching them again, like that first time in the garage. Shit, but he
wishes she could just be more bladey sensible sometimes on this
Black thing.

—Where you going?

—Find him, obviously.

—Find him where? Aw jeez. Wait.

He has to jog a little to catch up with her, already sneaking fast
down the path.

There is no answering whistle at the servants' quarters. Isaac hides
while Yvonne goes in to ask if anyone's seen him. She does the
same inside the big house. From upstairs, they look down into the
front garden, but they don't see him.

—He prolly smoked himself into a complete dwaal, Isaac tells
her. Prolly asleep under a tree somewhere.

To be in a dwaal is to be in a dreamwalking haze, and he'll drift
in on his own when he's sober again but, no, she insists on going
to look for him now. He checks his watch, tells her he'll have to be
heading back to work soon.

She thinks the Citroën is parked outside. —Let's go to your
car, she says.

—What for?

—To go look for him.

—That's dumb. We don't even know where to start.

Her face hardens.

—Oright, oright, he says. We can check if you like. But I came
on the bus today.

So they sneak down in the usual way, out through the garage,
and walk down the long driveway to Gilder Lane. As they walk
downhill he tries to hold her hand but she doesn't respond. They
have crossed the road to the park side. Yvonne screams: a long
syllable of a sound he's never heard come out of her before. She's
already running across the street. He goes after her, shouting her

name. Then he sees it also, on the pavement behind the parked cars.

She gets there first. Isaac looks back downhill and the smear of blood goes all the way down to the corner. Moses is belly down, dragging himself with one hand and the other tucked under himself. Grass roots are under his fingernails. The mineral smell of blood hovers so that Isaac is afraid to turn him over.

Yvonne has fallen to her knees and is holding his head in both hands. Isaac leans down to hear Moses saying, — . . . The man, he stab for me.

Yvonne starts to cry. —Why, why?

—Not to give. The change. Steal for money. I not let him go.

Yvonne's shoulders are shaking, her eyes wet. —Oh Moses man Moses you should have just given him the money! The bloody money, a pound! Oh my God.

That makes him arch his head up to shake it. As if what she's said is insane. —Never, never. Is *your* money . . .

When they roll him over gently, they find the stab wound is low on the right side, the shirt soaked through there and when they peel it up the wound shows as a tiny bright mouth, a puncture, not a slash. The liver, Isaac thinks. The blood that leaches out is plum dark.

Yvonne sprints back to telephone for an ambulance while Isaac waits with him, this mortally bleeding gardenboy. —It's oright, Moses, he says now and then. Moses closes his eyes and moans in his breath. Isaac is thinking how he mustn't get blood on his work clothes, he's thinking he's going to be late back for work. And what he keeps feeling are spikes of anger: because he doesn't want to feel sorry for this Black, this Black is not his problem, he doesn't want to get *involved*.

Meanwhile Moses keeps moaning and apologizing and the truth is he's not a bad one, he was being loyal, like Silas. He pats the poor bastard's shoulder. —Be ukay hey Moses. Be fine.

Yvonne comes back and he waits with her. It takes forever for the ambulance to show and when it does it turns out to be a White ambulance. They drive away with Yvonne screaming at them. She runs back to the house and eventually gets a Black taxi to come, to take Moses out to Orlando township where he's from. By the time the taxi arrives he is unconscious, lolling. Yvonne sobbing so hard Isaac fears she'll hurt herself, that she'll physically tear something in her chest.

When he gets back to work there is dried blood on his trousers and he's an hour late for the first time ever. He has to humiliate himself by making up some bullshit story for Franzie Labuschagne that Franzie can see right through, Franzie cutting him off with a crimp of the mouth and the disgusted words: —Ach, whatever, Isaac, just get to bladey work awready. It's even worse with Jack Miller: Jack just gives him that professional silence of his, the shaming ray of his disappointment.

30.

COMES THE WEEKEND. *Thee* weekend, and Isaac has planned out the route in The Wilds, made a list of everything that will go in the bag he will carry, decided what he will wear. He wanted to have big flowers like proteas but they'd get squashed in the bag and he worried about that till he thought of using some wild vygies that can be wrapped in a cloth. The bottle of champagne will be kept fresh with just a damp cloth and not ice cos the ice could melt and soak everything. To eat, he'll pack them a nice roast chicken with potatoes, apple strudel for dessert.

And don't in the name of God forget the ring. And what will the weather be like that day? What if it rains? So bring an umbrella – big umbrellas are romantic to share in the rain. Extra blanket if it's too cold. What if there's someone else sitting already on the rock he's got mapped out, or if there's idyats running round, noisy kids or such? So have a plan B just in case, a second location, and a third. Ready for anything . . .

But he's not ready for the Mad Queen telling him Yvonne will be attending a family function all day Saturday and on into the night, and that she's out just now.

—Oh, says Isaac, blinking. Oright. But I thought–

Queen's not interested in his thought or thoughts. Some family thing's come up. He doesn't push it, his plans can keep till next week. He hangs up the tickey box receiver and goes to work at the Reformatory and works savagely into the night, crashing

318

there around midnight, his body numb, his mind empty. He wakes up and goes on working for all of Sunday.

When he goes to his day job he finds that for the first time his mind wanders and his hands fail him. He damages three separate panels with his hammer and slapstick, making Jack Miller squint at him. Once, he catches Labuschagne watching from across the shop; when he looks at him, Labuschagne moves his eyes quickly away.

On Wednesday he goes out on his lunch break to wait for Yvonne and finds that the school bus does not deliver her as usual. Seeing this, he feels nauseous with disappointment. Wednesdays are their days! On Wednesdays she always comes straight home early, she doesn't have a last period or anything after school. But not this week. She could have told him she wasn't coming. He kicks a willow tree till the bark shreds. Then he wonders if she's ill. He makes a call from a tickey box but the maid tells him, Yvonne, she go for school. He can't understand it. What the hell has happened to the Linhursts? Did someone die?

At Lion Motors on the first payday of the new month, Hugo lets him know he'll be taking care of wages this week as well, not to worry himself since he's sent Silas on the road again with the trucks. Isaac can't seem to get particularly irritated by this information. He just nods, goes back to work. Working on smashed vehicles, wrecked machines, until he feels like a machine being wrecked himself, a biological structure with steel for bones and wire for nerves, being overused, over-revved. But the weekend sales have continued to be strong and the yard is almost completely stacked with wrecks now and Hugo says they'll have their crusher soon, they'll be able to hoard up even more of the scrap metal that will one day soon be more valuable than gold itself.

When he's home early like always for Shabbos dinner on Friday night, he waits till after to use the telephone at the front of the shop. Rively has gone out with Yankel Bernstein, Mame is doing dishes,

Tutte has gone to bed. The workshop is dark and he doesn't put on a light. Earlier he was in the sewing room where he uncovered his hiding place, in the corner behind the mirrors, the immigration forms in there, and the engagement ring, which he lifted and held to his lips. Now he feels nervous, his mouth dry, his hand trembling the receiver. It's because he's calling to invite her on the big day – ja? It's because he wants everything perfect – right? Not because he hasn't spoken to her for what seems like too long.

In the dark at the desk when he closes his eyes, for some reason unknown to him his mind keeps showing him flashes of Mama Kelo, that thick arm sticking out at him, those eyes swelling whitely from the clenched muscles of the face like a carved mask. Something bad's happened, he thinks. Then says to himself harshly: Oh shut up, shut up your Stupid head. You are fine. You are the same. You are good at your work and you will be a great panel beater, an artist, and you are one-third owner of a business that will make you into a millionaire. You're on your way, boy. You'll buy Mame a house so beautiful it will make her cry. And the call will come from Papendropolous and her sisters and their families will be brought to the house that you have built, a house so big they'll have enough room for them all and no more rent for any Greenburgs, no bond over our heads.

And most of all you have The Princess. You have Yvonne. Yvonne. Now he is thinking of her totally. The feel of her hair on his face, the column of her warm neck with the good breasts and the good hips and the good manners and the sweet soft musical voice. Just the sound of her voice, that will be enough. Because he is tired and he doesn't want to take the train out to the Reformatory to work all those long hours again, which he knows he has to; but if he can just hear her, just a little trace of her lip music, just a little burble of her good laughter in her ear, just that, it will be all right . . .

He has dialed the last number, the rotor spins back. He waits, swallowing. The mother answers. He can hear the ugliness in her voice, see her in the lounge with its glass cabinets full of vases and urns and cut crystal sugar bowls, see that she's wearing a folded cloth on her head with a peacock feather and a diamond in the middle of the forehead. In one breath he's asking please-can-I-speak-to-Yvonne-Mrs.-Linhurst.

—You mean *may* you speak, says Mad Queen. We presume you have the capability. But, devastating to report, Yvonne is not available. Yvonne—

There's a sound behind, muffled, then the swooshing of a hand rubbing the receiver.

—Mrs. Linhurst?

She comes back on: —Hold the line.

The tone of her voice means to shame him, to make him lesser, he can feel it. Trying to act as if he's never been to the house to fetch her daughter. Trying to make him into a crafty little Doornfontein schemer who has gone from carrying her boxes to stealing her Yvonne away. Well, choke on it you old bitch, you crinkled-up meshugena, cos I got her, I *have* her and there is nothing you can do about it, I've had my bare fingers deep inside of her and me and her are as close as two people can be, we love each other. Choke on that, you old klafte. *Love.*

When Yvonne picks up, he exhales without knowing he was holding his breath and it's like a slump of relief. —Hey hey, he says. She nearly told me you were out. It's our lucky night hey. And he laughs, a wild sound. She does not. Instead she says to him, in a voice flat and even formal: —Why would she do that?

—You know, he says. Your momsy.

—No, she says, slow and deliberate. No, I don't know.

— . . . Yvesy?

But his Yvesy isn't there; this is another Yvonne.

—Why do you keep ringing me?

—Yvesy, man . . . summin wrong? What's wrong?

Silence.

He tries to laugh again, a dying sound. —What's a matter hey? You oright?

A long nasal inhalation. —Isaac. It's just not a good idea.

His heart squeezes hard, sending tiny thumping noises up his neck and into the ear he is pressing so hard against the telephone. —What isn't? says his voice.

—This.

And the way she gives him the word *this*, so deadly seriously, so blunt and all-encompassing and unmistakable, it makes him feel like a trap door has opened under his chair and he is gone, gone, he's plunging, leaving his guts behind. He has the mad urge to giggle. —Why? he says instead. What?

—The whole thing, she says. It's very. It's too . . . It's gone too far. All right. All right Isaac?

—Whole thing? What? Is this from. Did your ma . . .

—*Christ*, she says, so that he knows he has used exactly the wrong words.

—No, no, ukay, not your mother, no, ukay.

—Don't grovel at me. I know what you said.

—I'm not *grovelling*, Jesus. I don't get this. Why are you. I mean, what did I do?

She sighs, huffs. —Look, Isaac, it's not one thing. It's only.

—Ja?

—It's not a game anymore. Pretend.

—A game?

—Oh God, you see, you can't even–

—Wait a second, wait a sec. I mean, Christ, who ever said a *game* . . .

— . . . Isaac, he is most likely going to die. If he hasn't already. If he isn't already dead!

It's good he's fallen into total silence. He might have blurted the word *who* aloud. She would have hung up.

—Ja, he says, putting on a long sigh. I know hey. Poor old Moses.

—*Poor old . . .*

Quickly: —I know, it's so sad hey. What happened. I mean I keep thinking of it hey.

—It's *our* fault.

That one stops him like a slap. The twistedness of it. Ours?

—It wouldn't have happened if it weren't, if we hadn't . . . we were . . .

He remembers it then, how close she was to coming like that. She had forgotten about Moses too. It's her guilt and it's mixed up with her other guilt about letting him, Isaac, do things, about wanting him to – maybe about wanting him altogether. See it: the boy with the clumpy orange hair and the freckles and the wide ears, sitting back there on the ledge in the sun in his work clothes and this Princess with her doll's face riding on his leg like some–

—It's *us*, she says.

—Us.

—*This*, yes!

—Ukay, I understand. In a way he's relaxed now, he has the reason. Nightmares, they always disperse if you wait long enough. He waits now.

—I have to go, she says.

—Oright fine, he says. But can you just hang on like another sec?

—No, Isaac. This is all. I want it to be finished now.

—Do you? Are you sure?

—Isaac, what was it? Our own little pretend world in the garden. Meanwhile you didn't even notice, I mean look what we caused, and you don't care, you don't, really, inside you *don't*.

—Do you know what happened to him?

—Like it matters to you.

—Hey, he says. Come off it. Be fair hey.

—No Isaac, I've had enough pretend. It's bad enough my parents, the nonsense they say about it. When he's already been replaced. And it never would've happened if you–

—If I wasn't even there.

—Exactly.

—So, it's my fault, only mine.

—You don't understand.

—That's true, I don't.

—Isaac, it's the fault of *pretending*. Being false. It's false of you right now, the same thing, acting like you care when I know, I *know*, what you really think, what you thought of him . . .

—Hey, Yvonne. Yvonne.

— . . .

—It's me, it's your Ize. I'm here, oright. I'm not perfect but I'm changing. Right? Is it right of you to treat someone – to just cut them like this? Is that right?

— . . .

—Hey?

—I don't know.

—Ja, he says. Let's just see each other, I mean talk proper.

—No, Isaac.

—Why not?

—I don't think so.

—Come on Yvesy.

—I'm going to go now, Isaac. I don't want you to telephone anymore.

—Yvonne.

—Leave me, Isaac. Goodbye.

He sits for a long time with the dead circle of the receiver pressed to his ear. Becomes aware in his hollow shock of the tiny parts of him that are still going on: the eyelids blinking, the heart drumming, the breath against his teeth. But something massive has torn. He doesn't want to move because then he'll feel the damage.

He's been in an accident.

31.

FOR THE FIRST TIME since the start of Lion Motors Isaac doesn't go into work at the Reformatory. On the telephone he tells Hugo he's ill. Hugo says not to worry, he has it all under the control. He advises Isaac to shine up. Isaac walks the route in The Wilds that he would have walked with her, drinking brandy, brooding, the ring in his pocket. He watches the sunset alone. On his cot there's no solace, only turning and twitching and the inability to do anything to stop the thoughts and images that dig at him like sharp claws. What she has told him is unreal, impossible; the engagement ring – that is a real thing. All that's happened is she's mistaken, she's just made a mistake. He has to correct her, that's all, bring her back into sanity. He gets up, paces. The whole of Sunday oozes by like a slow wound. When darkness comes he drinks brandy in the backyard the way he used to, sitting on the wall, staring dully at the Greyshirt's DeSoto Airflow. This is another night without sleep. Closer to morning he makes strong tea and drinks cup after cup. He goes to lie down when it gets light, so his parents won't ask questions. Then he dresses in work clothes and, haggard, telephones the shop. Gets Labuschagne on the line and tells him in a whisper of faked hoarseness that he is sick (yet how true!) and won't be coming in.

—Ja hey, Labuschagne says. What is it wrong with you now?

—I dunno. Just sick, something.

—Ja, sick of work, I think, lately.

—No.

—Isaac, I got my eye on you.

—Just a cold, Franzie. I promise.

— . . . Oright.

—Oright then.

A car worker without a car, he takes the bus out to Parktown. Waits there in that little park with willow trees down the road from The Castle. He never had such mad feelings inside him in all his life. There's this terrible wilding pain in his chest and a sense of overwhelming desperation; it's like the need to breathe only *she* won't let him. He feels like a dog wounded by its owner and in its pain all it can do is go back to the same owner for the caresses it has become dependent on, but there is no caress, only another kick. He knows his face must be white as soap.

Usually she gets a lift to school with the Cruel Duke but she won't this morning. There is no rational basis for this knowledge in him yet he knows it with no doubts: she'll take the bus today. He walks up and down behind the willows. The sun's pale rays start to thicken to a harsher yellow. He digs out another Max cigarette, the last of the pack. He doesn't remember smoking them all. What is he doing? Am I going mental here? Is this what it is to be truly mad in the head? If I saw myself I would laugh so hard at me, at how stupid, how pathetic. But I am in myself: this *is* me. His mouth so dry he can't dredge up any tobacco spit. He is chewing his nails in lieu of cigarettes when she comes down the street in her uniform: her green blazer and tartan skirt, the stockings on her long strong legs. She does not show shock or even mild surprise. She gives him cat's eyes, blank and observing, full of disdainful tranquility.

—What now? is what she says.

—No lift this morning hey?

She watches him.

—Why not hey?

—What is this, Isaac?

—They gone away?

She nods once then seems to try to erase the fact she's made this gesture by shaking herself.

—Where to, he says, Switzerland?

—Yes Switzerland, she tells him with her flat eyes and voice. Switzerland, America, Asia. The Med. London. Antarctica.

—That's nice, he says.

—And I'm going to school.

—I know.

—And you're going to work.

—Yes.

—So goodbye.

She steps around and keeps on.

—Yvonne.

He has to follow, double-stepping to catch up. —Yvonne, what did you want me to do hey? *I* never stabbed him. I was right here in this street tryna help. His blood was on my clothes. I went back to work and got kuk for that, you know that?

—Isaac, please.

—What?

—Come on. He's just. He's just a kaffir to you.

He has no words for this new cold rage in her.

—And you're just a con, she says. Like everyone. On your own you wouldn't have lifted a finger. If it wasn't for me. Tell the truth. It's nothing to you if he lives or if he dies.

He bites at lips so dry. —You know what I think on these things. I'm not perfect hey.

She stops. —Well neither am I!

Her eyes look wet now. —I'm eighteen, Isaac. I mean I am eighteen years old. You understand that right?

But he doesn't.

—Isaac, this just isn't . . . Isaac, just forget this all, right, forget it.

—What am I supposed to do?

She shakes her head.

He squeezes the hard small thing in his pocket so that his forearm aches. —Look at me standing here, he says. I love you Yvonne. I love you.

She starts walking again.

—It wasn't my fault!

She keeps going and he follows after. —He didn't die, did he?

She doesn't answer.

—Yvonne.

—How would we even know? God.

Then she stops again. —Why don't you go find out for me?

—Hey?

—Yes, go. Instead of words. Go on. Do *that* for me.

—For you, he says.

—Well look around. I'm the one in high school, mister. You're the one's supposed to be all grown-up, with the car and the money and the job. You *could* go.

She's facing him now, her green eyes level, a little pinched down in their staring.

—I don't have a car, he tells her. The one I's borrowing went back. I took the bus.

She blows a puff of air through her nose once, her chin lifting.
—See.

—I would.

—Listen, she says. *I'd* go. I have the guts and I'd drive us anywhere if I could, and to hell with school. But you, you don't mean anything. You're just words.

—I don't have one, Yvonne. I don't collect Cadillacs.

She watches him with her pinched-down eyes in a silence, then gives another snort, shakes her head so that the ends of her hair dance. —Yes but you're the same as him. You're both the same thing.

—How you ganna say that to me?

—Dadsy and his Cadsy, she says, looking off.

He reaches for a joke then, something to force some air and space and lightness between them, trying to smash at the dead weight of her cold negation. —We could always take *that*.

She doesn't smile and she doesn't laugh. She faces him.

He's not allowed even to stand on the driveway so he waits on the pavement under the municipal jacaranda trees till even after the garage door has rumbled up. She comes down the drive and waves to him without looking directly – her firm impervious distance a horror he must ignore and pretend not to be affected by.

—School sorted?

—I rang them. Said my parents will confirm when they get back.

—Will they?

—Never bloody mind that. Her agitated foot tapping, her eyes anywhere but on him, hideous Isaac.

—Oright, so . . . you ready?

She folds her arms. He waits a while then repeats himself. She shakes her head but goes uphill and he follows behind her. The garage door's still up, the garage empty but for the bulked sheepskin to the left in the open clean space. No chance of Moses hiding in any dark corners.

She says half in a mutter, —Why couldn't you get one? Borrow a different one?

—I just couldn't, oright. Look, if you wanna leave it, if it's too much . . .

He gets a direct look then, a hard loathing glare that in Jewish would be called a glotz.

He tries a shrug. —Anyway, where's the other car? If it was here, I'd rather . . . I mean. It makes no difference to me hey. It's.

—They've gone to the Drakensberg, she says. A motor holiday.

—Oh, he says. Nice.

She is rubbing her brow with the back of her hand, looking into the garage, muttering: —Phinneas is driving them . . . But there's no key for the . . . I mean he keeps it locked.

—I told you that's no problem.

Now he recognizes some fear in her face and it makes him feel calmer to know it's growing in her, with the reality of what they are doing on them like this. He goes past her, over to the sheepskin cover, bends to take hold of an edge, then remembers what Moses did that time, the straps underneath. Good old Moses. Lead us to the promised land hey won't you mate.

He looks back to say: —Wanna give me a hand with this?

She doesn't move.

—The easy part, he says.

They roll quietly to the bottom of the driveway, only the soft jouncing of the rubber on the flagstones. She goes back to shut the garage; meanwhile he gets out to open the bonnet. He stops. The automobile is immaculately clean and the morning light looks astonishingly beautiful on the cream white steel of its long form: in front a silver angel with backswept wings leans forward into an imagined wind; the swoop of the mudguards under which the whitewall tires nestle reminds him of one of Hugo's good fedoras; the long chassis and the silver lines detailing the bodywork speak to him of speed and power in a way that makes his skin ripple with gooseflesh. Like a statue chiselled from one block of pure new marble. He lifts the bonnet, the massive engine makes him whistle in his teeth. He touches a screwdriver between two points on the starter, that's all it takes, then a few tugs on the accelerator wire to make sure. Its rev sound is low and smooth and throbbing.

Yvonne is sitting in the passenger seat with her arms folded.

Now he is piloting the steel mass of this American driving machine down Gilder Lane. Now turning.

—How is it? she says.

—It floats.

—I don't mean that.

He corrects the drift to the centre; the feeling of being wrong, sitting on this side, is not diminishing.

—Go slowly.

—I keep looking the wrong way for the rearview.

He changes into third, gentle on the stick off the steering column. Everything smells of leather. There's a clock in the centre of the dashboard with horizontal lines of inset steel on either side and the nose of the automobile is very long ahead of them through the angled windshields, the silver windswept angel at the tip marking the view of a rich man's world.

—I keep wanting to change with the wrong hand.

—Are you all right with it?

—Ja, I just keep bumping the right hand, I mean my left one, which is the right one for changing, ha.

—Don't talk about it, just concentrate.

They are merging near Empire Road, the high road swooping down to the low, and Isaac has already looked over the wrong shoulder. His head whips back and he sees a car looping fast out into the oncoming lane to miss them, hears the distorted notes – *eeyow* – of the hooter as it passes. Fuck, is what he says.

—Be careful man!

—Is oright hey, he says in a while. I'm getting the hang now, serious.

He gives it a little more: the V16 surges, so quiet and so much power. Jesus but she is a dreamboat. Three tons but it's like on oiled ball bearings. Jesus but she's lovely. Oh I love cars, good cars like this, smooth as oil she is.

—Slow slow Isaac. Slow.

—Just a little bit, she wants to open up. She's a beauty. An American darling.

—Slow down now.

—Oright, oright. I'll easy on her. She wants to run me but I'll easy-easy on her. Yes darling I will.

He has a feeling Yvonne might be smiling so he glances across, but her face is set hard.

—Watch the bloody road.

—I will, says Isaac. Absolutely.

32.

THEY DRIVE SOUTH AND WEST FOR A LONG WHILE, to the far side of the city, and finally reach a road that passes along a rise to their left with a fence at the crest made of concrete boards. Where there are gaps in these boards there are glimpses of the Black world on the other side: the rocks on the roofs of rusted tin and cardboard, the red dust and rusted wire. Comes a road sign warning of Blacks crossing, a picture of them silhouetted on a road, and the words *PASOP NATURELLE VOOR – CAUTION NATIVES AHEAD.* Yvonne says it makes them seem like animals in a game reserve. What is it she would prefer, see them getting run down? But he nods. A little farther and they reach the crossing place, a crowd here of mothers with little ones strapped to their backs in blankets and sacks of mielie meal balanced on their clothed heads. Isaac slows. Now the smell tips through the windows: burning rubbish, sweetish taint of exposed sewage, sweat of many bodies. He eases the Cadillac to the roadside.

—What are you doing?

—You sure you want to do this?

—You're not?

—I'll go in, I'm not chicken or nothing, I'm just asking.

—There's nothing to ask.

He nods. We'll see, Princess. Princess ganna learn today. Blacks have meanwhile drifted closer to stare at this huge machine that could be made of polished ivory, so brilliant in the bright sun. He turns it very slowly, tires crackling on raw stony earth. His mouth mutters that he can't believe he's doing this and she, very quick, cuts back at him: —Doesn't matter if you believe it or not. Just keep going.

Then, as if truly enfolded in the swamping numbness of a dream, the Cadillac is away from the tarred road of the Whites and climbing a rise of baked red soil dotted with clumps of yellow grass and fat-leaved cacti. —Illegal for us hey, his mouth says. I think Whites can go in jail for coming here.

He'd forgotten that possibility.

—What? she says.

Watch your mouth, he thinks of himself, watch your thoughts from getting out, it feels a dream but it is no dream. He says: —Nothing. Then: —Jee-zus.

Ahead Blacks on the path turn to look over their shoulders at them and it occurs to Isaac this path isn't meant for cars, it's missing the parallel grooves that tires would have worn. No, Blacks have no cars. Some are on bicycles but mostly they are walking and mostly they stop to turn and to stare.

They start to pass them, waiting on the side, staring in. A woman in the blue and white uniform of her church, with a star pinned to her bosom on a strip of green felt. A man with khaki trousers and a horrified face under his hat, with goggling eyes and a mouth open like a pink flesh flower full of teeth. Boys and girls start running beside them, Isaac so slow and cautious they can almost keep up. Then a bicycle in the middle of the path ahead, the rider, a bareheaded boy, looks behind and almost falls at the sharking surprise of the Cadillac rising behind him. He pedals hard to the side, with his eyes never leaving them. As they pass, Isaac sees on the front of the bike how a live goat has been lashed with wire and twine, its legs folded tight to the ribs. The mouth bleating steadily, showing a blue tongue.

They crest. The path falls away to Orlando: clumped boxes in the dust and farther out concrete rows. Ahead on the path a line of small children in short pants, with bare feet. They don't move even when Isaac taps the hooter. Yvonne seems ready to get out and he almost catches her arm. Then an old man with the salt of a grey beard speckling his chin hurries from behind and takes the children aside in a chain of holding hands. In profile, Isaac sees how their bellies protrude and he thinks how well fed they must be, fat as little piglets they are, and what commie propaganda it is that they have nothing to eat.

The old man takes off his hat as they rumble past. Isaac lifts his hand. The old man salutes him. Isaac feels slightly better.

At the bottom of the hill is a dead tree still standing, the only one in sight, nothing more than a bare forked trunk, the trunk charred. Beyond, there's a lineup for a tap in the centre of a swamp of churned mud. People with pots and buckets of all sizes. Women who have hiked up their skirts to wait in the mud, men with trouser legs rolled to the knees, shoes in hand. Now as they get closer comes stronger that sweetrot tang of burning rubbish mingled with raw sewage. Under the forked tree men are sitting on wonky stools and barbers are clipping at their skulls. Mirrors dangle down on strings like strange crystalline fruits. Chicken legs yellow and singed rest on grilles over an open fire. Every single face watches them. Isaac steers wide round the marsh around the tap. So many eyes.

—Thought they'd all be at work, his mouth says. Be empty like.

Yvonne doesn't speak. Is her door locked? The dream feeling in Isaac not going away but the opposite, getting thicker, deeper. He's drowning in dream. They are passing hills of rubbish now, an undulating rubbish land of rotting things, smouldering things. Dunes of ash, newspapers, tires, scrap, jagged tin cans, flaps of cardboard, feathers, bones. Skinny dogs and children who were climbing and playing but have frozen to stare.

They cross a ditch full of dark fluid and when the tires splash through it he is ready for the stench of the shit yet it's still like a foul cloth forced down the back of the throat till he tastes the first acidic intimations of his own vomit. Insects ripple up in silver clouds. Isaac steers for a laneway through the shacks ahead, the boxes with stones holding down their roofs.

The Cadillac barely fits; faces come to the doorways, the hatch-like windows. He sees a tiny separate garden of dirt and twigs and coloured stones. Sees a planted white cross. Sees a stout woman with her fists buttressing her wide hips, squinting at them. Dry face under a beret, wrinkles and high cheekbones. In the rearview more children running, smiling. The open doors and the shaded worlds within. To bring a Cadillac here. Do you see what you've done? His heart has been kicking in him all the time but he only feels the force of it now. The sweat on his hot skin. Some little hands tap on the rear, the roof. The laneway goes on, on. He realizes it is impossible to turn around here. This dream of utter inversion: the White Black, the Black White, positive negative and negative positive. The insane wrongness of what he has allowed himself to be persuaded to do here keeps coming down like bricks on him, like tumbling rubble. Dustblasted earthiness, dirtafrica. Another species nests here. Not for him. It is not for him to be here.

And the dream feeling falls. Everything turns clear and hard. A need fills him like a scream. To get out. Get out, survive, leave, go. It shrieks in him so that his body twitches as if electrically pulsed.

—We have to go. This is mad.

She hasn't heard, she's rolling down the window. —Slow down hey. I've got to ask someone where he lives.

—Have to get out.

—Hello, she calls out to some children. Hello. Hi. Sowbona.

Isaac swears; yet he does slow a little. —Careful, they're like birds, he tells her. You start feeding one, there'll be ten milyun.

Little hands come through the window, little pale palms.

Yvonne giggles. Isaac accelerates. —Hey! What're you doing?

—You keep asking me that.

—Isaac!

—Well you weren't getting directions were you.

—Stop. Stop!

But ahead he sees another laneway opening, to the left. He shoots the Cadillac, Yvonne still telling him stop over and over.

—It's ukay, he tells her. But truly it's not. As he swings this big vehicle he finds the lane isn't wide enough to make the turn and he ends up having to stop at an angle. He puts it into reverse. Edges back, then a little forward. Again Yvonne asks him what he's doing. The most irritating question there is and blindingly bladey obvious: getting the hell out. Enough is enough and the panic is on him now, almost fully, it makes his scalp shrivel and parches his mouth, his armpits stream. When he revs forward again the tires rip up red clouds, but it's still too tight. He licks his dry lips, grinds back into reverse.

From out of the dust behind he sees in the sideview mirror a tall young man in neat pressed clothing. A flat cap and pleated trousers. Others behind him. He comes to Isaac's window, taps. Isaac ignores him.

—Isaac!

—Oright.

Slowly he lowers the glass. The young man, leaning down, says: —What kind is this? E-Chevrolet Special?

He has a triangular face, a thin chin with wide-set eyes under his cap, good-looking with caramel skin. —No, Isaac tells him. It's . . . something else.

—Why you have this side?

—American car. From America.

The young man has a way of staring down into Isaac's eyes without blinking. Almost as if under the influence of the bottle or the smoke, but the eyes are clear and unbloodshot. Isaac has never been stared at by a Black like this. He notices one eyebrow is spliced in two by a thin scar.

—What kind engine?

More young men keep coming out of the red dust behind him; they have an unhurried way of walking, leaning back from their steps, their arms dangling slack.

—Um. Big. Sixteen cylinder.

The young man whistles but it is not a sincere whistle. He moves his chin, pointing inside, past Isaac. —This one is your wife.

—Look, Isaac says. He doesn't have much breath. His chest so tight. —Look.

—Hello, Yvonne says, leaning across.

Isaac puts his hand on her shoulder, tries to press her back into her seat. She pushes his hand down.

The young man says, —You look for police?

—Me? What for?

The young man makes a laugh-like sound. His eyes never waver. —Police not here, he says.

—Beg a pardon?

—We looking for Mr. Luthuli, Yvonne tells him.

—Not police? the young man says. He has a sporting look now, he tugs on the brim of his flat cap.

—No, Isaac says.

—Yes, police.

—Not police.

—For Chlistmas now, the young man says.

—Pardon?

—Chlistmas time. Merry Chlistmas.

—Hu hu, not yet, Isaac says. Have a long time still.

The young man appears to grow serious, for his split eyebrow clenches in toward the other. —I am say for you. Is Chlistmas. Chlistmas today.

—I don't.

—*Today.*

—No, Isaac says, the word winded on his lips.

—Isaac, Yvonne says.

He feels the car rocking slightly. The dream feeling comes back but different, dualistic now: as if he is not only here in the dream but elsewhere also. It's not a useful perception.

—You know what is Chlistmas box? says the young man.

—What is what?

—Chlistmas box, for give present. Now you give for me my Chlistmas box.

—Hu hu, Isaac says.

—What is your name?

—Me? says Isaac. No one.

—You sixteen cylinder, says the young man. You give for me my Chlistmas box, sixteen cylinder.

—Good one, says Isaac.

—Yes, says the young man. You give. I want American car.

—Sure, sure, my mate.

—Shore yes. Why you laugh?

—Hu hu hu, says Isaac. He begins then without pre-thought to speak in Black: the Zulu phrases that Silas taught him come to his mouth with amazing fluidity. *We go now just and sorry trouble sorry.*

The young man ignores this. —I have say for you, he says. You give it.

Isaac has stopped looking at him. The faces of the other young men are at every other window, the same flat caps and direct eyes.

Tsotsis: it comes to him, the word, for these are them, the very ones, here and now. The newspaper term given flesh and life. Tsotsi: always it held for him a joking ring, the harmlessness of some little township gangster, a tsotsi, the joke of their strutting, lords of dungpiles.

But here, now, he finds nothing to disdain.

The young man – the tsotsi – is speaking again. Isaac searches past the handsome triangular face. Searches with eyes that are like hands grasping up out of drowning waters. He finds a woman passing behind. She has on a doek and overalls, she could be a maid on Beit Street. The motherliness of her thick hips. Isaac sucks a deep breath and shouts. —Hey! Hey mama! Hey!

The woman pauses, shades her eyes.

—Please! Mama can you help? Please!

She comes forward. Without looking at her, the tsotsi speaks the liquid full-mouth clacking of Black to her, not Zulu or Sesotho because Isaac doesn't understand a single word. The woman looks at him and takes a step back.

—No, no, please, Mama! says Isaac.

She leans down a little. —What is?

—I, he says. We. We come.

—Mr. Luthuli! Yvonne shouts past him. We looking for Mr. Luthuli. Moses.

—Heh? The woman dips in closer, to see Yvonne. Isaac can tell she had not noticed a girl in the car before, the way her face changes as she looks in.

He leans back and hisses to Yvonne: —Yes, tell her. Explain it. *Tell her.*

Yvonne says it again and the woman's eyes thin, her head cocks. —Luthuli?

—Yes, Moses Luthuli. We've come to see him, to help.

—Ohhh, says the woman.

—Yes, please, if you can help us, Yvonne says.

The woman talks to the tsotsi, he turns around and leans his back to the car, crossing his legs and scratching at his nostril (Isaac sees in the sideview). Now the woman is turning, calling a child. She bends to the little girl; the girl listens then runs.

The maid woman stays at their window beside the tsotsi and the tsotsi speaks to her but she does not look at him. He tries to bend down to Isaac again and she grips the door, her arms in his way. The tsotsi's voice gets louder, harder. But the woman does not let go. Her hand on the window frame is curled inside the car, thin mud-coloured fingers with fine paler lines like rings from the knuckles to the nail beds. Isaac looks at the hand and wants to kiss it. What's happening? Yvonne keeps saying.

Now the tsotsi is shouting. The woman is shaking her head in a kind of dumb rhythm. The tsotsi steps, giving room to his lanky elbows, shaking them out. Oh shit no, is what Isaac thinks. The girl comes back and behind her is a man wearing a black suit with a wine-coloured shirt with a white ring collar at the throat, one of those Christian ministers. He has a beard of tight curls along his jawline and his arms sweep as he speaks, speaking not just to the handsome tsotsi but to all of them, lifting his voice. They shift back, but not far. Pleated pants and flat caps and hands in pockets. One of them whistling a clever cutting note like a bird chirp.

When the minister's face drops to the window, Isaac can see the flecks of spit caught in the wires of his beard and his eyes are very big in his dark face. He shouts: —Go! Drive it!

—Can't, says Isaac.

But the minister has already skipped up onto the running board. —That way! Fust, man. Go fust. Ride it man!

So Isaac accelerates. The rear side of the Cadillac rakes the rusted iron corner of a box house, crumpling it in. The noise of this lifts an answering sound from the young men standing in the dust, as if in echo, a moan of outrage. Whistles break out. Yay! Yay! they shout. There's a thump from the back, a boot or a rock. The minister is shouting the word *go*. Isaac gives more gas and they bump up over some kind of cornerstone and come down hard and keep going. Behind, the tsotsis come running through the dust, whistling and throwing.

The minister has one hand inside pressed flat to the soft ceiling. Isaac gives it: the shacks blur: there are no signs here, the lanes twist. The piles of tin, the dust and wire. Then a more open space where Isaac can slow.

The minister's face dips in again. —Ow ow, he says. Who is it you people are searching for here, that you come in here like this?

Yvonne leans across. —Thank you so much.

The minister's face shaking. —Ow ow ow.

—It's Moses Luthuli, she says. He's been hurt.

—Luthuli.

—Yes, Moses.

—Yes yes. I shall direct you.

Behind the minister in the more open space is a listing concrete rectangle with a missing door; before it is a small lake of dark urine coated in slime and shimmering with insectile life.

The minister catches their staring. —What they give us for toilets, one for maybe fifty thousand persons. We have only last week a little girl who fell in and drowned to the death. In that.

—Christ.

—Yes, you can say Christ. Eight years old.

They go on more slowly. Past the urine swamp of the toilets are the grey concrete homes that he saw from the top of the crest before and these are made of pale breezeblocks with cracks but their walls don't reach all the way up to the roofs. The minister signals to stop, jumps down and walks ahead. They watch him from the car, knocking on a tin door: him in the sun with the sun shiny on his black coat sleeve and the door in shadow and all of the doors in the long row behind him in the same shadows in the pale concrete, the concrete facades all the same as if stamped by one machine.

Isaac looks at Yvonne. What to say? He tries her name. —He's coming, she says. He looks back and the minister is jog-stepping back. Yvonne gets out and then Isaac.

—See that one there, says the minister. Luthuli.

—Thank you so so much, says Yvonne.

The engine of the Cadillac is still running; with no key he won't chance shutting it off. —I'll stay here with the car, he says.

—It's all right, the minister says. I will look after it.

Isaac pulls on his nose. —Maybe better not, he says.

—*Isaac*, says Yvonne.

—Ja oright, he says. He puts his hand in his pocket and starts to bring out his wallet. The minister steps back, his face screws as if hit with spit. Yvonne is the one who says sorry. Isaac mumbles and follows her.

A woman with a woollen cap is at the front door. —I am the wife of Moses, he hears her saying to Yvonne.

Inside is a small room with a big bed on which four children are sitting. A girl with braids covers her mouth, swings her feet. Mrs. Luthuli is naming them, Yvonne making girlish noises, aw how nice. In Isaac there is a deep immediate knowing of this place, these people: it's Auntie Peaches and Auntie Marie again, it's himself at seven or eight years of age in this same kind of tiny room, pressed with others, warm bosom and soft lap, skin warmth and rickety chairs. The feel of memories that live in the body.

Mrs. Luthuli wants to give them tea now and Yvonne keeps saying no thank you, keeps asking about Moses. Slowly they edge through another door, an opening into narrow gloom and powerful stink.

The space is no bigger than a large walk-in closet with a single mattress on the ground. Something shifts on this mattress and the stench that has pricked Isaac's nostrils gets stronger: the rotpong of old food gone squishy with rancid juices, vomit and excrement in this closed space. He has to force himself to squat as Yvonne has. There is the shape of a dark skull against the pillow. The skull turns a little and its eyes – strangely alive and flickering – look at him.

—Moses, Yvonne says.

Isaac's eyes are adjusting: not a skull, not yet, there's still the thin skin stretched over the bones, all the meat sucked away, just skin over calcium and living orbs sunk deep in the sockets.

Yvonne says: —He's been to hospital?

—No hospital, says Mrs. Luthuli from the doorway behind. Only one doctor here.

—And did he see him? The doctor?

—Yes. He put his bandage. We must change. He putting also some powder but is almost finish, we need more.

Moses whispers. His torso bare but for the loops of bandage about his abdomen. In his whisper are little heaving sighs of air. After a time Isaac realizes these are his coughs, and that between them he is repeating the words *thank you*.

—We want you to get better, Yvonne says to him. Her eyes are running.

You'd think you'd get used to the stink, Isaac thinks. You'd think the longer you have to sit here the more your nose would get numb and used to it but no it doesn't, it gets worse and worse. Jesus Christ. What must be happening to a man's guts to make them stink like this, so bad till it's like a gas. I swear to God if it doesn't stop I'm going to coch up breakfast all over this poor stinking bastard lying here three-quarters dead already. Oh Jesus imagine having to lie here and die like this. Dying in the stink of your own rot on a filthy mattress, chunks of your body already turned to fertilizer. He is such a bladey goner, the poor bastard. I wish that he had died that day. This is worse for him and I would not have to be here, nearly getting us killed the both of us. It woulda been so much better and cleaner if he'd just pegged, finished and over with. I could take her to his grave somewhere and put a few nice flowers and finished and klaar with it. Oh God this is dirty dirty, oh my God this is sick.

Suddenly his skin wriggles: Moses has touched him. Moses has put one hand out of the gloom and up onto his knee. He can feel the germs swarming off the sticky hot palm and onto his trousers. He spots the tin bedpan at the end of the mattress then, the gelatinous ruby wetness nestled there, quietly offering its contribution to the waves of unbearable smell. Then the skull whispers. At him, Isaac Helger. Yvonne hisses at him. Slowly, holding his breath, he brings his face closer to the skull.

—Baas, baas.

—Ja, Moses.

—Pasop. Is bad people here also. Watch for her.

—Ja, I be careful hey Moses . . . thanks hey. We'll be oright.

—Moses, Moses, Yvonne says, bright and loud. I'm giving your wife something, all right?

Isaac is quick to pull up and look around, to get his face away. He sees Yvonne pressing cash into the woman's hand. —Oh God bless you, Mrs. Luthuli says. The Lord God bless you forever and ever amens. Her eyes too start to run.

Lifting her voice for Moses, Yvonne says, —For the doctor. And she can buy medicine. You're going to be all right, Moses. You are going to be strong again and come back to us. Yes you are Moses.

The skull whispers.

Now the wife is saying, —Oh my husband, he has so too much pains.

—You tell the doctor. Tell him you want medicine for the pain also. Can you telephone?

—We have one telephone here in Orlando.

—Give me pen and paper. I will give you our number . . . You must telephone to tell me how he is doing. Moses, Moses. You're going to get better. You are.

—Yes, the crying wife says.

Yvonne bends down and touches the skull. The skull slowly shows teeth. —I'm so sorry, Yvonne says. Her shoulders start to shake.

The skull rolls from side to side. Rotting whispers float up. —No, no, my medem. No, is not you.

Now Yvonne is dragging her sleeve across her eyes. —Don't be sorry Moses. You know I'm not a medem, I'm just a girl, I'm just Yvonne, I'm only . . .

The skull's eyes have closed. Mrs. Luthuli is holding on to Yvonne's arm. —He must to rest, to sleep, I think, she says.

They go back into the other room where Yvonne writes a telephone number. There is noise in the street outside. Yvonne is saying she's going to try and find a hospital. Many faces are at the window, the door. Someone pushes through to say that Minister Tshabelala says to come. Isaac has to pull Yvonne out. Mrs. Luthuli, crying into a hanky, follows them outside with the four children behind.

A crowd is around the Cadillac and the minister waves at Isaac and Yvonne with the whole of his right arm. —The other ones are coming, he says. You should go now.

—Which way to get out?

—That way, that way. Keep right. At the end, go left.

Isaac has to lead Yvonne around to the passenger side. She is shaking and she can't see, she has her hand against her face. When he puts her in he catches his shin on the running board. The pain is like a spark into his belly where the tinder of his irritation starts to flare. Her blubbing is so useless just like this whole nutso trip. A pair of bladey Stupids. He starts driving fast through the wider lanes between the concrete huts. Anger crushes out the other feelings that were in him from the sickness. Rage has always been this kind of an inner cleanser for him. With rage he can think properly and, stuff it, if Moses Luthuli wanted to get himself stabbed that's tough tits for him no one asked him to and what about Greyshirts that stab Jews what is that, nothing? And look at this, how they live, can't she see it? Why must they blame themselves for this? I mean another second and that Chlistmas box joker would have stabbed me in the neck with a sharpened bicycle spoke like they do and it woulda been me like Moses Luthuli, with *my* bowels full of pus. And Yvonne, man, they woulda been like dogs on a cooked chicken, ripping her up. What do you expect if you bring your White arse to Orlando one fine sunny morning *in a fuckun Cadillac.* I must be mad. I must actually be insane meshuga in my head, what am I doing here, *what am I doing?*

He bangs the steering wheel hard. He shouts.

—What are you doing? she says.

He keeps banging and shouting. —We're alive!

—What's wrong with you?

—Alive!

She turns away. Ahead is a berm with a fence topped by concrete planks. He recognizes it: the other side is the main road they came here on. Now they reach the berm and he turns so they run parallel with it and ahead of them he sees the young men with the flat caps, spread across in a broken line. Some of them are dragging things across or rolling tires. —Oh look it's them, Yvonne is saying. We should–

He's already changed down and she is punched back in her seat as he flattens the pedal. The distance collapses with her scream, like a telescope snapping closed so that suddenly the young men are there, diving hard away, mad swimmers in a sand race. Some junk smashes off the Cadillac's massive bulk: a bed frame whirls, a rusted oil drum bounds, warbling. Something metal gets churned under. Swerving, he hits the berm and comes off and starts to fishtail; he has to brake hard. As he rights it again, there are thumps on the roof; the rear window coughs a half brick onto the back seat. He crushes the pedal flat: the Cadillac makes slither noises at the rear then the tires bite and they are pressed back in their seats again by sixteen roaring cylinders. One tire is gone in front, the rubber slapping and the steel juddering. Isaac fights the wheel against the slewing of it but he does not come off the gas and the car is also dragging something under, a tin can rattle like some demented wedding flight. Ahead, maybe another half a mile, is a break in the berm. He turns through it and they scrape onto the tarred road, the White road.

He stops once only to change the wheel and to drag loose an old bicycle frame snagged with rusted wires, cutting his hand in the process. Yvonne will not speak or look at him. At The Castle she gets out and opens the garage door. He is waiting behind the wheel to put the car in but as soon as she steps in she pulls the garage door down. He gets out and bangs on the door. He goes back to the Cadillac and stalls it out. He walks around it, the mauled bodywork, the broken windows. He cocks his head: a two-week job, in his most considered professional opinion. Maybe leave a Gold Reef Panel Beating card for them under the wiper except there is no wiper anymore ha ha. He smirks a little but a joke needs someone else to ignite into real laughter; otherwise you're just a solitary madman. When he rings the bell at the gate there is no answer. He knocks twice more on the garage and he waits, sucking on his cut hand, and then he goes away.

33.

HE BUYS A BOTTLE OF BRANDY and sips it from a paper bag on the bench at the train station. In Brakpan he buys another one then takes a slow sipping walk. When he finishes the bottle he can see the shape of the Reformatory risen from the burnt plain to bulk against the silken noon sky. The sun is bright on the white parts of the wall where the old plaster hasn't cracked and fallen away. The gate is open under the LION MOTORS sign. Isaac drops the bag with the empty and walks in and sees a ring of workers in their blue overalls sitting on the grease-stained earth around a small fire. They have a plate of salt and are dipping intestines in the salt then turning them with twigs on a grille made of rusted wires.

Isaac looks past them at the wrecks, the broken cars on top of each other in stacks with pathways left between, like some demented library of industrial decay written in volumes of rusted steel. The stacks stretch out all the way to the walls and up to the building now. In front are the greased chains and pulleys on a heavy steel frame for the lifting of the wrecks. This is hard naked work here in the yard; this isn't at all the fine modulated skill of panel beating, it's butcher surgery and heave-ho, the small of the back aglow with constant pain and the skin of the hands getting thick as nicked leather gloves if it wishes to survive.

While he stands there looking with his brandied eyes, Nangi comes up, stepping quietly.

—What you all up to?

I see you, baas, says Nangi in Zulu. He squats calmly; Isaac sinks too. Nangi takes out a twist of snuff and Isaac watches him push a knob of it into one of his big nostrils then the other. He snorts hard, scrubs the nose with the pale flat of his palm.

—You supposed to do from that truck all across to the Ford by the other side. They haven't even been started, them.

Baas, nobody has worked today.

—The hell's going on?

Nangi takes off his cap and puts it on the earth and bows his head over it, the hair stands from his crown in brittle tufts. He starts to trace the sand beside the cap. —Baas, is it that you don't like how we are working?

—Hey? Whatchoo mean?

—Is baas not liking the working we are doing?

—Why?

—We are always working so hard baas.

—Ja, you are.

—Nobody is take for you, baas.

—I should bladey hope not.

—Baas, we are wanting to know why is it there is no more money for our work.

—Didn't Silas give you?

—No, baas. Silas, he not for here. He in Free State.

—Still?

—He was here, but baas Hugo, he send him again.

—And he didn't give you pay last week?

Nangi scrubs his nose.

—Hey?

Nangi holds up three fingers.

—No!

—Yes baas.

—You charfing me.

—No baas.

—Didn't Silas give it?

Nangi strokes the sand, slowly and evenly, back and forth, studying the motion.

—Oright, says Isaac.

Upstairs, Hugo is at the desk with his feet up, one hand toodling with an adding machine, his eyes hooded and tie undone. Isaac picks up a paper spike. Hugo puts his soles down; his grin still intact. —You shika aren't you.

—Ja, I'm a drunkard, Isaac says, climbing the desk.

—Careful with that thing. Hugo backs the wheeled chair away.

Isaac jumps down and Hugo stands. —You know, Isaac says, I have had but one helluva day. And you know what it is that will make me feel better? Sticking this right in your fat guts.

Backing away, Hugo expresses a desire to know what the hell it is that is going on.

—I don't like being bullshitted. Where you going, gunif?

Hugo stops. —I'm a gunif now?

—Three weeks' work, Isaac says. Not a penny. What else you call that?

—I think you better sober your head and put that thing down. What happened to your hand?

—I think you better not blink, says Isaac. He weaves the spike and Hugo jerks at it with both hands, very quick for such a rotund fellow; the spike falls. Isaac sinks a meaty slap across Hugo's ear. Hugo walks sideways, rubbing.

—That bladey hurt, you dick.

—Remember it, says Isaac. Those boys have got chuym loksh for nelly a month.

—What are you hukking?

—You told me you'd give the pay to Silas.

—You know, Hugo says, I reckon you been grafting too hard, boyki. Go and get some sleep. Your brain's gone soft like porridge.

—I'm fine.

—You're not fine. You are drunk. You should see your eyes man. Wait. Wait. It's the female isn't it?

Isaac stands there, breathing hard.

—Ja, what happened? She said no. Is that what happened? It is.

—She's just deciding, that's all. She'll be fine.

—I'm sure she will be, boyki, I'm absolutely sure. But you're upset.

—Did you give Silas the dosh, yay or nay?

—You upset. I understand now.

—Hugo, you know I told you give Silas the wages.

—You *told* me? Scuse me, junior, but why don't you go back outside in the yard and leave the financials to one who knows what the hell's potting.

Isaac gives a guttural sound off his palate. —Ja, the great financialist.

—I think it's better you go. Cos you got your heart broken, you gone all mad.

He feels the truth of what Hugo's said inside his chest. Broken. If he opens his mouth a sob might come out. He bites his lip to get back control, says: —Never mind me. You don't pay people, they don't work. How's that for financials?

—They been paid, don't you hassle.

—You gave Silas the cash?

—He got it, he got it.

—Look at me, Hugo. You telling me you put the actual cash in Silas's hand?

— . . . You smell like a brewery, man. Get off me.

—Hugo.

—He got the pay, it's organized.

—Then why didn't they?

—I dunno, maybe you better ask your Silas.

—Silas is absolute. If he got it, he paid them.

—Oh now you believe the kaffir over your partner.

—You didn't give him nothing.

Hugo walks a large circle around and picks up the chair, sits in it and leans back, his hands meshed behind his neck. —Don't get so aggro about these moonts, ukay? They been treated more than oright. If they wanna eff off, they can chuck. The yard's nicely packed already and when prices turn around there'll be cash flow enough for a hundred new grease monkeys. Your Silases.

Isaac shakes his head. —Oright. Why don't you come down and do some graft with me in the yard hey, if you reckon's so easy. Just you and me. Like to see you do what they do.

—Isaac, just relax yourself. You got this bee stuck in your bonnet about Silas, I dunno why. Maybe it is that whoever I organized to give it to Silas stuffed it up, it's possible, I been running around like a blue-arse fly so much – tryna make *you* rich, apparently which is a big crime of the century. While you worried more about your female, and look now what that's caused.

—Hugo.

—We'll ask Silas when he gets back. Anyway, take a chair, man, like a civilized. I got something for you I was ganna give it if you hadn't tried to murder me dead just now.

—Wasn't ganna *kill* you.

—Ha ha. Doesn't matter, honestly, it's nothing. Nothing. Makes me feel how you wanna take care of those boys, that's good man, you're a loyalty. You're a solid egg and I am sorry things haven't worked out with your chickie there. You know that ring–

—I don't wanna talk about that.

—I just mean if you not–

—I said shut up on that. It's ganna be fine.

—Course it is, ja, sorry. Look. I can see you at the end of your rope. You been working like ten kaffirs on fire. So even if

Silas got the money, what's the difference, if it's that important to you, you my partner, boyki, then here. I want you to be happy. Here.

While saying this he leans to the side as if breaking wind, one hand squirming in a trouser pocket. It brings out a fat roll of notes looped by a rubber band. Isaac catches the lob.

—Go ahead and give them, says Hugo. Give em double pay if you want, if that's what you think's right. There's plenty.

Isaac examines the money.

—You don't have to worry yourself on the financials, says Hugo. We are capitalizing bloody fantastic. I promise you that's chicken peck.

—Ukay, says Isaac. He pockets the roll.

—That's it, take it. But I'm telling you boyki, you look fermuttered, man, you worn out. You look in shock. I understand what it's like when a thing like that happens. Broken-hearted. But you shouldn't be drinking hey, you in this kind of state. What the female can do to a man.

Isaac says nothing.

—Always the bladey female, says Hugo. Sit down here a sec, boyki, I wanted to give you something. Sit man.

Isaac sits on the desk edge, bent forward, slumped and tired. Hears the jingle of keys and Hugo hands a key ring across, a key on it with a moulded base and a logo he doesn't recognize.

—It's a Cushman, boy.

—Hey?

—A Cushman!

—One a those scooter things.

—Ja man. I feel bad I had to take back that Citroën, so I thought here's a wild little toy old Isaac can fly on. He'll have a ball with it.

—I don't have a licence for one.

—Don't need a *licence*! Christ sake, you sound like a pensioner. Go and have a ball man.

Isaac turns the key over in his tough hands. So tired. He feels
Hugo's warm palm cupping the back of his neck, rubbing there.
—Listen boyki. You've taken too much strain with this female
business, I understand, plus with all this graft, it's been too much,
I can see. Why don't you have yourself a little holiday, take the
break from Lion Motors altogether. You need a break. Leave it all
to your partner Hugo to organize for a while. Let me have the
full weight on my shoulders and you worry about other things,
get yourself sorted, come back when you feeling better ukay?
What is a partner for otherwise?

Isaac finds himself nodding. They go downstairs together, out
the back through the hole in the wall, Hugo with his arm around
his shoulders, talking all the way, saying how he always knew this
part-time job on the side was going to start to fray at Isaac, it's
a wonder it didn't happen already, man he's only human, if he
goes on non-stop this way he'll die.

In the back stands a battered silver scooter that starts up at the
eighth kick (Isaac staggering a little with the brandy in his balance),
the motor sounding like four or five sewing machines tumbling
down stairs, squirting foul blue smoke. They have to shout over
this while Isaac buckles on a helmet that Hugo hands him, pulls
the goggles down over his eyes.

—Always did want to ride one a these.

—Easier than a tricycle, shouts Hugo. Then he holds out his
hand. —Let me have those few bucks hey, so I can take care of
the boys.

Isaac hesitates.

—You go on. Leave it to me, I'll sort them right now tonight.

—You will hey.

—Come on. Are we partners or are we partners? Lookit me.
I'm Hugo. It's no worries, my mate. You jol on home on this,
start yourself a good holiday. Rest up. Feel better in a while,
you'll see.

Isaac revs the little engine; the smoke stinks of burnt oil. He's tired and his eyes feel gritty with weariness behind the goggles. Let him have the load. Break away from the burden of this place. Almost in a movement of exhaustion he lifts and drops the roll of notes back into the plump palm. When he rides through to the front, one of the men by the fire stands up. By the cap, he knows it's Nangi. A wind picks up. Smoke slants off the fire against the squatting men who turn their faces aside. Isaac stops and Nangi comes up. Isaac takes a breath to speak then looks back and swears.

—What is? says Nangi.

Isaac shakes his head.

—What is?

—Not you, says Isaac. What's wrong with me? He U-turns and rides back, catches Hugo just going back inside.

—What s'matter?

—Nothing. Hop on the back here.

—Ha ha.

—Just hop on a sec.

—What for?

—I just wanna show you something.

Hugo makes a bitter face. —I dun understand.

—Come on. We partners. Take a sec.

Isaac turns the scooter around and walks it back to Hugo's feet. Revs it. —Come on awready, you wasting time standing here.

Hugo coughs against the exhaust, sticking his tongue out and pretend-choking himself. Then his mass settles on the back, the scooter dipping its tail so steeply it clangs. —Just slow now hey.

Isaac takes them back to Nangi in front where he draws up as Nangi rises. Hugo dismounts and Isaac tells him to go ahead.

—Go ahead what?

—You know what. Give the man his due.

Hugo stares at him. —But this isn't Silas, man!

—Nangi's okay.

Hugo looks at Nangi, looks away to the building, stirs some dust with his shoe.

Isaac grins and leans across, pokes him twice in his soft belly. —Inside all that, there's a good oke somewhere. Let him out, Hugo. Do the right thing and give em their bladey wages.

Hugo looks down, shakes his big head, starts to chuckle. —Oright, sure, here. If it's so important to you right here and now. He pulls out the cash, counts off the notes. —And you can keep the ring too, he mutters.

—Thanks, I will.

—My stuffing pleasure.

34.

THE UNMANLY CUSHMAN draws a few laughs from the okes at Gold Reef when Isaac pulls up on it. He expects that the work will go badly but right away he finds that his hands are good in the job: the concentration on the labour fills up the bad hollow feeling and this becomes a day when he and Jack Miller make smooth progress. They finish the whole side panel section of a smashed Chevrolet Phaeton and when Labuschagne comes over to check the cracked manifold and the engine block, Miller puts in a good word about Isaac that makes Labuschagne nod.

It goes on that way deeper into the month of August, Isaac working better and better, keeping away from the Reformatory as per Hugo's advice. His full return to the craft of panel beating is like an addict to his drug: unworried blissful days when he concentrates so absolutely on his careful work that he seems to dissolve right into it and there feels to be no difference between his tools and the steel and his own self, it's all just one floating bubble of creation. He starts early and ends late and is fresh and sharp at his labours so that the quality of his work takes an immediate jump that nobody can fail to notice, even Labuschagne. They decide to give him his first solo job: small damage to a 500cc Norton motorcyle with a sidecar.

He detaches the panels, sands the steel, custom-machining his own dolly to suit the unusual angle in the sidecar. He uses wooden mallets on the inside to do the rough work then goes on to Miller's trick of a bent file as a slapstick, tapping the panel with the tip of it to get the right sound from the dolly on the other side then beating with the flat. A file stamps a nice mark into the steel that an ordinary slapstick would not, showing him exactly where his blows are landing. As he works he presses the whole of his hand to the steel, feeling the map of it with the palm and all the fingers, gently, as if treasuring the face of a beautiful woman. But don't think of a woman, not that, never that.

A Thursday. The hammers clash on the panels in the shop, mostly drowning the big band sounds of the Glenn Miller Orchestra from the battered old wireless with its exposed valves. Isaac is kneeling on a greasy work mat beside the Norton, unbolting a mudguard, when he senses movement and turns to face four legs. He wipes his hands on his overalls as he stands. There is a man beside Labuschagne. The sight of him is like being shot in the chest. All his blood drops to his feet. The vast shape of the man so much wider and higher than Labuschagne and he can't bring himself to look straight at him, he's just a human mass at the edge of his vision. How could it be? Why here? Why now? *How?*

Labuschagne saying: —Hierdie is die nuwe werktuigkundige.

This is the new mechanic. Magnus Oberholzer. Magnus, this is Isaac.

—Ach nee, Oberholzer's voice says. Ons ken mos mekaar.

We know each other. Then in English: —How is you, Cohen?

—It's Helger, Isaac hears himself croak, finally looking, but not at the eyes, at the neck as thick around as a telephone pole. His heart in its thudding hurts as if a cruel fist is squeezing it.

Oberholzer brings up his hand to shake. —Well, he says. So luvely to see you here, my neighbour. He laughs. It should be a deep rumble, man of his vast size, but it comes out gaseous and high, almost a little like a pig's squeal.

Labuschagne says: —Neighbour!

—Oh ja, says Oberholzer. I'm from Doornfontein also.

—Is it a fact?

—Oh ja.

Slowly, Isaac is taking the hand, Oberholzer's enfolding his like crocodile jaws, huge. Someone calls Labuschagne and he steps away. Oberholzer smiles. —Ganna have good times working together hey Jewboy. I can't wait, can you?

He squeezes. Isaac's hand is strong, toughened by the heavy work, but Oberholzer is freakish: that impossible natural might that comes from wide bones and heavy meat, tidal power that bears down on Isaac like an ocean swell, crimping the knuckles.

Oberholzer angles his head and sucks up snot from the back of his throat and spits hard. —Ja, he tells Isaac. I really kahn wait to start here. Ganna be so good. I cannot wait.

Then Labuschagne comes back and Oberholzer lets go. Isaac keeps his face neutral. His hand throbs as if scalded. He restrains himself from rubbing it till they move away. Deep red marks he knows will bruise up like ink bands. Remembering what that steel grip once did to him before. He looks down at his laces, the oily blob of mucus there.

The end of the shift brings them their pay packets and they hand some of the notes to Labuschagne for his Quality Street tin then go wait outside, smoking, while he locks up. Isaac decides to skip the comradely drinks at the Great Britain Hotel. He's gone by the time Labuschagne comes out.

Oberholzer's presence in the shop makes a feeling of shock in Isaac that he ignores, day after day, pressing on with his good work, finishing off the Norton and then going back to working under Jack Miller on the Chev. He learns from him that Oberholzer came looking for a job out of the blue, a godsend to Labuschagne who has been looking for a good mechanic. It seems that Oberholzer knows his job, too. No complaints on him from the

okes, or from Labuschagne. It doesn't make sense to Isaac that
Oberholzer would have come here by chance but neither does it
seem sensible that he would have arrived just because Isaac is here
– what for? Maybe the gas incident is the answer to that. It happens one day after Jack Miller arrives. Isaac stands up from his
work to say good morning and sees the wrongness in Miller's face,
the folded arms. —Whatzit Jack?

—Bladey tank's empty.

—Hey?

Miller elbows towards the big oxyacetylene tanks racked on
wheels. —Tap got left open last night. You know how much
oxygen costs man?

—Me? Jack, I diden–

—You supposed to check, Isaac. I don't want to hear. The
whole bloody place can blow up like a bomb.

—Jack, seriously, it wasn't me.

—Don't want to hear. Let's just work oright.

The rest of the day his hands are not his hands. The soaring
feeling does not come, he's been thrown off. Where usually his
fingers are drawn into the work with a nimble intelligence of their
own, this day he has to wield them with his conscious mind. Doing
it this way is clumsy and full of errors, as if he's got thick gloves
on. He battles in vain to regain the deft feel, the easy confidence,
to focus his mind so that the energy will come and lift him and the
hours dissolve into a seamless moment but, no, he cannot take off,
he can't get over the injustice of the accusation.

When Miller curses at him for the first time, after he almost
destroys a panel with his clumsy banging, he knows it's justified.
But there's nothing he can do. On his locker that night there is a
cartoon from an Afrikaans newspaper cut out and stickytaped at
eye level. Showing a Jew with a trumpet nose and swindling hands
pickpocketing a Boer. But from above, a Nazi grips a Star of David
with its sharp point aimed down at the bald Jew's skull. Isaac rips

the paper off, whirls. The men in there look away. Again he does not go to the pub.

The weekend is another gloriously decadent interlude of sleeping in. He fights the temptation to head out to Parktown or to the Reformatory. Tries not to think about either of those places at all. When he returns to the shop, he finds that the boot panel of the Chev that he had almost straightened is now buckled in again. Sledgehammer marks. He waits for Oberholzer to arrive. Stares hard across the shop at him. Oberholzer waves, smiles. Isaac's breath comes in small gasps, his heart pumping hard under the tight cable of his throat. He goes back to work. Works badly. At the end of the day he finds two of his dollies are missing, including the one that he spent so much time machining himself. He catches a harsh lecture from Jack Miller. Isaac nods, packs up the rest of his tools carefully, and goes home without saying a word.

Tuesday: More tools go missing.

Wednesday: The oxygen tap has been left open again. By now Jack Miller knows something very strange is going on. He hardly meets Isaac's eyes.

Thursday: A drawing of a pig with a Semitic nose pinned to his locker. His mug on the tea table has paint in it. He glances around and Oberholzer is pointing from across the shop; other men turn and look at him and laugh. When he gets back to his station, Jack Miller is shaking his head.

Once again, after he gets his pay packet and pays into the kitty, he skips having a drink at the Great Britain Hotel. Oberholzer will be there, his giant shoulders taking up a mass of space at the bar, his booming laugh pressing on eardrums. He goes home and has powerful dreams of Yvonne in the night. He's swimming in lakes in shimmering caverns under mountains of slumber, chasing the pale jewel of her ankle, her thigh, her laughter held in bubbles.

He wakes to a hollowness. When his mind pronounces her name he knows he is in trouble. It's not finished, he tells himself. Let it rest, just wait and she will come back, she must. He has a bottle in the sewing room and he goes out to get it, telling himself he won't look at the ring in its hiding place behind the mirrors with the immigration forms – but then he does, clenching and unclenching the bright stone on the engraved silver hoop in his hand for a long time before putting it back. Outside, a dry African windstorm slings mine dust against metal roofs. He drinks from the bottle and looks at the Oberholzer place and considers going over there, banging on the door, wake the man up and demand from him, What is it you're doing? Got nothing better to do with your pathetic life than come all the way cross town and work at Gold Reef to give me shit? Why would you *do* that? What the hell's *wrong* with you?

I'm not scared to do it, he tells himself. I could. But his body doesn't move. His body hasn't forgotten the massive force of the man's bulk, like a sweeping wind, and that grip like a vise of industrial steel. So he drinks until there's no more to drink, till he feels drool on his chin. He weaves back inside and picks up the telephone and dials without pausing. It rings seven times and a man answers, the voice of broken sleep. —Zat Mr. Linhurst?

—Who is this?

—Look, Mr. Linhurst. I can tell you this cos I am a man. And you are a man.

—What?

—Hang on. Hold your horse, Linny. You a man, I'm a man. What I saying, a man he owns up hey. A man takes the responsibility.

—I don't like games. Who is this?

—You know, you know. The boyki from Doornfontein.

A silence.

—Ja, how things at the old Castle hey? Grounds in order? Queen get her medicine? Everything *chipper*?

—See here, you little drunkard.

—I wanna pologize for the Cadsy, okay Dadsy?

A woman's voice behind his now. Pecking. The muffled sound of a hand swooshing over the receiver. Then Linhurst says: —I'm going to ring the police.

—Police, says Isaac. Woo.

—If you dare talk to any of us again–

—Aw, Dukey.

—See here you little swine. We'll charge you with breaking in, with stealing the car, vandalism. With kidnapping and confinement. Get that through your drunken skull, can you understand how serious?

Isaac sways, breathing heavily. His lips slowly working, his tongue making sticky noises that echo back in the buzzing line. Kidnapping.

—The full weight of the law. I can make sure. I–

Isaac takes the telephone from his ear. He watches it for a time. The little voice buzzes. He puts the handle on the hook and goes to bed.

He does good work all day, and at closing time he finds a new little something waiting for him on his locker, an advert for Cushman motor scooters that's been torn out of a magazine, a picture of some woman sitting on the scooter with a fountain and a church behind. Someone has used a crayon to give her head a wild mop of orange hair. Her nose has been lengthened and elephant ears drawn on in dark ink.

Isaac looks at it and snorts. He takes it off and he holds it to his chest to show the room. —You okes only wish you had a chick as lekker as me. This sentence catches the right tone, snapping the room's tension, showing them he can take a joke, that he knows the Cushman is funny, and they laugh with him half in relief. He sees the heavy shape of Oberholzer for a second in the doorway, turning back out. Got you, you bustud.

This Friday night he goes with the okes to the Great Britain Hotel instead of home even though it's Shabbos supper, and all the way there he feels very good about his little triumph in the locker room on top of the good day of shop work. At this moment there is no thinking of Yvonne, there is nothing hollow in him. Only the full happy feeling from the way he worked well on the Chev and afterwards how he dismantled the trap that had been laid for him, turning it on its owner, using it to make himself popular for this night, with a couple of the okes even paying for his Scotches with jokes about where is his lipstick. The best is that there is no worry about going out to Brakpan that night; if he has uneasy thoughts about the Reformatory he lets them float off, like the Yvonne thoughts, floating away, the way he later on will drift in the steam of his hot bath.

In the night come the dreams of her laughter and her touch. He wakes early with a pang of need that is like the necessity to draw breath. He has to get up and walk around the workshop. It's in the middle of his chest, the feeling, hard as a cricket ball, a pain that cannot be shaken. He has to speak to her, to see her. Why does she not contact him? Every day she is falling further away, becoming a stranger. They were only just sitting together in the crisp air on the ledge talking and touching and loving, she was going to be his bride. That is real and this is not. He is stuck in the wrong reality, a left turn in a dream and he can't get back to waking. Why will she not contact him? Why? What must he do, what can he do, what is the right thing he must do and the wrong thing he must not? The gesture that could banish her from him forever versus the move that will bring her into his arms where she always should be? It's bad, he thinks. I've got this really bad.

Admitting this to himself brings on fresh nausea, his scalp shrivelling, a wave of weakness fluxing through the bowels.

He is bent over, heaving for breath, when his father comes in, ready for shul in his good clothes, and asks him if he is sick.

I'm worse than sick, Isaac thinks. I'm dying. He says, —No one rang for me hey Da?

He shakes his head. When?

Anytime, Isaac says in Jewish. Or a note? No one came here to see me, nothing, the post?

Isaac, what are you talking, the sun isn't even properly up yet.

He goes in to work Monday and when he gets there he finds waxen threads of bright lipstick drawn all over his tools. You don't mess with another man's tools: that's an iron rule of the shop. He's been like a patient who thinks he is clear of the disease but here is the fresh symptom, it's spreading and it's worse. This is not going to stop. A lipstick tube is still open beside the marked tools; beside it are puffballs of rouge and a dark little brush on a stick that Isaac thinks is what girls use for painting the eyes.

Aloud he says: —What the fuckun *hell*.

Jack Miller walks up with a mug of tea in his hand, chin pressing wide bulges of throat fat. —You telling me, he says. Listen, I don't need any more of this fucken crap, right?

Jack Miller is not a man to swear. This is only the second time that Isaac has ever heard him do it. —You better sort this out, he says. I am telling you.

Looking across the shop Isaac sees the faces watching him, sees Oberholzer sitting back in the corner: the smirk under the moustache.

He crosses to the office, raps on the open door.

—Gotta talk to you, boss.

Wearily, Labuschagne looks up. —I run a business here, man.

If this's about any other thing like this kuk for two-year-olds that's been going on, I don't wanna know it.

—But boss.

—Sort it out yourselves man. Running a business here.

Isaac takes himself to the tea table, to put his back to the shop. He's scooping sugars with a shaking hand when Vernon, the other apprentice, comes to fill his mug.

Isaac nudges, hisses. —The bladey hell man, what's going on now?

—It's not me hey.

—I know that. What the okes saying?

— . . .

—Hey? He nudges harder.

Vernon's glasses are fogging in the steam from the shrilling kettle in which his whisper is almost lost. —They say you queer.

—*What?*

—It's not *me*.

—Who told you that, a queer?

He shrugs. —Going around.

Isaac says the eff word three times. He forgets his tea – this isn't the time for the soothing of bladey tea – and he uses turps and rags to clean off his tools and takes the used rags with the rest of the lady crap to the big oil drum used for rubbish. He drags the bin out from the corner and he slams his rubbish in and kicks the drum hard enough to make them look at him, to scoop out a pause in the hammering. He fills his chest, shouts: —You better watch it hey! Whoever messing my stuff, I'm telling you. Telling you all now. Watch it!

He searches the faces, the stopped work, for Oberholzer, but can't find him. Someone somewhere gives a whistle, two long notes, one up one down, like the ones that get fired at passing girls. Someone else laughs: a different laugh to the locker room because this time Isaac is on the outside of it, he gets the teeth end of this cutting sound. Then someone else, invisible, maybe from under a car, gives out a call in falsetto. —Skattie, skattie wil jy my 'n soentjie gee op jou mooi Cushman neh?

Oh darling, darling, throw me a little kiss on the back of your sweet little Cushman won't you?

This time the cutting laughter comes from everywhere. Teeth and teeth. Red blood slams in his head: he makes a sound at them that is like a cat's howl. Now Labuschagne is coming towards him from the office, Labuschagne shouting at the shop to drop this kuk and get to work. Isaac goes to his station where Miller won't meet his eyes.

All day his work is very bad. What's happened is that the joke he made about being a girl on a Cushman has been turned around against him. This new queer thing is very bad and he must stop it now before it destroys him.

After his shift is over he can only breathe in the locker room once he sees there is nothing on the steel door. He decides he will not go to the Great Britain Hotel but straight home; and he packs up his tools to take with. When he reaches the Cushman parked in the back he finds the petrol tank is open and there are white granules all around the rim. In lipstick someone has written, *Suiker soontjie vur n skattebol.* Sugar kisses for a sweetheart. He doesn't try to start the engine. Maybe there is a chance of saving it if he drains and cleans the tank, but if it's been run already, the sugar will have clogged the filter, maybe even ruined the carb. The worst part is that the handwriting is different to the other from before.

Carrying his tool box, he takes the tram home.

35.

ALL NIGHT ISAAC HELGER squeaks around on his cot. He reckons now this is a past failure coming back to get him. He should have handled this monster Oberholzer the first time, after what he did when he moved in here. Gone back after and sorted him. But you left it and now it's ten times worse. He gets up and paces. There's no other way – the man's come looking for him, jamming him in a corner.

He goes into the kitchen and gets a breadknife, the biggest knife they have, serrated and rectangular with a pine handle. He goes on out into the tepid air, the white moonsplash. Walks into the alley with the blade. No light in the window at the back of number forty. Halfway there he stops: time ebbs and nothing changes. He stands that way for maybe half an hour, maybe a full one. Then the back door opens and she comes out. He slips quickly to the side, hunkers down. She should not be here this late according to her old habits which he used to watch with such glazed and drunken avidity. On the other hand he can see in the ambient streetlamp gloom that she has her cigarettes as she always did and she's wearing the same blue nightie with the bunny rabbit slippers that scrape softly on the road as she crosses to the DeSoto. She sits on the running board, her long thighs and pale manly knees sticking up. Lights her cigarette.

Shadowed, the knife close to his chest, Isaac glides against the wall. Now he is close enough to study the waxen pale flabbiness of her flesh, the shoulders as wide as a man's and that face, horse-narrow, squeezed between pillars of straight sandy hair. When she blows smoke it's past her nostrils, bottom lip overlapping the top. She glances his way, he freezes. Her eyes shrink to dots, she flicks back a strand of that straight hair. So white she is, so waxen, as if glommed together out of soft Sabbath candles.

—Hey, she says. Someone there?

Isaac moves off the wall. —Shh, he tells this woman of Ober-holzer's. He walks out, hears a faint buzzing from a lamp farther up the alley, the weak yellow glow fractured on the concrete. She doesn't move. He stands over her. Her eyes go up and down, she drags on the cigarette. —Ach, you.

From where he is he can't see the door. The skin down his side is crawling, a part of him imagining Magnus Oberholzer's eyes there, on him. He looks down at her, at the bread knife in his hand. Surprised to see how white the hand is around the handle, bloodless yet steady. He looks at her white throat.

She flicks ash at the knife. —What, you come to have another go at the tires? He told me all about that.

Isaac stands unmoving.

—Be my guest, she says. Her horsehead tossing sideways, the long hair flicking. —Think I care hey, not *my* tires.

As with motion, he has no words for this moment.

—What you staring me out for like that?

He has to crack through his tight throat: a croak, barely.

—What you ganna do?

—Give me a smoke.

She shakes her head.

—Give.

—No. Go buy your own. Then: —Everyone wants something.

—Give it to me.

—Of wat? she says. Afrikaans: Or else what?

He feels his pulses heavy in his neck. —Why?

—Hey?

—Why is he at my work? Why did he come there?

—You the one I should tell thank you that he does.

—Me?

—He was watching you always go off, your nice clean little uniform on, every morning bright early. Gold Reef Panel Beating there on the back all cute. That is what got him to go over there and ask for the job. He didn't like you thinking you better cos you work. All a you people. If you hadden kukked him off, he'd still be lazy at home all day.

—Me?

—Yes you, you. What you deaf also? He only went to work there cos a you.

—Jesus Christ.

—Ach, she says, and drops her cigarette and stands. The tower of her. —Know what? I don't even care what you do to the car. It's not mine this car. Nothing's mine. Go ask my ma-in-law, s'her car, if you want a fight. I don't even care.

She's so tall he is looking up at her, the tip of her slender horse nose. No tits to speak of, just nipples very pointy and clear under the thin blue nightie. A straight body with thick thighs and loose arse. She makes a flicking gesture, as if to send him onto the tires already, standing there with the knife out.

—Go inside call him and I'll wait here for him.

—Magnus? Man he so asleep. He's a working man. A smirk comes with the last words. —Thanks to you, boy.

—I'm not a boy.

—No, she says, her eyes dropping and rising. —I can see that.

She steps in close. Almost touching.

—Your husband, he says, and it's a wheeze, his voice, nothing more. He's such a scum. He's a bastard.

—Oh fuck *you*, she says. What you want here anyway? Hey?

He drops the knife at his side. So close she is. His arm rises slowly, slowly, with the drumming of his hot slow thoughts. It curls up behind her long head. Looking down at him, she smirks again. A toothless lip-pressed smirk. —Oright, she says. Oright. Lez try this. She tucks her cigarettes away somewhere in the nightie. But Yvonne, he thinks somewhere. Yvonne. Her mouth bends down against his. Yvonne doesn't matter, Yvonne is the cause of this, she deserves this.

He opens his mouth and stabs his tongue but she pulls back, a little. Again she brings her mouth in and again when he tries with the tongue she edges back. After a while he stops trying and they stand there, mouth almost to mouth, breathing each other. The pitch of her gradually shifts. Such a big woman: a kind of monster female. He is shocked to feel her wide strong hands gripping his arse. She turns him around to the dark side of the DeSoto away from the house and the streetlamp glow. She undoes his pants, so calm. They puddle to his boots. She pulls down the underwear and his cock snaps out like a bent spring released. She runs one fingernail along the back of it and his legs twitch and quiver. She curls her finger in the pubic hair and pulls until he comes up on his toes and winces. He feels so light and small beside her. She steps back and her hands go up under her nightie. She waddles, steps out of her panties. —Open your mouth, she says. Maak oop. Afrikaans, that language of orders: Open up.

He opens and she stuffs the panties in, past his teeth. —Yes, she says, almost hissing it. Yes, boy. Something seems to pop in Isaac's brain. Like a lightbulb full of sweet liquid. She slaps him and bites his neck then turns around and bends over in front of him, leaning on the car, hiking up the nightie around her belly. The arse is very white and round. She reaches up from under herself and takes hold of his cock. She pulls and he shuffles close with his ankles looped in the puddled trousers. His thing bumps the shadowed space between her white cheeks. She takes her hand back, he can see her straight hair hanging down, hears her spit onto her hand, sees her lick it like a cat. She brings it back, the touch hotslick now as if bleeding. Her long fingers slip over him loosely. She grips and slowly draws him inward, into the shadowed space, inside in, slow. A feeling like being peeled, the skin curling away to expose himself to her, nerve by nerve by nerve. It slips up his spine, shudders in his head, makes his jaw work against the soft wad of panties gripped there. When he feels the crinkly bush of his pubic hairs flatten against her flesh he puts his hands on the buttocks and pulls her apart and towards him and rams her and this is too much: his balls clench up and he spasms into her. She seems to stop, cautious. After a while he goes on. So much wetter now, opening, like a sodden flower to the uncaring sun. Fluid runs out and drips onto his thighs. He works calmly back and forth. Quite numb now but still hard as the steel tools of the shop. He starts to understand more of this: without the peeled feeling of the pleasure to overwhelm him he can think in the experience of it, a small measure of brutality in this detachment. He squeezes her soft white flesh, pinches and slaps it hard. He thumps on her back. It only makes her shudder, raises new sounds. He starts to club hard in her and the pleasure comes back and begins to climb.

Walking back afterwards he feels as he did when once he fell asleep in the Chains Park on Seimert Road and got sunburned all red. Waking up in the baked shell of himself. The shade a blindness after the shattering light, his skin radiating. This has some of that weak emptiness also; it had ended with her shocking him again by reaching up between her legs to jerk herself to a spasm like a man. He had not known it was possible like that, so raw. She told him she could not have babies; the risk hadn't remotely occurred to him. In the backyard he uses the whispering tap to wash his cock and balls in the cold water, over and over. Washing her juices from his privates as he once washed her husband's piss from his face. Dirt from dirt people. It's only then that he realizes he still has her chewed panties between his teeth.

——

In the morning he has an appetite for the French toast sprinkled with cinnamon and sugar that Mame sets in front of him. As she serves him she is listening to Rively translating the news on the wireless, a report about a big agreement signed now between Stalin and Hitler, the Communists and the Nazis getting into bed together, agreeing not to attack each other, which nobody seems to be able to understand as they're supposed to be such enemies. He tells his sister to send his regards to Comrade Yankel, look at what nice friends these commies are fond of making. For once she doesn't snap back at him but seems quiet and shocked so that he touches her back on the way out.

He whistles in the street. He slept well and the calm and ruthless feeling that he awoke with is still with him. When you make a proper decision. A machine feeling: cold and driving.

It stays in him as he carries his toolbox onto the tram. Someone he knows says hello and he ignores him. Walking up on Marshall Street he can see the front garage door is open knee high and he can hear the sound of banging and the angle grinders, see the flickering whiteness jerking shadows from the oxyacetylene torches.

Inside is the petrol smell, the warmth. He goes across to Miller and Miller looks up. —You need to go talk to boss.

Isaac looks at him. —What now?

—Listen, Isaac, I've just had enough. I don't care what you are. But this is a job.

—What I *am*?

Miller turns back to his work. Isaac goes to the office where Labuschagne tells him he is going to fire him. He doesn't want to hear what Isaac has to say. Isaac stands there unwinded, unshocked. Calm in his mood of brutal numbness. Labuschagne says that someone poured a can of pink paint over Isaac's workstation, wrote the word moffie, that bad word of the many bad words that there are for homos. Jack Miller had to clean it up first thing but a lot of the okes already saw. —You know how bad it is for the shop to have this kind of thing. It makes everyone unhappy, ay. I can't have it.

—Oberholzer, Isaac says.

—Hey?

—It's Magnus Oberholzer. Your new mechanic. You know it, I know it, everyone knows.

— . . . He's a good mechanic. What's your proof?

—He hates my guts.

—Why?

—Cos in Doornfontein, long time ago, we had some aggro. It goes back.

Labuschagne rubs his chin. He lights a Van Riebeeck. He does not have to say what Isaac knows: a mechanic, especially a good one, is worth more than any apprentice class A panel beater in this shop or any. So Isaac says, —Am I really finished, Franzie, or what?

Labuschagne clicks his jaw from side to side. —Dunno man. You started so good. I thought you ganna be one a the best. I dunno. He shakes his head. —Ja, nee. Can't have this . . . Alls I can say, uhkay, try to sort it with Magnus. He not such a bad ou hey. Try and sort it with him. Otherwise . . . He shakes his head.

—Otherwise I'm out.

— . . . Sort it oright? Try to go back to how you was before. I'm not ganna fire anyone today oright. But Isaac, it can't go on.

Isaac nods. He knew this himself; he's already decided. He works through the morning in the shell of his resolution. He doesn't have to look over to where Oberholzer is working on a brown six-cylinder Plymouth to feel that presence. When it's almost lunchtime he breaks early – Miller says nothing – and puts a roll of masking tape in his pocket, a handful of panel screws. Some bag dollies, a wedge.

In the toilet stall he strips off his overalls, his shirt. He pulls off a length of tape then pierces a dozen sharp screws through it then tapes it around his neck down over the collarbone, the backs of the short screws cool against his skin. He adds more layers of tape, some criss-crossing, packing it solid. Then he puts his foot up on the toilet and hikes the trousers. He moulds the bags of shot, the dollies, against his shin and tapes them in place. He takes off his boot and fits the wedge at the top of his foot, tapes it there and loosens the bootlaces and pulls the boot back on and tightens the laces over the bulge of the steel pressing up under the tongue. He puts his shirt back on carefully. Pats himself, bounces, to make sure all is firm. The last thing he does is check his pocket under his overalls for the thing that he put there this morning, that he brought with him from home, token of his calmly determined state. He moves it to an outer pocket.

Lunchtime is starting, the men peeling slowly away from their jobs, their stations. The clanging and shrieking slowly falling off to voices. Through this, Isaac walks. He stops fifteen feet away from the man who is wiping his huge hands on a rag, sitting on a bench.

—Oberholzer!

He sucks his lungs full: —Oberholzer!

Magnus Oberholzer straightens up, the dense moustache across the wide face, a neck like a tree stump sunk into the pack of the heavy shoulders so wide in the tan overalls, a belly over thick knees. He gives Isaac that smirk of his, the lips prodding forward.

—You been telling people I'm a queer!

—Is that what you are hey. I diden even hear that.

Isaac can feel the others catching wind now, drawing in, turning.

—You shit talk behind my back hey. Saying I'm a moffie.

—You know, says Oberholzer, now that you says it, I can see it. You always did look girly to me.

—You speak kuk man!

—Why you getting so worked up, Cohen? I'm only saying I never have seen a real queer before. And he laughs that high piglet snigger.

Isaac catches laughter from the sides too, some from behind. Bladey vultures. They're enjoying this. And Labuschagne has disappeared of course, so convenient. *Sort it out yourselves.* Well ja then, ukay, here it is.

Isaac says: —Maybe we should ask your wife about that hey.

Oberholzer jerks then: his head twists on the stump neck, cocking. —What say?

—Your wife, says Isaac loudly. Annabel. You go and ask Annabel your wife if I am a queer.

—Why? says Oberholzer. Does you borrow her makeup from her, ay, is that why?

Laughter, more of it than before. Oberholzer stands up slowly, a smooth unrushed movement like the swell of a great ocean wave. The size of the man, and the smirk: he lives for this, he's come here to the shop just to bait you till you break and he is not going anywhere.

Isaac says: —It's not makeup that I go to your Annabel to get.

—What is it, perfume?

The watchers laugh some more. Like a tennis match for them.

—Ask her, says Isaac. Ask her what I got from her last night. In the alley behind your house in Doornfontein there. Ja, go and ask *her.*

—Jewy boy, you mixed up. You were with your other queers in alleys last night.

—You wish, Isaac says. I was behind *your* house with *your* wife, number forty Buxton Street. I had her like a street whore.

—Ooh, someone behind says. Oo wah.

Otherwise it is silent.

Isaac glances to the sides, sees that some men are looking away, some at the floor. Their breathing has concentrated now, here is a new weight in the air and it is no longer the breezy feeling of a tennis match. When he looks back at Oberholzer's face he sees the lips under the moustache have curled in and gone white.

—Ja, Isaac says to the shop. His big wife Annabel. You check her big soft arse. I gave it to her twice bending over in the alley behind his house. I swearda God. Twice. That's the God's truth.

No one laughs or makes any sound. Then someone walks out. Someone else, sounds like Rustas, says: —Shouldn't say those things about a man's wife hey.

—It's true, Isaac says. He started. Calling me a queer and that's a lie. Stuffing up my tools and all bladey nonsense. But what I says about his wife is completely truth. His wife, she's a bladey slut. Not even. She fucks anyone like a animal for free.

People hiss.

—Hey hey, you better stop it, a voice says.

There's a soft woofing noise that men are making, a kind of muted bark that means to tamp Isaac's words down.

—That's not right, ay, says a voice that could be Christo the Italian, a panel beater.

Oberholzer takes a quick step toward Isaac, his face alive and bright, his lips curled in. Says, —Do you wanna fokken die? You dirty. You lying Jewboy piece a kuk.

—Is this lying? Isaac says. Is it?

He takes the panties from his pocket, holding them up, waving them. Someone whistles softly. Someone else says, —Ach no hey, no.

Isaac spreads the panties wide between his hands. —Look at the size of her, he says. Try and tell us you don't recognize these hey Magnus. They are prolly ones you bought a present for her hey. That alley slut that is your wife. That bitch in heat. You call me dirty – then she must love my dirty cock.

—Ooh wuh, someone behind breathes.

—Sal jy moor, jou poes! Oberholzer says. Flecks of spit shine in this fast shouted Afrikaans. I'll kill you, you cunt. —Sal jy dood slaan. Sal you derms uit jou gat uithal. I'll smash you dead. I'll rip your guts out through your arsehole.

And closes the space between them with three wide steps.

Isaac has wrapped the panties around his right fist. He sets and throws a long punch, from behind his shoulder, telegraphing it, throwing it a little slower than he can. Oberholzer's arm sweeps up. He smacks the punch down and away: that vast left hand, spread like open pincers, slugs into the side of Isaac's neck. The grip clamping there at once. Thumb into windpipe. Exactly as it happened on that other night long ago; night of piss and shame. A man can be relied on to always use a trick that works.

Isaac puts his hands over the other's hand as the power of it digs into the soft notch in his throat and twists into his neck. A second more and he'll be choking, paralyzed. He drives up his shoulder, feels the screws just under his overalls popping through the fabric, catching in the living flesh. Oberholzer jerks back; but Isaac's got the hand in tight. He grinds his shoulder, twisting hard. Oberholzer shouts. There's a flash of red as he gets the torn hand free. Isaac lets go, steps around lightly behind him as the giant sucks his hand to his belly, bending. Isaac aims his right foot, swung back like a soccer player shooting for goal. He drives from the hips. His leg, almost straight, comes up relaxed with the centrifugal drag of the taped shot pulling at the shin, sweeping up between Oberholzer's splayed thighs. The foot mostly disappears on the far side of him: it is the iron instep close to the ankle that slogs into the soft give of the scrotum. A lighter man would have been lifted. Oberholzer grunts, taking the full shock. Isaac steps back. Oberholzer turns, face drained. Still holding his bloodied hand to his belly. He takes a step, another. Isaac moves back, watching him. Oberholzer, showing teeth, lunges. Isaac dodges. Oberholzer goes to one knee. He holds himself, bloodying the crotch of his trousers. He bends slowly and vomits. One hand, the good one, against the shop floor. The other palm smears red on the groin, so bright. Dripping now.

Isaac steps around him again. Bends himself sideways and swings his weighted leg, a horizontal kick, wild and sweeping. The side of Oberholzer's mouth caves: teeth and tooth splinters in a pink spray squirt out of the far side. He does not fall over. He paws at his jaw with the torn hand. He rears up again but can't seem to get off the knee. Isaac toe-kicks him in the kidney. He grunts, folds low. The breath bubbling and whistling in the pink mess of his mouth. Isaac steps around and aims another kick. Arms grab him from behind and around the middle. —Is enough, Rustas keeps saying.

Someone else saying, —What did he do to him?

Isaac struggles. —Lee me, lee me go.

—Is finish, is over.

Others come across between them. Someone bends to Oberholzer. Blood and vomit on the concrete. Isaac unwraps the panties from his fist, throws them onto the mess. —Let him clean it! Let him clean it up!

—Okay, okay now, George Kazy says. Is finish, it finish now.

—Finish? I'll finish *him*! The redness swimming in Isaac's soul, obliterating. He breaks from the hands. —Ja! All a you! What happens if you bladey soek with me! Talk kuk around on me!

His voice so hoarse and startling it sounds even to him as though someone else is shrieking from inside the prison of his chest. Madman. Rabies Helger. He goes to the toilet, strips off his weapons. Throws away the used tape, pockets the shot and wedge. Scrubs the blood from his overalls with wet toilet paper. Then he lights a cigarette with hands shaking so much in the end he has to press his elbow against the wall to steady it. He smokes the whole cigarette quickly, then another. He finds he is very thirsty. He drinks from the tap till his belly is full. He goes back out. The shop is empty. He goes into the yard where the ruined scooter still stands. There are a few Blacks sitting against the wall with their eyes hooded against the hot sun.

One grins at him. Lifts his fist up and down in that graceful loose-jointed way they have. Each time he lifts the fist he whistles sharply once through his top teeth. Others grin. One sing-says in Zulu: You killed him today, the bull, the bull.

Another one chops the edge of one hand into the palm of the other, keeping time. Saying *chuh chuh chuh* with each blow. The first sings in Zulu: Esh what happened to the Boer bull today?

To the ground, to the ground, the others sing back.

Esh what happened to the Boer bull today?

Hospital, hospital.

What happened to the Boer bull today?

To doctors, doc-tuhs.

They laugh and whistle, stamp feet on the baked earth.

Isaac smiles at them, turns slowly. Goes back inside to wait for Labuschagne.

36.

FOR THE REST OF THE WEEK Oberholzer is absent and everyone seems to be suddenly intent on doing a good job and being
extra friendly and polite to everyone else at Gold Reef Panel
Beating, as if in compensation for the bad blood that was so
savagely spilled. The fight is also conspicuously not spoken about,
as if it never happened at all. Over the weekend Isaac reads in the
papers how Great Britain has now signed a promise with Poland
that if someone attacks Poland, Britain will backstop them. Mess
with them and you mess with us. It's just like the okes at the shop:
the only thing that really counts in this world is the fist. It gives
him a bitter feeling, this realization, which is not what he expected.
He thought he'd be high on his destruction of Oberholzer. He
considers going out to Parktown and half goes to the bus stop; he
has notions of going out to the Reformatory and half starts towards
the train station. In the end the weekend dissipates in time frit-
tered, in napping and walking, doing nothing but feeling itchy and
restless inside.

There's a surprise waiting for him at work. His scooter's been
repaired, body and engine better than it was, scrubbed and shining,
set out for him in front of the shop. Inside he finds that Magnus
Oberholzer is back, his face mutilated by black stitches and a great
swelling, as if he's holding a golf ball on one side between teeth that
are no longer there. Looking thinner too, maybe because he can't

eat solid food but must take his lunch through a straw. He is very pale and seems to have lost something else, something nameless and more essential than blood and weight.

Again, Isaac fails to feel the triumph he should, even though now it is Oberholzer who goes home after work and Isaac who goes to the Great Britain Hotel; even though when Isaac tells a joke the men all boom where before they wouldn't so much as smile; even though he has his scooter and his honour back; even though Isaac is the man and Oberholzer the fading boy now. No, it is not a fine triumph to know in your bones that men are worse than dogs, rolling on their backs for the stronger one, licking the arse of the superior. Being the strong now does not cheer him. Simple respect should have been his before, but he can't forget how it was when Oberholzer was the strong and he, Isaac, was made shameful and piteous. Ja, there is nothing lower in this world than the ordinary man.

Thursday, payday, also happens to be the last day of the month and when Isaac claims his pay packet, installing a portion of the cash in Labuschagne's dented Quality Street tin, he finds it hard to believe he's been away from the Reformatory for that long. It's time to head back tomorrow – the first of September – after work. But on Friday not much real work gets done at the shop because the okes keep stopping to crowd around the wireless. Shock news keeps shooting in from Europe all day: starting at about five in the morning the German military has ripped into Poland in a full-scale invasion. Tanks, dive-bombers, battleships – over one and a half million German troops relentlessly drive the Polish forces back. The okes at Gold Reef send out boys to get the special editions and read them with their greasy fingers and pass around the information in half-amazed whispers as if they're repeating sinister curses. Even Labuschagne fails to shout at them to get back to work. Late in the day they read a statement from Chamberlain in London, saying the nation is going to have to grit its teeth and see the struggle through. So it's going to be war, finally. Isaac eyes the Afrikaners in the shop, Labuschagne and Oberholzer and Rustas and Pienaar and the others – Nats they are, they'll never fight the Nazis, they'll never fight for Britain. It makes for an unease that he carries home.

The house on Buxton Street has guests, neighbourhood folks, who have gathered to listen to the good wireless and to be close to each other. Even Tutte listens in, despite it being Shabbos eve. Nobody says much and Mame rubs the back of Mrs. Geverson who keeps crying. The Geversons, it turns out, have relatives in Warsaw. The next day Isaac lets himself be persuaded to go to shul for the first time in however many years. An extra prayer service has been called and the place is jammed and a crowd lingers outside after the service. At home Mame is still at the wireless with Rively and Yankel Bernstein. A special session of the South African Parliament has been assembled. Prime Minister Hertzog wants to keep out of this war, but good old Jannie Smuts, his deputy, is for backing Britain all the way. Thank God for Jannie Smuts, Isaac reckons. But the United Party is now splitting apart. It's just like he was taught by Mrs. Winterbourne at Athens Boys High School in Bez Valley: there's good Afrikaners and bad ones. Now this war is flushing out which is which. Hertzog's going back to his old Nationalist roots, his old cronies, teaming up with Dr. Malan and all the same gruesome bunch that's in bed with the Greyshirts; but Smuts is lining up with the English. One side likes Hitler and Germany, the other is for the British Empire. They listen to the debate on the wireless and the incoming war news and in the morning they hear that Great Britain has declared war on Germany. France does the same but meanwhile the Germans keep steamrolling into Poland with their tanks and their dive-bombers, chopping up Polish cavalry, devouring astonishing amounts of territory. The reports speak of bombers targeting civilians, hitting convoys of refugees and city centres.

Neighbours come and go and sit together in the front room

and Mame serves them tea and honey cake. How different it is this time to how it was with the couchers; now Mame wants them here, now that all of them are falling into a nightmare together it's good to have company to share the horror. When he leaves the house that afternoon his head feels stuffed with the cotton wool of too much talk, too much worry. He rides his scooter out Brakpan way and beyond. It's later than he thought it was, the evening light glints off the distant shanties and shadows darken the scorched plain, the orange ball of the sun sliding towards the lift heads of the mines. The Reformatory makes a vast wedding cake with its tall walls and the box of the grey concrete building within. Up close, his mind feels a wrongness that his eyes cannot place at first. He pulls up before the high gate and lifts his riding goggles.

—I don't believe this.

The sign is gone. The gate is damaged and listing, with stanchions bulged out or twisted half free. He walks up and cups hands at both temples, scanning. Faint chinking sounds of labour from behind; the wrecks in front are unchanged from the last time he was here, only the chains and the iron hoisting stand are gone. He rattles the gate, shouts. The chinking lapses then goes on. He rattles some more, shouts louder. This time the chinking goes on without pause. There are some new padlocks through the gate lock's eye; his key can make no opening here. Breathing curses, he tracks around the wall, finds an old mattress humped in the weeds down by the stream. He drags it back, puffing filth and lice. Stands on the scooter to drape it over the barbed wire atop the gate and some of the jagged glass cemented to the wall beside it. He climbs up and over. At the top he sees how the spotlights have been smashed. He tears his trousers climbing down, almost falls badly.

On his way to the noise he pauses to pick up a chunk of bumper with a sharp point. He edges around the building between the stone and the high stacks of wrecked automobiles. Rainwater has puddled in the broken steel, turned the colour of rust, on which mosquitoes shimmer; milky pools of battery acid have also cratered. Around the corner he sees a man bent over an old engine, pulling with one hand and hammering with the other. He has on overalls but the top has been turned down so that it hangs like a skirt from his waist and his skin is the colour of crude oil, taut and supple over the shifting of the muscles of the back, the veins in the working arms. With every pull and stroke his stretched earlobes dance. Isaac puts down the chunk of bumper. As he crosses to the worker he sees other parts spread out on canvas, an open can of paint beside them with a brush, the parts fresh-marked with the yard symbols for make, year and model, some also marked left or right. Gearboxes, starters, generators, rear doors, fenders, mudguards.

—Silas.

He turns, nods. His face is drawn like a skull save for the purple mass over one eye that is mostly shut, save for cuts on his chest over which some rags are held with masking tape.

—Bladey hell.

—Hello baas.

—Man, what's going on?

Silas says nothing, his right hand holding the hammer and his left greased to the elbow.

—What you doing all yourself here? Where the others?

—I'm work myself now. I'm trying.

—What you mean trying?

—Have to try, says Silas. His mouth is dried white and cracked around the lips which keep on moving, he's talking softly to himself. He looks away from Isaac and seems to be staring at the wall and goes on talking softly for half a minute. Then he slowly looks back, slowly blinks. —Trying, he says.

—Where is Hugo?

Silas lifts his chin. The movement seems to make him sway back a little, then he turns, whispering to himself, and bends over the engine again. The chinking starts up as Isaac walks into the building through the hole in the back wall, the room full of used steel and rust, then up the stairs to the sales floor but there is no selling here. The floor is empty. Hugo's desk is there but bare, no calendar on the wall, no chairs, no adding machine or files or invoices. There seems to be some kind of a couch down at the far end. He crosses to the window to shout down to Silas when he hears a sound above, a whipping noise like the stroke of a cane, then a pock of impact. Chinks of green shine down where the tarpaulins patching the many ceiling holes are lit by daylight, between the rusted steel beams where the pigeons huddle in their nests of dried white dung. At the far end he finds not a couch but a bed made of rear car seats covered in wadded blankets, a smell of sourbody and old food, empty bottles on the concrete dust.

A stepladder rises under a daylight gap, the tarp above thrown back. He climbs into the sky. Across the open roof there is an upright oil drum and close to it, at the roof edge, is a car seat on which a man is rocking, his head tilted back. When Isaac gets closer he sees it's Hugo with his shirt unbuttoned and his legs apart, the fat of his loins packing his trousered groin like imminent childbirth. His eyes are closed against the waning sun and there is a bucket full of ice and beer bottles to his left. To his right rests a cricket bat. The eyes open when Isaac's long shadow falls over them.

—Howzit, Tiger. Heard your scooter. Matter of time. Keen young mind.

He reaches for a beer and leans forward, knocking the cap off in one motion against the edge of the low brick parapet before easing back. —I been drinking these then whacking the bottles for a six but I haven't got one yet. Lotta fun. You should try one.

—And how long you been doing this for?

—A while. Long enough. Not long enough.

Isaac has a look in the drum. There are charred papers and wood, a smell of burnt petrol. Over top, a grille with ossified black droplets of charred fat clinging to the wires like ticks. —Been having a braai up here, Hugo?

—Man's gotta eat.

Isaac walks around in front of him and sits on the ledge. Not easy for him to keep the trembling out of his voice. —What's the story?

—What do you reckon, keen young mind?

—Fuck you, Hugo. I mean *fuck you*.

He watches Hugo inverting the bottle of Lion Lager; the liquid goes down as if into a drain. Hugo grepses back up the spout, wipes his mouth, picks up the cricket bat, a Gray-Nicolls with a pigskin sheath, and flips up the bottle. Evening sun spangles in the brown glass, lots of wrist in the stroke that cuts the bat forward, making that whipping sound. The glass arcs in a high lob over the yard of wrecks. Breaks with a faint and pleasant tinkle somewhere in the right quadrant, but well short of the wall.

—Shit, says Hugo. Close, but I just never get there.

—Hey Hugo, says Isaac. You better look at me. I am telling you man. You better talk to me.

Hugo shakes his head loosely. —What's to say, Tiger? It's the twist. The bladey twist. Got me by the balls again.

Cash flow from the parts sales: into the races. Bank overdraft funds into the races. The races. The little-bit-of-ponies, so nothing and harmless. Creditors out of patience, lease payments past due. So does Hugo try to explain what Isaac keeps seeing but not truly believing.

—What about the staff? he says.

—There was no boodle for them, Tiger. They left.

—But you paid them last time I's here.

—Last payroll I made. When it started happening again they effed right off.

—Except for Silas.

—Ja well, his choice.

—His *what*?

—Calm down. It's life, man. Heads zu win, tails Zulus.

—Ja, I've heard that one. You a real jokester. I'm falling down on my back laughing.

—Well, says Hugo. Tops crying duzzen it?

He goes on. Capital assets, i.e. the trucks, have been repossessed. Nothing much complicated to his story. Hugo had played the races and often won; when he lost he needed to go back to make up for it. It fell to a decisive day. Simba Dawn was the sure thing that turned out not to be.

—*So* close, says Hugo. Sounding as if he's the one who's been grievously cheated. —I diden ever think a little bit of ponies could lead to the twist. Not the *ponies*.

Isaac has stood up and is pacing in front of the parapet, now and then kicking it hard. There's a bang from below and he peers over the edge, down onto Silas. —He's grafting his noble Zulu heart out, Hugo says. Trying to get parts together for one more sale. Believe me I told him a hundred times, Silas it's over, nothing we can do. The sales wouldn't be enough, never mind one with only a few dozen parts instead of a whole floor full. But he doesn't want to hear. He just been working for nothing like this since we hit the end. I think maybe he's one shy of a full load now. Cuckuroo-coo.

—What happened to the parts we had stored?

—Sold, all sold.

—Christ Hugo but you've stuck us up shtoch street but good hey. Really stuffed us up good and proper.

Hugo wheezes, leaning over, digs up two beers and flicks one to Isaac.

—End of the road, Tiger.

—Can't be.

—Blank wall. Ninety miles an hour.

Isaac looks below again —Poor bastard, he says. It's my fault he's here.

—Nobody's fault, says Hugo. It's the twist. He should get a medal, though. Lately we been getting visits from them human jackals in shitburg central over there. They can smell we going down like blood in the water. Guess who's been holding the fort, alone. I think they waiting for him to peg of exhaustion. Last night, I mean this morning, he's up on that gate throwing bricks for glory till they stabbed him off with some kind of long spear, I don't even know what. I was up here kipping. I went down and got a megaphone going and that seemed to chase em. But they'll be back hey. Jackals.

—*How?* How'd this happen man? All that capitalizing you kept saying. Kept telling me everything's so fine and fluent or whatever.

—I meant it. But it's the twist, boy. This is the twist. Always gets me.

—Why do you have to play with money, man? We were going so well. Why'd you have to take our money and play?

He feels a heat in his face that melts and runs, coming out through the eyes, the nose. He slumps down, puts the beer on the ground, fits his hot face into the curve of his palms.

—Boyki, boyki. Don't take it so bad. And don't blame the ponies. That playing saved our arses you don't know how many times. A couple of my streaks got us through the last two months alone. That's where that last bundle came from that you told me give the boys when you were here last.

For a long while Isaac rocks, his breath catching, making his shoulders jump. Then he wipes his eyes on his sleeve, says, —Whole fucken world is collapsing.

—Hey?

—War declared today, know that?

—Ja, I heard. What'd I always tell you? And we almost came

so close. Lookat this yard full of parts, man, of good scrap. It might as well be gold but there's eff all we can do to hold on to it. Not by end of month.

Isaac looks up. —Why not?

Hugo is looking down at the beer bottle wedged against his cushioning navel and his face in the evening sun is holding its fixed grin, but the eyes close and the grin makes Isaac think of dead rodents, how their front teeth show in the slack jaws. —Ja, he says in a straining voice that is not his own. Old Blezzy really stuffed it this time hey. Didn't he? He really bladey did. He starts to breathe heavily, his chest lifting up and down and a high wheezing sound oozes through the dead grin. At the corners of his closed eyes liquid starts to glint.

Isaac looks away. The wheezing sounds get higher and stronger then slacken off.

—What's happening at the end of the month, Hugo?

—Bailiff will be here and take possession. All of it. Auctioneer's already been to list. All our gold.

—Shit. Kuk. Shit.

—Can say that again.

—I thought the rent was bupkas here.

—Bupkas is still something. It adds up if you miss enough months. Everything adds. We past being in arrears. Now it's coming a court order and the tank is dry, Tiger. No bucks, no luck. Lose all our stock.

—Nothing?

—Nu–thing.

—Nothing?

—Well, plenny of creditors, ha. We filing bankruptcy for them, they can koosh us in tochus. But the stock has to stay here and the stock will not belong to us.

Big ants on the gritty roof are clustering at spots of spilled beer. Isaac studies them.

—Funny hey, says Hugo, how bad things come in September. Ever notice? September's evil. September's got it in for us.

Isaac rubs his face. —It's not the month, Hugo, it's you. What the hell man. What the hell are we ganna do?

—There's nothing, boyki. There's miracles.

—I got two pounds in my pocket I can give. How much you reckon we need?

—Nice one. Put a trip of noughts on that and we maybe talk.

—Bladey *hell*. You charfing me.

—No, I'm not. It's over, boyki.

Isaac thinks hard. —I could sell off the ring you gave me.

Hugo huffs laughter for a while. —Good one. You keep that. Might as well have a souvenir. Coupla few quid won't make any diff to anything. Shame about that though hey, the female. But you young. You'll find another. They come round like buses, remember. Keep it for the next. You may's well have something out of all your graft.

—No, says Isaac. It's still ours. I had it engraved and all. Still ours.

They sit in a long silence broken only by the faint and steady chinking of the mad labour below.

—I'm sorry, boyki, says Hugo. I am so so sorry.

His voice sounding strange again, strained and wheezing.

—Is it really over?

—Ja. Ja.

—So what you doing sitting here?

—Got nowhere else. Captain goes down with ship. Has to.

—Hugo, Hugo. You such a bladey shmock you know that.

—I know it, Tiger.

—I hate you.

—I know you do, boyki. I know you do.

37.

THE DEBATE IN PARLIAMENT GOES ON, Isaac following snatches of it on the wireless in the workshop and in the bar talk after work at the Great Britain Hotel. It comes down to a vote to stay neutral or not, Smuts versus Hertzog. It's a close thing. Smuts wins by just thirteen votes. There's talk Parliament might dissolve for another election: that's bad, could stir up a bladey civil war, who knows? But Hertzog moves aside, lets Smuts become the new Prime Minister, members crossing the floor to give his old party its power again, while Hertzog joins with Malan and the rest of the Nats and the Greyshirt lovers in opposition.

First thing Smuts does is declare war on Germany.

Outside Cohen's Café, the young okes start talking about this new recruitment centre that just opened on Small Street in town and how already lots of neighbourhood okes have gone in and signed up. There's not ganna be any conscription cos the Afrikaners might rebel. So they're ganna need volunteers big time for this war, and the boys of Doornfontein are all more than willing. On the way to the tram, Big Benny Dulut stops Isaac, tells him to come with him right then and there to sign up. That's what he's doing. To get a gun and learn to shoot it into fascist scumsuckers.

—I've got work to go to, Benny.

—Man, there's too many Greyshirts in there already, we need to make sure army stays with Smuts. You ever thought about it like that?

—Can't say I have, Isaac tells him.

—Rabies, man. The hell's happened to you? Come with me.

But after the conversations he's had lately with Mame he won't even consider it. Mame afflicted with back pain so bad it doesn't even help to lie down. Tutte says it's from all the sitting she's done bent over by the wireless all day. And all the worry.

When Isaac speaks to Mame now he tells her that the news of war is not all bad. Firstly, it hasn't affected backhome directly yet, nobody's invaded Lithuania. Soon the British and the French will come in and sort Germany out once and for all. And then, more important, Jan Smuts is Prime Minister again and he, Isaac, is sure that Smuts will let the Jews who have families in South Africa come here; he'll do it *because* of the war. Mame nods when he says these things and gives him a look that is skeptical but also has a sad kind of hope in it, as if she wants to believe but can't bring herself to. There's a fierce, almost desperate energy to Isaac's little speeches to her, fuelled by the secret of what is stored out back in the sewing room like some slow-ticking time bomb. —Listen, Ma, he says. This war is ganna make the business into a gold mine right. Like Hugo says it, we ganna be milking the cream soon. And I'm working hard at the shop also. So we ganna have that house soon, Ma, so soon. And then when Smuts lets them in . . . It's ganna happen, Ma, I can *feel* it, I just *know* it, it's *ganna* happen. When they let them in I am ganna have that house all ready for them hey. We'll choose one up in Linksfield all larney. Highlands North. We ganna have a front garden and a back garden too hey ma. We ganna have rooms for them, Ma, so many rooms . . . Are you listening to me Ma? It's ganna be oright, it *is*.

But it works on his nerves, the pain in his mame's face, so that he wakes up often in the middle of the night and goes to the sewing room and takes out the forms and broods over what he has written there. How long has it been since Papendropolous gave them to him, how many months exactly? The attorney telling him to hurry up and fill them in, then lay back and be patient for the deal to come through or not. So easy for him to say. And that was before war broke out. What worries him is that the war could have changed everything. The question gnaws. What is going *on* over there? When the pain from Mame's back gets so severe they have to call Dr. Allan to come prescribe her pills, Isaac goes to a tickey box.

Enough monkey business – this Papendropolous, who in hell is he anyway? Avrom is *my* blood. He asks the operator to place a person-to-person call to Avrom Suttner at Lion's Rock farm outside Bakerville. Like any trunk call, she says she will ring him back with his party when the line is available. He fills the booth with tobacco smoke, waiting half an hour, and when some idyat keeps tapping for a chance at the telephone, he tells him to eff off before he gets hurt. The idyat looks at him, then goes away. Maybe not such an idyat after all. The phone rings.

He picks up with his stomach full of what feels like broken glass churning around. But the voice on the end isn't his rich cousin, it's the attorney Papendropolous who asks him what the hell does he think that he is doing.

—I wasn't ringing for *you*.

—I speak for him. And you were told never do this.

—Ja, but that was before it was war, man. We just supposed to sit all lardy-da?

—War doesn't change it. You tried to contact.

—Well what was I supposed to do? We fucken dying over here!

—Shouting doesn't help.

—Ahh stuff you! And eff him too! You were never ganna come through with anything anyway!

Papendropolous says nothing and Isaac can hear his own hoarse breathing in his ear. Waiting to be cut off.

But Papendropolous says, —You lucky. Normally I would have put down on you by now, but.

—What?

—Truth is, I was about to get in touch with you.

Now his own breathing stops in his ear; he's biting down on his lip, close to blood.

—We're in our rights to call it off, but it's set now. Listen carefully. It's going to be sometime between the twenty-fifth and the twenty-seventh of this month.

—Twenty-fifth to twenty-seventh.

—That's right. That's a Monday to a Wednesday.

—When's twenty-fifth, two weeks?

Papendropolous doesn't speak and Isaac has a clear picture of the man grimacing there on the other end of the line. —It's . . . thirteen days. *Listen to me.* Don't say a word. Operators, other people, they listen in to calls. So don't speak, don't say any names aloud, just listen. There's a place you go after work sometimes. You know what I'm referring to?

—Ja. I think so.

—On the eighteenth of this month, a message will be left there for you to pick up.

—A message.

—That's right. Monday the eighteenth.

Isaac laughs. —You reckon I'm swallowing all this kuk, what am I, a Stupid? You seen too much bladey Hitchcock, man. This is just more a you stuffing us around.

There's a clicking sound, the man snapping his lips on his teeth, getting angry. —I'm about out of patience with you, he says.

—Oright, oright. Don't catch a hairy, mate. Just saying it sounds like a lot of rubbish what you telling me, messages.

The line is filled with Papendropolous's heavy breaths for a time. Then, saying the words clearly and separately: —You go to the place. You pick up the message. It will have the time and location. Read it and burn it.

Isaac snorts. —Burn it. No, you definitely charfing us. Tell me true now. You charfing us, man.

All of a sudden it's Papendropolous's turn for shouting. — Quiet! Quiet already and bloody listen!

Isaac doesn't speak; he notices his free hand has pulled a button off his shirt. It takes a while for Papendropolous's breathing to calm. He goes on in that separate-word way: —We've already contacted the other gentleman. Understand? Does that sound like charfing? It's been done. Now I'm warning you for the last time: Do not. Try to. Contact us. Again. All right?

—Ja oright man, oright.

—You remember everything else I told you, before?

—I . . . ja, I do.

—Good. So wait for it. Then take you-know-who. Step one and step two. All right?

—I'm not deaf, says Isaac. I can hear.

The following days feel dreamlike. Too much of a numbing dream to even think of running to share with Mame, he'd have to tell her how he's kept this secret for so long, he can't even imagine doing that yet, first make sure it's real and not truly the waking dream it feels to be. When he goes to the Great Britain Hotel he stares with dream eyes, wading with dream legs through air that feels as thick as the blood driven by his heavy beating heart. In the entrance, as he passes the reception desk, it seems to slowly tilt, all the cubbyholes and the hanging keys behind the man in the waistcoat tilting with it. You go up there and ask is there a message, do it in the daytime when no one else sees, slip it in your pocket to unseal later or else do it here, in the toilet.

A time and a location.

Charlie Steenkamp comes to him at the start of lunch break, Isaac swilling the rust flakes from his brow at the tap out back. Steenkamp is a short wiry man with teeth coated beige, the edge of a blue

tattoo showing just over the collar. Rumours have always hovered
like a bad smell about his person that he's really a Coloured passing as a White, for his hair is bush thick, his skin a bit too yellowish. Bit of coffee in the blood, Mame might have said.

Since the beating, he's been spending lunches sitting with
Magnus Oberholzer who no longer needs to take his nourishment
through a straw, whose stitches have come out, though he is still
pale and bruised and reduced. What Charlie Steenkamp says to
Isaac now is, —Man, old Magnus, he wanna shake his hand with
you hey.

Isaac looks at him. He lets the bitterness in him touch his face;
it's not hard.

—Says he sorry. Genuine. Wants it to be another way, fresh.

—So let *him* come tell me.

—Ach, don't be that hey. He duzzen wanna try it if you don't
want. He got some pride still hey, ha. But why not make chinas
with him and put aggro behind. Overs is overs and that. He not
such a bad ou. Genuine. I feel sorry . . .

—Well and good. Let him keep his side. I keep mine.

Charlie shrugs. —That's not very Christian hey.

—Ach, piss off, Isaac says. Go on, piss off.

He watches Charlie slouch away. But the gesture raises an
unease that stays with him. A bad feeling akin to guilt that makes
no sense, not until he's reading the paper and comes across an item
that makes his hand freeze as he turns the page. A photo of girls
and one oke standing in a row. The girls have tennis racquets and
white skirts with sleeveless jerseys. A pile of clothes in front and
in the centre of them he sees her – like a visual scream – the doll's
face etched in the grey dots, her pale hair band above. There is a
tall fellow beside her who has on a suit and tie. His arm is around
her waist all the way and her free arm is around his neck and they
are tight together and both of them are smiling.

DYNAMIC DUO NETS FOR NEEDY

(*Staff*) Tons of clothing will be provided for poor Natives this weekend thanks to the efforts of a Parktown girl and her legal-eagle beau, who staged a recent charity tournament at a local tennis club.

Yvonne Linhurst, 18, star pupil at Lord Vincent College, and barrister Alexander Campbell, 25, will serve an ace against Native poverty next week when some two tons of free clothing will be given away in the parking lot of the Newtown Market.

"In these terrible times of ours, we think it's more important than ever to try and do our bit for the less fortunate," said Mr. Campbell, rising star at the leading city firm of Linhurst Blackwell.

The clothing was gathered at a round robin tennis tournament held last week by the Fenleigh Ladies Lawn Tennis Society, which Miss Linhurst has been a member of since 1930.

Miss Linhurst, daughter of Cecil and Sylvaine of 18 Gilder Lane, Parktown, says the impetus for the project began after she first noticed how many of her friends were throwing away their used clothing.

"Alex and I both agreed it was an awful waste," said Miss Linhurst. "These are perfectly usable garments that get tossed out simply because they are going out of fashion. But to a child who is cold in the winter because they don't own a jersey to wear or warm socks and proper shoes for their feet—fashion is the last thing on their minds."

Not content with mere words, the dynamic pair soon decided to take action, settling on the idea of a charity tournament at Miss Linhurst's club, where many of her friends were also members. Players brought used clothing to donate in order to participate in the tourney, and the results so surpassed expectations that the lovebirds have already vowed to make it an annual event.

"I couldn't have done it without Alex," said Miss Linhurst. The fashionable couple first met while both doing work in another charitable assistance project, she said— and they've been happily courting ever since. "Alex pushes me to see things through. He's just wonderful that way, and always brings out the best in me."

Lower down Isaac reads how Miss Linhurst is *strikingly attractive* as well as *bright and well-spoken*, and with an interest in *affairs well beyond the feminine sphere* which makes her *one to watch*, with plans to enter the University of the Witwatersrand next year in order to study political science and history, *with a view to one day joining the Bar*, like her *beau* and her father, senior partner at Linhurst Blackwell. The firm started in the last century by William James Linhurst, Miss Linhurst's paternal grandfather, himself son of Robinson Ernest Linhurst, founder of the country's largest private railroad, later purchased by the government.

Isaac stares at the face of the man in the photo. A slim nose, a slicked side part, nicely cut suit with narrow waist and wide shoulders. After a long time he closes the paper and goes back to work.

At the end of shift they get their pay packets and Labuschagne comes round with the infamous Quality Street biscuit tin, the round tin painted with a jolly Christmas scene of the olden days, top hats and carriages, and packed with cash, for the bonus payout is due to be drawn the next day. They add even more notes and go wait outside as always, smoking; inside Labuschagne's locking up.

Charlie Steenkamp approaches Isaac again with the same shit about making sholem with Oberholzer. Isaac looks at him full of pain, the crazy need to hug someone suddenly on him like thirst or hunger. He shrugs and says okay. That bad feeling around Oberholzer from before that's like guilt, he knows what it is then:

it's from bringing the woman into it, that was bad, to take away a man's woman from him is to generate an unspeakable pain. *This* pain. Oberholzer needed to be taught a lesson, ja, but there wasn't any need to mention the man's wife also, humiliating him with it in front of everyone. The panties. The way it seems to Isaac right then is that nobody deserves that, not even a piece of kuk like Magnus Oberholzer.

Steenkamp is coming back with Oberholzer. Where the stitches came out has left a livid crescent on the pale face. They shaved his moustache and he hasn't grown one back; without it, he seems a reduced presence. A face that wants to belong in a shuffling crowd, not even trying to stand out.

—Isaac, I only want to say lez make overs overs. Oright? He puts out his hand. Isaac glances at the other one; criss-crossing scar tissue is still fresh there. Charlie has drifted up to Isaac's side, he presses his back.

—Don't touch me.

—Ach man. Make it okay. Finish the bad blood off.

—I said don't touch me.

—Uhkay, sorry, sorry.

—You come to tell me you learned your lesson.

Oberholzer looks at him a while then nods.

—Say it.

—I learn my lesson.

—Good.

Moving slowly, he shakes the hand. Oberholzer doesn't try to squeeze. He's always going to have that scarring on the one side, like Mame.

—Oright so it's over, Isaac says.

—Ja man, Oberholzer says. There's too much wars going on in the world as is. It's a blerry shame, not so?

—Ja oright, Isaac says, letting go. Is finished. Is klaar.

—Ja man, I buy you nice whisky.

—That's ukay.

—No man, we will have the drink.

They are talking softly, standing away from the others out of the street lights and in close to the garage wall. Oberholzer goes into a rambling story about his cousin from Witbank and how he ended up getting divorced all because he wouldn't say sorry, and how, no, his own father taught him a real man is a man who can say he is sorry. Meanwhile Labuschagne has come out and everyone moves off with him, heading for the pub. Oberholzer starts telling what could be a joke about three men stranded in the desert; it goes on and on. Eventually Isaac has to interrupt him, and they start off for the Great Britain Hotel also, Oberholzer walking slowly and talking ceaselessly in a flat dead voice. Once, Isaac looks back. —Hey where's your china?

—Hey?

—Charlie. He not coming?

—Oh ja. Prolly just went for smoke or the paper.

At the bar, Oberholzer finds them a quiet corner away from the others. As he buys Isaac a second triple whisky, Charlie appears. —Howzit ouens. Lekker to see everyone matey-mates again. All lekker like a cracker, hu hu. He touches Isaac's back, that irritating habit. When he moves away as Isaac sips, he gets a sudden fluttery feeling, his jacket swinging out. He puts down his drink, pats himself, his pockets.

—You oright?

He feels his wallet, his keys. —Ja, no. Fine.

—Cheers hey, Oberholzer says, turning with the drinks. Here is to happy future on us all.

—Ja, Isaac says, uneasy. Ja. Oright. Cheers.

They clink and drink. Isaac's feet shift, he looks down. —Listen man, Magnus. About your wife hey, what I said like . . .

Oberholzer looks at the bar. —Lez not talk about it.

—Nothing happened, ay, I made it all up.

Oberholzer says nothing.

—Got those underwears from somewhere else. So like, I want you to know, she would never even look at me, ukay?

Oberholzer nods without looking up, lifts his glass. They make another cheers; but Oberholzer still won't look him in the eyes. A press of feeling rises thick in Isaac's throat. They talk some more, then the big man wanders off to join the others while Isaac drinks on with Charlie.

At home the house is dark and everyone is out and at first he's unsure why before he remembers it's Rosh Hashanah today, Jewish New Year, and his parents and Rively have probably gone to the Altmans' for the special supper. Tutte's given up on asking him to take off work or come to shul for holidays, but Isaac's fairly sure at some point he'll get the annual lecture about the Days of Awe, the sacred time between the New Year and Yom Kippur, the Day of Atonement, now coming up soon. Ja, Days of Awe: when you have to cry and say you really really sorry to God and other people for all the sins you've done in the year, while you still can. Before your fate gets sealed on Yom Kippur.

That night a fearful dream wakes him on his cot. He's in a stone chamber with water pouring in, green and cold; he has a giant stone key and there are slots for it in the ceiling. He keeps trying to fit this heavy key into one of the impossible slots with the cold green water rising. Then from behind a hand pushes his head down. The more he struggles the more someone giggles, bubbling, off to the side.

In the morning he goes to work and there is something very wrong.

38.

WHEN ISAAC WALKS INTO THE SHOP he hits a motionless silence that stops him cold. The White workers in their clean tan overalls are all standing in a clump by the office over on the far side of the workshop to his left; the Black staff are lined along the rear wall. At first Isaac thinks something terrible to do with the war has happened, but no, not in this silence with the wireless off. As he walks across he sees that all of the dozen journeymen panel beaters are there, including Jack Miller plus the other apprentice, Vernon. He sees Bliksy the parts guy and Rustas the glass man, Eddie Tops the upholstery king, even Mornay Pienaar the paint man. When he reaches them and starts to say something, Miller tells him to be quiet, to wait.

Labuschagne's office door is open and he is behind the desk there, murmuring quietly into his telephone, writing with his free hand. After about five minutes he looks up and lifts his voice, wanting to know if everyone is here now. Voices tell him ja. He comes out and his face under the bowl cut is clumped and mottled.

— Never thought in all my life it could ever happen here to me. Okes, the kitty, she is gone. Some bastard went and diefed the kitty from its place must have been last night. Gone.

It's like the negative of a bomb going off, an implosion of silence in which Isaac can feel all of their attention sucked down to the tiny point of Labuschagne's mouth and what it will say next.

— Was full up too. Now it's stolen and gone. Twenty-five

404

years in the game I never had nothing to touch this. I'm ganna tell you right here, it has to be someone of us who done this. Because they knew how the kitty works and exactly where to go.

—In the safe in there your office right? says George Kazy.

Labuschagne spits on the ground, scratches under his chin. —Spose if I say right now it makes not a difference. Where it was . . . Rustas, gimme that.

He takes the steel bucket that Rustas extends with his golden hands, carries it to the wall behind where he turns it down and steps up. The electric clock on the wall comes into reach: he shifts it aside to show an uneven hole in the bricks, a hollow behind. —Hu! says Rustas.

—Crafty bladey bugger, says someone close behind Isaac.

Labuschagne lets the clock swing back, steps down. —If it was a stranger they woulda gone for the safe in the office, ja. But nothing else was even touched. Only kitty was taken . . .

—But no one but you even knew, says Dean van der Westhuizen, panel beater.

Labuschagne makes a fist and presses it to the palm until knuckles crack. —Look, he says. This is what can happen here. I am ganna bell the cops. They'll come and start with all the investigator shit what they do. But lemme tell you ouens, I do that and it's never ganna be the same. But I will do it. Unless a man wants to be a man. And you sticks your hand up. Says it was me, Franzie, I did it. Oright hey. Says you sorry and you can walk out. And know what? You can even keep the kitty.

—Hey hey hey whoah, says Rustas.

—No ways man! shouts Keith Chambers.

Labuschagne's palms are up. —No, no. That kitty can be the stuff-off pay. Take it for severance and go. I'm not saying nothing. You own up. You sez sorry and you fok off. That's it. I just want you out and then we go back to like it was. Even if you go to another shop for a job I won't even say what you did for a reference.

I'm not even ganna tell the owners, but that's only if you talk right now. Your chance to be a man. Own up and walk out. Otherwise it's the cops coming here and they go through all our lives. And lemme tell you, when we do hook the oke – and we will – he is not ganna walk outta here to go to jail neither. We ganna sort him our own way first. Sort him solid. So better for him to talk up right now.

He faces the Blacks. In Afrikaans: You hear me when I speak. You men all fokken get me?

They nod, some mumble ja bass. They keep back against the wall, as if they'd like to go farther but can't.

Dez Malcolmson calls out, —How would they know?

Labuschagne folds an ear forward. —How say?

—How could anyone know it was there? It's only you that locks up.

Labuschagne grimaces. —There's it, ay. There's it exactly.

He points up. A grimed skylight above him: a part of the shop Isaac's eyes have moved over hundreds or thousands of times but his mind has never noticed.

—Some clever monkey, he went up. And I know he came down through there cos it was all spiderwebs and all that's gone. He musta watched down on me, putting the kitty.

Rustas: —So could be anyone?

Labuschagne is shaking his head. —Had to be someone who knowed when it was time for me to stick the kitty in. A coupla minutes on a Thursday. He waits up there and sees, looking down. Then comes down and gyps it.

—Crafty bastard!

There's movement amongst them now, men looking sideways at other men. Then Jan Veld steps forward. —What the bladey hell, Franzie? How can you stand there and make an accusing against us man? Go fucken talk to *them*.

He means the Blacks flat against the wall. Their eyes start

rocking and now the men are edging towards them. Chambers picks up a jack handle and goes out ahead.

—Moer the lot a them till they give it back, says Eddie Tops.

—Make them tell.

—Lez get these boogs.

There's a bang, very loud. Isaac turns back and Labuschagne kicks the steel bucket again, crunching it against the wall. —Hey! Nobody does one bladey thing! You stand still! Everyone! Get back here. Dez, you. Jan. Keith. Eddie. I am telling you all I will bliksem the first oke touches anyone. This is my shop and I'm boss. Get over here.

He starts pacing, his face shining red now. One of his plate hands scratches at his chest, the other is on his hip.

—I ganna be the first one in line if it's one of the boys done it. You okes know I don't take no shit from any a them for a second. But fair is fair. I'm not having one of my boys buggered up by you ouens for no reason. I tell you straight, first one to start with gets fired. Uhkay. Uhkay Keith?

Chambers mutters.

—Hey! I'm talking a you.

—Oright.

—Now I'm ganna be honest with youse all. I know my boys. Most a been with us since the beginning. Before I lock up, they all go home. They got trains they got and they can't miss em, if they in town after dark they get picked up by the cops. That's why I always let them go by five, so they have time and they don't disappear in jail for six months. Now it woulda been a helluva job for one a them to come back and wait here. And then what, hide all night? And if it was one of the boys, why just the kitty hey? Why not anything else he could get his hands on not nailed down?

There's a silence.

—You see it? says Labuschagne in his animal pacing. Plus everyone here knows we got watchman patrol what sticks some dogs in here and the yard and leaves em overnight. Now I been on the line with Ricardo the barkeeper already this morning, and he remembers good who he served last night and he remembers every one of us was there. Every one.

—So then how could it be us? says Rustas.

—This's what I'm working out, says Labuschagne. What I reckon it was, when you ouens was all outside waiting for me, someone climbs up outside onto the roof and watches down through here, seeing what I does. When I leave, he climbs down and grabs it. Then he climbs back out and goes to the bar like nothing.

—Bladey sly bastard!

Now the Whites are looking at each other again. One or two fools grinning like it's all a joke. But the grins soon slide away from the hard looks of the others, turning sickly.

—Had to be someone small hey, a voice says.

Labuschagne stops his pacing. Looks back to the electric clock. —We got work to do today. So I'm giving the oke who done it, giving him . . . two minutes. Two minutes more from right now. Be a man or I go in the office and bell the cops. And when they do find out it's you, God help you. That is all I can say. God help you. And they *will* catch you.

Silence. The second hand on the big electric clock face drops a quarter turn, then another. Men glancing to their left and right. Watching their feet. Other men with folded arms biting at their bottom lips. Isaac like Labuschagne puts his hands on his hips. He is thinking he'd like to get his hands on the one who did it, thinking who was it, who could it be? Who's the most monkey-like, to clamber down from that skylight? Feeling more secretly a slight admiration for the audacity and enterprise of this burglar . . .

—Boss. Franzie.

A vast scarred hand is in the air. The silence folds in on him.

—Ek het iets, he says. I have something. He swallows, his pale throat moving, goes on in the same Afrikaans: I don't want to throw an accusation. I only want to help for everyone. But I did see something last night.

—Wat het jy gesien? asks Labuschagne.

I saw . . . ach, I don't know if it's right to say. I don't have proof of anything.

Tell us.

And also, because of what's happened . . . with him. This looks bad. Like I am looking for revenge. But I am not a revenge looker. I only want to tell the truth.

What are you prattling for? Say your piece.

—Gister aand, he starts, then in English repeats: —Last night. Last night I seen him.

Isaac's scalp has shrivelled; his chest goes cold.

—I seen him going around. Isaac.

They look at him now. Be calm, Isaac says in himself.

Labuschagne: —What you mean going around?

Oberholzer points. —Down by that way. Where you can go by the alley there. You could climb up . . .

—You saw him go round?

—Ja, I seen it. Look, I only saying. I don't know nuffing. Is only what I did see. Sorry, Isaac.

—Bullshit, Isaac says. You bladey full of stinking bullshit.

—Did you go round? Labuschagne says to Isaac.

—Didn't go effing nowheres man. This. This kuk-stirrer over here. This . . . He is pointing, his finger shaking. The words plug under his Adam's apple like boiling milk in a corked bottleneck. He has to swallow hard to go on. —This bastard is bladey bullshitting through his arse cos he is just trying to get back from the donnering I gave him. And I'll give him another one if he doesn't shut his lying trap.

Oberholzer turns up his huge paws. Shrugs. —I'm not saying he did nothing hey. I only says what I seen.

—Kuk! Rubbish! Isaac says. Blinking fast. —Last night. Hey last night, you *know* I shook your hand . . . we were talking . . .

Now Oberholzer lets out a little snigger, that high piglet sound of his. —Ja really, last night we were chatty hey. We were pals and mates and best chinas all a sudden.

And someone snorts, someone barks a laughing note. Heads are shaking. How crazy. They're looking at Isaac and he feels scooping disbelief. —You . . . you a liar! Is all he can shout back. —Bladey liar!

—No, Oberholzer says. We don't shake hands. We don't chat. I seen you going round down there last night. You know you were, Isaac. Why don't you just tell that honest?

—Scuse me, scuse us hey boss.

A new voice from the back. Everyone looks. It's Charlie Steenkamp. Isaac's heart drums; his mouth parches. —Scuse hey sir. I have to say, hey. I have to say I also seen it.

—Seen what? Labuschagne says.

—Seen it how Isaac went that way. Down to go around like. When we was all standing outside having smokes and whatnot, waiting for you.

—You lie, Isaac says. You lie like your bladey breath stinks. Now he is shouting: —It's his china! It's his little china, him and Oberholzer, come on, they best mates. They cooking up a bladey story together here man.

—No seriously hey, Charlie says. I'm only saying what I seen. I was standing to one side. I wasn't even near Magnus.

—Oh stuff you, Charlie, Isaac says. I am ganna kill you. You so dead, you lying bastard.

—Oright, Labuschagne says. Stop with the threatening now.

—But they telling lies on me, boss! What am I supposed to do?

—Why would they tell lies?

—They mates. They big chinas. They cooked up something

here against me can't you see? So obvious. To get back for me
donnering Magnus.

—Listen Isaac, Labuschagne says. This's serious hey. Did you
go down there last night?

—I told you what I did, boss. It was Magnus came up to me,
Charlie before, he said we should shake hands, make friends
and that.

Charlie laughs, a low cackle: —I diden say that, man! Who in
the right mind is ganna say that? Everyone knows you two are like
cats and dogs.

The murmuring is all around, the watching faces going hard,
serious. He senses the ones closest to him subtly shifting off. As if
he's been identified as the carrier of some contagious mutilating
virus, some gripping strain of leprosy.

He says, —Magnus comes over to me and shook hands and we
were talking. Didn't you all see? Some of you okes musta seen it . . .

He looks around, finds Miller looking at the floor. No one
speaks.

—But that's what happened, he says.

—Well think well on it, Labuschagne says. Maybe you did go
down there. To have a piss or something. No one is saying you did
nothing else. If you tell a lie about that then we not ganna believe
other things. If you went down there, it's fine to say.

—I didn't go anywhere!

—Oright. Uhkay.

—I'm telling you they tryna cook up a story to get me back
for what I did to him.

—I don't cook up nuffing but my pap and my boerewors with
gravy, Charlie says.

No one laughs.

—Just calm hey, Labuschagne says. Just calm it down hey
man. We ganna get the facts here. Now you say these two, Charlie
and Magnus, they is both lying.

—I . . .

—Yes or no.

—Yes.

—Uhkay. Magnus, he say he's seen you go around while I was in here locking up. Charlie says same. Lemme ask. Did anyone here remember seeing how Isaac got to the bar?

—What the hell?

—Shut up a sec. Does anyone remember if he came late?

No one speaks.

—I want to know who walked there with him. Anyone?

—He did, Isaac says.

—Who?

—Magnus!

—Yasis, Magnus says. Now who is the liar?

—Stuff you, Isaac says. I'm ganna smash you ten times harder.

—Come try with your tricks again. I want you to.

—You see! He's tryna get me back.

—Ja, says Magnus. And he hates my guts, this little devil. So he try and tell everyone now how we was such big chommies last night? Please.

Now others start to speak, to shout.

—Hang on, hang on, Labuschagne is saying, calming the air with his long arms out. Facts is facts. These men say they seen Isaac go round. Later he was at the bar. But no one has seen him get there.

—I went there with Oberholzer, Isaac says.

—Nuh, nuh, I'm sorry, says Charlie Steenkamp. Me and Magnus walked to the bar together last night, and Isaac wazzen with us. That I can vouch.

—Ach please! says Isaac. This is getting just stupid.

Labuschagne stares hard at him.

—Don't you know, Oberholzer calls, these Jews, they reckon they got all the brains in the world. They bought them up wholesale.

Some laugh. Labuschagne shouts, Everyone shut up! in Afrikaans, and quiet does fall. —Does anyone remember seeing when Isaac got there, who was he drinking with?

No one speaks.

—Okes, come on, says Isaac. I didn't do nothing!

—Lez just bell the cops already, says Tops. We have to start work don't we boss.

—Hey Isaac, Pienaar calls, singsonging. Ize–ik. Where did you stick the kitty hey?

Someone laughs. —Ja Isaac, just give it back hey.

Heat flames his head, his shoulders. —Stuff you all, okes.

—Wait, wait, Labuschagne says. There's no ladder left. To climb back up he woulda gone off the door here or something. He must have had two hands to climb. He must climb bladey quick. And if he is in a hurry for outside, he doesn't have a satchel or nothing.

—Unless he did and he left it on the roof behind, says Bliksy.

—Ach he coulda stuck it anywhere, says Rustas.

—Ja, maybe, maybe, says Labuschagne. But probably I say not. Prolly he got the kitty in his hands in here. Has to go quick-quick . . . looking around . . .

It's too much: Isaac shouts, —I didn't goddamn do a thing man! Almost sobbing out the last syllable.

There's a silence.

—Then, says Malcolmson, you got nothing to worry about.

Pienaar from the back: —Ja man, just relax.

—*You* relax. Not you being called a thief.

—Shhh. Labuschagne is rubbing his chin. —Wait, wait. Where would I stick it? What is the safest place? . . .

The silence again, but heavier now, a sense of everyone's locked attention on the boss.

—Lockers, says Kazy.

Again Isaac's control slips, he feels his face twisting as if he's bitten glass. —Ach come off it, he says. We wasting such time here. All this Sherlock Holmes jazz. Just get the cops, man. I don't even care.

—Lockers is easy to check, says Oberholzer.

—You just shut your lying beak, Isaac says to him. You big lump a shit. Ganna sort you after, I guarantee you that.

—What's a matter, Isaac? calls Charlie Steenkamp. Is it you scared?

—Eff you, Isaac says. I show you all my locker right bladey now. Right now.

He steps out. Labuschagne nods, okay. Isaac crosses to the alcove behind the toilets where the steel lockers are set in the wall, pulling his keys out as he does. Something there, a flickering, under his thoughts, some irritant, pricks up at him. He grabs the cool padlock. When he plugs the key in he feels others close in behind, hears Labuschagne telling them move, step back, so he can see proper what's going on. When Isaac turns the key and undoes the lock and takes it from the bracket, Labuschagne says, —If it's ukay with you, lemme open it.

—Absolute fine. Do what you want. It's just an empty bladey locker, Christ.

The steel door swings out.

It is empty but at the bottom are some newspapers in a stack. Isaac looks at them. A few newspapers, were they always there at the bottom like that? He doesn't think so, but he can't remember, maybe, ja, maybe they were. They look old. He never looks down anyway, underneath where the clothes hang. All of this in a flash of thought and feeling that doesn't matter because he has already surged forward. Redly ferocious is the sense of rectitude in his bones now. Show these accusing bustuds how wrong they are, these swine. He bangs on the empty shelves. —See? See? I am not the bladey stuffing liar here. I'm not a thief. I was at the bar. You should check that big ox's locker now.

—Ja, says Oberholzer, behind. Like I could climb through the roof.

—Ha, someone says.

Then it hits Isaac. —No, it's Charlie, he says. Charlie. He's the one. He did the . . .

Remembering the feel of his jacket lifted away at the bar, Charlie there beside him, and Charlie touching his back. How he had checked his pockets, his keys, Jesus, his *keys*.

Labuschagne has bent to the newspapers.

—Wait, Isaac says. Stop.

—Ooh his newspapers, says Oberholzer, quick and smooth.

Isaac's skin goes cold. —Not mine, he says. You don't. Understand.

Labuschagne is pulling at them. It looks like a neat stack. But as he pulls there is something wrong about the way all the papers move together. He lifts the top few. Pauses. Whistles. Men press forward.

—Oh my bladey Christ, says Malcolmson.

—Would you have a look at that, says Veld.

—Hell. Hell.

They can all see that a round hole has been cut out of all the papers except the top few. The stacked cuts make a space in the middle of the pile that even Isaac in the roar of his numb shock recognizes as ingenious. In the space sits a round tin of Quality Street chocolates. Labuschagne lifts the cut papers away from it with grave care.

—Yasis, that is clever hey.

—Yas, that crafty bugger.

—Hold these, Dave. Labuschagne puts the papers carefully onto the arms of panel beater David Rogers, like a man placing evidence in a court of law.

—That. That isn't mine, Isaac hears his voice saying.

—Shut up, says someone behind him. When Isaac turns an arm snakes his neck, tightens. Faces are in close, bodies. He struggles. They grip his arms. They bang into the lockers and they wrap his legs with their legs and lock him solidly.

From back in the shop he can hear the shouts. —They got him! They got him! It's Isaac!

—That bladey fucken little Jew. I knew it was him all the time.

—He's a vicious little bastard, watch him for knives.

—Fucken hell, I knew you can't trust em.

Isaac tries to yell but the arm strangles his throat and pinches off his voice. Labuschagne is opening the tin then. The cash notes are packed in, unsurprising. —Looks like it's all here.

Labuschagne turns to Isaac, his head shaking. His face is long, hollowness under the eyes. One of his platesize hands swings up with all the fingers stiff to stab into Isaac's chest. —I told you when you first started, remember? I had a feeling about you. I said you ever try anything – what did I say to you? – said I kill you. Man, I kill you. You think I'm a stupud? You think that I am such a stupud?

Different eyes sliding away as he tumbles, a cat in a falling cage. The sharp bone of a forearm is dug in under his Adam's apple, the rest of him lifted. Get him outside. Get him in the yard. And what he thinks of then, strangely, is Mama Kelo with her dog that had once been his, rescued, and the way her eyes puffed in the sockets when she'd stopped, pointed. He squirms and the tough arms clamp tighter. A fish in a braided net. A stick man in vises. Someone punches him in the belly where he is stretched. It burns like spilled flame. Another punch goes into his groin, oddly it doesn't hurt as much at first, just throbs out a slower sickly nausea through his bowels.

The rear door clattering up, morning light on the dirt. Then tumbling under sky. They drive him into the ground and spread his limbs. Boots are standing on his hands and arms, his legs. Some heavy bastard kneeling on one forearm. A voice wants someone to bring a razor.

Someone else: —Wat gaan jy doen?

What are you going to do?

Something warm plops on his cheek. He looks up to see Charlie Steenkamp hawking again; when he spits a second time Isaac moves his face and gets hit across the nostril and the green spit runs over his top lip so that he gets a taste of it, salty and tobacco foul.

—Gaan hom sny?

You going to cut him?

Someone leans down and slaps him, rubs sand in his face. He writhes. Men are coward dogs and he is down now. Some bastard keeps kicking, kicking him, hard in the left side. Chambers.

—Sny hom, ja.

Cut him, yes.

They leave his face alone. He sees someone light a cigarette, sun in his eyes making them all silhouettes. He says, —Hey let me up, okes. I didn't do nothing.

Someone repeats this in singing falsetto. —He didn't do nothing. Fuckun queer.

A kick: bright pain right on the sore rib.

—Fuck you! says Isaac.

—Shut your face, thief.

—Get the cops, says Isaac.

The falsetto: —Get the co-ops.

—Okes, hold his mouth open. I wanna piss right down his throat.

—Someone go take a shit and bring some fresh.

That makes them laugh. The sense of pushing each other to go further, daring.

—Where's that razor?

—Get the cops, Isaac says. I want the cops. Panic makes him bulge upwards off the ground, but their weight has him staked on his back with the sun in his eyes. That kneeling bastard has moved to his thigh and the pressing kneecap starts to kill there.

—The cops is too easy for you, Jewboy.

—But shit, you see how he was lying before like anything, with a straight face.

—They do that hey. You can't stuffing trust them.

Isaac is looking for faces now. Just connect with one, one human being, one set of eyes. —Vernon! Rastas! Dezzy! Come on okes!

It's me, he thinks, Isaac Helger. But then it's not. It's like with Yvonne: one day you are her beloved and the next you are a nothing. Wake from the dream and find the real. He makes eye contact with Chambers. —Keithy, please man. Come on hey. This is wrong.

Chambers sinks beside his head. —You oright, Ize?

—No man help me. Tell them stop.

Chambers strokes his head like he's a pet. —Shh, shhh, he says. What's a matter? Then he scoops up a handful of yard dirt, sand saturated with black grease and boot filth, and grinds it into Isaac's mouth. —There we are, for you, Jewboy. That's it. Eat it nice.

What Isaac is thinking of as he fights to keep his teeth closed against the vile grit, feeling his lips tear in places, the sand against his gums, up his nose, what he keeps thinking of is the Felder brothers so long ago in Dusat. How the goys chopped them up and threw them in the fire. Cos you can't ever rely on the goyim, sooner or later they will turn on you, every single one of them, they will, and here it is. Mame, I shoulda listened to you only you.

—Nothing lower than to take a kitty, ay.

—The scum.

—Here.

A small point of unbearable pain on his right arm, near the crook. So bad his whole body convulses a half inch off the ground against the pinning boots. He smells burning meat. He twists his head to see a big hand grinding a lit cigarette out in his skin. The face behind the smirk: pale Oberholzer with the pink scars. Isaac's scream makes dirt spray.

Now his head is lifted from behind and hands are on his eyes, gripping him in darkness. He hears the whispering of steel. Scraping cutting pain in the scalp. More things are being stuffed in his mouth, not sand, something fibrous and loose, like strings. It goes on and he starts choking.

He tries to buck but this time they've got him locked. Through fingers he can make out some faces. Chambers, Malcolmson, Veld, Bliksy, Christo Terelli, even Tops. Most of them are standing back, some laughing, some looking disgusted. All the times they asked how he was doing. All the drinks and the jokes. He can't breathe. Where did those parts of them go, what are they now? He can't breathe. Was this their truest self always waiting to come out? Can't *breathe*.

Labuschagne's voice: —Oright now. Let him up.

—Shit no, boss. We haven't even started nothing.

—This is a business and you all late.

—We haven't done nothing good to him yet.

—Looks pretty messed up to me.

—He's getting it easy, boss.

—We finished here. We got work to get to. Let him up.

The weights lift off. Blood tingles into his numb arms and legs and the limbs start to ache brutally, pulsing where the knees and boot heels pressed. He rolls over, roughly, retches up sand and blood and orange strands. What he realizes is it's his own hair, so much orange.

—Hey. Hey Jewboy. He looks up. It's Magnus Oberholzer and Isaac turns his head at once but not quick enough and the boot catches him behind the temple. His brain rings a high note that goes on in one ear.

Labuschagne's voice. —Oright, oright enough. Go in. In, okes.

Isaac lurches up.

Labuschagne: —Get off the property.

Isaac starts to speak.

—You want me to soek them back on you? I said eff off. Out of my shop. You a disgrace. A disgrace to your family and everyone.

Labuschagne turns him and keeps shoving all the way to the gate in the chainlink fence, where Isaac stops. —My tools.

Labuschagne has bunched his overalls in both fists; he lifts Isaac to his toes. —Why? he says. Why man? Why'd you have to do it?

Isaac sees that his lips are trembling, the man's eyes full of hurt.

—I didn't, he tells him.

Labuschagne shoves him out backwards through the gate and slams it after. He goes down hard on the raw earth. He rolls, squats there for a minute, like an African. He fingers his hair, the blood on bare skin. But I just came to work, he thinks. I just walked in here this morning to work, I'm a panel beater apprentice class A. He gets up, the muscles in his legs twitching.

There is a wide unpaved alley between Gold Reef and the garage next door, with Marshall Street at the end where he sees the traffic. He starts down it. There's a hollow with a pool of oily water and there are clouds there as if it's cupping a portion of fallen sky; over this cloud as he watches there floats a balloon with a darkened horror face, some brutal beast of a fallen world with the top half white as the belly of a leech and bleeding and the bottom smeared in soil and blood.

He starts to shake, to feel so very cold, his teeth clicking. A pressure seeks to spurt from his bowels. He sits down carefully next to the puddle, holding himself. Going forward to the street is not possible. He will stay here and sit and kuk his pants and eventually something will happen to him.

In time the gate clangs behind and he hears steps. He does nothing but hunch his disfigured head down into his shoulders.

—Isaac.

He doesn't move but for his shaking.

—Isaac. Here. Isaac. Here man.

The speaker moves around, sinks: it's Jack Miller. —Get this down you hey. He has a tin mug, steaming. Isaac looks at him, dumb. Miller cups a hand behind his neck, feeds him the hot tea. A double heat: tang of alcohol folded in the sweet milkiness under the steam. He coughs some up. —Slowly, slowly, Miller says. Some more. Ja, you need it. There's it, there's it. Get this poison in you. Nice.

The sweet double heat fills his belly and Miller rubs his back. The shaking eases. Miller has a rag saturated with hot water and wipes the dirt off Isaac's face, the blood off his scalp. —People is animals sometimes, he says.

—Jack, I didn't. I swear to God.

—Never mind that hey. It's finished. It duzzen matter. Here. I brought you your tool kit. And this is my hat. You keep it. I moved that scooter in the back behind the shed, if you go round the other side no one will see you. It's got the keys and your helmet and goggles.

Isaac looks up at him, his fish mouth and his soft chins. How much he learned of the beautiful craft, how much twisted metal they righted, how many accidents of time and fate undone. Undo this now Jack. Fix it. Help me.

He starts to cry.

Jack Miller rubs his shoulder. —It's oright. You a youngster. It'll be oright. Youngsters bounce, they don't break, any parent knows it. Put the hat on now and go around and go home. It'll grow back no time, you'll see.

—You. You don't believe me, Jack.

Miller shrugs. —Duzzen matter now. Anyway I know who you are, Isaac. People who are good can sometimes make a bad mistake.

Isaac wipes his arm across his face, fresh blood and tears in one long smear. —That bastard Charlie Steenkamp pickpocketed my key . . . stuck that thing in my locker, so sly, the two a them . . .

—Shh, is oright, Miller says. I got three boys you know. They younger than you but one is getting up your age. People, they can be animals sometimes. You go home now, have a nice rest.

He stands, the empty mug in one hand. —Goodbye Isaac. You got talent in your hands, don't forget. God bless.

39.

GOD DOESN'T BLESS, instead He seems to have noticed that it's been a bad day for Isaac Helger and decides to add to its gloom by muffling the morning sun with black and purple thunderclouds and a scratching wind. The bruised sky starts to spit on him as he rides into Doornfontein, turns off Buxton Street, shuts the scooter and walks across the alley in the failing light. He keeps to the side of the yard, away from the kitchen window. The house boils with neighbourhood guests – no one's working on this Rosh Hashanah Friday. Over their voices he catches the bass murmuring of the wireless, that toxic trumpet of ill news. Today the news is all about the Soviets maybe coming into the war in Poland and what will France and Britain do about that.

From the shed he collects a mirror. In the outhouse he closes the door and puts on the light to hold the looking glass before his face, to bow his head to it, as if in worship of the horror on his scalp. Lord, they've sheared me like a lamb. They cut me and marked me but good. Then he vomits.

He has a half-pint of brandy that he picked up on the way home, he drinks deeply then blots toilet paper with the alcohol and dabs the wounds, the little razor cuts where there should be hair, the weird lunar surface of a pale skull studded with bits of orange stubble. His lips aren't bad at all, little cuts inside, and there's only a small knot on the skull behind the temple. What hurts is a bruise on his thigh and the smeared pain in the ribs on the left, and most of all the deep cigarette burn on his inner forearm. It starts to rain hard outside: heavy drumming on the tin roof.

The hat that Jack Miller gave him was too big for him, he left it back there behind the shop where he voided his bowels and started the scooter. He thinks of a watch cap that might be in the sewing room. He puts out the light and runs the five paces there through splashing rain. It's best to leave the light off, but the gloom is too heavy to see. He wraps the light bulb in some fabric and gains enough weak illumination for his search. Bad things happen and there must be a reason, a cause. Searching for a cap to cover his abused scalp is a physical analogue of the way his mind gropes to answer why, why me now? He thinks of the Torah story, the one brother who killed the other and tried to hide from God, then got a branding on his face to mark him out for all time. But what-all did I do? Nothing. They come at you not for what you do but what you are, a Jew. Like the peasants down the hill in Dusat, singing and drinking. You are marked from the word go, boy, never forget it. Yvonne didn't drop you like a hot stone because you didn't cry for Moses or cos you poor, no man, face it, she dropped you cos you a Jew and that's what you are, wherever you go, wherever you work, whatever you want to do, they'll be looking to sink you, trick you, take you down and piss on you and spit on you. Never forget those faces. What people are underneath. Take away the laws and the cops that stop them and you know what it is they will do to us. You can be ten times better than them and it won't matter cos there're so many more of them.

There's a smell of faint burning, the globe is starting to smoulder in its wrapping. He puts out the light and stands by the window, watching rain. You just had your future amputated, mate. How's that feel hey? What's left now, Mr. Ex–shoe store clerk? Forget panel beating shops, apprenticing, your name will go around the pubs and they'll all say, ja, Helger the thief, another Jewish crook.

This thought moves into his body and he hunches with it, a cramp that squeezes tears from his face, his heart. Oh Tutte, I'm really sorry. How is he going to tell him? The way Abel touched those tools and got down the brandy bottle that time. The *properly job*. And now.

And Mame – there's one thing he does have to give, the little shard of hopeful news for her that she doesn't know about yet: the immigration papers, the message coming on the eighteenth. Maybe. If it's true.

But to tell her anything else. About the business. About *this*, today – no, God, unthinkable. No.

Facing it: he no longer has a sacred trade, no longer has a gold-mine business, no longer has a gorgeous wife to love forever. It's like the war where no one can stop the Germans, they just keep coming. Bad fate like stormtroopers has taken all three fronts of his life.

What have you got, what have you got left? You were ugly to start with and now you're even uglier, a pauper monster with a bad name. He feels very tired and lies down on the thin carpet. He pulls some fabric over himself and rolls onto his unhurting side, putting his hands between his thighs, and falls asleep at once. As if his overloaded nerves simply switch themselves off. When he wakes he's stiff and his body aches in its throbbing places; the rain is still whispering and it's still dark. He looks at the clock, sees he's been out for hours. He hears the whine of the kitchen door, voices. He gets up and edges to the window and looks across the yard. Lots of neighbourhood folks remain there in the kitchen. After they're all gone maybe get Mame alone and tell her about Papendropolous, but how to do that without telling anything else? And what if it's all bullshit? This lawyer – he does not trust him at the deepest level.

Someone comes out of the outhouse and enters the house. As the kitchen door closes he sees that one of the people standing round the table in there is Blumenthal the laundryman, fellow

Dusater, who's told him more about Mame's secrets than anyone on earth. He watches the kitchen window, Blumenthal's heavy-jawed profile easy to track even through the rippling of the rainwater on the glass, the man smoking a cigarette, nodding. The man knows the family. He knows the sisters and he must have known the brother who ran away. Maybe even knows Avrom Suttner himself. That's a thought he stays with, thinking first how good it would be to confirm the truth of the immigration meeting with Avrom directly, if he somehow could. And then the sudden leap of an idea that's been brewing underneath, simple and true and real now: cousin Avrom could save Lion Motors. He could. If he wanted, he could. Isaac turns this around in his mind, being real. Look at it: Lion Motors is still savable. If Avrom is truly giving help with the immigration, then why not the business? The lawyer said at the beginning in the back of the car how Avrom likes what I've done, supporting me, ukay then. If he could put it to Avrom straight, as a straight business proposition, that the wrecks are ganna turn into gold, a sure thing, a solid investment which he'll get every penny back plus so much more . . . then ja, there must be a chance here, there *is*.

But how to reach the man, how to get round that fucken lawyer. You try and you get cut off forever. No contact means no contact. But there's always a way. If you find that lion inside yourself like he said to do. Means the guts to go after it. But not being a Stupid about it, not just ringing and asking, no. Get some other way, find some means of appealing to his cousin Avrom . . .

He comes back to the sight of Blumenthal. Ask this man about Avrom and especially Avrom's father that Mame would never talk about. Whatever can be learned about Avrom Suttner and the father Hershel Moskevitch could maybe be the angle he needs, the little something that makes all the difference. A family detail that could put him in with Avrom, past that cocky mamzor of a lawyer.

He turns to the small room, the dark fabric stacked up high in cool rolls to the left, the sewing table containing the Singer machine now stored away inverted under the flat top. He still can't find the bladey watch cap. He pulls on the scooter helmet. In the yard under the rain he goes through the narrow gap behind the outhouse to reach the house wall then edges along the bricks to the kitchen window. Blumenthal's still there, hukking away to someone he can't make out. Isaac flicks some little stones gently at the glass; at the fourth Blumenthal frowns and has a look. Isaac puts out his hand, catches the man's eye. Blumenthal's mouth opens. Isaac puts a finger to his lips and points to the yard, makes a round-the-corner move with his arm then presses his lips again. Blumenthal stares at him. Isaac nods fiercely. Okay? Okay?

Isaac stands in the rain, his helmet dripping. Blumenthal comes around the tin hut of the sewing room, mopping water from his brow with the back of his sleeve. —Yitzchok, vos macht du dorten?

—Not doing anything here. I just wanna ask you something.

—Du kookt azay veiss in ponnim.

—I'm not sick, I'm fine.

—Vos?

I lost my job today, Isaac says, going into Yiddish also.

Ai. Woe. Woe. I'm sorry to hear. And on Rosh Hashanah also.

Don't say a thing to my parents.

I won't.

Want to ask you. You know my uncle Hershel, back in Dusat. Want to ask about him and the boy he had.

Hershel?

Sure, my ma's older brother. Hershel Moskevitch. He ran away to Vilna.

Brother? Vilna? No-o.

He was the older brother, maybe it was before your time. I know he died young.

Blumenthal smears more water from his heavy-jawed face. He shakes his head. Isaac leans closer, catches the hint of Mame's sweet herring on the man's breath mingled with the tobacco and brandy. He takes hold of his arms. Just tell me. It's all right. I already know it.

Youngster, I don't want to mix in with this business. Your mother, ask her. Ask your father.

Just tell me straight. It's important.

Blumenthal takes a half step back; Isaac pulls him in, shakes the arms. Tell me straight!

But Blumenthal keeps shaking his big jaw, slowly but definitely. Isaac, Isaac, cool down. I'm speaking God's truth. Everyone knew your grandfather with his six girls. And believe me if anyone ran away to Vilna everyone would have known. In Dusat there couldn't be secrets.

Six girls, says Isaac. What are you saying? What about Hershel?

I'm not saying egg noodles. I'm telling you Zalman the butcher had girls, that's it, cut and salted.

No son?

Did you hear me?

You're sure?

Enough enough. Take your hands off me. This is going somewhere I don't want to go. I'm not here to stir trouble.

—Kayn tzores, says Isaac, letting go. No trouble.

From inside the sewing room, Isaac watches Blumenthal leaving in the rain through the gateway in the low brick wall. He turns to face the fabric rolls and the sewing table and the random goods piled against the tin wall behind, the shapes of stacked broken chairs, bedposts, crown mouldings, and in the corner the frames and the never-dusted mirrors. It fits, what he said. No record of Avrom, you've always known it. So Mame lied. Everyone lies. You can't depend on no one. Not Yvonne, not the okes at the shop, not Hugo. Who *is* Avrom? God knows. Of course he's not ganna help, you *child*. He never was: all this talk of leaving messages for him – another bladey lie. All this immigration kuk is just some pie in the stuffing sky. Just some strange struggle going on between Avrom-whoever-he-is and Gitelle, that he has no real idea about. Chances are there's no money at all and never was. Think: all of a sudden when he tries to ring him up the lawyer bells back to say, Oh ja, I was just about to ring *you*. Kuk! They playing me like a toy. Not even related to us! His heart clouts and clouts at his ribs. The lying scum at the shop setting him up with the kitty, and no one even believes the truth in a liar's world. Everyone's out to get you in the end.

He finds that he is biting into his fist. He pulls it away from the teeth, the flesh indented. A powerful urge vaults in him. He picks his way to the back corner, shifts the mirrors and squats; part of the tin wall at the bottom can bend away. Behind is a little suede bag and a big yellow envelope. He takes the little bag and tips the ring out onto his palm. It's not very bright in the darkness. He finds that he is making a low keening sound. He looks around and gets some heavy cutting shears off the table. He grips the ring in the blades and drives it against the hard floor and twists it. A sob comes out of him. When the silver snaps he takes fresh bites with the shears. He stamps with his heel, grinding. Everything, he thinks. All of it. He pulls out the envelope, removes the papers and puts on the light. He wants to hold the forms to the hot bulb till they run with flames and dribble ashes, what suits these lying bladey filthy lies. When she told him that time in the car outside the bank to make everything clean between them it wasn't clean it was filth she was giving him. The same as it was when Yvonne held him close in her room, feeding him all of those meaningless whispers. And when they hid stolen money in the Jewboy's locker.

The papers bump the light and it sways on the cord. The words *Vance, Johnson and Smythe, Attorneys at Law* moving in and out of shadow. Papendropolous saying, on the telephone, about *the other gentleman*. The other gentleman – that means the lawyer, the one supposed to have the cash in a safe, waiting. Three numbers to call him and a letter of release for the funds. *If* it's true. If. Slowly, he lowers the papers. He finds the legal letter and reads it and goes to the window and looks out at the yard. He stands that way for an hour. The rain picks up, so hard it's like buckets of water are being dashed against the glass. It's getting late, more hunched-over guests keep leaving through the yard, running home to get ready for dinner with their families in these Days of Awe.

He goes on standing and he watches the back door open and Mame comes out. Watches her run towards him through the rain with an umbrella open above her, a stout Yiddisher mame in a print dress with blue flowers and short sleeves, slippers splashing, the bulb of the hanky she always keeps in her sleeve against the soft upper arm that jiggles as she moves. Her rectangular face bent forward so that he does not see the scar. Yes, please come here, Mame. Please run here to me.

She cuts across to the outhouse.

There's a space of nothingness, when he fades out of wherever he is standing and fades back to see her disappearing into the house. Some kind of standing swoon, some kind of sleep on his feet. As if a thought can be so heavy he must black away from its very looming.

We've already contacted the other gentleman.

His mind circles the meaning in these six words. Are you a lion or are you a sheep? That's what *he* told me to be. So decide it. A Stupid or a Clever, a lion or a lamb, no other way. When everyone lies through their filthy teeth and takes and takes from you. Decide it. When the world comes to feed on you and it's only yourself even when all your life all you tried to do was your best, to be a good son. It's only yourself now. This is only you. Forget everyone else. Even her. Time to be strong for you. Afterwards when it comes time for charity *then* you can help them all. Mame and her family. With houses and boat tickets and visas, it doesn't matter. They don't need it now like you do. They've been waiting so long let them wait a bit more. Now is the time to take hold of the gold that is in your hands, you understand that? That you've worked yourself halfway to the death for. If you don't at least *try* to survive there will be nothing for you and nothing for anyone else either. Don't be a Stupid, Isaac, worse than a bladerfool. To go and admit it to her and to *be* that – never never never.

He goes on standing.

We've already contacted the other gentleman.

Man, there's nothing there. But there *might* be. Sitting there.

The whole idea falls to him then, not in a rush but calmly, fully – as complete in every detail as an intricate gift from the devil's own hand.

When he moves, he feels dazed: amazing how much time has passed in the relentless wash of his circling thoughts, a whirlpool current he was powerless to slow or to stand apart from. He disbelieves the little clock on the table. The darkness gathering outside is the evening spreading above the rain clouds. His body is stiff from the standing and it hurts badly in the places where the men hurt him at the shop. He licks the burn but it goes on stinging. His ribs twang some notes of agony when he sits by the sewing table to open a drawer. She keeps her order book here, and notepads. He tears off a clean sheet from a notepad. The sewing table has another lamp that she uses for working at night. He puts it on. Takes up a pen and dates the page. He looks down at the sheet for a long time.

Then, in careful block letters without pausing, he writes:

I, GITELLE HELGER, GIVE FULL AUTHORITY TO MY SON,
ISAAC HELGER, TO SIGN ON MY BEHALF WITH THE LAWYER
MR. VANCE OF VANCE, JOHNSON AND SMYTHE, ATTOR-
NEYS AT LAW. AS THE REASON FOR WHICH IS ILLNESS THAT
I CANNOT ATTEND.
ALL HAS BEEN ARRANGED IN ACCORDENCE WITH MY
PROPER WISHES.
Translated from mouth by Isaac Helger, signed,
Signed by Gitelle Helger,

After he has written this he reads it over with his lips moving, nine times. Then he signs his name. He gets up and takes a sheet of glass off the wall and puts it on the sewing table with a small part overhanging. He finds a loose carbon copy of a page from Mame's order book, where she has signed off an order completed, under other notes made in her quick unvowelled Hebrew characters. He uses some tape from the drawer to stick the page on the under-side of the overhanging glass. Then he puts the sewing lamp close under it on a footstool. When he puts his letter on top of the glass her writing underneath shows through and he copies the signature precisely. He takes another sheet and composes in Yiddish, carefully copying each Hebrew letter by sliding the sheet around over the original. He signs that one with her mark also.

When he looks up there is a tight feeling in his head, as if some tiny vital screw like the screws his father works with has been turned and turned till there's hardly room for his pulses to twitch in his temples.

He goes to the door; sheets of rain still rake the yard. He puts out his hand and cups a little cold water to his face. You'll be all right. Things will be all right. For everyone, in the end.

He looks around for something to keep the papers dry.

40.

IN THE HOUSE ON THIS SABBATH NIGHT, this second night of holy Rosh Hashanah, he knows that Rively and Mame and Tutte will be at the kitchen table with a white tablecloth and candles in silver candlesticks and a platter of fried latkes and another of gefilte fish and maybe a third of chopped herring with grated onion and crumbled egg. Maybe there'll be guests, the Altmans. They'll dip apple slices in honey and wish each other a sweet new year, next year in Jerusalem; but he knows they won't wait for him, they'll assume he's gone to work late at the Reformatory.

He has his papers inside a satchel on his back and has wrapped a sheet of oilcloth from the sewing room around himself and is driving the scooter through the rain. Shops in Doornfontein are closed. He finds what he needs in the Oriental district in the rougher part of Vrededorp that people call Fietas, gaining strange looks when he walks into a shop on Fourteenth Street with his helmet on and won't take it off for a fitting. He uses a nearby tickey box that smells of curry. There are some badly shivering moments before he lifts his hand off the hook.

Ten minutes after he has hung up he is still standing there: the dazed feeling. He had not truly believed. Then he drives through this rain that will not ease to an office building in town, on Diagonal Street.

———

There are night lights on in a marble lobby, crystal sconces crowded by shadows in the cool stone. A statue of a woman with her hair swept back in clean lines reminds Isaac of the ornament on a certain automobile bonnet. Don't think of *that*, it's not any coincidence, just the modern style: smooth chrome face of the 1930s, after which comes what nobody knows. He shakes the rain from the coat he bought with the other things at the churu shop. The night boy who lets him in takes the coat to hang up, then crumples a bronze lattice in front of the lift doors and the engine shrills to life. As Isaac is ridden up he is thinking there is still time to stop. Five, six. Now seven. Still time to say no and turn back. He is shown to a shadowed couch at the end of the hall against a window with a potted fern beside. He waits but does not sit. It takes over an hour before he hears the lift shrilling and humming again. He watches a man with no hat and an unbuttoned jacket come towards him. He whispers Isaac's name, as if this dark hour will tolerate no full-voiced heartiness. Isaac whispers back in the same illicit spirit and the man unlocks an office door.

Mr. Vance has a full red face with a snub nose and chestnut hair that sits like moss above the wispy eyebrows. He came from a party, he tells Isaac, not sounding happy. He has small eyes and they keep flicking at something over Isaac's head. —I didn't realize, Vance says, that you are of the Islamic faith.

Isaac taps his own brow, the white fabric there. —Jay man, he says, sliding on his best Indian accent, we coming straight from de Bombay, long time, we Helgers.

Mr. Vance doesn't laugh.

Isaac cackles enough for two, his voice sounding even to his own ears more than a little hysterical. Calm yourself. —Nu nu, he says. Only kidding. This is a yarmulke hey. Jewish as all get-all.

Mr. Vance frowns.

—Ja, I'm religious, me, says Isaac. He looks sideways and sees his own reflection in the window with a view of the city outside, other dark buildings with pasted-on rectangles of yellow. What he sees on his reflected self makes him almost jerk in his seat. He's got on a woven white skullcap that cups the whole top of his head, protecting his abused scalp from public view, yes, but now in the reflection he can see – what is that, bladey Arab writing? – alien symbols woven into its fabric, Christ, shapes he hadn't noticed in the Fourteenth Street shop when he was in such a hurry and this was the only cap on sale.

—Religious, he mumbles again.

Mr. Vance creaks back in his chair, made of lacquered red leather in buttoned squares with wings at the top that frame his head like some manner of pagan Anglo-Saxon throne. He says, —I was given to understand that Mrs. Helger–

—Ja that's my mother. It's there, it's there. A hunned percent.

—Yes.

But Mr. Vance does not look down at the papers before him, the typed letter authorizing release of funds, the two homemade letters in ink.

—And she is ill, you say.

—There's it. Sick as a dog, poor woman.

—Mr. Helger.

—Isaac, please. Mr. Helger's my father.

Mr. Vance pokes at the two ink letters; they've been slightly dampened by the journey.

—The one is the original she wrote. In Jewish, like, which is the language of her birth. The other one, I made a proper translation.

—I'm afraid before I can release any funds I'm going to need her signature.

—It's there. Look at it.

—I'm going to need to see her sign. My instructions were specific. She needs to sign for the imbursement.

—But she can't, she's sick.

—Well then, he says. Another time. And please make sure of
her presence. Office hours might be more appropriate too, I have
to say.

—Well, I was told anytime.

Mr. Vance taps the desk. —That is true. However.

—You know, says Isaac, you taking this very casual.

—Beg your pardon?

Isaac leans forward. —You know what this is for?

Vance says it's not his concern; it's a blind trust and he has his
instructions.

Isaac says, —It's for saving people's lives, you understand?

Vance shakes his head, his eyelids dipping. —Please don't tell
me what it's not my concern to know.

Isaac leans over the desk. —Listen, you gotta get me organized
here. You better. I'm telling you for your own good.

Mr. Vance favours Isaac with a toothless smile. —In my con-
siderable experience, threats are never wise.

—Who's threatening?

Mr. Vance goes on smiling.

Isaac says, —Listen, you know who gave this money.

—No, says Vance.

—Bull fucken shit, says Isaac. You know bladey well. And
I'm telling you – do you want to make this man unhappy? This
money is for close relatives, ukay. I don't care you say you know
it or not, you got the blood of his family right there on your
fancy desk. And I do reckon you understand very well what I am
saying. There's a war now. Think on that. Now I don't know
what your story here is, stuck up with some rule or whatever, but
you can pick up the telephone right now and call my mother
Mrs. Helger – na na wait, lemme finish – ring her and I promise
if she can talk she'll talk, from her bladey sickbed and all.

Mr. Vance has stopped smiling. He fits his fingertips together
under his bottom lip.

Isaac taps an imaginary watch. —You ask me why I'm coming middle a the night. Office hours you say. Office hours! Look at me, I only got *an hour*. I got *no time*. There's a *very important* gentleman waiting and Ma is sick in bed. You couldn't understand her anyway, I have to translate. There's the letter. You can phone. You can also phone you-know-exactly-who, and maybe you better if you ganna tell me no, cos guess who'll be ringing *you* very soon after he gets the word of what happened. That you would not help us, his blood. When it's war and emergency. Cos a signature and telephone call is not good enough for you. I don't know who you are but I wouldn't want to be you if that happens.

Mr. Vance puts his fingers on the desktop where they ripple gently. His mouth works as if he's rolling a bit of mouthwash around in it. Then he puffs out air. —I thought, he says, that religious Jews won't do business on a Friday night, the Sabbath. And today is a Jewish holiday isn't it?

—We do it if it's emergency, says Isaac. Are you listening one word what I'm saying? *Emergency*.

Mr. Vance nods slowly.

—Life and death, says Isaac.

Mr. Vance goes on nodding. He shifts around some more invisible mouthwash and puffs out some more air. Then he picks up the letter with the Hebrew characters and looks at it and then lifts the other. His left hand extends to the telephone.

Isaac watches him lift it, heart knocking, face neutral.

Vance says, —Rubin, can you bring the lift back up please? I need to go down to the vault.

He hangs up and looks at Isaac. —Emergency eh? he says.

—There it is, says Isaac.

41.

THAT MENTAL SWOON that he had before in the sewing room comes back to him on the road. He finds that he has left town long behind and the rain has stopped yet he cannot remember the drive to this point. The clouds break and a pregnant moon hovers through, silvering the washed land. Presently he runs out of petrol. He's been so much in his own head that he hadn't even looked at the gauge. He starts pushing the scooter and grows tired. He sees a couple palm trees off the road ahead and pushes the scooter around the back of them. Somewhere close a dog starts yapping. He puts the scooter on the stand and lays down the oilcloth and falls on it. Tired not just in the body but also in a deepbruised deepinside way. Soul tired. The burn on his arm bites at him like a snake.

After a time he pulls the envelopes from his satchel. The darker one is from the sewing room, the other is from Vance and has a rubber band around it and is bulked with the brickettes inside. To hold it gives a feeling like an electric current through his belly. He puts it down. His hands turn back the flap of the other one. Don't. He pulls out the forms. Don't. Bright African moon is strong enough to read his own hand. Don't. Trudel-Sora Melkin. Dvora Kirtzbacher. Rochel-Dor Kreb.

Orli.

Friedke.

Who is this one, who is that. Say the names, Isaac. Tell me.

438

Yes Mame.

These are your real aunties, Isaac, your only aunties. Never forget it.

Family, Isaac. The most important thing.

A pang, very old and long forgotten, spikes through him. A clear memory rides with this feeling, of the graveyard in Dusat on that last day. He and Mame and Rively stopped on the way out of the village to stand by the graves and say goodbye. Raining then too. The lindens and the white birch trees gave shelter from the wet but they were creaking and sighing from the wind off the lake and he felt warm and safe leaning against Mame's strong thigh while his face was cooled by the fresh wind. The old gravestones were scary but he was safe with Mame from the old dark stones with their chalky crumbled edges, with the little glasses around them in which candle flames fluttered like things trying to escape, making small dancing shadows on the stones. He wasn't able to understand why everyone was crying if no one had gone to heaven. Mame was happy, though. The cart was waiting for them with their suitcases with the goose-feather pillows tied on. They were going on a holiday boat, an adventure, to see Tutte. It gave him prickling chills up and down thinking about it, like the feeling of getting sick but different. The fresh wind was cold in the face and he was warm in his new coat and the birches hissed like snakes under the rain and all the bags in the cart belonged to them and they were going on a boat to see Tutte. Every boy has a tutte and they were going to see his. He was lifted up and passed to his aunties and his uncles and everyone kissed him. He didn't like it, they kept kissing and kissing, and he kept wiping his face with his arms and every time he did that they laughed. Some of them were crying and laughing at the same time, wiping their eyes. Goodbye little monarch, they said. Their big faces were too close and smelled funny. Goodbye you handsome clever monarch, goodbye. They squeezed him too hard and he didn't understand the crying because no one had gone to heaven, they were only going on holiday to the train station where he'd never been, going to a steam train and then a boat to meet his tutte. That was all.

Now Isaac can't find his breath. He keeps trying but no air will come in. He finds that he is standing up and the pages are at his feet, it's as if his windpipe has locked on him. Like trying to suck air through a stone. His legs kick and twitch and he jigs around in a panic, then finally it releases and he draws in a long gargling breath that is like the snore of an old man. He pants hard, bending over. The papers have spread on the oilcloth. Every one of them is like a giant white eye, unblinking, staring at him alone. These are the Days of Awe when sin is tallied and fates are sealed. He feels his windpipe starting to lock again. He stamps on the papers, trying to blot them, twisting them into the cloth, shutting the white eyes. It's not enough. He bends and grabs them up with both hands as if to throttle them, grinds them into a ball, crushing. Feeling his own spit on the backs of his hands, hearing his own racking gasps. He digs out his cigarette matches and strikes one and holds the shaking ball of paper to it. Flame catches and spreads. He drops the ball on the earth. Watches the yellow knives of the flames working. There. It's done. Now forget it. It warms his shins. He feels sick, but he can breathe.

He wakes curled up in the oilcloth and shivering, his body stiff and aching, wet with dew. He pushes the scooter and the sun dries him as it rises. He finds a petrol station and fills up and rides on. He reaches the Reformatory and is relieved to see it still has a gate intact at all; but he can't find a mattress or a blanket to put over the barbed wire and the razor glass. In the end he keeps banging on the gate with a rock, hoping for someone to come. It's possible no one is here. Anything being possible in this falling falling life of his.

It is Silas who comes. Silas as thin and hard as braided wire so that the collar of his overalls hangs loose around his shrunken neck.

I see you, Isaac says in Zulu.

Silas unlocks.

Is the fat one still here?

Silas nods.

When he turns after letting Isaac in, Isaac cups his shoulder. —Don't worry hey. Everything ganna change now. Promise you.

Silas blinks, his unfocused eyes drifting.

—No really, look at me, says Isaac. Look at me, Silas. I promise you.

Silas nods and goes on.

Hugo is cooking a fry-up for breakfast in his underpants with his socks held up by clips, wrinkled scrotum adangle as he squats before a fire. This is on the second floor where Isaac sees he's erected a tarpaulin like a Bedouin tent over his bed made of flattened car seats, the tarpaulin spattered on top with bird dung and the girders full of avian burbling. Without looking up, he bids Isaac a hale good morning. Says that the bird racket gets him up with the sun, bladey flying rats, he wishes he had that shotgun the albino ran off with.

—When I's a kid I used to shoot em with my catty, says Isaac. Dead eye. Never missed.

Hugo farts gently. Isaac peers over the pan that appears to be made of a hubcap with a handle welded on. Inside, grumbling and bubbling in grease, are half a dozen shiny egg yolks, some chops and fat sausages. —You joining us, boyki? Pass me that bottle of Worcester.

—Us?

—Me and Silas the noble, who else. What's that on your head? You look worse'n hell.

—No blowout parts sale today?

—Ach, the poor shit. He put so much into it but last night he hit a twist of his own.

Isaac waits, the smell of the fatty eggs queasing at his guts.

—Ja, he had those few good parts he just about died to take out, had em out all nice and covered from the rain. Too bad this was the night he finally couldn't keep himself awake.

—The jackals hey.

—Everyone's twist has a different flavour, says Hugo Bleznik. They come over last night and they stole those parts right from under his nose. It's a wonder he didn't off himself when he got up. Poor bastard. There is one helluva big heart in that little negro, I tell you, one helluva heart. Sling me the salt also there hey Tiger. There's a boy.

Isaac watches him tipping in a dark shower of Worcestershire sauce then snowing a layer of sodium onto the selfsame feast. —Speaking of Silas the noble, you wanna go give him a shout? Tell him grub's up.

—I don't think so.

Hugo looks up. —Hey?

—Got something important I wanna discuss.

—Look at you. What's this now?

—Wanna talk business, says Isaac. Serious business.

Hugo, pants on now, is digging in the desk for the agreement that'd first been adumbrated in ink on the back of a Miracle Glow circular, when Isaac had insisted on the name Lion Motors. He straightens, saying here it is, asking, what, did Isaac reckon there was something in the fine print might save their Yiddisher arses? Cos if he did, boy was he wrong. He starts reading from it, a typed and stapled document from his lawyer, three pages long.

—Hugo, stop. I'm ganna tell it to you plain, ukay. I want to buy you out.

Hugo looks at him in an investigative way.

—You want what now?

—The shares what you got for Lion Motors, I want em.

Hugo's head slants one way, then the other. Like Isaac's speaking Swahili. —You don't look like you tryna be funny.

—I'm not.

—Man, what the hell is that thing on your head anyway, like a yarmy or what?

—Not a yarmy. You hear what I said?

—What's wrong with your hair there? Plus you got like a mad look in your eyeballs, I am telling you. What *is* that thing, you come outta hospital or what?

—No.

—The female again, same one or someone new.

—No. I made a decision.

—Hey?

—Hugo. I want you to sign me over the shares.

—Sign you over. Before, you said buy out.

—Buy out, sign over. Whichever. Oright? Please.

—World a difference, boyki. Why, what's happened? You come into some dosh? Some rich uncle I never heard of?

That makes Isaac look down, makes weakness flood through his body. He leans his shoulder to the wall beside the window. He looks out and down, sees the new day gracing old wrecks down there in the pocked mud. Smashed machines. Rust. Batteries leaching acid. Life is bladey hard. Know that? Mame always told me that but I don't think I listened hard enough.

—Look, he says. I maybe got a few quid together . . .

—How much?

— . . . Not much.

—How much is it?

—It's not that. It's more like this investor, ukay.

—Investor.

—But he wants me to have the company, like. He doesn't want to back a partnership. Just me.

Hugo walks off a bit then comes back with a finger that wags.
—Sounds very effing fishy to me.

—Don't look at me. Those are his terms.

—Who is this?

Isaac shakes his head.

Hugo wrinkles his nose. —I'm smelling horse manure, boychik.
Do I look like I fell off the turnip truck yesterday?

—What difference does it make, Hugo? We dead anyway.

—What *we*? You telling me to eff off man, out of my own
firm! That I started from nothing!

—Hey hey. Just turn it down oright, I got a helluva head.

—Ja, with that churu cap on or whatever I am not surprised.
What the hell's happened a you? Are you seriously feeling well?
Are you sure this rich uncle a yours isn't all in your brain?

—It's genuine, Hugo.

—And so now you wanna push me out. Me, who started the
whole thing. Me. Who did you a kindness letting you in part-time
or'd you forget so convenient?

—I bought my way in, Hugo. A hundred pounds cash. Or did
you forget?

—Ja, that mystery cash. Is this from the same place?

—Hugo. What difference does it make?

—Huge! Huge!

—Just hang on. Ukay. It's not me, ukay. Me, I can appreciate
you might be cheesed. But let's just say this investor, he's heard
about you and your ponies, and that he doesn't trust no more
that you won't run round and do the same thing again. It's not in
my hands.

—Well who the bladey hell would tell him all about that?

Isaac doesn't speak.

Hugo paces. —But how much are we talking here? You keep
avoiding.

—Hugo, it doesn't matter how much.

—When someone says that, it's *all* that matters. I know what I'm talking boyki. You tryna blow sand in my eyes. Summin reeks fishy as anchovette paste.

Isaac rubs his aching neck. —Hey Hugo. What are you even hukking me about here? You are a man sitting in his gutkes with birds crapping on his head. You frying your breakfast in a hubcap. Next couple weeks, bailiff is coming.

Hugo looks at him and his blue eyes are moist, the big head trembles. —I can't believe you'd want to ditch me. After all what I done for you. You know how hard I've tried for you. Remember when I rang and rang? You worked in a bladey shoe shop. And then even *I* came to your house to convince. *I* had to convince to do *you* the favour. Remember? And now you wanna take the favour that you wouldn't have if it wasn't for me and steal it from me like some bladey gunif.

Isaac sighs. Finds a seat on the window ledge, puts his hand on his knees and bends forward.

—Just be honest with me, says Hugo. That's all I want. I deserve that.

—What? says Isaac to the floor.

—Who is it?

Isaac shakes his head.

—Is it real?

—It's real.

—How much is it? I mean is it enough? Need a lot more than a few hundred.

—It's enough.

—How much?

—I got the money.

A long silence. Hugo staring. —What you mean you got it? You said someone interested. Have you got it or is it just talk? Cos if you don't have it, it won't do you nothing to have my shares of bankrupt. You should do the opposite. Get your name off the firm so you not the bankrupt, have that on your neck for the rest a your life. You—

—Hugo.

—I mean, cos when you say you have when you don't have it, when you—

—Hugo!

Isaac has the satchel open. He upends it and the fat envelope with its rubber band drops out.

Hugo goes pale.

—Tell me and take your pay and let's be on our way. I'm sick and I'm tired. I had enough, Hugo.

Hugo's eyes don't leave the envelope; he laces his pudgy arms across his chest. —Na, you charfing me. You tryna run a game on old Blezzy. What's in there?

Isaac shakes his head; it feels like something's grating in the bones of his neck. —No games. This is the dosh. Cold cash latkes. What do you want?

—How much is there?

—A lot. More than a grand. Well more.

—I don't believe it.

—I don't care what you believe.

Hugo rocks on his heels, watching the package as if it's a coiled mamba. —And if I leave, then what? What you ganna do?

—That's my problem.

Hugo starts to nod, chewing his bottom lip. —Oright, he says. Oright, Mr. Thousands. Oright. You gimme five thousand pounds. I want five thousand cash right now.

—I'm being fucken serious here Hugo.

—So'm I.

—Don't be stupid.

—That's my price. The cost of stabbing your only true mate right in his back. Only oke who ever tried his best to do right by you.

Isaac puts his hands on the edge of the desk and walks his feet backwards, letting his head droop.

—And if I go, says Hugo, what you reckon's ganna happen? This isn't some part-time game you can do on the side. You an apprentice panel beater! Can you handle the contracts? Be honest. The accounts, the creditors. Do you even know what you'll need to do to get out from under this mess, the people you have to see? You don't have the first clue. Listen a me, boychik. We partners for a reason. You got the hands and you run the shop and I do the rest. And you only have to show up here part-time and you still keep another job on the side. I mean come off it! Who else would make a deal like that? I been good to you. You know it. I know it. What are you standing here talking buy me out? If it's not an investor, I mean if you got the gelt right *there*.

Isaac jerks up straight, bangs the desk hard with the flats of his hands. —Cos everyone always fucks me around!

His voice echoes, a hoarse and breaking sound. Like a kid crying. Nothing ever goes the way it should. He trembles.

Hugo looks at him, then speaks more softly. —Isaac, I know I ballsed up. I know I stuffed a good thing out of sight. I know all of it. Believe me, what you reckon I do all day out here sitting and brooding? You think I haven't almost jumped off that roof? You have no idea what hell this is for Blezzy. Look at me, man. Look at me, Ize. I am finished with ponies. I'm finished *finished* with all that.

Isaac rubs his jaw on his shoulder. Feels hot and sick.

Hugo's voice is turning funny now, straining and high like it was the last time when he was up there whacking bottles. —I swear to God, Isaac. I swear on the souls of my late parents, uvuh sholem. On the both a them, Isaac. Isaac, if you serious and you have the money to save this place then, God's sake man, let's use it together and save this place and get moving forward together like we was. We had a twist oright, we ran into a twist. But gimme the chance here, man. I'm on the bones of my arse. Isaac look at me. Gimme the chance and let's do this together. Let me beat the twist. I want to beat the twist just once. I do. Isaac . . . Hey, you not looking at me. *Isaac.*

When they call Silas to them it's not to receive his cold breakfast only but also to sign on the changes they've written up to the two copies of the agreement. Isaac watches him marking his name carefully as their sole witness. Silas Mabuza.

—Good job you can write your name hey, says Hugo. And you know what you just signed there? A miracle, mate. Mazel tov. How'd you say mazel tov in Zulu?

Silas stands there looking at him from those hollowed sunken eyes: if ever a corpse had walked such a look would be its lawful own. Isaac studies the amended agreements one more time. Switched now so that two-thirds of Lion Motors is his, one-third Hugo's. He puts the papers on the desk and puts the pen on the line for his name.

—Go ahead boyki, says Hugo. Go ahead and finish it.

But Isaac doesn't move.

—Boyki.

He looks up. —I'm ganna depend on you, Hugo.

—You can, Tiger. You can.

Isaac looks down again. —I'm a Stupid, Hugo.

—Hey?

—Am I a Stupid?

—Boyki, you the last thing in the world from stupid. We about to become very rich men.

—I hope so, says Isaac. And he signs.

By noon, Silas Mabuza has washed and dressed in clean street clothes. Hugo too is spruced with a clean suit and even a felt carnation in his hatband. There's a dented '34 Dodge sedan with the spare wheel missing from the side that still has half a tank, and they stand beside it talking in soft serious voices.

Isaac counts the cash notes, enough money for all the staff's back pay, plus bonuses, plus their first three weeks' future pay. He hands all this money over to Silas who accepts it with a grave face and solemnly buttons it under his jacket before climbing into the Dodge.

—Oright boyki, says Hugo. We got to get going now.

He knows that Hugo has to see the landlord and the truck dealers, the rail freight company; most of all he has to do the rounds of his more mysterious creditors. Altogether, the sum of fifteen hundred pounds should more than cover it, with any balance to be banked as working capital, perhaps some used to purchase a crane or a compactor. Hugo's keen to head out there as soon as possible to start signing more new contracts while they still can.

—We talked and talked on this already, says Hugo. It goes straight into account. There's a branch I know will be open. I'll set up a meeting with manager and I'll ring you with the time. Then I'll see the lawyer to put this agreement all typed proper and that. Then I'll go and sort the urgent. I'll use cheques when I can, then you can see everything yourself, and Monday morning you go in there and you sit down with manager and get all the signing powers that you want. It's your baby now, you king of Lion. That paper's official. Oright? And absolutely no ponies, no nothing, for Blezzy. Swear on my life. You ganna see every contract I collect if you want. Oright?

Isaac nods.

—Oright?

Isaac nods again. One thing, Hugo has asked no questions about Isaac's secret source. Maybe he doesn't want to know, maybe he knows Isaac won't say.

—I'll organize today in Brakpan for some watchmen to come out here and keep an eye till when Silas and them get back. As soon as Silas is on his way back he's ganna let me know and I'll bell you, you might have to come here to supervise when they arrive.

—I'll be here.

—I mean you might have to organize to miss work.

Isaac shakes his head. —There's no more work.

—What you mean?

—I left panel beating, Hugo. Lion Motors is all I got now.

Hugo puts his soft hand on Isaac's shoulder. —Boyki, boyki, whyn't you say something before? Man, I'm not ganna let you down. You can depend on old Blezzy. You believe me hey? You can.

—Ja, says Isaac. I do believe you.

He presses the envelope full of cash to Hugo's chest but Hugo doesn't move, just stands nodding slightly, his warm hand pulsing on Isaac's shoulder, his blue eyes close. —I dun know how you did it, but you saved our arses, Tiger. Saved our dead arses. I'll never forget this long as I live.

He takes the envelope and gets in the Dodge. Isaac watches the floating red dust the car leaves behind till all of it has settled and the Reformatory feels gutted with silence. He scratches the woollen balaclava that Hugo dug up for him to replace the Indian skullcap, checks he has the keys to lock up, then he climbs onto the scooter and starts the long ride home.

42.

IN THE HOUSE ON BUXTON STREET the wireless for a change is not muttering, and the workshop is empty with his father gone to shul. He stops next to the workbench, lets his hand drift over his father's tools, the tiny screwdrivers, the rags tinged with mineral oil, the lathe attached to the electric motor. The monocle of his father's loupe is right in front of the seat, as if he's just set it down for the moment. Low voices make him look up. The kitchen. He goes softly and slowly, half expecting guests there. But when he stands in the doorway, he sees the table has a plate of quartered oranges and a pot of tea. Mame is seated with her back to him and Rively and Yankel Bernstein are on the opposite side and they stare at him without speaking.

—Whyn't you go to shul? he says to Rively.

Mame twists around in her seat and he looks down at her. Mame with her sunken eyes and her scar, her hair held down with some clips and her plump arm over the back of the chair. —Isaacluh! she says. And he wants to cry, the bulge of a sob lifts like a wave to the base of his throat. He tries to say the word *Mame* but not even the sob comes out. The problem of not being able to breathe again seems to teeter in his chest.

—Ver you been? Voz kookst du? Vot iz?

He shakes his head and moves to the table, Mame telling him to sit down. He blows his nose with a serviette, a way to close his eyes. Seated, he manages to croak: —Fine. I'm ukay, Ma. Rively meanwhile keeps asking him what's wrong, saying he looks like hell.

— Speak for yourself, Isaac tells her. And it's true they have a strange air, a kind of pale tension in their faces that he senses has nothing to do with him and everything with what they've been talking about.

— We were both at a meeting, Yankel Bernstein tells Isaac.

— We were just telling Ma, says Rively.

Now Mame scrapes her chair around towards his, he feels her hand on his thigh, patting. She says his name twice and he looks at her with his eyes unfocused and makes himself smile, his face wooden, then he looks away. Take off your funny hat, why you wearing a hat, take off your coat, sit nicely. What is it Isaac? What's the matter?

He grunts, slips off his jacket and hangs it on the back of the seat.

— This was a Hashomer meeting, says Yankel. They had an important speaker, why we went.

The good white tablecloth that would have been laid out the night before is not here now, Mame has put down the cheap one that is soft and knitted like a thin blanket, squares of yellow. Mame is rubbing his arm. He feels sick, sick. Mame says, He works so hard, my boy. Sit and relax and I'll warm you some nice chicken. Something to drink? What do you want?

He shakes his head. He can feel her wanting him to look at her, into her brown and weary eyes. What happened to your neck here? Her fingertips brush scratches someone put on him in the yard at Gold Reef.

— Nothing, Ma. From work.

What is this you're wearing on your head? He ducks his head from her reaching hand.

— We were just telling Mame about it, says Rively.

— You should hear this, says Yankel. About this speaker. Everyone should.

Isaac attends to him, not because he wants to but to avoid facing Mame. What a mistake to have sat. —Who was he? he asks.

—Her, says Rively. She's a Jew from Poland. Who got out.

Polackers, says Mame, they talk Jewish so funny. Everything is *oi* instead of *uy*. Like straw is stuck up their noses. They say *shuh* instead of *suh*.

—We understood her, says Rively. Beser nit.

Beser nit: words that mean too bad that we did. We wish that we hadn't. Words with a weight that Isaac doesn't want to feel. No, he thinks. It's enough. I can't. It's enough. Don't.

—Yuh yuh yuh, says Mame. She puts her plump elbows on the table and covers her mouth with both hands. Rively moves her chair around and leans over and rubs Mame's back.

—What is this? says Isaac.

Rively keeps rubbing her back and Mame says: —Me used to have a Polacker in Dusat. Mishus Turnikov. She was. She.

—What the hell? says Isaac. What's going on?

Rively says: —This woman who spoke, she got out of Warsaw. She's married to an American, that's how she managed a visa. But she told us what the Germans are doing to Jews over there. Isaac, their army is shooting Jews like stray dogs.

—She is still in absolute shock, you could see, says Yankel. She left so many people behind. She doesn't reckon she'll ever see them again.

—Ja but she will, Isaac hears himself say. After this war. Of course she will.

—She doesn't think so, says Yankel. And she should know.

Mame's face is entirely covered by her hands now. Rively keeps rubbing her back.

Isaac hears his voice: —You said yourself she's in shock. Not thinking proper. People say things.

—No, Isaac, says Rively. It's really bad, like we have no conception. She told how any Jew under the Germans feels what they're like, and it's worse than hate, it's determination. That's what she said. Their determination is worse than hate. She saw them burning shuls. In front of her eyes they were beating Jews to death in the street. People hanging from lampposts. She says it's just starting, that's what she kept saying. Just starting.

Mame gives off a sound, muffled in her hands.

Isaac's heart goes wild in his chest. —But Dusat's not even under Germans!

Rively rocks back, blinking. His voice had boomed of its own.

—Not yet, says Yankel. But they've already taken part of Lithuania right, and who's going to stop them getting the rest? Not Stalin. The Soviets betrayed us all, signing that deal with the Nazis. Shame on them, shame on *me* for believing in Russia. No. It's a matter of time, I reckon. Matter of luck.

—Matter matter matter. You sound like a bladey stuck record, man!

—Isaac, says Rively.

—I'm just being real, says Yankel. You the one stuck like a ostrich head.

—What did you say?

Yankel shakes his head. —Nothing.

Isaac jerks up out of his seat. His legs bang the table hard enough to make tea slop everywhere.

—Isaac! says Rively. S'matter with you? She moves against Mame, curling her arm around her and pulling her close.

Isaac's hand is stabbing his finger over the table like a piston. He shouts, spraying spit: —You're a bladey troublemaker Bernstein! I knew it from day one! Look what you doing to my ma, making her cry! You and your stuffing politics. I had enough!

—Isaac! says Rively. What's wrong with you? She cradles Mame closer.

Yankel's mouth opens and shuts and he leans back, blinking behind his spectacles. Isaac is roaring: —You come with your shit

to my house and take my sister away from shul where she should
be and you bring in this effing politics and make my mother cry,
make everyone all scared, what the hell's a matter with you,
what's wrong with your stuffing brain you idiot, can't you see
what you *doing*?

Yankel gets up, stumbling a little. He looks at Rively and
Mame huddled and he stutters apologies.

Isaac mimics. —He's so-so-sorry. After you the one made her
cry!

He goes around the table fast, and Rively shouts something,
just a sound, an avian squawk. He wants to grab gangly Yankel,
take chunks of his shirt in both fists the way Labuschagne grabbed
him, haul him around and send him through the back door
sprawling into the yard. But Yankel moves the other way, backing
through the door to the workshop with his long arms outstretched.

When Isaac grabs at him a finger snags in the balaclava and he
feels sudden air on his scalp. He shoves Yankel as hard as he can
and Yankel sits down. Behind him there is a shriek. He turns:
Mame's face behind her pointing hand has become a twisted
lumpen thing, all the flesh cratering away from the teeth and the
eyes, the scar bright as fresh blood. She's pointing at Isaac's face,
straight at it, his head. And then she goes soft and Rively holds her
as she lolls.

Isaac takes a step towards them but Rively screams at him to
get away. —*Get out, you animal.*

He turns back on Yankel, sees him scooting to his feet, his hand
out. —I'm sorry hey, calm down. Jesus, what happened to you?

Yet still the stupid shmock refuses to leave at once. —Lemme
just talk to your sister. Isaac now at last has his fists full of Yankel's
clothes and lifts and rams him into the front door. —Can I just say
goodbye to Rively?

—Mate, I'll put you through the fucken window. Open that
door.

—What happened to you, your hair?

Isaac gets the door open. —I'mna kill you any second.

—You joining the army hey, says Yankel. That it? They shaved you by the army didn't they? Good for you. We ganna try to get into Palestine otherwise I would be signing up also, I–

Isaac butts him in his chest. Yankel grunts, his arms windmilling as he falls out. Isaac slams the door, locks it.

When he gets back to the kitchen it's empty. The door of his parents' room opens and Rively runs out, one hand covering her mouth. —I hate you, you animal, is what she says, and then she is past, going on to the front.

—That's right, he shouts after. You go too. The both a you! Just leave Ma all alone, doesn't matter.

At the door Rively shouts back: —You did it to her! You! You mad! I'm ganna get Dr. Allan.

The door opens and he gets a look at Yankel's shocked idiot face before it slams. He goes to Ma's room and knocks softly. Then he remembers his bare head. He goes back to the kitchen, finds the balaclava, puts it on and adjusts himself in the window reflection.

Mame is lying on her back, this bedroom with rose-coloured curtains holding the daylight at bay, the bed with big dark wood headboard and a bedspread covering it all like a shroud, only a narrow gap between the bed and the sideboard with the mirror, Mame's legs packed like thick sausages in the flesh-coloured stockings below the skirt hem. She's lying on her back with a scarf over her face. He stands beside her and takes her hand, squeezes it.

—Yitzchok?

—I'm here Mame. How you feeling?

I caught a fright, she says.

Yes Mame.

I looked at you and I saw a terror thing. My mind, Yitzchok. My mind is full of terror things. Dreams.

No Mame, it's not your mind.

She doesn't speak.

Mame? I had an accident at work.

She stirs. He tries to relax her, to settle her back down, but her other hand takes the scarf off her face. She squirms her shoulders and comes up a little higher on the bed to look at him. What happened, are you hurt?

No. Yes. A little bit.

She touches his face where the cheekbone is bruised. —Duyner oremer kepillah. Your poor little head.

Yes, something fell on me. I was under the car.

Oh God.

I'm all right. But the – from the battery, you know, what we call acid. It burned my hair.

Your hair?

Yes Mame.

That's why you have the funny hat.

Yes Mame.

Let me see.

They had to cut it off Mame. I don't have any more hair.

Oh your beautiful red hair. Messiah hair.

Here it is Mame. He dips his head and she pulls off the balaclava.

Ai Isaac, no, Isaac.

He starts to cry. It's all right Mame, it will grow back.

My Isaac, she says. My champion Isaac. He feels her warm palm spreading over his crown. For you Isaac my love, I will kill any bull, you know that. You are my precious one, my rainbow.

He leans down and kisses her head and feels that his tears have wet her forehead. Mame, we'll have a house for our own.

Don't talk it, Isaac.

Why not, Mame, it's true.

No, Isaac. I can't think this way anymore. It hurts me too much. Let me see you. Oh my God. Seeing you like this, it was like a fall from a height. My heart.

It's fine, Rively's gone to get Dr. Allan.

Listen to me. I saw it like this before, such a head with no hair, and the cuts. In a dream. And this on your arm.

I burned it. With a soldering iron, by accident.

My dream.

Only a dream, Ma.

It wasn't you. It was so many of them. And with them it was Friedke and Orli and Dvora and Rochel-Dor. It was Trudel-Sora. The husbands, Pinchus and Yossel. All my sisters and even the children. In the dream they were walking in smoke and none of them had any hair. I spoke to them but they couldn't see me. They were just walking walking with eyes that couldn't see. All of their beautiful hair was gone, they didn't look like people anymore. And now it happens to you in life.

An accident, Mame.

What can it mean, Isaac? What does it mean?

It doesn't mean anything Mame, it's just a dream.

Isaac, I want you to do something for me.

Yes Mame.

Go and get the pictures.

He tugs at a loose thread on his knee. Mame, I don't think we should look right now.

You're right.

Mame?

Get them and I want you to put them away somewhere I can't find them.

He presses a hand to his face.

I have to stop looking, Isaac, all the time. Put them away. It's eating me up alive. Let me try to think of other things. There is nothing we can do. I went to see Avrom. You saw what I did, everything I could.

Yes Mame. I saw.

Everything, she says. Now it must be Avrom. Please God, Avrom. Let God whisper in his heart, like Tutte says He does. Let him decide . . .

Her eyes close again and her breath gradually slows.

It's all right, Mame, Isaac whispers. All right.

43.

THERE ARE MANY PEOPLE standing outside the synagogue, people in their Shabbos best – crowds come now in these Days of Awe and war. They go quiet as he walks up and past, wearing a work shirt, no jacket, a satchel on his back and balaclava rolled up over a bloodless and haggard face. When he pushes in the David-Star'd double doors he sees the back of the singing chuzen on the bimah and the yellow light streaming down from above the ladies' gallery. The Ten Commandments affixed to a post behind the bimah stare at him. Kibud av v'em: Honour father and mother. He watches for his father in the usual place and the heads of the men pivot, one to the other, nudging down the word. Above him the ladies' hats dip and rotate like vast birds, sensing the feed of his commotion, a scraplet of gossip for the quick lipstick beaks. His father has seen him now, and risen, taking his cane off the pew. Isaac backs out to wait.

In the corner of the lobby by the women's staircase, Abel grips his shoulders. What is it? What's happened?

Mame, she's not feeling well. Rively's gone to get the doctor.

What happened?

She's all right. Only she fainted.

Fainted?

But she's all right now. In bed.

And you? Why the bag? What's this on your head?

It's nothing . . . Tutte.

What?

Tutte.

What is it my boy? What's wrong?

Tutte, can you do something for me?

Of course.

Give me your blessing.

My what?

Like in the Torah.

What are you saying now?

I remember that. In the Torah, they are always asking for a blessing from the father. Isn't it? Can't you give me yours?

Isaac, what's wrong?

Will you bless me, Tutte?

Of course I will my boy.

I'm going away, Tutte.

What are you talking, Isaac?

I've joined the army.

Ai ai ai.

Don't, Tutte.

Isaacluh, Isaacluh, Isaacluh, what have you done?

I've already done it, Tutte. I signed. I have to go, today, now.

Why? Why? Why?

Will you bless me Tutte?

You can't just go!

I'm not going home Tutte. I can't go home. I'm leaving from here, I won't be back. Tell Mame that I am so sorry I couldn't tell her goodbye, I couldn't because she isn't well, I didn't want to upset her.

For a long time his father grips him. His body rocks and Isaac can feel the way the pain must be hitting in racking waves, coming up from deep within him. He keeps saying the word *no*, and Isaac keeps saying *I have to, I have to, Tutte.*

You don't know what it is, an army, he says. Not the army, Isaac, never. Not the war.

I've already joined, Tutte.

How a lie can feel more solid than the truth when it makes its own. The rightness of it calms him right through. It's how it should be, Tutte, he says.

And your work?

I left my work.

And the business?

I don't care about business. I have to go.

But why, my God, why, out of the blue? It's mad.

Because I deserve it, Isaac says. It's what I deserve.

What does that mean?

I can't undo what's done.

What are you saying?

Will you bless me, Tutte? Will you bless me before I go?

They stand talking closely, his father arguing with him, gripping him, until gradually Isaac can feel him giving up, feel him understanding that the decision is made, his boy is going, there is nothing he can do. Then Isaac sweeps off the balaclava, saying they did this to him at the recruitment place. And when Tutte sees this final evidence of Isaac's utter commitment, he at last consents to bless: he touches his forehead to Isaac's there in the lobby of the synagogue with the faint sounds of the chuzen's braided wailing seeping through the wooden doors to the sanctuary, and he whispers in Hebrew, asking The Name God Almighty to bless this only son of his, to look over him and guard him and protect him, and please please O Lord if it pleases You, bring him back home alive and well to us where we will always be waiting, always.

Thank you Tutte, he whispers. Thank you so much.

PART THREE

Greenside

44.

FROM HIS LETTERS she knew Tobruk was the name of the place; when it fell to the Germans in June her heart shrivelled. Ten thousand South African troops caught up there in the desert at the far end of Africa, the papers said. Was winter frost in Johannesburg when the telegram arrived; her tears hissed on the coal stove in the kitchen, reading the words *missing in action*. Another two months limped by, torturing her, before a second note could confirm him as a prisoner of war. Alive still, blessedly, in this year of death and mayhem, nineteen hundred and forty-two.

Two years later they hired a driver and took the Altmans' Austin sedan out to the Waterkloof airforce base near Pretoria. It was good weather to watch it descend, a converted Lancaster bomber easing from a sky with no clouds. He came through in his uniform, a kit bag over his shoulder. There was no sign of disorientation or surprise: he looked taller, harder. He had always been wiry but now he was gaunt, ground out, his skeletal face the face of a man in that it no longer contained other possibilities as a youth's – ever mobile – always does. This final face of his had set hard, without twinkle or smile, with features that now seemed a little smeared and flattened as if by the sanding pressure of events, the eyes puffed and a little slitted, like the eyes of a fighting terrier taken from the pit. When she hugged him his body felt like a piece of warmed steel. She winced when his arms squeezed back, like pinching cables.

His new room was Rively's old, with her married to Yankel Bernstein and settled in Palestine now. The teddy bears were packed away, the walls whitened by a new coat of paint; Gitelle had sewed a duvet cover and spent on real goose feather pillows. But that night when he woke them with his screams she found he had gone to sleep on the floor with an old blanket, the bed untouched.

For months he slept late and bathed little. His hair grew shaggy, his face always prickled. She would clip out job notices and ask him questions and cook him good meals; he ignored the clippings, mumbled his answers, vomited often after eating. In the afternoons he would go out and when he came back at night he bore the rank whiff of liquor in his pores. She went to the army for help; they sent a Captain Lewis – nice youngster – who went into his room for an hour. Afterwards Isaac had a shave at a barber, a haircut, bought himself a nice new jersey to wear. But in the night was the screaming and the next day he lay in bed till noon and went again to the liquor when the sun fell.

Captain Lewis had said to her that Isaac escaped twice from that prisoner camp there in Sicily. Once for sixteen days: he'd eaten grass, ruining his gut. They sent him to a facility run by the SS; it took the Red Cross a month to get him transferred back. Lucky. Captain Lewis repeated the letters SS and gave her a look from the tops of his eyes that she pretended to understand.

When the German surrender came in June it made no effect on Isaac's slide. His body stank; his beard grew rife, oily. There were purple eyes and scratched knuckles. She tried intercepting his army cheque in the mail. He told her if she did it again he'd move to the pub. The pub. Next day she followed after him like a spy. Through Joubert Park into town, to the Regent Hotel by the corner of Plein and Loveday streets, three storeys in need of fresh paint. Through the lettered window she saw drinkers on stools who looked up with dead grins for her son, Isaac slotting himself into the line of them as if machined to fit. Came a hitch in her heart and breath, an ice ripple. Who these men are, it's the same as it was. Parasites.

45.

HE'S THERE WITH JOHNNY NO-TEETH and Serge the gimp,
stuttering Manny and cross-eyed Rolph, Stevie Pimples. His
third one of the day is in front of him for he has only just arrived
and he's saving it, making himself wait for the square cool feel of
the glass in his hand, then the cold burning trail down into the
belly and the flare of pain in his weak stomach before the banked
heat can trickle into his blood and throb up behind the eyes.
Making himself wait, ja, knowing it is there, the saliva loose
under his tongue with the anticipation of it. But also starting to
feel the other two (whiskies knocked back like always as soon as
he sat) working in him, that early groping feeling behind his
eyes, and in a few minutes he knows the smoky heat will find its
way into the chambers of his heart and his heart will open up
and his mouth will smile: the day will turn easy as the sunlight
pooling on the sawdusted floorboards over there by the window
where Barney's cat lies on its side and he can just sit and be and
breathe and drink. All the bleary chatter will meld into one long
afternoon song and the shadows will get long and he won't care
about anything but the sweet warmth cradling his soul, numbing his thoughts. He reaches slowly for the glass; the door
jingles. Behind the bar Barney looks up from his paper: —No
ladies, madam.

But Mame is already walking in. It is Mame, right? There's
a second where Isaac thinks truly he is making her up but she

keeps coming, none other. She has a burlap sack in one hand and her handbag in the other. She walks to the bar beside Isaac and when she puts the sack down on it, it makes a clunking sound.

Farther down the bar some of the jollyboys are singing that old sad Afrikaner war song in their hoarse cigarette voices, full of longing and lostlove: *My Sarie Marais is so ver van my haart. / Maa'k hoop om haar weer te sien. / Sy het in die wyk van die Mooirivier gewoon. / Nog voor die oorlog het begin.*

> *My Sarie Marais is so far from my heart*
> *But I long to see her again.*
> *She lived near the Mooi River*
> *Back then before the war began.*

Then the sadsweet chorus:

> *Oh bring me back to the old Transvaal,*
> *There where my Sarie lives,*
> *There under in the corn fields by the green thorn tree,*
> *There lives my Sarie Marais*

—Hello Ma, Isaac says.

Barney says, —Ladies out please. Ize, you know.

—Ja ja ja, she's going, Isaac says.

She speaks in Jewish: Look at me, your mother.

—Hello, my mother. Go home hey please. Far away to the old Transvaal.

Will you come with?

His attention is on the full drink on the bar before him and he licks his lip and scratches his chin through the beard. Mame, he says. Please go home will you?

Will you come with?

—Ja sure, he says. I'll be right along. You go ahead.

She shifts the sack on the bar and again he hears something heavy clunk and scrape. You think I never had before drunkards in my life?

He looks at Barney who's shaking his head. —Sorry hey Barns.

—What sorry, he says. She just has to go, Ize.

Manny with his veinous mushroom nose on the other stool starts to say something to Mame and Isaac backhands him a medium one across the collarbone. —About-face, Isaac says. Manny complies.

They were on your father like leeches, Mame is saying. And now it's the same with you.

Isaac picks up the glass and tilts it to the light, angling the molten gold. Funny she would say leeches. Probably she's never smelled a burn ward. Used to stick leeches on them there to try to get the blood working. The rotting smell and the screams when they came to take them to surgery to cut another piece off. Lying there under leeches in their stink. They were sad bastards, ja, but even they had it easy, compared to certain other ones. Certain others. —Cheers. L'chaim.

He tilts his head back with closed eyes, feels the cold of the glass on the bottom lip then grunts as it spins out of his hand.

—Hey hey! says Barney. That's it! You get out madam! I don't care who you are. Out. Out.

—No Ma, Isaac says gently. No Ma, you shouldn't do a thing like that. That's a big sin. The glass rocks unbroken on the bar; Isaac rights it then wipes his fingertips in the puddle on the wood and puts them in his mouth. This time when Mame slaps at his mouth he leans back and catches only a wee whiff of air. She reaches into the sack.

—Oh boy, he says.

—Hey missus, says Barney. I'm ganna have to come round and show you out if you don't go right now. I'm serious.

Isaac says, —I wouldn't if I were you, Barn.

Ma brings out a hatchet. New. Sharp.

—Here we go, says Isaac. He has been dabbing a napkin in the spilled Scotch and water, now he tilts his head and squeezes the good juices out onto his tongue.

—Yitzchok!

—Ja Ma?

Look at me.

Isaac looks at Barney instead: Barney seems a trifle pale. —What is this? he says.

—It's how my mame deals with drunks, Isaac tells him. Turns them into firewood. I hope you got insurance, Barn.

—Put that thing down, missus, says Barney. For serious now.

Mame is not, it seems, overly interested in what Barney bartender has to say or not to say. The hatchet she has taken out of the burlap sack is a smaller tool than the wood axe that Isaac remembers still so clearly even after, what was it, eighteen, nineteen years? In one part of his mind Mame will always be standing with that thing behind her skirt and talking so coyly to the couchers in the cluttered workshop, telling them it's time to leave and them laughing up at her, trying to send her back to the kitchen for another plate of schmaltz herring or sliced polony. That axe had needed two hands and was half as tall as her; this one has a handle and is only maybe a foot long but the steel blade looks very bright and fine. She has it in her strong right hand, held at the base of the handle, and she is shaking it at him like a protest sign and her soft but strong upper arm is jiggling a little in the shirt sleeve of her dress.

Isaac says, —What you tryna do with that, hey Ma? You'll get yourself arrested. Send me another one there, Barn, a double.

—Let her leave first. Get her out. Or you can go with her.

Isaac sighs. —Mame, Mame. Vos toost du?

Mother, mother, what are you doing? An old question in his life. Then he says, This place isn't your couch, Mame. If you break things they'll take you to jail.

I won't cut what isn't mine.

Cut?

Mame places her left hand on the bar, palm flat and fingers spread wide. Look at me, Isaac.

—Oh jeez, he says. Whatzit now?

Yes indeed he is not seeing things as he does in the night and yes indeed the hatchet still looks sharp as a new knife edge and, indeed yes, she has lifted it higher and is aiming that cutting edge down at her own flesh, her brown wrist with a plump hand affixed, a few freckles on the back, five stocky splayed fingers on the solid wood of the bar underneath.

—Ganna cut it off, Ma?

—The hell's going on here? says Barney.

She says, You think I'm joking, Isaac?

—She's ganna do a Captain Hook, he tells Barney. Chop a doodle doo. I suggest you fetch a bucket with lots of ice, my mate.

Isaac, she says. I won't leave you here. You come home with me.

—Just gimme that thing, Ma. Give it a me and stop performing like a meshugena.

I want you to come home with me. I want this to stop.

Isaac says, —I'm not hurting no one.

Look at me, Isaac, my eyes. This is nothing for me, to bleed. I bleed every day for you.

Studying the bar, Isaac begins to laugh, his head shaking.

You come with me and you promise on your life never to come back here.

He must have been laughing harder than he realizes because his eyes get full of wetness, the grain of the bar blurring. He wipes at them and senses Barney edging towards her, his hands busy under the bar. —Just relax, Barn.

—What's she saying?

—Says she ganna chop off her bladey hand if I don't go with her.

—Then bladey go.

—There's the thing, Barn. I just don't happen to want to.

—Missus, says Barney, just put it down, ay. Stop acting mad.

Isaac looks at his mother and watches with a sick unfolding in his innards as she lifts her chin at him, stretching the scar tissue. He sighs. —Ja, he says. She's not acting, Barn. She's ganna do it. Better get a tourniquet too.

He glances to his left. Along the silent bar the heads look down in a staggered formation that makes him think of dominoes. When he looks back at her she asks him again in Jewish, Are you coming with me?

—The big question, he says.

I give you till five, Mame says. One. Two.

—What is that, counting? says Barney.

—There you go, says Isaac.

—Druy, says Mame.

—What the hell is this shit, man? says Barney.

—Another of the big questions, says Isaac. I got lots more.

—Fier, says Mame.

Isaac looks at the sharp edge of the hatchet; it barely trembles; the scar on her face still stretched. He yawns, lifting his arms. —Oright Ma, he says to the roof. Let's go. You win.

—Fimf! says Mame.

And Isaac feels his guts swoop and jerks around to catch the hatchet flashing at the living meat and bone of her forearm. He screams then, starting to jerk from his stool. But Barney has already lunged, stabbing the truncheon from behind the bar across the hand and the blade hits it, biting deep. He jerks it back and the hatchet, caught, comes with and he snatches it in with his other hand.

Isaac shouts: —Didn't you goddamn hear me Ma? I said I'm going with you!

Mame looks at him, her brown eyes like two dark washed stones glittering against sunlight. That's another thing, she says. How is a person supposed to understand you when you go around mumbling like an old man all day? You've got to start speaking up, Isaac. You've got to start behaving like you're alive.

46.

SHE WON'T LET HIM FLUSH after vomiting, she checks the bowl to note what doesn't stay down. No bread, no milk. She feeds him hard-boiled eggs, some porridge unbuttered and unsalted. Skinless chicken well cooked, plain rice. Marrow bone in broth. He starts to eke on a little weight. She has a new task for him every day. Light manual labour, the kind she says men enjoy, not sweeping or scrubbing but the fixing up of broken things. One instance: an old nail barrel she found in the street that he strips and sands and de-rusts with steel wool; he rubs raw linseed oil into the pine staves till they shine a honey glow, and paints the hoops silver. He works in the yard with his shirt off, using a table made from an old door set on folding trestle legs. After a while he starts to like this simple work of his hands and the feel of the sunlight and air on his skin. Likes the way she brings him tea and looks in on him every hour through the afternoon. At night she puts Epsom salts in a hot bath for him and shaves his face and trims his hair if it's needed. After supper she reads him the newspaper, translating the stories into Jewish with the dictionary on her lap while he lies on his old cot in Rively's old room, the cot hard enough for him to be comfortable on and at least keeping him off the floor, and more often than not he passes into sleep with the steady burble of her reading voice in his ears. He holds a silent gratitude that they don't come into his room anymore when he wakes screaming but leave him instead the space to fall back asleep in his own time. Grateful too that they do not try to wake him early in the morning and make no mention of his sleeping in late; and the empties that sometimes roll around under the cot get periodically cleaned away without comment. He hasn't gone once back to the pub.

In time he begins to feel a strength take root inside himself and then he is ashamed if he thinks back on how he has been. One day he stands in the alleyway, looking along it and is not aware of Mame watching him till he turns. —There used to be that DeSoto.

That couple, she says. With Mrs. Smith. They moved out.

—When?

Mame shrugs. Long time already. Things change.

Now, gradually, there steals into him the urge to go back to work again, stronger day to day. Perhaps Mame can sense this new stage in the vitality germinating within him for she sits him down and places some papers in front of him that she says are very important for him to see. She says that she hopes he doesn't mind but when he was away she went through his things and organized them nicely, including his papers. There is something that she found folded in his jacket pocket that she has always kept. Remember how he left that day without even taking his jacket with him? It was on the back of the kitchen chair. She points to it, the very one.

And the papers, she says, They were in the pocket.

He looks at the first page and sees it is the articles of incorporation with regard to the *business enterprise hereinafter referred to by its trading name as "LION MOTORS PTY. LTD." or "Lion Motors"*, and that changes have been made to the text in pen, initialled by three parties and signed at the bottom of each by same.

Memories. He turns the contract over quickly. The stuff underneath is all ads scissored neatly from the weekend papers and from barbershop magazines like *Radio Fun Time* and *Polisie Nuus* and *He Man Monthly*. Full- or half-page ads, none smaller. Each with a vast photograph of vast Hugo, and his arms, in one, are widespread like some overweight Jesus in a three-piece with silky lining. RADIATORS? IT'S A BLOWOUT! CARBS, SHOCKS, SPARKS? WE GOT "EM" ALL AS "GOOD AS NEW" OR MY NAME'S NOT BLEZNIK!!! There were photos of parts in what looked like a warehouse and salesmen behind a counter. Convenient parking located on De La Ray Street. Three other locations. The company name stops him: Bleznik AutoMetals.

When he looks up Mame is leaning over the table. I spoke with Mr. Rothstein.

Who?

The lawyer.

Isaac's nose twitches; he sits back.

Hope you don't mind.

Isaac says nothing.

He says if it was the same what the firm had to start, the what-you-call-them, assets, then half, more, is yours.

He doesn't look at her.

—Yitzchok?

He stands up. —Don't talk to me about this. I don't want to see this again.

Where you going?

That night he finds a crowded snooker hall in Jeppe that serves only house beer by the pitcher. Two hours later the police arrive to bright blood on the green tables, broken cues, splintered teeth lying where flung billiard balls sit on the vomitory carpet. Isaac is released with a warning and dropped off at emergency where they give him an X-ray and a dozen stitches to close the gash across his knuckles and a package of painkillers. He proposes to one nurse and gets kicked by another for sticking his hand up her skirt.

It's dawn when he comes in through the back door at home, easing the door closed quietly before seeing Gitelle asleep upright in a kitchen chair, waiting for him. He looks at her in the pale blue light through the window: she is sitting with her chair against the counter and her head leaned sideways resting against the bottom of the wall cabinet, her one arm flat on the counter and her other folded over her lap, her eyes closed and mouth slightly open. He stands without moving, watching her for a long time. She is wearing a white nightgown and her plump feet are like small bricks in the slippers beneath its hem. He watches the way her chest lifts so slightly with every inhalation, how her lips blow outward with the opposite. The shallowness of her fluttering life. Under the hair clipped down, her plain unhandsome mutilated face in its heavy stillness seems dense as thick leather, a thing of flesh made for enduring. How much that tough face has had to take from this life of hers and how she was here, now, waiting for him and only him.

He cannot look anymore and turns away. To stop the mewling sounds that come up his throat he jams fingers between his teeth. A part of him wants to rip the stitches off his other hand, to bleed as he should. He grips the door frame to stop that hand moving and he watches her, his fingers aching in the squeezing teeth.

The very least you could do for her. The very least, you traitor scum.

47.

ON THE MORNING that Isaac has his stitches removed he puts on his best khaki trousers and nicely ironed tan shirt plus a good hat and takes a short bus ride up to Vrededorp. This is the headquarters of Bleznik AutoMetals and says so in red letters on a white sign six foot tall. The building takes up a block of its own on De La Ray Street, made of yellow brick and with green sliding doors in front and a big walled yard behind. When Isaac asks the lady with spectacles to see the man himself, he is told Mr. Bleznik is not immediately available. Maybe the manager, a Mr. Teasedale, could be of some assistance?

—That's all right. I'll wait for Bleznik.

—It could be a long time, sir. What is it that's your problem exactly?

—The problem isn't mine, Isaac says. You tell Bleznik that Malan is here. Malan from the Receiver of Revenue's office. Tell him if I don't see him as soon as possible, I'm not the one who'll regret it. You understand?

—Yes sir, certainly.

They show him up carpeted stairs to an office where he stands looking down through barred windows onto the open yard where wrecked automobiles are piled in stacks such as he remembers so well. There is a crane below, farther out a crusher and several parked two-ton trucks. In half an hour there are steps and a voice behind him that seems not to have been changed by the passage of the war years. —Would you like to sit down, Mr. Malan?

Without turning around, Isaac says, —I reckon you the one should be sitting down for this, Mr. Bleznik.

—Ha ha, says the voice. Well let's have a cuppie tea should we? And you can call me–

Isaac has his hat off, facing around. —Hugo. I know.

Hugo is more tanned and fleshier, his stomach and the fat under his chin have grown and his face has a good rich buttery shine to it and his clothes are soft and well cut, fitting his thick body tightly, a dark blue suit and a striped tie, a smooth hat matching the shade of the suit, no hatband.

Of course the face does not cease its grinning but Isaac sees the flicker behind it as if a light is being briefly dimmed behind a curtain; then it shines again even brighter. —Boyki! Holy fuckerolee! Come here man!

He advances with arms spread for a hug into his soft bulk that goes on and on, the flats of his hands thumping Isaac so much that when he speaks his voice vibrates. —Oright, oright, easy. I survived the war, what a you tryna finish me off now?

Hugo pushes him back, hands on his shoulders. Isaac can just see the shape of a chunky gold watch under his left eye, the bright gems marking the dial. —Tiger, you thin as a stick but I tell you what, I'd hate to get a klup from you – your muscles are like bladey rocks man! . . . What the hell you tell them downstairs, Malan from Revenue, you tryna give old Blezzy heart failure man! Cheeky bugger, I should throttle you. Since how long have you been back?

—A few months.

—Months! Why in hell didn't you ring me up straightaway? Isaac smiles.

—Come on, says Bleznik. Let me take you out for the biggest steak you ever had in your life. You need some vleis on your bones, I say.

He starts for the door but Isaac drifts calmly in front of it.
—Couple things I'd like to chat on first, Hugo.

—Ja man, absolutely. Let's go ta lunch and you can fire away.

—Not right away, says Isaac.

—What, you don't believe in free lunches? Ha ha. Don't worry Tiger, it's all on Blezzy.

—That's generous of you, Hugo.

Hugo puts his hand past Isaac, to the doorknob. Isaac catches it in a friendly fashion. —Maybe talk a little business first hey.

Hugo hesitates. Isaac's grip pulses ever so slightly.

—Why not hey? says Hugo.

—Exactly, says Isaac.

Hugo is full of good news: it starts hosing out of him before he's even sat behind the desk. That Isaac has absolutely nothing to worry about even though he knows Isaac must be concerned, nothing to worry about at all.

Isaac doesn't sit. He leans his shoulder on the wall beside the window, says: —Why would I be worried?

—Listen, Hugo says. I look after my friends, ask anyone. You tell me what job you'd like and you got it, hunned percent. Sit. Siddown.

—Job, says Isaac.

—Absolutely, name it. You want to run this yard, it's yours. Hugo Bleznik doesn't forget his friends.

—A steak *and* a job, says Isaac. I think you overdoing it.

—Hey?

Isaac looks out the window. He straightens the fingers of his left hand and rubs the fingernails with the ball of his thumb. —I seen your ad there in the paper. Doing well hey.

—Ja, I am thanks. Didn't come easy lemme tell you. Lot of hard graft went into it.

—Is that a fact?

—You know, Tiger, I'm not sure what it is, but I reckon I am picking up a very slight negative tone off you. Is there summin I said wrong?

—Tiger, says Isaac.

—Hey?

—Still calling me Tiger, Isaac says, coming off the wall.

—Why not, you prefer different?

—I wanna know what happened to lion.

—Lion?

—Lion.

—Ha ha, says Hugo.

Isaac sits on the desk, beside Hugo. Hugo leans back but his blue eyes flick to the telephone. Isaac reaches across and slides it away to the far side.

—Ja, those old Lion Motor days hey, says Hugo. Those were some times, I'll never forget.

—Won't you?

—Well. Too bad we couldn't make a go of it. But you learn from your mistakes hey. You dust yourself off and get back on the trail. You shine up like I always say.

—Perseverance, says Isaac.

—There's it!

Isaac takes a folded paper out of his jacket. —See this. This perseveres.

—Hey?

Isaac unfolds it, holds it out.

Hugo lifts some ivory-frame half-moon reading glasses from his pocket that Isaac never remembers him needing before; he polishes the lenses, slides them on. —Would you look at that. Isn't it the old contract hey? Ja, remember when. Poor old Silas, what he went through. Ja . . . those days. Silas, he still with me, know that? Those were rough times hey boyki. Bones of our arses. But we don't have to worry no more.

—We don't, do we.

Hugo takes off the glasses to lean across and pat Isaac's thigh. —I'm telling you Tiger! Name your job, man. Name your job. I look after my friends.

—Hugo, says Isaac.

—What?

—Hugo.

—What?

—That was my money. I put in fifteen hundred pounds. Solid. Plus another one hundred before, the first time when we started Lion. That is sixteen hundred quid, china.

—Boyki.

—Maybe you changed the name of this firm but it's still the same thing. And majority still belongs to me. You signed your name to that.

Hugo laughs. He creaks back in the seat and laughs for most of half a minute. —Ja Tiger, you got me there. This is ten times better than Malan from the Receiver's office. Ten times. S'good one.

—Is it?

—Ja perfect, you got me beautiful.

—Too bad I'm not charfing.

Hugo takes a hanky out and blows his nose and rubs his mouth with it, his chin, takes his time stuffing it back into his vest pocket. —Tiger, that other firm was dissolved how many years ago now. Get serious. This one's a – what you say – a separate enterprise. Sorry, but this paper you got means sweet blow all. In case you forgetting, you the one who disappeared on me without a word. Left me without a ball to carry. Some partner hey. But who keeps grudges?

Isaac says, —More'n a grand and a half in my hard cash. My labour.

Hugo is already shaking his head. —Really disfortunate, but all that capital went down with the ship when Lion couldn't make it, gluggedy glug. This firm here I started fresh with my own capitalizing which I raised and was no cherry garden I can tell you.

—I spose you got all the papers showing that.

—What papers? More than half a decade ago now, boyki-woyki.

—That's not what a lawyer says.

—Lawyer?

—That's right.

Hugo laughs. —A lawyer now already? Wow. Listen boyki, whoever told you you could go to court over this is paddling up his arsehole. I got plenty lawyers and believe me they can keep this thing arguing for much longer than you got money to pay your guy. Some people would be offended by what you saying but I am telling you don't worry. What are we arguing for? I'm ganna look after you, I'll set you up so beautiful just cos I don't forget those days. And hey, I know you were in the war and all, but let's not make a bad flavour here and hurt my good feeling. No more meshugena talk about Lion Motors ukay? Those was solid good times but Lion is dead and buried years ago.

Isaac nods for a long while, not looking at Hugo. —The war, he says. You talk about the war.

—Ja, well.

—Saw a lot of things.

—Hey? Ja, I spose you did hey.

Isaac is looking down at his feet, one finger tracing the line of the fresh scar on the knuckles. —While you were working here in your nice office. This one place I was in for a while, there they used to make people eat each other. I don't mean that as a whatchacallit, a symbol. I mean they used to tie someone down and leave him and other people was starving, they would cut out their liver and eat it while they was alive.

—Jesus, says Hugo.

—Changes you, says Isaac. You see a thing like that happen.

Makes you think, nobody is ever ganna take a bite out of *me*. You know?

He turns his eyes back on Hugo and Hugo says nothing. —Way I see it, you in the motor game today cos you had all that stock and all those contracts to get you started. You had my sixteen hundred and all my sweat and blood that I put in. Never mind anything else.

Hugo's shaking his head.

—Now you can pay me out what that's worth, that's fine, says Isaac. Or leave it as a half share in this business and bygones be bygones and Monday morning we start running it together. I say we shake on that.

Hugo studies Isaac's hand with sadness filtering into the blue eyes over his grin. His head has not stopped its steady shaking. —Boyki, boyki, he says. I'm sorry you feel this way.

—You sure?

Hugo turns up his palms.

Isaac says, —Oright then. Only one thing left.

—Hey?

—You keep the contract and I'll take an eye off you.

—Hey?

—Like the Torah says. Eye for an eye. I reckon that's fair.

He taps the contract but never drops his fixed stare from Hugo's left eye.

—What? says Hugo, huffing a little bit but failing to take flight into full laughter. You religious now?

Isaac smiles. —That's another thing I seen in the war. Eyeballs ripped out. It's not that hard, really. If they want to stick me in prison for it, that's ukay too. I go happy if I go right, know what I mean? Doesn't matter much to me, after what I been through.

—Ha ha, says Hugo, huffing.

Isaac smiles and waits. His hand drifts to the desktop. There is no invoice spike like that other time at the Reformatory long ago but there is a stapler here and he picks it up without dropping his stare and holds it in his lap.

For a time Hugo shifts in his chair, making the leather creak. Suddenly he points at Isaac's face. —Ahhh nailed you! he says. Nailed you didn't I.

—Absolutely, says Isaac. You got me good.

—Had you going.

—That you did.

—Thought old Blezzy was tryna do the dirty on you, diden you?

—You had me for sure.

—Put it there, my partner.

—All the way, says Isaac, thin-lipped, shaking the soft hand as Hugo rises.

—So good to have you back, says Hugo, his grin perhaps a little shaky and his words lightly panted. So good. Maybe now we go get that steak hey? Not liver – ha ha. Tell you what, all a sudden I could do with a nice Scotch or two. Celebration. The war hero is home.

—I reckon, says Isaac, we should get our new papers signed and squared away first.

Hugo's grin holds.

—Wouldn't you say? says Isaac, and gives off an implacable grin of his own.

48.

IN THE BEGINNING the partnership is split as it was before, with Hugo handling the deal making, the advertising, the office management, and Isaac running the yards (including the one at the Reformatory, a property Hugo had long ago bought) and the staff, which reunites him with Silas Mabuza. But it's Isaac who begins to understand what is happening long before Hugo admits it to himself – Isaac with his nose in the grease and his ears on the streets, his body tuned by the torments of the war into one vibrating nerve of survival. Not that it takes an especial instinct to see what is plain: how the prices on used parts and scrap metal are sinking quickly to more reasonable levels now that factories are turning back to civilian production, now that new models of civilian automobiles – closed for the war effort – are once again flooding the market. What had made Hugo rich will no longer. Yet he continues to spend on promotions and to bank on the market share he has won for his name to carry high sales volumes on a continuous wave into the future. He doesn't see, maybe doesn't want to, that the shortages are over, the world is shining up again and will hold no particular loyalty to Bleznik AutoMetals.

And all the time, too, Isaac is noticing how much new competition is being born every day, for more than a good few returning soldiers have gone into business for themselves, and starting up a garage is a common choice, with few barriers to entry save for the mechanical knowledge that many have gained in the army. Such garages often developed into tow-truck operations and some became dealers in scrap metal and parts. Isaac watches them sprouting everywhere like tough weeds in the city's cracks. But when he tries to get Hugo to listen to him he receives only that familiarly dismissive wave from the back of Hugo's pudgy hand. What does he know, what has he done? It's Hugo who has built Bleznik AutoMetals to its number one position. Isaac says he doesn't care about any number one: the only number that counts is net profit. Hugo tells him to go back to the grease pits where he belongs.

Isaac goes. In these early years he still feels weak, still respectful of Hugo's wartime achievement (NUMBER ONE IN JHB!!!), is still drinking. Steadily, Hugo's contracts for farmland wrecks become meaningless – no longer worth the price of the shipping. And sales continue to fall; yet rather than close locations and lay off staff Hugo spends all the cash he's made in the war to prop them up and begins even to borrow. Number one, number one.

At least there's no more gambling, Isaac thinks. For himself, he goes on working hard every day with his hands, keeping to long hours and few distractions, letting the manual labour of stripping wrecks with the boys in the yard slowly re-energize his haunted spirit. His stomach gradually heals itself too and, though he is still thin and hard as a rail, his mame's good cooking has put meat into the crannies of his face and around his neck so that he does not seem the starkly gaunt figure worthy of a double take that he had been on his return.

In the summer of 1947 there comes a crisis weekend: Isaac has a meeting with the accountant without telling Hugo, then he calls Hugo to join him at the office where they can all face the facts of life together, recorded there in plain and unforgiving ink. After all the shouting is done it is Isaac who prevails, pulling out the papers he made Hugo sign that first day in the Vrededorp office, pointing out the magical number of fifty-one percent allotted to his name.

The next month the company restructures under a name both new and old: Lion Metals. All properties are sold off except for the Vrededorp building. Staff is cut and debt reduced. Remembering his days as a panel beater, Isaac knows the importance of the insurance companies, the ones who used to send all the work to Gold Reef. Now he sees they are the key to locking up a future supply of wrecks to be turned into parts and scrap metal. Yes, there may be a thousand little towing operations in Johannesburg at the moment, but the insurance companies, themselves consolidating, will not for long deal with such a petty multitude. In time one firm must become the largest, one firm must dominate. Isaac knows which it must be, will be. The war has hardened him to function in a world of eater and eaten – the world Avrom Suttner once revealed to him, prepared him for.

It becomes Hugo's job to concentrate on charming insurance men with long lunches and discreet gifts. In the meantime Isaac starts getting aggressive about finding towing jobs to keep up the cash flow. The key here is to be first on the scene at an accident and this they try to achieve by bribing police radio dispatchers to give them a ring. They aren't the only ones pursuing this tactic and after a second driver comes back to the Vrededorp yard with a lump like a golf ball on his head instead of the salvage job, Isaac takes to following his trucks in his car, bringing Silas along. If there is any sort of hassle with another tow truck trying to chup away their business, they both pull balaclavas down over their faces and come out of nowhere fast, Silas with a traditional assegai, a stabbing spear, two feet of razor steel shaped like a diamond, and Isaac with a jack handle. While Isaac interacts with the other crew (vigorously or mildly, depending on their attitudes), Silas darts around with the assegai, opening up at least two of their tires before anyone can realize what is happening.

By the end of that year, Lion Metals has secured several lucrative insurance contracts and they no longer have to chase after towing business and can send their trucks out to collect their wrecks in a civilized manner from either the police impound lot or another tow company's. Hugo's charm has won and is continuing to win the necessary battles. The more insurance work they do the more they receive. They have a relatively smaller business now than before (when Hugo was NUMBER ONE!!!) but it makes a solid profit and its growth is steady. Still, Hugo mopes: no longer is he the star of the half-page ads. Isaac cheers him by offering to sell out some of his share of the business so that Hugo can have majority control.

—Now why would you do a thing like that?

—Only one reason in the world.

49.

A FAINT VARIANT OF The Pain had always been with Gitelle,
only hardly ever severe enough to disrupt her life: just a sense of
pressure in the lower back and under the floating ribs on the
right side, as if some phantom had its knuckles pressed against
her from the inside. Sometimes back spasms would flair up, true,
as they had during that worrying time right before the war, but
who doesn't get back spasms? They always subsided and seemed
unconnected to the feeling. She would later not be able to remember exactly how long the faint pressure had been with her – years,
yes, but how many? – but she would never forget the day that it
mutated. Enlarged.

It had happened after she and Abel had gone to the Alhambra to
watch a special screening of a film that was prohibited most strictly
to those under the age of twenty, presented by Hashomer Hatzair
raising funds for the Yishuv, the Jewish community in Palestine
suffering badly under the twin ills of British occupation and Arab
attacks. But the film had no scenery of the Holy Land, nor was it
concerned with the immediate present. It showed instead scenes
taken by film crews at the liberation of Buchenwald and other slave
labour camps and industrialized liquidation centres, though Gitelle
never saw the others. Buchenwald was enough. There was a
bulldozer sloughing hillocks of naked bodies into a pit, the bony
limbs of men and women entangled, the mouths hanging open in
the skull faces, a yawn of death with eyes rolled back, shaved skulls

lolling on stick necks, shin bones and backbones and the scooping hollows in the pelvic girdles still covered with skin, bodies humped on the bulldozer blade like so many bundles of wet straw. She stumbled out of that dark and flickering chamber of horrors, went home and collapsed. Abel found her writhing on the floor. Till that point, she had continued to send letters to Dusat. Perhaps some relatives lived yet under the Soviets; the stories of mass graves in the forests of der haym could not apply to her own. But the film made her body accept what the mind had long since suspected. Old weak points hurt the most when the body is stressed and that is perhaps why the pressure sites in the back and ribs flared into such an unendurably skewering flame. Dr. Allan came and examined, tapping her kidneys, pressing her belly. The Pain had receded a little and she was left with a script for painkillers and told to drink lots of weak tea. The doctor was certain it, like the back spasms of long ago, was nothing but the shock of what she had seen, but he prescribed a few tests to be sure, a visit to the weekend clinic he kept at Johannesburg General Hospital.

Abel thanked him and telephoned Isaac who rushed home from work. Gitelle was badly upset. It was nothing, they both told her, nothing, like the doctor said. But in truth she could see that neither of them quite believed it.

50.

NOW IT IS LATE FEBRUARY in the year 1948, trace beginnings of the cooling season in the air in high-up Johannesburg where the sky is hazy and the grasses brown and dry. Isaac is walking on the banks of the Emmarentia Dam, a reservoir in the northern suburbs bottling the waters of the Braamfontein Spruit. Ducks bob, fishermen hunker with odd hats in the willow shade of the muddy banks, little bits of bread mashed on their lines to make them visible. —It's quiet here, he says to Maureen Venter.

—Oh absolutely.

Maureen is a short and worried lady with long brown hair and big square glasses, a tweed skirt suit. Newest agent for the Golden Era Realty Corporation, specializing in suburban developments. She takes him in her car to see the next house, five minutes from the dam across the avenue named after ex–Prime Minister Hertzog and into Greenside. There are many elegant art deco–style homes here, most dating from before the war, but the house she brings him to is newly built, a bungalow in the modernist style with a slanted tile roof on a corner lot. It was erected after the neighbours decided to subdivide their immense garden, gifting the plot with many mature trees and flower beds and a fine kikuyu-grass lawn.

Isaac likes the nice high wall enclosing the garden. A little orchard of a sort stands in one corner, peach trees with grey trunks speckled with nuggets of dried sap; across on the other side stand two dark-trunked plum trees with maroon leaves; and in between, against the garden wall, is a pomegranate tree with tough sharp-edged leaves.

Isaac stops on the path to the front door. —I think I'm ganna take it.

Maureen gives her laugh that is not a laugh but a nervous giggle like an involuntary twitching of the lungs. —You haven't even seen the inside, meneer.

—I don't think I have to.

It's the tranquil span of this corner lot that draws him, a quarter acre of open lawn from the carport behind the main gate sweeping around to a fifteen-foot hedge marking the boundary with the next house. Down that way on the far side there is a gap in the brick wall with some steps down to street level to a garden gate, both cute and secure, onto Shaka Road. It all feels safe and green to him, a section of defended countryish land in these tranquil suburbs, so far from the jabber and mire of the inner-city streets. He can see his mame sitting there in the cool of the shade in summertime. The bee noises in the pollen'd air, the quiet wind in the bending leaves. They go inside.

Big rooms have huge windows to flood them with natural light; the master bedroom has its own bathroom and there are two other bedrooms off a passageway opposite another bathroom and a study. The kitchen has two doors and like the one at Buxton Street opens onto a concrete yard but this yard is expansive and has a solid brick hut for the girl, while a tall wooden fence privatizes its connection to the neighbouring property behind. Isaac goes out front again and stands in the garden and sees how there is plenty of room to build an extension between the carport and the house. It could be a kind of private wing. He sees it.

—What are they asking? he says.

—Nine two.

More than double what a basic house would go for. He reaches into his jacket and takes out his chequebook. Miss Venter giggles.

—I'll give ten to make sure. Who should I make it out to?

—We have to go back to the office, she says. There's a lot of things . . .

—Like what?

—Lots of things, Meneer Helger!

—Like what?

—Ach, first approval of the bond, then all the paper for putting in the offer.

—Bond, says Isaac. Listen. I don't take bonds. I give them.

And he smiles at her and begins to laugh.

—What's it, meneer?

—Nothing, nothing hey. It's just someone else once said that before me. I've come a helluva long way for the taste of the same words in my own mouth. So now you tell me who to make this out to, and don't worry about no bonds or papers or nothing else. Don't you worry.

At the end of that month the transaction goes through and work begins under Isaac's directions on the extension. He tells no one about this project, not even Hugo, with whom he now lives, having long ago moved out of Buxton Street to take a room in the shambling monstrosity of a home (neo-Grecian statues in fake marble, furry carpets, rotting ponds) in Northcliff, which Hugo got at a discount since the previous family all had their White throats cut by unknown assailants in an infamously bloody mass slaughter the previous year. (What the hell do I care? was Hugo's line. It's only a few stains).

By April, the work is finished, the extra wing freshly painted. Isaac walks through the bare rooms of his new house, running his hands on the clean white walls of what will be his parents' bedroom. The bathroom is almost as big, with a beautiful ceramic bathtub on claw feet. All their lives they've had tin baths and a bladey outhouse – now let them luxuriate, let them have ease in their autumn years. The oak closet has a full-length mirror on the door and he stands looking at himself. A young man of property, dark suit this day, with hands in the jacket pockets, a good fedora and some orange hair touching the bat wings of his ears, freckles over the fleshy nose. He likes to think these days that in his suits he has a certain wiry resemblance to the popular American singer and movie actor Frank Sinatra, the same doggish thrust around the mouth, a certain brute narrowness to the eyes, but he knows that's wishful: in truth it's only the feeling of confidence from the business and the work behind him that would make him see himself this way. He lights a cigarette and turns away. No more mirrors. And don't you cry, there's nothing to cry about.

The following week the drapes and the carpeting go in, then the furniture, every piece chosen by him. There is a new Bakelite wireless and a refrigerator, an electric stove, an extra-large geyser so they will never run out of hot water. Some antique clocks he knows Tutte will enjoy, including a grandfather clock from Russia.

At work he gets an odd message, the secretary telling him that Miss Venter from the real estate says someone has been asking her questions about him. —About me? What kinda questions?

—She didn't say.

But when he phones her she says it was a misunderstanding, that she just wanted to wish him well with the purchase and make sure everything was going well with it. —It's fine, he says. Perfect.

She giggles a lot before ringing off.

The final touch is a maid for the back room and he interviews a dozen before he finds the right one, a gentle and calm Basotho lady named Gloria, with a church badge on her overalls, whom he thinks just right for Mame and Tutte. She will start work in May, as well as a gardenboy who will visit every Thursday. Meanwhile, he has the lawyer draw up new papers, transferring title to his mother's name. He places these documents on the shining pine table in the living room, with a new silver pen. He wants to show them their house, their new lives, and then have it end with the signing, the beautiful surprise of this gift he has been working all his life to give.

And it is a very fine omen that Mame has been feeling well lately. She will have to go into the hospital for a kind of surgery that has no purpose other than to look inside her, but Dr. Allan says she will be fine and they must believe him. In the meantime Isaac invites them most casually to come and visit him on Sunday; they have not been to where he lives yet, he says, and it's really past time. He will come in the car and he will fetch them for Sunday morning tea and then he will bring them back home afterwards. They both agree, though it takes a little pressuring as Mame has dress work to catch up on.

On the Saturday he begins to feel his nerves. Debates with himself whether to buy the fresh flowers this day or wait till tomorrow, have them be as fresh as possible. He picks up a vase of fine crystal – Lalique it is, making him wince to remember the Mad Queen – and then decides to do the flowers as well. He drives to the new house and arranges the flowers in the crystal vase on the table with the title papers in front of it, proteas exactly like the ones he once bought her the night she threw them in the rubbish, and vivid strelitzias with their long green necks and beaked buds of jungle colours. He puts fresh water in the vase to keep the flowers nourished overnight and then he goes home and has a bad night shot full of sleeplessness and thrashing.

Finally he gets up around half past five and makes coffee on the kitchen stove. He can hear a woman's voice and her silvery laughter, Hugo busy with someone new in the main bedroom. He goes out before the noises get too gruesome and has a cigarette in his bathrobe, looking at the overgrown garden and the mildewed ponds. The sky turns the colour of an eggshell and the security lights are very bright against its pale looming.

Around half past nine, Isaac has a shower, then shaves and dresses in his best suit. He spit-shines his shoes in the hallway. He takes the keys to Hugo's Chev coupe. The sun is bright, the bonnet gleams. He puts the top down, puts on the radio and drives to Doornfontein. Coming down Harrow Road, they start playing the new Frank Sinatra song called bim-bam something and he takes it as another good omen to feel the imprint of that wiry successful American over his own image, the similarity between them in his good suit in a shining convertible.

He parks on Buxton Street, a space halfway down the block. The old lady down there at number forty, the chutusta with the unlikely name of Smith, auntie of Oberholzer's wife, is bent over, watering a pot plant with cats on the stairs. He whistles and gives his biggest wave, his sweetest Sunday morning smile. She stares at him and her small mouth tenses, then she goes inside. There is losers and there is winners, Isaac thinks. Good night Greyshirts, good night. Hardies to you. Your cities are burned, your country is gone, your day is done, and we're still here.

He's whistling that Sinatra tune as he leaves his car. There is an older-model Studebaker parked two spaces ahead with a squat man leaning against it, smoking a cigarette. Something familiar about him to Isaac as he draws up, about the car also. As he looks, slowing, the back door opens and a short hatless man emerges, bald spot flashing as he straightens. Sad dark eyes behind a spaniel nose.

—Holy shit.

—Morning.

—The hell *you* doing here?

Isaac looks up then down the street as if an answer could be read there, but it's only Sunday morning empty.

—I've just been in, had a word with your people.

—Hey?

—You didn't forget about me did you? Forget about our friend?

Isaac stands with his mouth open: nothing comes out. His heart roars blood like an express train and the red mass slams his head, his eyes swell in their sockets, pulses crash both ears.

—You must have known what you did would catch you again, Isaac. What did you think? That we wouldn't know?

Isaac's voice comes out hoarse, the words half coughed. —Know what?

—Let's not play nursery games, Isaac. I was just in with them. He nods towards the house, reaches into a pocket, takes out two sheets of paper and holds them up beside his olive face. Notepad paper lined from folds. Block letters in English on one, Hebrew script the other. Signatures on both. —Showed them these, says Papendropolous.

Isaac feels can-opened, gouged, inverted.

—Did she write this or not? Did she sign? I came here to make perfectly sure.

Isaac finds himself taking a step forward, reaching for the papers. Papendropolous eases back and the man on the car moves in, his chin rolling a little towards his shoulder, hands coming out of his pockets.

Isaac wheezes, his mouth wordless. Papendropolous folds the papers back away, says: —We were never exactly sure. You went off and I tried to contact you, I came back to Vance and we thought then we understood what had happened. But you were gone.

He feels so weak, so dizzy.

—You were gone, Isaac. The chance for that meeting was too. And there wasn't another one.

A near whisper: —What've you done?

Papendropolous shrugs. —I reckon that question's for you my friend.

—What are you doing here now? *Why?*

His nose briefly wrinkles. —Came here to get the truth and to tell the truth. That's my brief. Now I can go home.

Isaac steps sideways and the squat man steps with him, his face right in close. Paused at the car door, Papendropolous turns back to say, —Why do you care, Isaac?

—I don't need lectures. I asked a question.

Papendropolous brushes his lips, as if cleaning them for the words: —It was noticed how well you're doing. Told you before once, there are eyes all over. I know what you're coming here for today. That would have been unjust. Now the record is set.

—He did this?

—Of course. It's his money, not so? Be grateful you don't have to pay it back, with interest. And penalties.

Isaac's heart rams at the ribs like a wild trapped thing, a dangerous anger chokes at him, makes his fingers into claws. The man puts a thick forearm against his chest.

—Well who the bladey hell does *he* think he is hey? Who the fuck is *he* anyway? I don't even know who!

Papendropolous winces a little, standing in the jaws of the car door with one foot on the running board, and rubs a spot behind his ear. —Look. He is not the same man he was when you met him. Everyone has changed. I'm not involved in his affairs anymore. Nobody is.

—What does that mean?

—This's a last matter he's asked me to deal with. I came as a favour. I'm otherwise not associated. I don't live out there anymore. Believe me Isaac, he's only interested in trying to set this old wrong right. In the truth. He wanted to know it, and he asked me to deliver it in the right way, to put it to you where it counts. And that's done now. So goodbye.

—*Fuck you.* He's just a sick bastard and a shit. The lot a you.

—No. He's changed. Everything there's changed.

—A fucken bastard to do this! You all are!

—We make our own beds, says Papendropolous. Good luck Isaac.

51.

HE STANDS IN FRONT of the door for a long time. When he was little he stood this way, with a puppy on a string. He knocks. Nobody comes. He knocks harder without effect. Through the window the front room looks empty of life. He goes to the side, the alleyway.

When he turns the corner his father is coming down towards him. His father in a pair of black trousers with a white shirt, no hat. His limping crippled father moving faster than Isaac has ever seen him, his right hand clawing at the brick wall for balance and his right leg swinging almost straight like some great hip-clutched staff, lurching under him as his left arm flails spastically for balance but not only, the motion also seems a kind of ripping assault on the air and the hairs are wild around the oval of his skull. Isaac stops. Six feet away his father also stops, his hand against the wall, and there is spittle at the corners of his mouth and his eyes are huge in his bony face.

—No, he says in English. No. You have to go.

A strange weak feeling, like smoke into the blood, like nerve strings being cut, a slackness. Isaac asks him in a voice that doesn't belong to him what he's talking about. It feels as if his throat is closing.

—You get avay.

This is his mild father, crippled and pious, gently backbent to daily labours, but now and here he is not the same man. Some demon has invaded and transformed. Some manner of shuddering in the neck and eyes that are red-rimmed and moist as if bitten by smoke.

—Tutte, he says. Daddy, what?

—You don't call me Daddy.

And Isaac's distant fading voice (how dizzy he is, how drained!) says, —Why? Why not, Tutte? What is it?

His father advances, clawing with the hand on the bricks.

Isaac shrinks back, backing away down the alley and with every step the weakness grows and he feels it for what it is, that he is becoming a child again, an eight-year-old, a five-year-old. His father keeps shuffling at him, scratching along the wall like some outraged mancrab of a creature, those eyes all wrong in that shuddering face.

—Neyn Tutte. No Daddy.

—You not my son.

—Please don't say that, Daddy please.

—Go. Don't come again.

—What did he say to you? The lawyer.

Abel lunges with a ferocious speed which Isaac would never have believed possible and the side of Isaac's face bursts with a white crack. He staggers. His father has fallen over. He takes a step to help him up but the old man presses himself up off the alley floor and hops at him again.

She would give her life for you. For you!

Isaac backs away.

Blood money! Thief! Murderer!

Clutching his face, numb and faint, Isaac Helger stumbles away. From the alley, from his father, from Doornfontein.

52.

ACROSS THE HARD PAN of this dry land there scratches a black Humber, a red plume behind; a fat man driving and a thin one beside. *Is it like what it was up there?* No of course: in those white dunes of true desert no thirsting scrub or dirty huddle of mewling sheep could dare to exist, only flies, so far as he could ever tell. *Flies?* Yes they thrive in that parchboned kingdom of their dark lord. We ate them on our bully beef, uncaring, and we killed them with the DDT guns and filled the tin basins like hillocks of piled raisins and burned them with the gasoline and they unfolded their greasy smudges in revenge, the taint of unclean insect death to coat our dreams with mirror eyes, sky towers of humming. *How hot, truly?* Dry air baked like steel plate that radiates from the touch of an oxyacetylene torch flamed bluewhite. Water rations and orders not to drink till direly parched. *Was it unendurable to your wholesome young soul?* It had seemed so but it was paradise in retrospect when later I would but have prayed for the release of the desert. *Is that the nature of blind time?* Of course: all is blind, past comparisons useless to the future. Any life is like the point of a knife slicing into blank time and always bleeding surprises. *Are you satisfied with your weapon?* I'm tired of your questions. Why do you wear a hood? Why does your voice buzz so, why do you sit behind my left shoulder?

Isaac wakes and rubs his face. Hugo looks over. —Oright?

   —Ja, good.

—Just saw a sign said three miles.

Isaac studies the dry land. —Looks all the bladey same to me.

—Looks a bit like it did? Hey? Up there?

Isaac stares at his doughy profile. —Kind of a bladey question is that?

—Why you getting all high horse, it's just a question. Here.

He has an open bottle between his legs; Isaac shakes his head. Now is the time to be only sober and sharp. They have come all this way and here he must not blunt himself with brandy nor with stupid talk.

When they reach the town he finds the one he recalls is gone. All the tin booths of the diamond dealers with their flags are just empty stretches, the canteens and rooming houses, the whores and the corner crowds, all has transmogrified into red dust and been blown off on the flaying wind. Only a few brick buildings stand, and the large one that used to have the sign Orange River Trading Co. on it now looks to be a kind of hotel, from a window of which a man watches down, shirtless and unshaven. They drive through and on.

—Oright gimme a knock, he says.

Bleznik hands him the bottle and he drinks and he wipes his mouth. —I shoulda come by myself, he says.

—Don't insult me, Tiger. Partners are partners.

—Yuh yuh, says Isaac. But there is truth there that his cynicism cannot melt. Hugo has fed and cared for him for two weeks when he might have lain in his dark room and merely died. Hugo who helps him still now, on this, having gotten him what he needs and brought him to where he must be, which has required more than its fair share of guts, this opening up of a channel of meaning for meaningless rage.

A little under two hours falls away and they come to the place where there had been the eucalyptuses in that endless line but now it's as if a cosmic dentist has paid a visit with twisting pliers and the land is bare with only gravel dimples to indicate where the great trunks once rooted. They drive alongside this absence to the old archway; but the arch too is gone. The asphalt road is covered in much sand, a little pitted and warped but otherwise intact. As they pass onto it Isaac tells Hugo to stop and he gets out. In a ditch he fishes up some rusted chain, drawing out a splintered piece of wood still attached, with the letters *LEEU* branded on, start of Leeuklip, Lion's Rock. Hugo has rolled down his window, his hat off. —Everything changes hey boyki. He mops with a hanky at his sweating watermelon of a head. —This place also.

Isaac looks at him and can see in his face the gladness. It doesn't irritate him, reckoning he'd be just as relieved if roles were switched. They rumble on but Isaac makes him slow enough that they do not raise a column of dust from the sandy road. Very carefully he steers over cattle grids rusted and caved. —There's nothing, nothing, he keeps saying. Like an incantation that is saving their lives and maybe their lives are indeed being preserved, though by this very decay rather than with anything his mere voice could ever work. When the land starts to rise, Isaac stops him again and gets out with the binoculars. He goes up ahead of the car, bent over, then belly-crawls to a rock at the top. Distant lies the white house and behind it the hilly ground then in far distance the range of low blunt mountains. He checks the sun then slides the binoculars from their case. A mush of blended colours blooms in the glass; he corrects the focus ring till everything hardens sharp and clear, so close-seeming it's as if he might brush the dusty rocks and the dry grass with his fingertips. He tracks to the left, from his angle he comes first across what had been the garages before. Now he sees only a ruin of boards and broken breezeblocks. He runs into white blur and adjusts again and the house jumps at him so sharp-etched in afternoon sun it seems razor cut from the blurred light behind. He sees the windows are gone and the white paint is peeled where it is not blotched with the tapering serpentine marks of bird lime; the front doorway holds no door.

When he takes down the glasses he goes on watching for a time and almost misses the smoke, faint above the hilly country behind. Pale vapours easing to nothingness in the still air. He watches it for some time.

Cloud shadows roll over the vacant khaki earth like the silent passage of sky whales. Some manner of carnivorous bird angles in blue infinity. He worms his way off the lip and side-shuffles bent over back down to the Humber. —Listen man. I want you to wait there for one hour.

—Hey?

—Just listen. An hour, not less. Then drive on to the house. Park there in front when you get there and just wait.

—What you ganna do?

—I'm going by foot, being careful.

—Why, what's it look like, you see em?

He shakes his head. —Man, it's a ghost house, falling a pieces. Ops me that bag hey.

—I knew it would be. So what you being a paranoid for?

—I'm not any paranoid, I just know survival. Give, ops, let's go.

He takes the sack, Santa Claus for paranoid survivors: The four handguns Hugo was able to get – no rifle or shotgun – with sundry clips and loose ammunition. A Luger and heavy Colt forty-five, a little twenty-two darling of an Astra, a Spanish gun made for the purses of ladies from Parktown, with a pearl handle and an engraved frame. And a Webley ex-service revolver. There are some holsters too, one that clips on a belt, one that goes around an ankle, one with straps for the armpit. There's a bayonet in a sheath, wire cutters, tape, strong fishing line, a knobkerrie for breaking heads of the kind Silas would no doubt approve, solid stinkwood with a heavy globe carved out of the top of the staff.

A balaclava and a tin of black shoe polish, a canvas satchel folded up, a canteen of water.

There seem to be a lot of nine-mil bullets so he loads the Luger first and its spares, holsters the weapon in his armpit. He loads the Webley and straps it to his ankle. He loads the Colt and the twenty-two. The black Colt is too big for the remaining holster so he leaves it and puts the little gun in one jacket pocket and the knife with the fishing line and the wire cutters in the other. Puts the canteen strap over his shoulder and the binoculars on the other one, ignoring the satchel.

Hugo, watching him, says: —Captain America, ready for action aye-aye. Those rock dassies and bundu sheep won't have a bladey chance, I tell you what.

—One hour, says Isaac, rising. And there's more than sheep down there.

—Hey? You see something?

—Just do like I say.

He loops out and marches, bent over on level country, preferring the wrinkles in the earth, the gullies and grasses, or using the little koppies as a screen wherever he can, away from sightlines on the higher ground ahead. He starts to sweat, to blink against it. A man in khaki trousers and a bush jacket, pleated trousers with a broad-brimmed hat, crossing the dusted veld. He comes up on the south side of the house, finds a crag in the land in which to hunker. Oright boychik. He takes off his hat and rubs his hair to let the air in against the wet scalp. Think it right through now, don't go rush like a Stupid. He peers again at it: the roof is in worse shape than he'd seen in the glasses, the thatch pancaked in like a failed soufflé. At this distance he can even make out one encrusted window frame and how bergs of fractured glass still cling inside. Just go around. No. Why not? Cos I don't want to. Then maybe you deserve you getting your arse shot off. Nobody's ganna effing shoot me. Wanna bet, ha. Ja, what I bet is I know exactly where that smoke is coming from. Where he is. And maybe the other ones, the ones you have to worry for.

He hunkers again and takes off his hat. Think it through. See what could happen; try remember what it was before and think what it'll be again.

After a time he takes out the twenty-two and holds it next to the hat and looks at both. Then he fits the little pistol into the sunken crown of the hat and puts the hat back on. Feels strange but it'll do. Let them call you a paranoid maniac after you walk out, fine by me. Can call me Kobus stuffing van der Merwe for all I stuffing care, long as I'm breathing. He looks over the edge and has a drink of water then goes on, the binoculars and canteen knocking together on their straps till he separates them.

The house in its Cape Dutch silhouette throws a block shadow forward away from the angle of the sun, the beautiful clear-scorching light of Africa. A shadow illusion of wholeness that beckons then degenerates, like nearing a woman with long hair from across a bar who looks beautiful and young but reveals herself to be more aged and haggard with every step closer.

Isaac sees the innards of broken walls, beams slanted to the ground. The thing entire as if kneeling in slowed motion back to earth like a headshot elephant. How resentful nature is, fierce in its destructions of anything that would try to rise and assert a shape first made in the mind of man, that would so dare.

He has to duck to enter. Bird wings slap in the overhead tangle of gloom slatted with breaks of sky glare; powder dribbles of thatch crust, splinters and rust everywhere. A steadier cooing as he goes, glints of outraged avian eyes blackly tracking him. The smell is moulder as of wet towels rotten and more faintly of woodsmoke and char. Floorboards all prised away, doors too. A shape scuttles left, rat or sand snake. He stops and tries to fit his memory of the staircase and grand room but feels all turned around in this cavern weirdness of crumbling things. Farther to the back, more light: guano as thick as carpet, a blackened firepit, yellow dried pages of some torn book and scattered green curls of broken bottle glass, ropy dried turds, some tin cans rustsplotched, jagged.

Curiously the rear door is still there, the brasswork long thieved but the door propped without hinges. He hovers there then reaches for the Luger then his hand stops. Don't depend on Nazi iron: the ill luck it might bestow. He bends and takes out the Webley instead. He climbs through a side window with care and goes forward bentover down the sandy semi-grassed slope to where the garages and living quarters for the men had been. Those he remembers in the car with the rifles and the bats at their feet.

It's deader than any doornail, mate. All this playing soldier for nothing but the lizards. Stupid. Maybe. He has that survivor nerve, and it keeps sounding in him like the alarm note of some plucked instrument overtaut.

He pokes his foot in the rubble and looks up. Those wisps of smoke over the near hills are no longer. He puts the revolver back in the ankle holster and marches on.

The light is tending to late afternoon green. Vast spaces of open veld. Distantly some flat-topped trees with leaves dark putrescent green in coloration, and closer in are the thorn bushes the Afrikaners call wait-a-bits for the way they like to hook a thorn in your shirt like some detaining finger urging you to linger. He passes the tall red pillars of anthills harder than any concrete. The flutter of a weaver bird near a nest shaped like a calabash. The male builds it for the female who'll peck it to shreds if it's not up to snuff according to the standards of her taste. A cicada starts to buzz that mind-drilling shrill in a grass thicket shoulder high. He wonders if there are baboons in this country. Strutting friends of the hills with scimitar teeth. But it's not the animals he's armed himself against.

The rhythm of picked steps in the gift of utter silence, motion of breath and rasping soles. It's not as if he has to call up the place in his head to find the way. He goes bodily, drawn. Finds the donga and climbs down to the salt white sand and follows it, along where once water, soft mystery, somehow cleaved this stony earth. Ahead the donga kinks left. He relaxes and his arms swing. When he comes to the turn there's a quick sharp whistle behind and above his left shoulder.

53.

A VOICE SAYS: —Jay man, you got yourself a licence or what?

He knows by the Coloured accent who it is before he starts to turn.

—Slowly slowly, says the voice.

He lifts his arms. —Can I turn round?

—What is it you scheme you are doing here?

Isaac pivots gently. —What licence?

—Trespass licence, meneer, says the man he knows is called Andre but cannot locate on the rock face. Seeing him only when he speaks again: —Big ears. Remember me?

Isaac nods. —Long time.

Andre comes off the ledge from his squatting: a lean hunkered man with splayed knees and a rifle in one hand, stock nestled in the hip, brown trousers and veldskoene and dark denim shirt with sleeves rolled up the forearms. The last time he had a suit and a homburg, now he wears a slouch hat of stained leather and there's grey in the curls that show under it. But the flat yellowed wrinkled face with those Asiatic eyes, the wide high cheekbones that speak of the blood of the Khoi or even San people, is still the very same.

As is the quicksilver motion of his slipping down. Isaac's heart pulses hard. His body now too remembering, how it was that day long ago when Andre stepped out and back and seemed only to touch that knifeman on the neck and how that gentleman fell and snored in the dust, his wrist like a wishbone for Andre's twisting heel.

Andre is lanky, lean of neck and more wrinkled there too, and as he crosses to hands-up Isaac, Isaac sees he's got a kit bag with a strap slung crosswise from the shoulder. He says: —This time is no visiting. Youse going to have to bugger straight off and not come back, hear.

—I hear, says Isaac. How'd you know I was in here? Been tracking me hey?

Andre snorts. —My mate, I diden need no track. You come in like elephants through a glass factory.

The man saying this with his hard eyes on Isaac all the time and his smooth strides bringing him in with the rifle levelled from the hip: a professional of violence, probably his whole life. Ja, but I been through a few things myself. A few little twists and turns that'd make the rest of his hottentot hair turn just as grey to even think of.

He's stopped in front of him, easy, telling Isaac as he once before did to put both his arms out. The same procedures a man will use, the tricks he stays with always if they work.

Isaac's arms rise and Andre keeps the rifle on him and pats with the free hand, draws out the Luger and whistles, tucks it into his belt at the kidney. —The other one, he says. Where that revolver hiding?

—Been watching me also hey?

—What you think? You not the only one with binocs.

—Why you still here man? Watching out for the man?

—There's no man, he's long gone.

—Then why'd you say visiting? Before.

He makes a clicking noise, his left hand busy at the back of Isaac's belt then starts to pat the thighs, to move down, squatting. —Don't be too clever for your own self, he says. Alls you do is turn round jump in that black car and you and your friend go back to Joburg. There's nothing here. Only me. And what is this?

His hand on the ankle holster. Isaac says: —*Don't you fucken move.*

Andre looks slowly up at him, calm. Isaac holding the twenty-two on his eye, hammer back. The rifle barrel is off to Isaac's left. —You quick, ja, says Isaac. But I wouldn't I was you. Put it down flat and turn round slow.

Andre appears to be studying not the little Astra barrel maybe four inches from his face but Isaac's eyes behind them. Reading them. Maybe there comes a little touch of hurt into his own.

—I wouldn't, says Isaac.

—Where'd that little stukkie come out from?

—My hat.

Chh: a guttural snort of a laugh. —His *hat*. I like that one. Man pulls rabbits.

—Put it down now.

—That what you been doing hey. Magician? All these years?

—I changed, says Isaac. You know I'll do it like nothing. Out here.

—Nothing changes. Was what you always was.

—Hu-uh.

—You just never knew it yet.

—Kuk. Things change. Lookit this place. You.

—Same underneath, says Andre. Just more true now.

—Put it fucken down, Andre. I'm serious. I'm asking last time for your sake.

—Man I wasn't ganna hurt you.

—I won't either. Why would I? I'm not here for you.

—I'm the only one there is here.

—Andre.

He nods very slowly, sets the rifle down to his right and Isaac steps on it without looking and Andre smiles faintly, sadly, and turns. Isaac tells him to lie flat, arms out, and he goes on his belly and stretches. Such long arms: a sallow bloodbone crucifix of a man on the white sand.

Isaac takes back the Luger, then gets his knife out and cuts the kit bag strap and takes it off him and throws it to one side.

—You didn't have to do that man. That's a good bag that.

—I'll get you nother one. You just don't bladey move one tick.

He steps away with the rifle – a Mauser, bolt-action – on the side where he can't be seen and tells him again not to move then puts down the rifle and makes a loop of slip knot on one short length of fishing line and picks up the rifle and comes back and makes him cross his wrists behind him. He snares the wrists and pulls it tight, keeps the rifle's muzzle pressed between the shoulder blades and, one-handed, winds more snare around the loop then tucks it between the wrists and underneath and draws it out, stepping back with the short length of it.

—You don't have to do all this, jong. You got the guns.

Isaac tells him get up.

—Careful you don't skiet me on accident.

—Don't you worry, says Isaac. I was in the war.

—Oh you were hey, says Andre. Well now that make me feel so much better.

A last turn and they go on and the dead end is there a few hundred feet ahead, the circling amphitheatre of natural stone as he remembers it, with one section of sheet rock to the left, pinkish in the light, rising at a shallow angle to a crest above, thin bands of differing colours undulating through its ancient grain. Isaac stops, jerking on the snare line to draw Andre up. He whispers: —Better tell me what's over the hump.

Andre's shoulders move. —There's nothing.

—Think I'm a Stupid?

There's a bark and Isaac looks up to see an orange short-haired dog with long legs and good muscles, a Rhodesian Ridgeback or a Boerboel, looks like. It barks again: hoarse echoing.

Isaac swears. —Nothing hey?

Andre whistles three quick times. The dog runs in, its tail beating like a lady's fan and tongue flopping. —Ah voetsak! hisses Isaac. Piss off, you chuzesa hoont.

—What you call him now?

—What he is. A chuzesa hoont.

—What that mean?

—Means he's a dirty thing like a pig and I might have to put him down in a minute.

—Ach don't do that man. That's only Chester. Just lemme sort him.

Isaac considers then steps back, tells Andre to kneel. Chester comes to him to receive soothing noises and awkward caresses from a lowered cheek and chin. Isaac steps on the snare line, slings the rifle, takes out more fishing line, starts to knot a new snare. Andre glances back. —You'll hurt him with that.

—Don't look at me.

—No man just leave him, he's harmless.

—And we get over there with him barking more and I get my head shot right off, congratulations.

—Nobody ganna shoot you man.

—Then who's there?

—Nobody.

Isaac has finished the loop of the snare. He clicks his tongue and the dog looks at him.

—Ach don't man, please.

—Like you just leave your dog behind. Like he wouldn't come with if there was nobody down there. Here Chester. Here.

—Ja-no, uhkay, there is, says Andre. There's someone.

Isaac waits.

— . . . Is only him. I promise you. Jus him.

—What's he doing there?

—You'll see. Things is different.

—If you here, the others must be also.

Andre shakes his head. —The olden days is long finished, if you haven't noticed.

—But not for you.

—Mister, he says. Alls I do is keeps a lookout for him now. He doesn't want nothing to do with anyone anymore, nothing.

—So what you looking out for?

—Maybe there's troublemakers don't like to forget, think they still like to want to find him. I deals with them if they do come.

—Like me, says Isaac, and grins to himself like a bared skull. He watches the ridge, considering. —Just him and you hey.

—Ja, that's the truth. Man, what you doing here? Are you here to hurt him? What for, man? He—

Isaac brings the rifle up. —Oright, stand. Let's go.

They go on again with Isaac holding the snare line behind the bound wrists, keeping the rifle on his spine. As they climb Chester runs circles, barking a little. There's cover to the left at the top – a column of reddish rock rising like a tree trunk – that Isaac steers him into. When they're in the shade of it, Isaac waits, watching the dog settle out on the ridge, sitting flat-arsed to cock its head to a scratching back paw behind the ear.

Isaac eases one eye past the edge of the rock. More of the thin upright rocks stand like trees sparse on the gradient. At the base of the crater there squats the great yellow mass with the vertical crack running three-quarters of its length to make uneven halves that once reminded him of mating elephants though he knows that it's called Lion's Rock. Before when he was brought here the land was bare of all but grit and wind and orange sunlight; but now built against this rock of the lion is an abode of sorts, a small hut made of corrugated metal with a slanted roof jabbing up the snub of a jagged-rimmed chimney. From the left of this hut there stretches a slant of canvas to tent poles, mosquito netting hangs to the ground and enclosed in it Isaac can see the backs of children sitting in two rows on the ground. He watches and makes out the legs of an adult near the front. He looks past the tent to where there is a windmill up on the higher ground of the far slope. A pipe runs to a tin-walled reservoir sunk at the base. A little farther along is a Ford truck.

He turns to Andre. —There's kids there.

—Ja.

—You said just him. What else you lie about?

—Ach no man, those just some pickaninnies he teaching.

—Teaching?

—To read and that. Sums.

—Where they come from?

—Ach, they country kids. They around. Maybe some children from the herders he used to have. They come for lessons.

—What happens to all those head a cattle he had?

—They olden days those.

He watches them, outside the tent now, the man touching the heads of the Black children, bending to them, picking them up, throwing some of them high to giggle and sink back to his catching hands. The man with short pants and a cap of white hair and white hair on his face too now, his body much thinner. The children cross to the reservoir and drop their clothes and splash in the water. When they leave they go up over the far side as the man enters the shack. In time the chimney begins to sweat smoke; spheres of faint white that climb unfurling, that pass to nothing in drowning blue.

The three of them move down to the hut. A bound prisoner of mixed blood pressed forward by the barrel of a White man's gun and a circling flop-tongued hound bred for the hunting of lions: African tableau. Freed of all laws but those of veld and thorn and claw. None to exact judgment save the vulture's savage eye.

When they reach the hut Isaac puts the barrel of the Mauser over Andre's shoulder and raps with it on the sheet metal door then steps back with the rifle levelled.

Andre shouts: —He got a gun here, Av!

Isaac swears, swings the barrel into Andre's head. Then raises his own voice. —Come out, Avrom! It's Isaac Helger!

A silence.

Then his voice: —Andre, Andre, are you okay?

—He's ukay, Isaac says. He got a big bladey mouth, s'all. You come out now.

Chester won't stop barking.

—Andre, says the voice. Let me hear him if he's okay. Andre!

—Ja, I'm not hurt, Av, he says. He got me tied on the hands.

Av? Isaac thinks. How strange this familiarity rings in a servant's mouth.

—You get out here now, Isaac says. I wanna talk to you. Come out hands up. Come out or your boy's ganna get it.

—Don't! Leave him, leave him! comes the shout back, immediate. I'm coming.

—Well do it then.

Chester will not let cease his echoing barks. A sound like a chisel on the base of Isaac's skull. The door opens and the barking stops. Chester runs to the man who steps out.

54.

AVROM SUTTNER IN THE DOORWAY with short cargo pants and work shirt and beard of white curls to hide the pockmarks on the bulldog cheeks. A belly no longer. Dark-ringed eyes deep sunk and watchful; they hardly flicker to the gun but do linger on Andre where he is held.

Isaac says: —I come to see you, *cousin.*

—What for?

—I think you know well what for.

He says to Andre. —Are you hurt?

—Get over there, says Isaac.

He is at first unsure what to do with Andre and considers hog-tying him with the fishing line but tying a man that way can injure him badly so he settles for locking his hands to the coal stove. This is a stove of thick black cast iron set about in the middle of the hut. Seems Avrom was just getting a fire going, twigs thrown over old coals which must have been from the earlier fire, casting the smoke that Isaac had watched climb past the hawks.

He looks around the tight space: there's a sink with razors on the rim and a mattress bed, shirts on hangers from a string wired across the room, a table and some chairs, kerosene lanterns. Isaac studies it all for a while. The way he locks Andre is to use a padlock he takes from the door. He makes Andre sit before the stove and makes Avrom tie off the snare line. After he checks it's solid he puts the lock through a gap in the stove's cast iron front and through the snare line binding the wrists. The stove is bolted to a concrete base and will go nowhere. All during the last part of this procedure Avrom had to kneel with his head against the wall; now Isaac takes him outside, into the brightness. Isaac closes the door and closes the hasp then bends a teaspoon through the eye to keep it shut. He makes Avrom walk well out in front of the rifle. Avrom mumbling in his beard.

—What's that you saying?

—That's for God only to know.

—Ja, you better pray, Isaac says. I bladey would if I were you.

He walks him down out of earshot of the hut, Chester padding alongside. One seriously stupid dog so far as Isaac can tell, who cannot sense a friend apart from a stranger with a gun. When they reach the reservoir he stops and Avrom turns, stands there looking at him with no expression in his eyes. Isaac says, —How you living out here? Food and that.

—We don't need much, Avrom says.

We, says Isaac in Jewish.

—We shoot buck. There's gemsbok, impala. Kudu. And Andre goes to town once a month.

—I went through your house. What was a house.

—That doesn't matter to me anymore.

Thinking of Hugo Bleznik Isaac says, —What doesn't matter that you lost it all? What, was it the races? Cards?

Avrom shakes his head, his face screwing sideways to show disgust. —I never gambled. And I never lost. I gave. I understood.

Isaac slants his head. —What the hell you talking now?

—I got rid of that life, says Avrom. Voz too heavy to carry, so I put it down one day. We live simple here, alone. The world can have its wars, its madness. We stay out of it. Try to do good every day and to thank God.

Then he speaks a line of Hebrew that Isaac misses. —Hey?

—From Torah, says Avrom. Don't you know it? The only way to cancel old bad is with new good.

Isaac snorts. —That why you teaching these pickaninnies?

—I try to do good, Isaac.

—Ja such good. Like send your lawyer shark to Joburg just to take a rip out of my mame and my life. For what? What *good* was that hey?

Avrom says: —She deserved to know. At least. And you too.

—What does that mean?

He shrugs. —I got rid all my things. They weigh too much. And things on my mind also.

—Got rid of. That's horseshit. You still got plenty.

—Neyn. Almost all I gave away. I don't want. We don't need it.

—*We* again, says Isaac. Funny, I saw clothes for two in there, two razor blades. But only one bed. Where does your boy sleep?

—Andre's not anyone's boy.

—You live out here with no women. The two of you.

—With no one, says Avrom.

—Summin not right, says Isaac. And you talking religious to me? That's chutzpah. Meanwhile you plot to mess up my life but good. I think you sick in the head, man.

There's no evil here, says Avrom in Jewish. I made my peace with God and He understands me. And I never did anything to you.

Isaac feels his face tighten. He lifts the rifle. —Never did nothing to me! You liar! You sent that Papenopo-prick to my mother just to tell her I took that money, just to give me a shtoch. From spite! What else! Something I did nine years ago when I was just a kid, just trying to survive. You even told me to! *Eat or get eaten* you said. All that lion jazz. Here by this rock. You the one who even gave me her money in my hand! Now you send your Greek to her after everything. Just to tell her what I did. You don't even know what you've done you bladey bastard! What I been through! When I was just ready to give her the house. You sick, man. You a sick sick bastard. What you have done to her. And our family.

Avrom lifts a hand to his beard and the stocky fingers probe in there, at the pockmarks beneath the springy grey. The shouting and the rifle do not seem to have bothered him; he moves his jaw sideways, sawing one way then the other, a thinking gesture, apparently. Then, still in Jewish:

What did you think? That the truth would never come out? You ask me why. Because new truth cancels old lies and I felt it was time. There's been too many lies around Gitelle for too long. But you're the one who should ask yourself the question why. After Gitelle left I couldn't sleep or eat. She started something in my mind. I saw I was wrong. That lion. Listen, we don't have to worry about lions in this country. It's money that eats you up here, not lions. I chased it all my life. There's a lot I have to be sorry for. Maybe I deserve you coming back on me, for what I put in your head.

—Man if you cared so much you could've sent more money for them afterwards.

Avrom is shaking his head. It was too late. By the time we found out what had happened, the war had spread. And the truth is I didn't want to lose more then, for nothing. I thought: I gave, I tried, it was enough. But don't try and paint over the truth. Their blood is on your hands, Isaac. No one else.

Isaac has a raw pang: he could cry. —I did what I had to do! Like you taught me!

It's better that she has the truth. She needed to have the truth.

—Truth. *You* the fucken liar. You not even my cousin! I don't even know what you are!

The mouth in the beard crimps, pressing blood from the lips so that they pale. Why do you say that?

—Because there's no Hershel. Never was. You and Mame both bullshitted me to my face. You not even family. Just some big macher she asked for a favour. So you got no business at all telling them things now. Getting your nose in my real family. You nothing to us.

He's shaking his head again. Look, you've got it all mixed upside down here, Isaac. I–

—Shuttup, Isaac says. You killed her.

His hand drops from his beard, his chin dangles and he stares with naked wide-open eyes.

—No, she's not dead yet but she is dying and you are what done it to her. Instead of the house I was going to give her you give her news like that. She'll never talk to me again. My father neither. But I found out how sick she is through my sister, from stuffing Palestine all the way it had to come. How they found a cancer in Mame, a big one. They can't do nothing and she's ganna die. And she won't even see me cos she thinks I killed her sisters. That's what you've done.

—Didn't *you*?

—Stuff you. I didn't kill nobody. You gave her this shock.

—Hashem knows the truth, Yitzchok.

—Don't God me. Since when are you going around Godding all a sudden? I see right through you man. You not my blood, you just some scum I don't even know.

—Yitzchok–

—I'm here to settle with you, Avrom Suttner.

Avrom watches him. —What does that mean?

—Get in the water.

Isaac, better listen to me.

He lifts the rifle. —Close your mouth. I won't tell you twice. Get your arse in that water.

55.

WHEN AVROM IS IN THE RESERVOIR, he clutches the side to keep his head above water, the reservoir sunken so that Isaac stands over him. Chester the clueless hound wanders near with a fanning tail. Isaac kicks dust at him and he moves off. He looks down at Avrom, sees a wet man shivering in bloodwarm water, a man trying to keep the fear out of his eyes. He fires into the water beside him. Avrom twitches, the surface bulges and slaps over the rim. The shot is numbingly loud and the sound zigzags high-pitched off the rock walls. Behind him Chester begins to bark and there's another sound, a raw shout from inside the hut then a wild banging that becomes steadier.

Stop, Avrom says to Isaac. Stop. Stop.

He has one hand up, the palm aimed at the barrel as if it could shield him from an eight-millimetre bullet.

—Please, he says.

Isaac works the bolt, aims at the chest. —Go under, he says.

—Ah vos?

—Under.

Avrom takes a breath and submerges. Isaac puts the rifle down. Behind him in the hut the banging accelerates; Isaac glances back. The dog is frozen halfway between hut and rifle, one paw lifted, one ear bowed, its nose switching sides.

Isaac rolls his sleeves and watches the form through the ripples. Time keeps passing. When Avrom starts to rise, he jams his hands through the water and grips the white hair and holds him. Avrom fights at once. Isaac holds him with all the strength of his hands and arms toughened by years of manual labour, with the leverage the height gives him. Avrom pulls hard on the side but Isaac keeps twisting his neck over and down. After half a minute he lets Avrom's face break into air and gasp maybe a tenth of a breath before shoving him under again. One of Avrom's hands claws at Isaac's face and he looks away to protect his eyes and the fingernails scratch his neck.

This time he holds him till he can feel his strength oozing away. He lifts the face and Avrom heaves in air and starts to cough, Isaac's fingers still bunched in his white dark-rooted hair. —Don't, says Avrom. Don't please.

—Who are you? How'd you know my mother?

Not like this.

The words spark in Isaac, fire off a movement of red anger, and he forces him under again as if performing some demonic baptism, holds him till he feels him slackening, then lifts again. —What's a matter? he says. You don't want to live, you had enough, you want to die? Hey? What you saying? Hey? *Cousin.*

—You cruel, says Avrom, coughing.

—No, Isaac says. The world is. When he starts to push him down this time, he tells him: —Better hope there's someone ganna say Kaddish for you.

It's this invocation of the death prayer that seems to hit him hardest: Isaac sees it light up his eyes with a spurt of new terror. He fights hard again, locking his neck, clamped hands hauling on the lip of the reservoir, his feet kicking at the side. Isaac twists and slowly forces him down.

At the last, when his mouth is half under, he shouts: —Okay! I'm not. Cousin. I tell you! I—

Isaac presses him under. Holds him stiffly there. One more good dunk to be sure. One more good measure of payback then let him up and let's have the real truth that you say you love so much. *Been too many lies around Gitelle for too long*. My arse. It's you who's the liar. These thoughts lend new rage to his tough hands. Avrom tries to buck up in waves but it doesn't help him. Water churns. From behind, the banging sounds like steel on steel now and Isaac looks around to see the dog at the hut, sniffing at the bottom of the door.

When he turns back and lets go, Avrom fails to rise; instead the body slumps at once, slips away from him like a sodden blanket and curls up on the bottom. He curses and jumps in. Fool must have opened his mouth and sucked in a breath of water, for the body is waterlogged, heavy and awkward to lift. It takes long panicked moments of bobbing and jamming and thrusting off his tiptoes to get the man's mass up over the tin edge. Then he climbs out and scrambles around and drags him down onto the warm stone ground where the sand coats his side. Isaac puts him on his belly and thumps his back. Water flows out of his mouth. He turns him back over and presses the chest. Avrom spasms, his legs kicking. He gasps. Isaac sits him up and he retches watery vomit down his front. Behind them the banging from the hut changes to a sudden crash. Chester is barking and moving between the hut and Isaac. Isaac looks at the hut's sheet metal door and there's another crash and the door bulges. He curses and picks up the rifle. The door bulges again, then again. The next time the hasp snaps off and Andre comes out headfirst, tumbling hard, a slab of black iron attached to his rear like some demented tail, sliding and thumping musically on the earth behind. Bright red flash of much blood there.

Isaac runs at him with the rifle.

56.

IN THE HUT Avrom wraps canvas strips around the lacerations on Andre's wrists. Behind them the coal stove is twisted on its base of concrete, its front end torn or kicked completely off, ashen coals scattered. From his seat at the table Isaac watches the tenderness in the way that Avrom winds the soft clean fabric, his left hand bracing Andre's forearm with a touch so gentle it seems more apt for crystal stems or frozen petals.

Isaac says, —When I go, I go. Credit for a debit and books closed. We even.

—Just go, says Avrom. Leave us alone. His voice is hoarse from the retching, his face bloodless, the lips twitching.

—You not ganna try follow me after? Find me?

Avrom falls back into Jewish as if the effort of the other language is too much for his state: We're not leaving this place. It's you who's done the wrong.

—You could send your people.

There's no more my people. Can't you see that?

Isaac switches languages also, drawing closer. If you want me to go, better spill your guts. Don't push me to do more evil here today.

Avrom says nothing: his attention to Andre's wounds absolute. When he is finished, he helps Andre to lie down on the mattress and nods his head and Isaac follows him out, still cradling the rifle. On his way Isaac takes two cigarettes from a pack on the table, and a box of Lion matches. There's a crate near the front door and Avrom sits. Chester comes to him and puts his chin on the thigh. Avrom strokes the dog's skull with both hands. Isaac tucks one cigarette behind his ear, lights the other, putting one foot up on the corner of the crate. Avrom speaks without facing him, speaking downward as if to the dog. Tell me what you think you know about your mother.

I know what happened to her when she was young, if that's what you mean.

Do you?

The seventeenth of April.

Avrom looks at him, nods. What exactly?

Isaac shrugs, tells him what is engraved in him from the words of Blumenthal. How there were fires in Dusat. Easter time. A young woman named Hanna Seft with blond hair like a goy went to the cathedral on the hill, found out a pogrom was coming and gave the Jews time to run or hide, all except for the Felder brothers.

Avrom nods.

My mother I found out was called The Saint before. So religious. Afterwards, she never went to shul again. She never has. Because of what happened to her, which made the veil for years, till she could find a doctor here to help.

Avrom nods again. The story of the great heroine Hanna Seft. How she saved the Jews of Dusat.

Why'd you say it like that?

You never said what happened exactly. What accident with Gitelle.

Isaac draws on the cigarette, his eyes slitting. He picks a tobacco fleck off the edge of his lip. She told me she fell off a cart, trying to get away that day.

You believe her?

—Just tell me what you fuckun know already.

Avrom nods, presses the dog's head, nods again, and starts to tell Isaac of how it was his mother Gitelle Helger who was in truth the one who told Hanna Seft about the pogrom coming on April the seventeenth. Who told Hanna to pretend she had sneaked into the church to hear of it, as a cover story. Yes, it was Gitelle The Saint who truly gave the alarm. Gitelle The Saint who happened to know of it because her sister, Rochel-Dor, was told by a certain young gentleman, Antanas Kavaliauskas, who happened to be a Lithuanian and a goy, a carpenter by trade. He had met Rochel-Dor Moskevitch when she was riding her bicycle in the woods and came across him framing a new cottage by himself. She had stopped to watch him work and he'd given her a piece of cheese, and that was the start of it. A simple piece of cheese that Rochel-Dor had hesitated to taste, knowing it might not be kosher. Afterwards, they began to meet in the woods all the time. No one would have known of it if she hadn't become pregnant.

—Pregnant! says Isaac. What complete kuk you sprouting. By a goy, come on!

It's the truth. Listen.

He goes on, telling how Rochel-Dor was almost ready to hang herself but she confided in her sister Gitelle instead and Gitelle was the one who decided to help her, help them both in secret. She knew an old Tatar woman and she took Rochel-Dor there. Ruta is a kind of flowering Lithuanian weed, with pretty yellow flowers that hold a poison that can kill a baby in the womb. Gitelle took her sister to the old Tatar and for three days she drank ruta tea and put ruta poultices in herself. Her problem was ended but Gitelle's began: she could hardly live with the sin she had participated in committing, the ending of a life, even though there had been no other choice in that time and place. She became even more pious, penitential, spending all of her spare time in rocking prayer at the synagogue on Maskevitcher Gass. Months later Antanas Kavaliauskas warned Rochel-Dor about the planned pogrom and Gitelle enlisted Hanna Seft to spread the warning to

everyone else. In her heart Gitelle felt the pogrom was a punishment
for the abortion, for her sister's sin with Antanas. She decided to
stay behind, in the synagogue.

—Wait now. You mean you saying she didn't try run away on
no cart?

That's right. She went to the shul.

—Why would she?

She wasn't trying to hide in there. She was going to protect
God's house with her prayers. Like a penance she gave to herself,
Saint Gitelle. And that was how the gang who broke in found her,
praying in there. They were searching for Jewish gold. Believed
Jews have gold in vaults under their temples. She was facing
Jerusalem. Her eyes were closed . . .

Isaac yanks his foot from the crate. Kicks at a stone, walks
off a few paces, finds he has bitten the filter in half. He spits the
cigarette away, puts his knuckle in between the teeth instead.

Avrom: Should I go on?

How do you know this? How could you?

I know. It's the truth. Do you want the truth?

Isaac nods without fully turning. Tasting a little knuckle
blood.

Avrom starts telling how after they had found that there was no
gold the gang took it out on her. Defiled her for hours. When they
were finished they debated killing her so she could never testify to
their crime. But then they thought, being powerfully drunk and
illiterate themselves, that . . . cutting out her tongue would do fine . . .

Avrom pauses. You sure you want to know it all?

Isaac grunts just once, a harsh sound, from deep in his chest;
the dog's tail twitches and its eyes roll to watch him but its head
doesn't move from between Avrom's kneading hands.

They had knives but they needed a pair of pliers which could
not be found. Someone had some fish hooks and they gave those
a try. They didn't get her tongue properly but ended up ripping

the side of her mouth open so that her teeth and gums were exposed, she was shedding so much blood they got scared and left her, they thought to die. She survived by cauterizing her own wound with a copper menorah made redhot in the fire they'd started. Before passing out, she put the flames out with a rug, saving the building.

Isaac crushes the heel of his palm to one eye then the other. How do you know this?

Avrom's hands stroking the dog's soft face and Chester still looking up at Isaac, only now with hooded eyes that seem about to close in their contentment. Isaac lights the second cigarette. How?

Because I've been told it all. Wait. You'll see.

Now he tells of how when Gitelle's face had healed there was a permanent gash in it through which saliva sprayed whenever she spoke, her moving teeth visible there in the jaw's working. She wore the veil and slushed her words and she could never bring herself to return to the sight of her torment. Who knows what she felt towards God then? Whether she continued to pray to Him in her heart or had lost all of her faith? Though (Avrom says) I think not, because of what happened next.

Two months after the rape she had to admit, finally, that what had happened to Rochel-Dor was happening to her. This time she was the confider of the dread secret. The old Tatar woman was where she'd always been; they made plans. But every time the day came near, Gitelle weakened. This must have been the kernel of faith still, fear of The Holy One and the Law. Or maybe having been brutalized to the edge of her existence she revered life even more strongly. Is it right to snuff an infant like some candle flame only because it's been conceived in pain? It was not the tiny one's fault. Innocence should be protected. So Rochel-Dor helped Gitelle conceal her pregnancy until it could be concealed no longer and then she helped her invent a reason to travel to Vilna that the rest of the family would not find suspicious. They went together and Gitelle had the child and they were able to find a childless Jewish couple to take that baby from them and raise it as their own.

Do you know, says Avrom, we're really talking about a child herself.

You can't know all this, says Isaac. How could you know?

She was fifteen or sixteen, no more.

Isaac drops the cigarette, heelgrinds it. —Bladey liar.

No, it's all true. I *know* it is.

Isaac watches him, his body so tense the whole of it trembles.

Avrom sighs. He turns on the crate, looks at Isaac squarely for the first time since he started talking. The couple took the child to Skopishok, where they came from. Later the husband died and it was the mother who raised the child. Her name was Suttner.

Suttner.

Yes, your mother never had a brother called Hershel, you're right, that's a fairy tale. She made it up as an excuse for that trip when you drove her here, something believable for you, that would seem to make sense. She came inside first that day. While you waited outside she asked me to pretend with her.

But why?

To hide the truth.

I don't understand.

Isaac, I know the real story because the story is mine.

Yours?

You don't see?

Isaac stares, narrow-eyed, unbreathing.

It's me, says Avrom. I'm the child that Gitelle had and gave away. She isn't my auntie and we are not cousins. Gitelle is my mother, just like she's yours. We're brothers, Isaac. Brothers.

57.

WALKING BACK OVER ROUGH GROUND through the fading light toward the ruin of the farmhouse, other truths come to Isaac, as if these won this day have not been enough. Truths within the truth. What Avrom Suttner, secret child, secret half brother, has not recognized even in himself, especially in himself. He thinks he is at peace in his self-humbled life, he thinks that he served the truth by telling Gitelle about what Isaac did with the money meant for her sisters, but he is not serving truth, no, he is serving the loathing like acid that he will not admit is at his core. He's a child of rape: seared, branded. Product of most gruesome tortures, conceived not from holy love but satanic defilement. And then Gitelle gave him away like the shameful object he is. Now for him to destroy her with this news, and not only her but Isaac too – the legitimate son, the heir to her open love that she dared to bring to see him, even to rub his face in – must be to tap a well of deep satisfaction, to close off a circle of revenge. Avrom has been hitting out at the world for all his life and now he is withdrawing from it, but they are both movements in hatred, a kind of bitter warfare, whether he can admit it or not.

In the end, before he left, Isaac had tried hard to get him to come with, to make a visit to Joburg in order to look upon Gitelle's ailing suffering face at least once more before she passed. To speak to some measure of final peace between them. (And more: what Isaac had not said was that he could use his halfbrother as a means to intercede with Gitelle now, to get her to see him and forgive *him*, to change her iron mind, though he doubted that this or anything would work.)

Avrom had refused.

Isaac thinks: He tells himself this is his holy place, where he does nothing but good. What shit. It's just another way of spitting at the world, that's all. I see it now. What shit. I know exactly what he is.

58.

SHE LIVED THEN AS ALWAYS in the same little brick cottage in rows of such cottages. Beit Street, corner Buxton, Doornfontein, an Afrikaans word meaning *fountain of thorns*. A neighbourhood of Jews where the pale dust from mine dumps off the northern breeze settled on their lives, their arriving and their leaving, their praying, their teaching, their trading, their loving and hating and dying.

They had cut her open and peered inside and closed her up and sent her home with tablets of morphine. She lay in the cool bedroom with the drapes pulled when she felt bad and when she was better she would get up to go to her sewing room or into Abel's workshop to greet the customers. Or she would pick up her carrying bag and walk out into the white glare of Beit Street to do the marketing she always had, the meat from Goldenberg's, the eggs from Shapiro, the milk and flour and vegetables from Samson unless the Indian was having a special on.

Sometimes she would ready herself to go out and by the time she reached the bedroom door she wasn't feeling well again and had to lie down. Other times she might make it outside, walking with her hair combed nicely and still moist, her dress clean and bright, hanging on her thinned frame, her once strong hand now bony and dry as desiccated fruit curled around the handles of her carrying bag. She would feel how good the fresh air was on her face and how good the heat of the sun, and how fine its vivid light looked on the faces of the people and the buildings. She could smell the petrol of the cars and hear the chinging of the bicycle bells. Then the smell of the fish on ice from Sidelovitz the fishmonger as she passed, and then the feel of the rough grain of the carrots and the pumpkins, growing things of the earth, still with the red sand clinging to their crannies, from the grocery stand two doors farther down. Those times, feeling as well as she ever had, she would smile at people who greeted her. They were always more friendly to her than was natural and instead of *How are you?* they asked her *How are you feeling these days Mrs. Helger?* and she would tell them fine, I'm fine. And they would touch her, sometimes, and tell her she was going to be all right. And when she went on she could sense the fear in their looking after her, in their low talking. She knew too that some avoided her, ran from her. She had become more than just a human being; she was also a kind of living symbol for what the world can do to you without excuse or warning, an object of dread contemplation.

But those times out in the street, walking without pain, she would know that she really was all right and of course was going to continue to be all right and how stupid it was of people to even have to think to wish her otherwise. The idea of dying then was as remote and ridiculous as some rumour about someone else. The illness somehow had nothing to do with her, it was as if all of those medical ordeals, those visits in doctors' offices and hospital wards, had happened to another person and she had watched *that* woman go through it with bored detachment, it didn't mean *her*, the real Gitelle, of course not. Not the strong unpained healing woman walking in the now through the colours and motions of her home street as she always had. Even if they think they are right, I am the expert of me and they are wrong. Look at everything I have been through in this life and survived and I am still here. Still a young woman!

But then The Pain would come and all would change. If she was on the street when she started to feel it she would have to turn around and hurry home; but sometimes on the way home she would get better again and turn back for the shops. Sometimes the badness would reappear, and once more she'd turn for home. It could go on like that, back and forth switching her directions, five or six or seven times. Such was the sadistic way of this cowardly sideways disease, creeping, scuttling, named rightly after a crab with its method of rushing out of a hole to ambush, with awful pinching claws. Or else Gitelle might think of a cat and how it played with a captive bird. Allowing her the illusion of hopping to freedom before pouncing; chewing a limb and letting her go once more.

Because when The Pain hit fully it was so brutal and so large she could scarcely believe such a depth of hurt possible. A pain that throbbed barbed and electric, stinging and bruising at the same time, a pain through every part of her, even into the jelly of her very eyeballs, and twisting alive in the capsules of every joint and sawing like a demented madman with a blunt saw at every sinew and artery and corpuscle so that even with the morphine tablets given her still she cried out, the tears squeezed from her crumpled face as if she was a child again, her pride gone.

At those times there was no question of death bypassing her – she was being torn out of her life in its jaws, shaken and pierced without mercy. At such times she had more than once whispered to Abel to give her a lethal dose, to end it. But he would not, because once the pain had eased she would be up again, soon making the old jokes with the customers in the workshop, asking how they were, how their children were doing.

But all this time – pain or no pain – she would not relent in her refusal to see Isaac. All her life Isaac had been a part of her, the best part, the part that shone out into a better future, and she would never have believed that any force on earth could have succeeded in amputating him from her, at least not without also destroying her. Yet she had done this very thing to herself and, more than that, though she dearly wanted to undo it and make things as they were before, she found it impossible. It wasn't that she had to dwell on her sisters or put their memories together with the pictures in her mind of what must have happened to them in order to drum up outrage and anguish; wasn't that she felt cindering anger against Isaac, not at all. It was more basic, almost physical: she simply could not see him. A part of her would not allow her even to try. Maybe she couldn't begin to face what he was. Maybe because facing what he had done to her would force her into facing what she had done to herself, since she knew she was responsible for making him into the man that he was – and that he had done it in his own way *for her*. He was the fruit that she had borne and now that she had found out that the fruit was full of poison she did not wish to bite it or even look at it ever again. What did it say about her? She would never know because she would not admit him back into her life.

So she went on not seeing her son and feeling well and strong sometimes and feeling agony and imminent death at others and only a little time passed before all of it came to a quick end.

Gitelle died on a Tuesday, in the afternoon. She had taken some radishes and a boiled egg for her lunch and was on her way back to the sewing room when she'd felt the stirring of the illness and gone to the bedroom instead and taken some of her tablets and lain down on the bed. The curtains were drawn and it was dim but still she put a cloth over her eyes so that she might have complete darkness. It was twenty minutes to three. From the workshop she could hear the faint sounds of Abel mending broken time, the whirr of his lathe not unlike her own sewing machine's. She expected the doorbell to jingle and wondered who might come in next, Mrs. Cooper or that Berkowitz she had never liked. These thoughts she knew were distractions because the deeper part of her was bracing herself for an attack of The Pain. The waiting for The Pain and the fear of its return were in some ways even more exhausting than the attack itself. Behind her closed eyelids under the cloth she began to pray, and this time she used a line from a prayer that she had not thought of in years, yet it floated into her mind now like a snatch of a song she could not stop replaying. She heard again how the men at the synagogue in Dusat used to sing it, almost baying it to the heavens. *Kudosh, kudosh, kudosh. Adonai Tsevaot.* Holy holy holy is the Lord of Hosts. Quite suddenly she felt herself begin to die. She knew it was happening now. She was grateful that there was no pain. She wondered if she would try to cry out so that Abel could come to her but she didn't think she would be able to and she lay still and memories rose through her like a silvered rush of bubbles ascending through dark waters. She saw the face of her father Zalman, the pious butcher with his sad black eyes. She saw herself again on the cart with little Rively and Isaac leaving Dusat for the train station at Obeliai and how Isaac wanted to stand up on the luggage and she kept having to turn around and make him sit down. She saw Branka the Shabbos maid in the kitchen chopping onions to throw into the stewpot on the pripachik and all of her sisters at the long table with their father at the head. She saw Dvora combing her long straight hair the colour of autumn leaves and Orli's gulping laugh, her head going backwards. And she saw Abel coming up the path that day to see her when the sky was as blue as fresh paint and deeper than any ocean with a cold wind off the lake going into the green pines and making them hiss and creak, Abel limping but resolute, refusing to use a stick, and she was standing at the window next to the front door in her good dress with a bow, her hands touching her veil, and watching him come to see her and wondering in herself if he was really the man for her, studying him so carefully as if a vital clue might appear. And then the memories of what had happened to her that seventeenth day of April also burbled up through her, and she saw herself and felt an immense pang of pity, a deep piteous sadness as the hands tore at her, as her blood poured out.

But then she was realizing that she was apart from all of these memories and they seemed no longer real, and in place of what she thought was the mass and solidity of her self came only a feeling of emptiness and space. The memories were more and more distant. They were no longer bubbles in dark waters but tiny particles of dust in a vastness of space. It was as if there was nothing inside of her that was real, only this empty space through which the dust of a few sensations was quickly drifting, fading, while the space kept growing more and more vast, the fading dust more tiny and distant. She had nothing solid in her, nothing to endure or hold on to, she was dispersing, dispersing. There was a prick of panic then and she spoke to herself. I don't understand, she said. No one told me. She wanted to throw off the cloth on her eyes but she couldn't. Then she had the strange powerful feeling that a baby was on her breast, healthy and warm. My Yitzchok, she thought. And she knew that she had to see him, Isaac. Had to forgive him, nothing was more important, how could she have forgotten, why had she not seen him and told him this, why? When forgiveness was the one solid act that could have endured.

She exerted herself mightily.

Slowly her head lifted, her shoulders.

She said, I have to live long enough to see Isaac once more.

Her hand shifted a little towards the cloth then she felt heavy and fell back, back, and died, her head twisting and her mouth lolling wide open so that when Abel came later to look in on her the first thing he saw in the dim light of that curtained room was that angled gape so rigid-looking and frightful that it stabbed him with horror through his heart, the face of his wife twisted towards one of the bedposts so that he knew she was gone even before he'd crossed to her with three of his limping steps.

59.

OF COURSE IT HAD BEEN IMPOSSIBLE for Rively to see her mother before she died as all during the month of May there was war in the Holy Land; the British had withdrawn and Arab armies moved in fast to eliminate the state of Israel in its cradle. Rively was evacuated with her two children, Shulamit and Ezra, from her kibbutz, Kfar Etzion, but Yankel stayed on. The kibbutz was overrun by the Arab Legion, using armoured cars and artillery. A hundred Jewish fighters put down their weapons and surrendered; the Arabs machine-gunned them, used grenades to finish off survivors. Wounded, Yankel Bernstein crawled into a culvert. He watched the legs of the soldiers passing not two feet from his sweating face. At nightfall he escaped. It was another week before he found his way back to Rively and she was able to try to get to South Africa.

Though Jews bury their dead quickly, Abel delayed the funeral to give her the time to fly down. She found him mourning alone, still refusing to see Isaac in honour of his late wife's wishes. She told him unless Isaac came to the funeral she would not herself attend. So Abel relented and Rively told Isaac to come.

It was a sweet and pleasant Johannesburg day, bright and cool. The sycamore trees shed their whirling seeds to the fresh wind and Abel came early with Rively for some private prayers at the West Park Cemetery near Northcliff in the northern suburbs, towards whose peaceful spaces Gitelle had always craved. He had dressed in a black suit and fitted a big cupping black yarmulke under his hat. When the car with Rively came he picked up a pocket watch, a beautiful gold instrument on which he had engraved Gitelle's name, and the time on it was set to seventeen minutes past four, to the moment when he had looked in on her and found this most vital of women transformed into a corpse. The first thing he'd done was to gently roll her head back to the centre, then he'd lifted it so that her jaw closed and he'd puffed the pillow and settled the head higher to keep it that way.

Now Rively parked at the cemetery and they walked up to the graveside on a path through the white headstones, a slight incline that Rively wanted to help him with, but he pushed her arm off and stabbed his walking stick and limped firmly all the way up on his own. The grave was dug: beside it stood a wide mound of red soil with three long-handled shovels stuck in it like flagpoles. In the near distance, the workers – Blacks in blue overalls with woollen caps – were sitting under oak trees, quietly talking and smoking.

Abel looked into the grave, the open rectangle rimmed by grass and a frame of steel tubes with winches at the corners. He saw the soil was muddy and waterlogged at the very bottom and he had a terrible feeling in his body of how it would be for her down there in the cold wet clay, the blackness covering her bones, the worms gnawing through the wood to find her rotting flesh. He imagined himself being in the coffin, thought that if he had been given the choice he would have switched places with her; she had loved life more than he, she had suffered more also, let her have the years ahead.

Abel took out a small siddur, a daily prayer book, and holding it with both hands against his sternum, he began to rock and to recite the mourner's Kaddish. He prayed as he always did, concentrating on each word as if it were the smallest broken cog in a tiny wristwatch. As he sometimes did, he felt what he thought of as the voice of God underneath his own, a divine whisper, an intimation of formless harmony that opened a prickling down the back of his neck. He prayed to God to grant mercy on Gitelle's soul and to give him strength to endure the grief for this day, also to help him to make sholem – peace – between himself and his son.

When he was finished, they walked back to the cemetery building where the bodies were kept before burial.

Isaac was waiting for them there, pacing at the foot of the stairs. He was wearing a dark double-breasted suit, one hand in his trouser pocket under the jacket flap, the other ferrying a cigarette to and from his lips. His head was down as he paced and his hat brim hid his eyes, but Abel knew at once it was him by the quick jerky way of the walking, by the wild flash of orange hair against the tops of the wide ears and down the back of his neck. My son.

Rively's arm was touching his own and he felt it tense but inside he felt only a kind of relief, a letting go; his only thought was of how insane it would be to turn away from his own son, especially now. He went quickly to Isaac who heard him and spun – surprised at them coming from the other side, away from the cars – looking up now with his sharp quick eyes, his pale freckled face open and vulnerable, waiting. Without breaking his limping stride Abel clasped him close then kissed him on the lips and the cheek and squeezed him again. He felt Isaac begin to cry and it broke open something within his own chest and he too began to sob. They clung that way for a long while, until he felt Rively's soft hand on his back, heard her voice whispering, saying this was how it should be, yes, a family together. How Mame would have wanted it. Truly.

The funeral was not a large one, but there were more there than Abel had anticipated. Many old Dusaters. He was surprised to see how many of the old couchers had showed up, like Taysh and Shmulkin and Leitener, the same men whom she had once chased out into the street with an axe, bless her. Some of them were amongst the few who shed open tears. How strange the world is, you never know what people really are inside. The men took turns as pallbearers all the way to the grave. At the graveside, prayers were spoken. The coffin with Gitelle's corpse had been placed on straps held by the winch frame; after the prayers the winches were released and the coffin sank. Abel limped up and bent over the pit. From his pocket he took out the gold watch, let it dangle the length of its fine chain, and the light was bright and glinting on the golden links. Bending over his good leg, he lowered the watch towards the coffin. Isaac came forward quickly and held him so he wouldn't overbalance. He dropped the watch the last few feet and it fell on the coffin with a solid knock. Gold returning to the element from which it had been dug, just as all flesh had once risen from the selfsame clay. When Abel straightened up he said to the faces in Jewish, All her life, the wife of a watchmaker, she never had one herself. That was our Gitelle. Now I leave her with this one so when she rises again, she won't be late for Messiah in Jerusalem.

Then he grasped the long handle of a shovel, turned it over and threw a load of red soil onto the box; it made a rasping hollow sound, burying the bright watch and most of the chain. He dug into the soil and threw on another shovelful, then another. Isaac stepped in and took another shovel and they both went on for a time, digging and covering, then Hugo Bleznik, wheezing, took up the third shovel and added more dirt. After a time others lined up and they passed the shovels so that most of the men there had a chance to help with the burial, burying and burying until the job was done.

60.

IT WAS DURING THE SEVEN DAYS of sitting shiva at the house on Buxton Street, when they would hold prayers every evening and Rively would make sandwiches and tea for those who came to give their respects, that Isaac first began to talk to Abel about coming to live with him at the house he'd bought in Greenside.

He said he had almost sold the house after what had happened, but in the end had decided he was going to keep it. He had built on a private extra wing that would suit Abel perfectly. Abel said he couldn't see how he could leave his workshop. Isaac said he shouldn't, he should keep Buxton Street as a business address and Isaac would make sure he had a car and a driver to bring him to work and take him home every weekday.

Abel said he would miss the Lions Shul. Isaac said there was a new shul in Emmarentia that he could walk to on Shabbos. By the end of the shiva Rively had joined in on Isaac's side. Tutte, she said, what do you want to live here alone as a stone for? You two should stay together. You're the only two Helgers left.

Abel said he would think about it. Two months later, when Isaac came to see him at the workshop, he agreed to go, but only if Isaac would let him pay rent for his separate room. —I will keep it my independence, he said, showing off the English word.

—Ja, Daddy. Of course.

The following week Silas Mabuza came with a Chev truck plus three workers and loaded up Abel's few possessions. A separate car

took Abel north and west. First along Seimert Road where the
Lions Shul still held his heart, then across the city on Smit Street
and Empire Road and then to Barry Hertzog Avenue. That took
them up in a great sweep to the suburb of jacaranda trees and art
deco houses with high walls.

The new house was on the corner of Shaka and Clovelly, it had
brick walls and a black gate of wrought iron, the house was hidden
behind its garden and its carport. The room that Isaac had built and
prepared for him had blue carpets in the latest style and a bay
window looking out onto the garden. They set his bed in the corner
opposite the mirrored closet and the bathroom door; the walls had
been hung with numerous clocks, making Abel smile to regard.

From the door of his room he looked out across the dining
room with its large teak table to a sideboard with a framed mirror
above. Everything was clean and new and spacious: the most
immaculate and serene dwelling of his life.

By late afternoon the unpacking was finished and Abel went to
the kitchen to make himself a cup of tea. The maid was there,
peeling potatoes and tenderizing kosher lamb chops for supper that
night. He said hello and asked her name; she answered Gloria, had
a shy and nurturing smile. She wanted to make the tea for him but
he shook his head. He made his tea Russian-style in a glass with
a blob of jam. Sadly, he couldn't find real tea with a strainer, had to
use a few of the modern tea bags instead; three of them still left him
with a weak brew. He noticed Gloria watching with her smile and
interested eyes. —This tea, he said. No good! Not like Russian!

She made a pantomime of burning her hand and offered him
a mug with a handle. Abel shook his head, picked up the steaming
glass by the rim and took it into the garden.

Across the broad lawn were two trees in front of the garden wall
with dark trunks and dark maroon leaves. A brick patio lay before
them with garden furniture made of rigid wire painted white, with
green cushions tied on by ribbons. He sat and murmured the blessing

then sipped his tea. Though the air was cool, blobs of sunlight through the trees kept his body warm and he dozed a little and had a gentle dreamlet in which Gitelle was calling him. When he woke he meditated on the fact that she could have spent her last weeks here instead of in Doornfontein; if it had not been for the cutting off of Isaac, this would have been home, she would have lived the dream she had for so long held. But the dream had included her sisters, their families, and without them, what was it, really? Without love and people what are mere things? But he was to blame as much as her or Isaac. Ashamed now of how he had lost his temper with Isaac. Of how he had not tried to talk her into changing her mind, though that would have been like trying to bend stone. He smiled to himself, remembering that, the force of that vital will of hers.

It was growing darker and in the streets outside a woman's voice started singing for people to come out and buy her green mielies, green *miel-ies*. Abel was still sitting under the trees when Isaac came home from work, crossing the lawn in his work shirt, denims and steel-toed boots. —You settled in nice, Da?

—Vunderful, Abel said.

—We having lamb for supper. I told the girl you like lamb hey.

—Ich veys, he said. I know. I spoke with her already, Gloria. She seems a nice woman.

Isaac nodded, looked around. —Nice out here hey.

—Very nice, said Abel. I hed a shnooze. But the Jewish phrase was more musical, so he said it too: —Chupped a dremel.

I snatched a little dream.

They went in, Abel feeling as they crossed the lawn how Isaac was walking slowly so as not to outpace his walking-stick limp, which irritated him mildly. Inside Abel sat in the lounge beside the new eight-valve radio, tall as a man's waist, while Isaac went to wash and change. When he came back, fresh and wet-haired, he called Gloria. —Bring us two whisky sodas please won't you.

—No, no, Abel said.

—Ja Da, you'll have one. Must. A l'chaim to your first day here.

—Oykay. Yes.

When the drinks came, Isaac looked at Gloria and said, —Did the police come again?

She shook her head.

He said, —Don't worry. I'm ganna talk to you about it.

She nodded, her round dark face under her doek giving that motherly smile again, then went back to the kitchen.

Abel said, —Voz iz mit der police?

Isaac told him how Gloria's husband had been staying over a few nights every week but a neighbour had reported them and the police had raided the backyard while Isaac was out. He'd avoided arrest only by jumping over the wall in his underpants. They'd sent Alsatian dogs after him.

They can do that? Just come in?

Isaac shrugged. —Look who's in charge now.

Abel knew he meant the new government. The elections at the end of May had brought the Nationalist Afrikaners control of the country; lots of these men were former Greyshirts. Men who'd prayed for Hitler's victory, open Nazis. Lots had sat in jail during the war for treason, put there by Smuts who was now out of power.

Abel said, You think it will be bad for us?

—Naw, I reckon not. Reckon they need every White vote they can get. They don't have to inspect our pricks to see if we been clipped or not.

Abel wagged his finger at his son, laughing but shaking his head.

—Ahh what the hell, said Isaac. Enough worry. Here's mazel tov to you hey Da. Your new place.

They clinked glasses. —Oon mazel tov af dier mein zoon.

And good wishes on you too my son.

They drank and listened to the news, then Isaac turned it off.

He said, Tutte, there's something I never told you. I went to see
Avrom Suttner. Not so long ago.

Abel said, Did you?

He told me a lot of things.

Abel nodded.

Isaac said, Do you know–

I know, I know, Abel said quickly.

About everything?

Of course.

Isaac scratched his nose. He told me . . . he's my brother.

Then looked up, almost guiltily; but Abel only nodded. Yes.

I tried to get him to visit Mame. But.

I know.

You know that I tried?

I know that he wouldn't have come.

Isaac sipped his drink and shook his head again. —Aw it's
some life hey Da, isn't it?

Abel smiled at him. Worrying is not for the young.

Isaac smiled back. —I'm going out after supper. A date like.

—Vos iz?

—A date. It's taking out a girl. To bioscope. A nice one I met
at a dance last week.

Good, good, Abel told him. Maybe it's a wife you have found.

Isaac laughed. —Ja, sure.

You never know.

Tutte, I'm in no rush.

Why not? Have some children for this big house.

—One day, ja, for sure. One day.

Abel raised his glass and drank the last of the whisky. The
taste was sweet and smoky and the liquor warmed his belly.

Isaac said, —Another sundowner, Da?

—Ah vos?

—What they call these.

The drink?

—Ja, if you having one at the end of the day.

—How do you say?

—Sundowner.

—Zundoonyer?

—Ja. Cos you have it like when the sun goes down hey. Ven der zoon gayn arunter.

—Uh huh. Abel turned to look through the lace, the windows facing the garden. The light was changing out there, turning redyellow and bright orange, like a spillage of molten gold. —Yes, I see.

Isaac called Gloria but she didn't come. He got up and went into the kitchen. After a moment Abel got up and followed after, wanting to tell him to make it a weak whisky, that first one was already touching his head. The kitchen was empty and he heard voices outside. He went to the window and looked out, saw his son talking with Gloria in the backyard, nodding as she spoke. Then Abel heard him say, —Next time if the police come you put him inside the house.

Gloria shook her head. —No, no, he can't.

—You put him inside, tell him go into the spare room. Don't tell anyone and no one will be able to touch him, they can't come into my house, I won't let them, you understand me?

—You can get for troubles, seh, said Gloria.

—Lemme worry about that, ukay. And I told you a hundred times, I'm not sir, I'm Isaac. So if they come again you have a key now, you have my permission you hide him in that damn spare room till they go. Oright?

Gloria covered her mouth and nose with her hands.

—It's ukay, he said. He patted her shoulder. It's ukay. Here. This for you and your husband. Isaac dipped into his pocket and brought out his wallet. Abel watched him count out notes. Again Gloria shook her head.

—Take it, it's ukay. Take.

She looked at the money and then she took it and held it against her and her lips bent inward over her teeth. She looked away and started to cry. Isaac touched her shoulder again. —Hey please now, it's not a big deal hey. It's not a big deal.

Abel went back into the lounge and stood by the window. He heard Isaac making drinks in the kitchen and turned when he emerged, a glass in each hand. —Ready?

Abel nodded, accepted his drink, faced back to the setting sun.

Isaac said, —Should we do it proper hey Da? Go outside and have a look?

Abel smiled.

Outside on the far side of the lawn the maroon trees were already lit by flames that were not flames: burning but unharmed, life frozen in a blaze. Abel knew this miracle would turn to cold and black with astonishing speed; but tomorrow it would be back again.

—Cheers, Da, l'chaim.

—L'chaim.

As he lifted his glass, Isaac touched his wrist and said in Jewish, This is your place now Tutte. It belongs to us, the Helgers, like Mame always wanted. Forever.

It's a beautiful place, Abel said.

I know it's not Parktown, said Isaac. Not yet.

Don't speak foolish, said Abel. I couldn't have dreamed better. You've done it.

Isaac seemed to tremble, his voice a rough whisper. —Thank you, Da.

From inside came Gloria's call and, faintly, the smell of good roasting spring lamb with gravy and potatoes. The two men had one final look around the sun-gilded garden, over the burning trees, then they touched glasses and drank and turned to go back inside.

Rively: *An Epilogue*

SHE IMAGINED THE WOMAN as wizened, tiny, rough-hewn. But her bulk and her eyes were soft. Her apartment was full of growing things. They sat at the window table with dates and coffee, an open pack of Nadiv cigarettes and a plastic lighter. On the woman's side was a file they both kept ignoring. They spoke Hebrew but slanted off into Yiddish, now and then reaching for more haimisher feelings. Of course she cried; the woman – Mrs. Sonya Ponnis – did not. They talked about their children, the times; they were circling the unseeable, what had brought her here on the long train ride from her kibbutz in the south, then a jolting Egged bus up the sloping roads of this bay city squatting on its blunt mountain.

Ten years old, I remember him, the shochet Zalman Moskevitch.

My grandfather. But not me you don't remember.

You and your mother left in what again?

It was three of us, 1924.

I was ten years old. So many children in my mind.

—Uni m'vinuh, Rively said. I understand.

I *don't*, said Mrs. Ponnis. But she wasn't talking about any lapses in her memory, Rively felt; she meant it all. So they came to a deep silence and Rively was suddenly afraid to push her words out into it, like a child at the edge of a great cold ocean. She made a small noise, the equivalent of a prodding toe.

What happened to us – you've heard before. Same old horror story. The only difference is this village was yours. Ours. Your face belonged there, we have the same look. We can sing the same songs, remember the same smells. Same love in our hearts. Broken hearts.

I want to know, said Rively.

To know? It's gone.

But exactly what happened.

Of course, said Mrs. Ponnis. She turned brisk, mashed a cigarette in a saucer. Began to talk about June 1941, more than twenty years ago now, but still fresh as yesterday morning in her mind. How in Kovno the local boys pulled random Jews off the street into the infamous Lietukis Garage – did Rively know this? – and beat them to death with tire irons; how a crowd formed to clap and cheer, women holding up children for a better view.

Mrs. Ponnis opened the file and slid across some prints of photographs. Rively saw bodies sprawled, pooled blood. A tall blond youth posed with a metal bar, satisfaction in his face. Mrs. Ponnis said someone there started playing an accordion and the crowd sang the national anthem. I'm showing you this so you can see the feeling in the country from the beginning, the fever that boiled in our neighbours for our blood. The German conquest was just an excuse for them, they didn't need orders. To them every Jew was a Communist deserving execution. And long before the special death squad with all of its Lithuanian volunteers and their little arm bands even got to Dusat, our neighbours had already forced us out of our houses, herded us into the barns under the bridge. You remember the bridge?

Rively bit her wrist.

We had to work in the fields for them, like animals. My father got sick. My mother told me run away. There was nowhere to go. I ran into the woods at night. I was lucky. Spoke good Russian. An Orthodox Christian family in a fishing village near us took me in and hid me as one of their own, and that's how I survived.

Rively nodded, waiting for the rest.

Mrs. Ponnis slid another photograph across.

—Zeh hoo?

That is the creature, yes. Jäger.

It was a black-and-white of a man in SS uniform, moustache, cropped hair in a side part with shaved sides.

He's been living in Germany all this time, working on a farm. Under his own name. They finally arrested him just a while ago, March 1959 it was. For war crimes. He killed himself before the trial. A coward as well as a murderer of little children, of women and unarmed men.

Rively stared. She said, The man in charge of finishing off the Jews of Dusat.

He had so many happy helpers. You know, his right hand was an officer called Hamann.

No!

Yes.

God, said Rively. *Hamann*: it was an evil name in the Torah, the name of a villain in the book of Esther who had sought to wipe out the Jews of Persia in ancient times, a reviled name the congregation drowned out with jeers when it was read aloud on Purim. She felt a seam of cold flowing through her, opened by this glimpse of a hidden structure beneath all things, webs of mystic connection.

I'm going to show you something you need to be ready for.

That's why I came.

Do you read German?

Enough to understand, from Yiddish.

The Soviets found this in the archives. It's genuine. They held on to it till now for their own reasons. They call it the Jäger Report.

Now Mrs. Ponnis slid across some pages in a neat stack. The top one read:

The Commander of the Security Police and the SD

Einsatzkommando 3   Kauen, December 1, 1941

| SECRET REICH MATTER! | 5 copies

                                                    4th copy

Complete tabulation of executions carried out in the
Einsatzkommando 3 zone up to December 1, 1941

Take-over of the security police tasks in Lithuania by
Einsatzkommando 3 on July 2, 1941

(Einsatzkommando 3 took over the Vilnius area on August 9, 1941
and the Schaulen area on October 2, 1941. Up to this time,
Einsatzkommando 9 handled Vilnius and Einsatzkommando 2
handled Schaulen.)

Executions carried out by Lithuanian partisans on my instructions
and under my command:

July 4,41   – Kauen – Fort VII – 416 Jews, 47 Jewesses   463
July 6,41   – Kauen – Fort VII – Jews   2 514

Following deployment of a raiding commando under the leadership
of SS First Lieutenant Hamann and 8 to 10 reliable men from
Einsatzkommando 3, the following operations were carried out in
collaboration with Lithuanian partisans:

July 7,41   Mariampole   Jews   32
July 8,41   "   14 " and 5 Comm. functionaries 19
July 8,41   Girkalinei   Comm. functionaries   6
July 9,41   Wendziogala   32 Jews, 2 Jewesses,
                              1 fem. Lithuanian, 2 Lith. Comm.,
                              1 Russ. Commumist   38

July 9,41	Kauen — Fort-VII	21 Jews, 3 Jewesses	24
July 14,41	Mariampole	21 " , 1 Russ.,	
		9 Lith. Comm.	31
July 17,41	Babtei	8 Comm. functionaries	
		(of which 6 Jews)	8
July 18,41	Mariampole	39 Jews, 14 Jewesses	53
July 19,41	Kauen — Fort VII	17 " , 2 " , 4 Lith. Comm.,	
		2 fem. Comm. Lithuanian,	
		1 Germ. Comm.	26
July 21,41	Panevezys	59 Jews, 11 Jewesses,	
		1 fem. Lithuanian,	
		1 Pole, 22 Lith. Comm.,	
		9 Russ. Comm.	103
July 22,41	"	1 Jew	1
July 23,41	Kedainiai	83 Jews, 12 Jewesses,	
		14 Russ. Comm., 15 Lith. Comm.,	
		1 Russ. O-Politruk	125
July 25,41	Mariampole	90 Jews, 13 Jewesses	103
July 28,41	Panevezys	234 " , 15 " , 19 Russ. Comm.,	
		20 Lith. Comm.	288
	Carry-forward		3 834

There were another five sheets of this stuff under this first one, the same lists, the ballooning total. Almost all of the victims were categorized as Jews, Jewesses or Jewish Children.

The final total on the sixth page was this: 137, 346.

She read it again, sounding the number to herself in carefully separated units. Then came three more pages with conclusions, over the signature of SS Standartenführer Jäger.

I can state today that the goal of solving the Jewish
problem for Lithuania has been achieved by Einsatzkommando 3. In Lithuania, there are no more Jews, other
than the Work Jews, including their families. They are:

In Schaulen	around	4 500
In Kauen	"	15 000
In Wilna	"	15 000

I also wanted to kill these Work Jews, including their
families, which however brought upon me acrimonious
challenges from the civil administration (the Reichskom-
misar) . . . The still available Work Jews and female
Work Jews are urgently required and I can foresee that
post-winter, this manpower will still be most urgently
required. I am of the view that sterilization of the
male Work Jews should begin immediately to prevent
reproduction. Should a Jewess nonetheless become pregnant, she is to be liquidated.

After Rively had finished, she began to read it again and
then she stopped. Mrs. Ponnis was smoking another cigarette,
looking out the window. Rively felt that she, herself, had turned
into a different person to the one she was before she'd started
reading. The world did not feel as it had before. This was temporary,
she hoped.

She said, I don't see Dusat on the list. Dusetos.

Mrs. Ponnis reached over and found the third page, ran her
finger down it:

	Carry-forward		16 152
August 22,41	Aglona	Mentally ill: 269 men,	
		227 women,	
		48 children	544
August 23,41	Panevezys	1312 Jews, 4602 Jewesses	
		1609 Jewish children	7 523
August 18 to 22,41	Dist. Rasainiai	466 Jews, 440 Jewesses,	
		1020 Jewish children	1 926
August 25,41	Obeliai	112 Jews, 627 Jewesses,	
		421 Jewish children	1 160
August 25 and 26,41	Seduva	230 Jews, 275 Jewesses,	
		159 Jewish children	664
August 26,41	Zarasai	767 Jews, 1113 Jewesses,	
		1 Lith. Comm.,	
		687 Jewish children,	
		1 fem. Russ. Comm.	2 569

Mrs. Ponnis said: The Dusaters were all included in the Zarasai killing. They marched them miles into the woods of Deguciai, near Saviciunai village. A long deep pit, like a trench, was dug there. They made them strip and stand at the edge of it, and when they shot them they fell in.

Rively was motionless for a minute, staring down at the ink. That very day. Her aunties, their husbands, the children.

It's an important document, said Mrs. Ponnis. In a way, it's where it all started. They killed over a hundred thirty-five thousand human beings in a few weeks, without mercy. Extinguished the Lithuanian Jews. A thousand years of history, more, gone. Vilna was the Jerusalem of the North. Our yeshivas famous for their genius. What *this* showed *them* is that it could be done. That people wanted to help them to do it – the Lithuanians were doing it even before the Germans took over – and that it was logistically possible. That nobody anywhere else cared, or made much of a fuss about it. It was the first time they started killing children in masses. And women, old people. All the rest of it – the camps, the gas – followed from this, like a fire from a spark.

A sound came out of Rively, the noise of some inner cracking.

Mrs. Ponnis sniffed. This is how it is for us.

At the door she handed the file over. Are you going to show it to your children?

—Loh yoduat, said Rively. I don't know.

You should. All your family should know.

Rively looked down. Not my brother, she softly said.

What?

She shook her head. I have a brother, Isaac. Lives in South Africa.

Yes?

He has a good life there. He's done well, and he looks after our father also.

And so?

She shook her head again. No. I think . . . It's better I let him go on in peace. In happiness. Isaac doesn't need this.

We all need the truth.

Not him.

Mrs. Ponnis watched her. Maybe, she said, maybe you're right. Life is forward. Life is now.

Ai, my God.

What?

You sounded just like her then, Gitelle, rest in peace.

Is that such a surprise?

They hugged and Rively left, walking in a daze till she emerged onto the crest of Mount Carmel. The view scooped away to mineral waters, a Mediterranean horizon of pale blue, waveless under the white kites of swooping birds. She sat on a bench, opened the file across her lap. After a time her eyes closed. Mame, Mame. Memories of Dusat long buried came up as if ploughed from her psyche's deepest soil. One came so vividly it felt alive in her: How when she was sick Mame used to feed her warm milk from their cow Baideluh three times a day. Baideluh lived on straw in the shed behind the house, Baideluh loved them so much. When they sold her to Minsker before they left for South Africa she used to wander back and stand lowing at the window till Mame went out in her nightgown in the pre-dawn mist, to lead her back to the Minsker place near Yoffe's mill, rubbing her side and talking nicely to her as they went.

Softly, Rively began to speak the words of a remembrance prayer, repeating them like a chant. *Give certain rest on the wings of Thy holy presence / Tie the rope of life to the souls of the dead.* The salt wind breathed on her: she paid attention to it but there was no whispering in its motion as her father used to promise her, no murmur from the divine penetrating all things. No: the wind felt only cold, the bench hard. She opened her eyes and looked down at the numbered souls, the erased places. The face of a child was trying to smile, and then soil fell on it. All things have an end and that was her Dusat's, it had happened, the centuries of life had terminated. She would have been there also, in the pit, but for her mother's determination to emigrate. She looked up and Haifa Bay stretched wide its mute jaws of sky and water, a toothless eater of worlds, alive and dead. She had not ceased in the chanting of her words of prayer. To try to sanctify the unholy: you do what you can. Bring light to dark. Lead a Jewish life in a Jewish country. For you, Mame. To be as strong as you were.

Acknowledgements

My most profound gratitude goes to my late grandmother, Hanna Raizel Bonert (1901–1995), for suffusing my childhood with absolute love, as well as the memories and stories of her home village, Dusat/Dusetos. This gratitude extends to all the Jews of Dusat, the community that so nourished her, including, of course, her late husband, Koppel Bonert (1886–1970), the grandfather I never knew, though I am his namesake.

I am also grateful to Sara Weiss-Slep for collecting and publishing the oral histories of many of the survivors of Dusat's Jewish community in a volume called *Ayara Hayeta B'Lita; Dusiat B'Rei Hazichronot* (S. Segal & Co., Tel Aviv, Israel, 1989). An English translation by Judy Grossman, *There Was a Shtetl in Lithuania; Dusiat Reflected in Reminiscences*, is currently accessible on the web. This wonderful historical resource has been a great inspiration to me in the writing of this book. I also want to thank Sara for receiving me with such warmth and hospitality when I visited her in Haifa, Israel, where she continues to tirelessly maintain her ever-expanding archive of Dusat-related information.

Many thanks to Gord McFee of the Holocaust History Project, for kindly granting permission to make use of his English translation of "The Jaeger Report" (which is available online).

The epigraph quotation from *Hamelitz* is adapted from a translation by the late Chaim Gershater that appears in *The Jews in South Africa, A History*, (Pages 70-71, Geoffrey Cumberlege/ Oxford University Press, Cape Town, 1955, edited by Gustav Saron and Louis Hotz).

Thanks to Don Fehr and to Ellen Levine of Trident Media.

I am deeply grateful to all at Knopf Canada – especially Anne Collins, Louise Dennys and Craig Pyette, for reading and accepting the manuscript, and to Craig again for helping me to refine it with his many excellent suggestions.

I reserve another huge thank you, and much appreciation, for Jenna Johnson of Houghton Mifflin Harcourt in New York, for so enthusiastically embracing this book, and for her valuable and perspicacious insights all through the editorial process.

Pasey Bonert lent me essential assistance in getting the details right – yet another reason to say thanks, Dad. And thanks also to my mom, Avril, for her untiring support.

Finally, I want to thank Nicole Tataj for always being there for me.

KENNETH BONERT's short stories have appeared in *Grain* and *The Fiddlehead*. His story "Packers and Movers" was short-listed for the Journey Prize and his novella "Peacekeepers, 1995" appeared in *McSweeney's 25*. *The Lion Seeker* is his first novel. A one-time journalist, his articles have appeared in the *Globe and Mail*, *National Post* and other publications. Born in South Africa, he now calls Toronto home.